BREAKING RYAN BAYLOR

CH Maddington

CONTENTS

To all those who have ever struggled to find themselves.

You're out there; I promise.

BREAKING RYAN
BAYLOR PLAYLIST

Available on **Spotify**

"All Downhill From Here" by New Found Glory

"Turn Off the Light" by Nelly Furtado

"If It Means a Lot to You" by A Day to Remember

"Monster" by Skillet

"Nobody Praying for Me" by Seether

"Breakdown" by Seether

"Monsters (featuring blackbear) by All Time Low

"Dear Maria, Count Me In" by All Time Low

"Wish You Were Here" by Incubus

"Falling Apart" by TRUSTCompany

"Saying Sorry" by Hawthorne Heights

"Make Damn Sure" by Taking Back Sunday

"Like a Stone" by Audioslave

"The Kill" by Thirty Seconds to Mars

"I'm Not Okay (I Promise)" by My Chemical Romance

"Time After Time by Cyndi Lauper

"BURN IT DOWN" by Linkin Park

 "What It Is to Burn" by Finch

"Bad Motherfucker" by Machine Gun Kelly and Kid Rock

"STAY (with The Kid LAROI)" by Justin Bieber

"Bones" by Young Guns

"Cold" by Crossfade

"Blurry" by Puddle of Mudd

"When Worlds Collide" by Powerman 5000

"Tears Don't Fall" by Bullet for My Valentine

"Rich Flex" by 21 Savage and Drake

"Someone Like You" by Adele

"Beautiful Liar" Beyonce and Shakira

"I Can't Stop Thinking About You" by Sting

"You're So Last Summer" by Taking Back Sunday

"The Red" by Chevelle

"Team" by Lorde

"Just Friends" by Boy Matthews and Hayden James

"Friends" by J. Cole

"Summer Years" by Death Cab for Cutie

"Here Comes the Sun" by the Beatles

"Let it Hurt" by Rascal Flatts

"I Forgive You" by Kelly Clarkson

"Sandpaper and Silk" by Hawthorne Heights

"Treat You Better" by Shawn Mendes

"Delicate" by Taylor Swift

"Stay Fly" by Three 6 Mafia (Ty's Rookie Lap)

FOREWORD

This is the story that my characters told to me. That's my writing style: I create characters, I allow them to tell me their stories, and I simply record what they have to say.

This is a story on which I worked tirelessly, and I still think about it every single day, hoping I did it justice.

This is a story that helped bring me back to life and rediscover my passion for writing, and the only thing I ask of you is that you go into it with an open mind and an open heart.
It's a realistic rollercoaster ride of emotion, a story about finding yourself and figuring out who you're meant to be, and hope you enjoy reading it.

However, please heed the following <u>trigger warnings</u> before diving in:

-Reference to sexual assault/abuse (*not* graphic)

-Reference to cheating

-Reference to divorce

-Reference to death of a parent

-Reference to abortion

-Physical assault

-Illicit drug use

-Alcohol use

-Sex addiction

-Strong language (like, **a lot**. F-bombs aplenty)

-Explicit sexual content, including same-sex scenes and group

-Anxiety/panic attacks

If you're good with all that?

Happy reading!

-CH Maddington

A FUTURE FIGHT (1)

His bedroom door slamming shut was a recently familiar sound to which she'd grown accustomed. It shocked her that it was still on the hinges, to be honest. Tonight's trigger events resulted in a heated argument on the first part of the freezing walk back from the club, silence for the second part, and then this.

Whatever this was.

She tossed her phone onto the counter, crossed her arms, and waited, wondering if she would get the silent treatment, the abs, or both. Right on cue, his door flew open. Seconds later, he was standing in front of her, now shirtless.

Don't look at him.

Don't look at him.

"Amara..."

"Ry, I'm not doing this with you right now," she asserted instinctively, avoiding eye contact with him at all costs. She'd known from the moment she'd met those eyes with her own that they held the potential to be dangerous in ways for which she couldn't have possibly prepared.

And then, of course, there was the matter of his abs.

"I was out of line. I'm sorry. Can we just talk?"

"We have nothing to talk about."

He closed his eyes and leaned against the refrigerator, one arm up over his head. "I think we do."

"You know what happens when we 'talk', Ryan."

She grabbed a water bottle off the countertop and began to fill it up at the fridge where he was leaning. It was about halfway full before she felt his other arm slip around her hips, his chest pressing against her back, and his chin resting on top of her head. "Ryan, don't."

"Do you love him?"

"I don't love him, Ryan."

"I love you, Amara."

"No, you don't. You're just drunk."

"Tell me how to fix this. I wanna fix this."

"This isn't yours to fix, Ryan." She capped the bottle, wriggled out of his grasp, grabbed her phone, and headed for her bedroom, closing the door behind her. She flung herself onto her bed and lit up her screen, where a single text awaited.

J: You still coming over?

And now, on top of everything else, she had to deal with this.

She set her phone on the nightstand, sighed, and pulled the blanket up over her head. Though desperate to fall asleep and forget that this whole night happened, it was impossible; tonight's argument kept playing on repeat.

And it had gotten ugly.

"Hey, wait up!" he called, jogging to catch up with her after she'd tried unsuccessfully to sneak home from the bar. *"Um, so what the hell was that tonight? Still just friends?"*

She turned around to face him, maintaining her pace and distance in front of him. *"You know, I'm surprised you noticed anything at all since you had a thousand girls literally groping you all night long."*

"They're fans, Amara. That's a little different."

"Fans." She laughed bitterly. *"Right. Everything with you is*

always a little different, isn't it?"

"Yeah, it is a little different, just like the way you moaned on his cock versus mine. Or are we just not gonna talk about that because it makes you uncomfortable?"

As difficult as it was, she knew better than to give him the reaction he wanted and just kept walking. *"Mar, come on, stop. Hey!"* he snapped, clutching her arm a little too hard and pulling her towards him. *"So, was this happening the whole time I was out in Worcester?"*

"Ry, don't."

"It was, wasn't it? Are you in love with him?"

"No, but I'm about 99 percent sure you are."

He rolled his eyes and tightened his grip. *"Stop it. I'll ask you again: are you in love with him?"*

She peeled back his hand and shoved it away. *"You want me to say yes, don't you?"*

"If it's the truth, then yeah, I guess I do."

"The truth. Like that matters."

"It does to me. Especially when it has to do with you and him."

"You're way too obsessed with what goes on between me and him. Why?"

"Because you keep telling me you guys are just friends when I know the truth. I wanna hear it from you."

"Fine. You want the truth?" She hesitated. *"We're just friends who hook up. A lot."*

He laughed bitterly. *"Right. It couldn't be more obvious that you're in love with him."*

"Grow the fuck up, Ryan!" she yelled, catching the attention of some drunken passersby, who immediately began to cheer. *"You wouldn't know the first fucking thing about being in love. And newsflash: you and me? We're not together anymore. Not that we ever should have been in the first place. But we're not, and you need to accept that and move on."*

She stormed off, but he followed. *"It's kinda hard to move on when you constantly lead me on. Maybe you should stop messing with my fucking head if you don't want me."*

She turned around to face him. *"I don't want you? Are you out of your mind? I haven't stopped wanting you since the second I saw you. This has nothing to do with whether I want you."*

"Then why did you give up on me? On us?"

"You know why, Ryan. Don't play dumb."

"He's three years younger than me!" he yelled.

"And I'm not with him either!" she yelled back.

"It's just strange, you know? We invite him into our bed, we break up immediately after, then I come back from Worcester, and suddenly you're making out with him in the middle of a club."

"You invited him into our bed. Don't ever forget that. Not me. You. I agreed to play within your little boundaries, and you changed the rules. And I think we both know why you changed them. You're just not ready to admit it yet."

He reached up and grabbed her face with both of his hands and pressed his forehead to hers. *"Yeah, it's because we both know you were gonna end up on his cock either way. I just got out ahead of the heartbreak...babe."* She pushed him away. *"Oh, sorry, I forgot. That's his 'lil pet name for you. What should I call you? Come on, you're a writer. Is there a word for a cold-hearted bitch who broke my heart but continues to shit all over it for fun?"*

She shook her head, disgusted, and stormed off again. *"You're fucked up, Baylor!"* she shouted.

"You think?" he yelled, chasing after her. *"Yeah, 'cause you've got your shit together, Miss 'I'm divorced and prey on younger guys because I can't get anyone my own age.' The younger and stupider, the easier they fall for your bullshit lies. Right, Amara?"*

She stopped, whipped her head around, and glared at him. His eyes were waiting for hers; they always were. And for the briefest of moments, she caved, allowing herself to see in them the guy she'd almost instantly and stupidly fallen for over the past few months instead of this stranger who stood before her now.

And no matter how hard she tried to get past it, every time she looked at him, it was always front and center: the persistent, agonizing fact that he was 18 years younger, and how much that age gap complicated just about everything between them.

As much as he'd hated it, his anger often begged him to say something hurtful to her, and he wished to God he was strong enough to tell it no. *"I'm sorry,"* he mouthed, knowing he'd taken it too far.

"Fuck you," she hissed. *"You wanna bring my divorce into this? You wanna say hurtful shit? Nice to meet you, Ryan. At least*

I'm not some pathetic slut who's completely incapable of love. And for the record: I don't 'prey' on anyone. They come willingly. You'd know better than anyone."

"Oh, that's rich. The woman who only bangs guys half her age calling me a pathetic slut. What's next for you, Amara? You gonna start hanging outside the high school during dismissal?"

"You're disgusting."

"And you're a fucking liar. Nice to meet you, Amara. I may not have been the best boyfriend in the world, but I never," he said, grabbing the sides of her face and forcing her to look at him, *"I never lied to you about how I felt. Ever. I know there's something more going on between you two."*

She threw her hands up. *"And what if there is, huh? Then what, Ryan?"*

"Then Amara? You can both go fuck yourselves."

They walked back home, fighting the freezing wind the entire time. And though it was in complete silence, when he reached his arm around her and rested it on her shoulder, she didn't push it away.

She groaned, flopping angrily onto her side and squeezing her eyes shut, wondering how the hell they'd become this obscure version of themselves, and more importantly, if things could ever go back to the way they were before.

It couldn't have been more than a minute later when she got up and went to her bedroom door, sensing that he was there. Before she could even get it all the way open, his hands were around the back of her head, with hers clutching either side of his torso as their lips mashed together chaotically.

Within seconds, he had her flat against the mattress, pinned under him, his hips rocking slowly into hers. She knew they couldn't keep doing this; they were on course to destroy each other, but she'd reached that pivotal point where it was beyond her capabilities to tell him no.

He ran a hand up to her throat. Squeezing gently, he moved his other hand between her legs, then whispered into her ear, "You know you're always gonna end up right back here with me."

And as far as she knew, he was right.

AMARA MCDONOUGH (2)

"You're not serious. Right? Please tell me you're joking."

"What do you mean? The timing is perfect."

"Right," Amara said, scrolling through the browser on her phone while she chatted with her cousin on speaker. "I'm literally staring at something called Elite Prospects right now, which says he signed a 1.8 million, two-year contract. Tell me again why the hell he even needs a roommate."

"Because it's a two-way, entry-level contract, and he was just assigned to us two days ago, last-minute. He didn't make the final cut. On a two-way contract, they only make the big money if and when they're called up. If they're assigned to the minors, their salaries drop dramatically."

She sighed. "Nick: he's a kid. He's..." she scrolled to his

birthdate, paused for a quick bit of mental math, and then snickered. "He's 23? He's 23, Nick!"

"And?"

"This is insane. Isn't there a teammate he can room with?"

"It was a last-minute decision. Everyone else is already living somewhere. I helped him find a place, completely turnkey, but he wants to split it with someone. You literally just show up, sign the contract, and drop your bags. No stress."

She hung her head, running her fingers through her hair. "This is *such* a bad idea."

"Mar, you're impossible," he replied, frustrated.

"That's the word on the street."

"Look: you wanted out? This is your out. You come here, you start over. Yes, parts of Bridgeport are a dump, but this is Downtown. It's up-and-coming. There are plenty of bars in the area. You'll have no issue finding a bartending job, if that's what you wanna do, and you can still write on the side. Listen, you asked me to help you find a place to live. Well, I found you one."

"No, you found me a fuckin' frat boy to shack up with. You do understand that I'm 41 years old, right? Like, you remember that part?"

"Don't make this difficult. This is your do-over. I know some athletes have a reputation for being scumbags..."

"Some?" she sneered, mentally running through the list of all the athletes she'd dated.

Yep. All scumbags.

"Yes. Some. And trust me: some of them are. OK, a lot of them are. But I promise you, you won't meet a more down-to-earth guy than Baylor, honest to God. He's easy to talk to and kinda goofy. You'll really like him. And I know your history. You gotta trust that I wouldn't put you in a dicey situation. Amara, he's nice."

"Yup," she said, scrolling through the Google image search she'd just run on him. "That's uh, certainly one way to describe him." *Gorgeous, blonde, blue-eyed, tatted, and built like a brick shithouse would be another,* she thought. "And you're sure he knows he's getting a baggage-hauling divorced woman who's literally old enough to be his mother?

"Yes."

"And he's cool with all of this?"

"One hundred percent. I told him I'd let him know soon so he could start looking elsewhere if he had to. He's a good dude. There are some guys I wouldn't even want you in the same room with. But Baylor? You have nothing to worry about with him."

"Mmhmm," she mumbled. "I need to think about it."

"You're still coming out here Thursday, right? I'm picking you up?"

"Yup, don't have much of a choice. I sold my car. Closing on the house Thursday, and I'm officially 41, divorced, carless, homeless, jobless, and on my way to Connecticut."

"Well, I can't do anything about most of that, but you don't have to be homeless if you don't wanna be. Let me know as soon as you can, OK? I gotta go."

"Nick?" she asked before he could hang up. "He's legit? No drama, no bullshit?"

"Positive."

"Fine. Tell him…" she sighed. "Tell him I'm in."

And that was how she found herself living in Downtown Bridgeport, Connecticut with 23-year-old New York Islanders prospect Ryan Baylor.

RYAN BAYLOR (3)

"Thanks, man. I really appreciate it," he said, handing the Uber driver $100. After all, the poor guy had been sitting out there for 25 minutes while he made four trips up to his sixth-floor apartment and back to get all 12 of his bags. It was the least he could do, even though the ride over from Long Island already cost him over $300. What was another $100?

As he stepped onto the elevator and hit the '6' button once more, he suddenly felt a pit in his stomach that damn near doubled him over. He put his bag down, slumped against the side of the elevator, and prayed that it didn't stop until his floor.

Get your shit together, Baylor, he told himself, as he grabbed his final bag, got off, and walked to his apartment door.

He should've been excited for this next part of his journey, but, in true Ryan Baylor fashion, that was impossible. All he could do was ruminate over every single mistake he'd made in training camp, wondering which one was the deciding factor in him being sent down to the minors.

The minors.

The two-word combination made him shudder. He still couldn't believe it. This was already year two of his almost two-million-dollar, entry-level NHL contract, and he'd yet to see a dime of it, minus a sizable signing bonus. Year one had been spent playing Division 1 NCAA at The University of Minnesota as a junior. After their devastating loss in the finals, he'd hoped for the opportunity to prove himself in some games in with the New York Islanders, but neither they nor Bridgeport had made the postseason, so back home he went until training camp started in September.

"Listen, sweetie. Things are about to change. Your life is about to shift drastically. You've gotta be willing and ready to change with it, and unfortunately, that means biding your time," his mom had told him, helping him to focus on his breathing as he broke down into a full-blown, 2:30 a.m. panic attack at the kitchen table.

Ryan Baylor was skilled in many things, but patience or the ability to handle things that didn't go precisely how he'd planned were not two of them. For most of his life, everything had always come somewhat easily to him, especially hockey. When it didn't, his anxiety would spike, sometimes nearly to the point of incapacitating him. He hid it well from the rest of the world for the most part, but his mother knew him probably better than anyone, and there was no hiding it from her.

"Your days of being the big fish in the little pond are done, babe. You're gonna have to fight for your spot now. You need to earn it. And you will, but it's gonna be a hell of a battle."

And she was right. Ryan was used to being the biggest fish in the small pond. Hell, he'd been captain of the Golden Gophers for his sophomore and junior years, his sophomore year being one of the best on record for the school in the past 10 years, and the best in school history for a defenseman. He'd put up 17 goals and 29 points in 35 games and had taken complete control of the penalty kill special team, earning him the 41st pick overall in the second round of the NHL draft. That fact had taken at least some of the pressure off him for his junior year, his last year playing NCAA, where he could just focus on playing his best hockey without the added stress of worrying about what the immediate future held.

Fast forward a year, where this immediate future of playing minor league hockey was now staring him boldly in the face? He'd be lying if he said he was pleased with what he saw.

As he shut the door behind him, his phone buzzed.

N: I'm picking her up tomorrow around 1. We'll be over after.

N: She's really looking forward to meeting you.

R: Sounds good. Looking forward to meeting her, too.

He replied right away, but in reality, this was just one more thing contributing to the constant uneasiness that was slowly consuming him. Nick McDonough was the athletic trainer for Bridgeport and had been at camp. At 32, he was on the younger side, and he and Ryan spent a lot of downtime talking. He was grateful that at least he knew someone here, because he'd literally never met another soul on this team; he'd heard of a lot of the guys, knew them by name, but that's it.

The Bridgeport Islanders were a well-established team: a mixture of older guys finishing out their careers, several guys on AHL-only contracts, a handful of guys called up from the Worcester Railers, the ECHL affiliate, and a few younger prospects who hadn't been at camp, as it had been decided they'd start the season there due to coming off recent injuries. He was very lucky to be heading there though: out of the six prospects at camp, only two made the big club, and the other three were sent out to Worcester. He knew himself well enough to know that there was not a chance he'd have recovered from that.

After learning that he didn't make the final cut and dealing with the whirlwind of emotions that came with that, he began to panic about finding an affordable living option, as it didn't seem that the big money would be rolling in anytime soon. Nick had helped him locate an amazing, fully furnished apartment in a building Downtown where some of the other younger guys were living. On only his AHL salary, he wasn't sure he could swing it without a roommate, so Nick hooked him up with one of those, too.

And so, there he sat, engulfed in silence, his entire 23 years of blood, sweat, and tears reduced to a roster spot in a development league and 12 bags. Alone with his own thoughts could be a dangerous place; he knew that. Thankfully, he wouldn't be alone for too much longer. His new roommate, Nick's cousin, would be here in less than 24 hours. He'd be lying if he said he wasn't a little apprehensive about the upcoming living situation: a 23-year-old single guy and a much older, recently divorced woman was an odd combination for sure. But he trusted Nick, and he was used to living just about anywhere, having played juniors and been through a few different billet families. He laughed to himself, thinking about the conversation he'd had with his 27-year-old brother that morning.

"Wait, she's how old?"

"She's...41, I think."

"Bro. And she's recently divorced? Holy hell, Ryan. Jackpot! Is she hot?"

"I mean, sorta? I guess. I found her Instagram, but it's private, so there's only one pic that I can see. She's OK. Definitely not ugly, but not really my type."

"So, what you mean is she isn't blonde and completely, 100 percent fake from the top of her head down to her toenails?"

He rolled his eyes, then shrugged. His brother knew him

too well. "I mean, I guess she's cute. I don't know. She's old though."

"So? When's that ever stopped you before? Juniors tournament hotel room ringing any bells?"

"Stop it. That was one time and a huge mistake. I mean, it was a really fuckin' hot mistake though."

"Exactly! And dude: over 40 and divorced? Do you even have any idea what kind of sexual awakening that woman is probably experiencing right now? You do know they go through a 'slut phase', right? It's like a rite of passage for divorced chicks. Screw this, I'm coming to visit. I'm not even kidding. I'm literally on my way right now."

"Right," he smirked, shaking his head. He knew his brother was just trying to make him laugh, keep his spirits up. But he also knew what an unapologetic pervert Luke could be. "And I'm sure Shan will be totally cool with it."

"Need to know basis, bro. Different state, doesn't count. Yo: send me her Insta."

"Get the fuck outta here!"

"I know you. I give it a couple weeks tops before you smash her, if that. I'm calling it right now. And I guarantee you it's gonna be, hands down, the best shit you've ever had in your life."

"Eww. I'm hanging up now."

"Wait. Ry?"

"What?"

"I love you, man."

"Love you too, Luke."

And there it was: homesickness hit him like a ton of bricks, as he had no clue when he'd even see Luke or his mom again. Their dad had passed away unexpectedly in a car accident when Ryan was 17 and living with one of his billet families while playing juniors. He'd taken the rest of that year off and moved back home to be with his mom. As soon as he returned the following year, Luke and his then girlfriend, now fiancée Shannon moved in. He said it was because they were saving up money for a wedding and a house, but Ryan knew it was because he was leaving again, and Luke didn't want their mom to be alone.

He stopped himself from going any further with these thoughts, deciding that this was an emotional rollercoaster he didn't have the energy to ride right now. Instead, he focused on busying himself, as there was more than enough to do. And just as he'd started going through his first bag, he swore he heard someone at the door.

Shit, maybe Luke was serious, he thought briefly, though he was utterly perplexed at who the hell could be knocking on his door right now, six floors up, in an unfamiliar city where he knew absolutely no one.

He opened the door to find two young guys standing there. Both were tall, roughly the same height as his six-foot, three-inch self, and on the slimmer side with dark hair. The slightly shorter one's longer, wavy hair poked out from under the sides of the gray beanie he was wearing. He had a lollipop stick hanging out of the side of his mouth and held a six-pack of some kind of beer, while the slightly taller one held a bouquet of pink and purple flowers.

"Don't get too excited. Is not for you," Flowers said with a heavy Russian accent.

"Osi. For real? That's how you greet the kid? How about hi?"

"Yes. This too. Hi."

"Hi?" Ryan half-asked, as Beanie shoved the six-pack his way.

"You're the rookie, right? Ryan Baylor?"

"That's me."

Beanie threw his hands up. "Surprise! Meet your teammates. This is Osi, formally Aleksey Osinov. I'm Hayes. Tyler Hayes, but my mom's literally the only person in the world who I'll allow to routinely call me Tyler."

Ryan swung the door open. "Uh, yeah. Hey. Come on in. It's kind of a mess right now. I just got in a bit ago, but uh, thanks," he said, setting the beer down on the counter and mentally adding "unexpected visitors" to the list of everything that currently had him on the brink of another panic attack. "How, uh, how did you know I was..."

"Dunny," Hayes replied. "Nick. We're down on the fourth floor. He said you're gonna be living with his cousin or some shit?"

"Yeah. She'll be here tomorrow."

"Nice. Heard she went through a wicked divorce. Yo, Osi?" Hayes nudged him.

"Yes. This for her," he said, handing Ryan the flowers.

"Right. Thanks. I guess I should, uh, put them in water," he said, heading to the kitchen to look for something to stick them in.

"I don't fuckin' know, I guess. Just make sure she knows they're from the two hotties on the fourth floor and not the dusty rook, eh?" Hayes twirled the lollipop stick as he looked around. "I thought you said it was a mess in here. Looks pretty put together to me. You should see our place. Most days we're lucky if we can find the front door."

"This is because you are pig," Osi chimed in, and Hayes flipped him both middle fingers.

Ryan smirked. "Yeah, it's fully furnished. Sheets, towels, kitchen stuff. All included."

"I mean, that's cool. Makes it easy. So, how'd you even end up living with Nick's much older female cousin? That's kinda weird, eh? What are you, 22, 23?"

"I'm 23. And it...just sort of happened."

And how'd you end up such a nosy little shit? Ryan thought, partially annoyed as Hayes grabbed a beer, twisted the cap off, and had a seat at one of the counter stools. Just as he was about to drink it, Osi grabbed it from his hand. "Nope. Can't have yet. Two more months."

Hayes swatted him and grabbed it back. "Shut it. Yes, I'm the only guy on the team who can't get into a bar yet. Meanwhile, back in Canada, I've been going to bars for almost two years. So stupid."

"Oh, you're Canadian? So, this right here is like the

beginning of a bad joke," Ryan quipped awkwardly. "You know. An American, a Canadian, and a Russian walk into a bar."

"No. American and Russian walk into bar. Canadian have to wait outside!" Osi replied immediately, giggling as he said it, which made Ryan laugh as well. He liked this guy already.

"Piss off!" Hayes shot back, pulling the lollipop out of his mouth, taking a quick swig, and immediately sticking it back in. He must've noticed Ryan staring because he said, "I'm not an animal, guy. Just trying really hard to quit vaping," as he pulled it out and waved it around before sticking it back into his mouth. "And I've got a little bit of an oral fixation."

"Well, that can be a very good thing," Ryan remarked, his eyes widening immediately after he said it. He damn sure hadn't intended to flirt with his new teammate but realized that's exactly how it came out. "I mean, I bet the birds don't mind."

Hayes stared blankly at him for a few seconds, then shook his head. "Nah, I'm sure they wouldn't. But there's only one bird for me," he said, reaching into his back pocket for his phone.

"3, 2, 1..." Osi quietly counted down to the exact moment when Hayes proudly thrust his phone in front of Ryan's face.

"Not bad, eh, Rook?" Hayes bragged, showing off a picture of him and his incredibly hot, half-naked girlfriend. "That's my girl Jenna. She's..."

"Instagram model. 500 thousand followers. Is 28 years old. Together for nine months. Is love of his life," Osi finished for him, rolling his eyes. "You will hear this five more times before we leave."

"I can't help it. I miss her. No idea when I'll even see her again. She's back in Ontario, and it sucks. You got a girl, Rook? Or a guy. I mean, hey: no judgment here."

Yup. He definitely thinks you were flirting with him. Great job, Baylor.

"Ah, of course you do," Hayes decided, pointing to where Ryan's black compression t-shirt clung to his incredibly well-defined midsection. "Kid's out here lookin' like a fuckin' Greek god."

Ryan laughed uncomfortably, and ran his fingers through his hair, unsure if this was an appropriate time to tell the guys he just met that at 23, he'd never actually *been* in a real relationship before. It wasn't for lack of opportunity; girls tossed themselves at him on a regular basis, and he indulged just as regularly. Ryan Baylor's toxic trait was that he liked to play, and the chase was his favorite part of the game. Getting them into bed, which never took long at all, seemed to flip a switch that made him immediately lose all interest, so much so that his nickname in college was "Ghost."

There had only been two girls who'd somehow managed to garner his attention post-sex. And both, after he'd worked up the courage to spill his guts and go for it, had let Ryan know in no uncertain terms he wasn't "boyfriend material." He wasn't sure what that even meant, but with that, a fuckboy was born, with him determining that it beat having the shit repeatedly kicked out of his fragile heart.

"Nah, nothing going on in the girl department at the moment," he finally said.

"Well listen, that's probably a good thing. Because you're about to have chicks of all ages, and I do mean *all* ages, throwing themselves at you like it's their full-time job. You? They're gonna sweat you hard. Buckle up, Rook. It gets very tempting, for real. Some of these women are so hot," he said, closing his eyes and pretending to bite down on his hand. "I'll flirt a bit, but at the end of the day, I'm not a cheater. You enjoy that shit, though. Osi does, right, Osi?"

Osi nodded and shrugged. "Every time and again. Is nice."

"So anyway, we won't keep you. Just wanted to introduce ourselves and let you know we're here. A few of the other guys will be over tomorrow night for a little pre-season get-together. You should come. And, uh, bring Nick's cousin, too, if she's down. I wanna see how hot…I mean, I would like to meet her," Hayes said with a sideways smirk and a wink. "Catch you later, Rook."

"Was nice to meet you," Osi said, reaching out to shake Ryan's hand. "Bridgeport is like big family. We are happy you are part of it."

"Thanks, man," Ryan said, and they exchanged numbers before they left. As soon as Ryan closed the door, he immediately popped onto Instagram and unfollowed Hayes's girlfriend. He knew she'd looked familiar.

Whoops.

He was about 75 percent sure he hadn't banged her and that she was just a "spank bank" follow, but better to be safe.

He set his phone down, cracked open a beer, and got back to unpacking his bags. Some of the uneasiness he'd been struggling with started to lift, although the jury was still out on Tyler Hayes.

THE MEETING (4)

"So, this will cover both of us, the other tenant Ryan and me, until January. I am gonna need that in writing from you though," Amara said, adjusting her glasses as she signed the lease paperwork for the apartment and cut a check for almost $11,000.

"Of course. Give me just a moment." The building clerk took the check and left to grab some paperwork from the printer.

Nick nudged her. "Are you sure? That's like, a ridiculous chunk of change, Mar."

"Yes. And it's fine. It's from my car anyway. I've still got a good amount from the house, not to mention that I'm gonna have alimony rolling in for two years. It's the least I can do for the poor kid since he's getting stuck living with some decrepit old lady." She shrugged. "Honestly, it's cool that he's cool with this. We'll call it compensation for the fact that he's about to have random pairs of reading glasses stashed in every crevice of his apartment."

Amara was far from a decrepit old lady; she knew that. Though 41, she didn't feel it and was probably in the best shape of her life. Having your entire world ripped out from under your feet and your heart shattered into a million irreparable pieces, as it turned out, was pretty dope motivation to work out.

It took her a while to get there, though. The crippling depression and anxiety that followed her ex-husband's cheating almost a year ago and their divorce five months ago wasn't pretty. There had been days-long stretches when she literally didn't get out of bed, shower, or even eat.

It was exacerbated by the fact that all her friends were also *his* friends and thus disappeared quickly after everything went down between them. Pair that with the fact that she didn't talk to almost anyone in her family: the loneliness had been downright unbearable at times, and she surprised even herself that she'd made it out alive.

Nick had been her rock. Her cousin on her late father's side, he was the only person related to her that she kept in contact with. He would constantly check up on her, even though in Connecticut, he was on the opposite side of the country from where she was living just outside of Seattle. He'd spent countless hours on the phone with her, sometimes just listening to her cry, scream, or whatever she needed to do.

When she told him about a week ago that she felt like she was suffocating and needed a fresh start, he offered to help her figure things out and invited her to move to Connecticut, where she'd at least be close to him and his fiancée, Mark. She'd have been welcome to stay with them, but their place was a studio, and there was literally nowhere for her to go.

"I promise you, Mar, I will hook you up with something amazing."

Now, bags in hand, she and Nick were in the elevator

headed there.

"Hey. It's all good. He's very easy to get along with. Honestly? He's kind of a dork."

"I can't help it. I haven't lived with another human being besides my ex since my parents, Nick. And even when I was married, I was alone most of the time. I don't know how the hell to be someone's roommate, let alone a 23-year-old kid. What if I constantly get in his way? What if I'm like," she gasped, "an unintentional cockblock? Girls are probably gonna think he lives with his mother! Or, what if he gets a girlfriend and she's weirded out by all this? You know, I didn't think this through. This might be a bad idea."

The elevator dinged, and the doors opened to the sixth floor. "Welp, it's a little too late now, bitch. Now grab your bags and let's go." She did as Nick instructed, and it felt like the longest walk of her life. She literally had no idea what she was doing or why she'd thought this was a good idea. As they approached the door, she put her bags down and went to knock, but Nick stopped her.

"Get your key. This is your place, too. You don't need to knock."

"Right," she said, as she fumbled with the lock. She finally got it and pushed the door open into the kitchen, which was beautifully upgraded with all newer, stainless-steel appliances, mahogany cabinetry, and white marble countertops. "Nick. Oh my God," she whispered.

"What'd you think, I was gonna put you up in some slum? I got you, girl."

"This is unbelievable," she gasped, rounding the corner to the living room, which was just as beautiful. She set her bags down and looked around, taking it all in. It even had a gray leather sectional with a chaise; she'd always wanted a chaise. She envisioned herself curled up with a blanket while writing and watching the Connecticut snowfall through the sliding glass balcony doors. "This is just..."

"Really nice, isn't it?" An unfamiliar voice startled her,

causing her to jump and spin around. "Sorry. Didn't mean to scare you."

"No, it's...fine," she managed to get out as her eyes immediately locked with his. They were blue with the slightest hint of gray, and they were guarded by a curious sadness. The feeling she got throughout her body served as a warning that they were a place in which she could get into trouble if she wasn't careful.

She lowered her gaze just enough to see that he had on a pair of black sweatpants and a gray undershirt that clung to his body for dear life, revealing part of a large chest tattoo that spilled over into a half-sleeved upper right arm, all of it done entirely in jet black ink. His blonde hair was a wet, matted-down mess, and she could smell that he'd just gotten out of the shower, picking up on a mixture of fresh cologne and deodorant.

She gulped.

"Baylor, what's up?" Nick said, patting him on the shoulder with one hand and reaching in for a handshake with the other.

Ryan shook Nick's hand, but his eyes stayed right with Amara's. "Good seeing you, Nick."

"So, I found this lady on the way over here and she looked like she needed a home. Ryan Baylor, meet your new roommate..."

"Amara," Ryan cut him off, his eyes still locked with hers. "That's a beautiful name."

"I...yeah," she stuttered, physically unable to pull her eyes away from his, let alone make words. "Yeah. Thanks."

Boy, this is going well.

He pulled his hand away from Nick's and extended both arms out, inviting her in for a hug.

Oh, OK. We're doing this.

She tentatively approached him and reached out; due to their height difference, her arms ended up around his waist as his closed tightly around her upper back.

"Wow," she said aloud, as they pulled away from each other after a few seconds. "You are hard. I mean, not *hard* like, you...your abs. I mean..."

"You'll have to excuse my cousin. Apparently, this is her first time seeing an actual man live and in person," Nick teased. She watched a huge smile creep over Ryan's face as he blushed.

"I just..."

She looked at Ryan, then back at Nick, who gave her a look that she's pretty sure translated to, "What the actual fuck is wrong with you?"

"Shut it, Nicholas."

"Well listen, as much as I hate to miss the rest of this shit show, Mark and I have to go for food tasting at the venue. Just how I want to spend my Saturday, sitting in traffic on the Belt Parkway. I swear, I'll be so happy when all of this wedding crap is over. He's driving me bonkers. Like, can we just go to the courthouse?"

"When's the wedding again?" Ryan asked.

"November, right at the week-long break. So about two months. Not soon enough." He made his way over to Amara and leaned in, hugging her and kissing the top of her head. "Have fun getting settled in, and try not to embarrass yourself any further in front of this stud, OK?" He laughed, shaking his head. "*You are hard!* Loser."

She punched his arm as she walked him over to the door. "You are an ass."

"Love you too! And I'll see you at our first practice Monday, Baylor. Have fun with," he opened the door with one hand and made a circular motion toward Amara with the other, "all of that." He left the apartment, closing the door behind him and leaving just the two of them standing in the kitchen, where an awkward silence ensued.

"Oh, um, so these flowers are yours," he finally said, pointing to the bouquet that he'd half-assedly crammed into a plastic pitcher. "I didn't know what to put them in, obviously. But I was told to tell you that they're not from the dusty rook.

They're from the two hotties on the fourth floor."

Amara shook her head and shrugged. "I can honestly say that I don't understand a single word you just said."

They both laughed. "A couple of my teammates live two floors down. They came to visit last night and brought those for you. Nick filled them in on…you know, this whole situation."

"Of course he did," she said, rolling her eyes. "Quite the gossip, that one. If you have any secrets, keep them far from my cousin, OK?" She peered into the pitcher and smirked, looking over at him.

Holy shit, could he be more beautiful?

"Nice attempt at a vase though. I'm surprised they're not sticking out of the toilet tank."

"Give me some credit. At least I knew to put them in water."

She rooted around in the cabinets, finally locating a vase and transferring them into it, as another awkward silence came over them.

"OK," she finally said, slapping her hands against the countertop. "Here it is. So, this is a little weird for me. I haven't lived with anyone besides my ex-husband, like ever. I am gonna try my best not to get in your way or make this any weirder for you than it probably already is. I'm sorry, but do you have *any* idea how gorgeous you are? Wow, I just said that out loud, didn't I? And I'm rambling. I do that when I'm nervous. Oh my God," she said, burying her face in her hands and leaning onto her elbows on the kitchen countertop. "I'm sorry."

"Nah, it's fine. Really. I've been living with random strange people since I was 15, so I'm basically a pro. It's just part of the game. I mean, not that you're strange. Honestly, I'm glad it's a pretty woman and not some psychopath. That's, you know, assuming that you're not also a psychopath." He shrugged, and as she lifted her head, he smiled at her. "Seriously, it's not that weird for me. Just another living situation. Anyway, wanna see your room?" He motioned for her to come with him, so she did. "I thought you should have the room with the bathroom in it. I'll just use the spare one in the hallway. It's not a big deal."

"Thanks," she said, as he pointed towards her door. "You didn't have to. That's sweet."

"I try. But don't get it twisted. I'm a monumental pain in the ass. I mean it. I look all cute and innocent, but give it a week and you'll wanna murder me."

"Mmm, I doubt that," she said, tucking her long, dark hair behind her ear and taking another inventory of his body. He was seriously perfection. "I mean it though, Ryan, I won't be in your way, OK? Do your thing, whatever that looks like, and don't worry about me. You won't even know I'm here," she said, as she cracked open the door to her room. "Oh, side note: the apartment's been paid up through January, so you don't need to worry about rent until then. We can talk about splitting up the other bills later."

He looked at her, utterly confused. "Wow. Um, why? I mean, thanks. But why would you do that?"

"It's just a small way for me to say thank you for letting me live here. I was…I *really* needed to get away from where I was, and it's cool of you to agree to this is all. Anyway, I guess I should start unpacking my stuff," she said, as she turned to walk back down the hall to retrieve her bags from the living room.

He reached his hand out and grabbed her arm lightly, stopping her. "Can I at least, I don't know, take you to dinner as a thank you?"

She smirked and shook her head. "I don't think so."

He sighed. "You're gonna be difficult, aren't you?"

"You have no idea."

"Well, I'm persistent, annoying, whatever you wanna call it. And you're not just gonna hide out in your room all the time. We're gonna get to know each other. I'm telling you, soon, you won't even remember what your life was like before you met me."

"Is that right?" she asked, though she didn't doubt it for a moment.

"Yup, you'll see. I'm a good time, girl," he said, flashing her the cheesiest grin. "Anyway, I'm heading out in a little bit, but some of the guys are having a get-together at their place tonight, and they asked me to bring you. That is if you wanna come."

"Would this by any chance be the fourth-floor hotties?"

"Yeah. I mean, you should at least come by and say thanks for the flowers." He shrugged. "It's only polite."

"I'll consider it," she said, as she realized his hand was still touching her arm. She pulled away gently and continued her way into the living room.

"Good," she heard him say, followed by the sound of his bedroom door closing a few seconds later.

She couldn't explain it, but Nick had been right about him; he was very easy to talk to. In the short amount of time they'd spent together, she felt comfortable, something she hadn't felt in a very long time.

OLD HABITS (5)

"Was that good, baby?"

Ryan lifted his head, which had been pressed firmly against the back of the couch, and opened his eyes. "Mmm. Yeah. Thanks," he sighed, watching her peel her face out of his lap, wipe her mouth, and sit up.

"Good," she said, as she reached for her bra and put it back on. Even though he'd just nutted, he couldn't stop staring at her massive, natural rack. "Because I really liked doing it." She pulled her shirt over her head and they both sat silently for a bit. "So, I mean, are we gonna do anything else besides hook up?"

Here it comes, he thought, as he mentally prepared "the speech."

She continued. "It's just, I really like you, and I thought maybe we could, I don't know, get to know each other."

He snickered. *You really like me? You're an Instagram puck slut who's sucked my dick twice now, once within literally a half-hour of meeting me.* He decided that was probably too harsh, even though he knew all these girls were after two things: sex and money. "Listen..." He searched his brain for a name, but it wasn't coming.

"Tori?" she said, annoyed.

"Tori. This was fun. You're fun. And so beautiful. I've just...got a lot going on right now. The season is about to start and I'm gonna be super-busy. I'm just not looking for..."

"Anything serious right now. Right," she said, getting up from the couch and smoothing out her black leather miniskirt. "Well, then I guess you better go. I would hate to keep you."

"OK then." He stood up, fastened his pants, adjusted his crotch, and grabbed his phone from the end table. He was experienced at making speedy, awkward post-hookup exits. "I'll just...this way," he said, pointing toward the door.

"Ugh, you pro athletes are literally all the same!" she whined, as she pushed past him on the way to the front door and opened it for him.

"That's a shame," he said, turning around to face her. "Because, wow, you seem so different from all the other girls who chase us around for sex on social media." The door slammed in his face, and he instantly hated himself.

He'd broken the rule, the one fucking rule, and went back; he knew better than that.

He'd met Tori at a bar last week after she'd DM'd him on Instagram that she "enjoyed watching him at the Islanders training camp and would really like to see *more* of him." It was incredibly lame, but she was a smokeshow and he was horny as shit.

Within a half-hour, they stumbled their drunk asses into Ryan's hotel room, while his poor camp roommate slept in the bed next to them, or at least pretended to. Since they were both pretty lit and neither of them had a condom, it ended up just being a lot of touching, kissing, and a very lengthy, sloppy blowjob from which he barely came.

28

Because she was so hot, he was willing to give it one more shot to see if he could seal the deal. When it ended again with her going down on him, he figured he was wasting his time, though this time she let him fuck her giant tits for a bit beforehand. It wasn't easy to call it quits with her: a blonde with a huge rack, a face full of fillers, and three percent body fat was essentially Ryan Baylor's kryptonite. But this one definitely wasn't worth the trouble, especially since the head wasn't even that good.

Her place was about a 20-minute walk from his. He'd thought about getting an Uber but decided to walk instead to clear his head a bit.

How much longer you gonna pull this stupid shit, Baylor?

He felt the mental breakdown coming, as he struggled to accept that, though this was who he was, it wasn't who he wanted to be anymore. He kept thinking about what Hayes said, how even more girls were gonna be throwing themselves at him soon. That would excite any normal 23-year-old, but not Ryan. He'd been whoring himself out like it was his full-time job since he ditched his V-card at age 18.

It happened in a hotel room with the 38-year-old mom of some kid he'd just played against at a juniors tournament, who'd slipped him her hotel name and room number in the lobby after the game.

"Confession time: I probably should've been watching my son, but fuck. I couldn't take my eyes off you for a second. Here. Come by around seven if you wanna, you know...play." Against his better judgment, he'd skipped out on the team dinner and made the trip to meet up with her, naïvely assuming they'd maybe just make out a little and he'd have a fun little story to tell the boys.

When he got there, after pacing outside for about 10 minutes while working up the balls to knock, she immediately pulled him inside, pushed him onto the bed, and ripped his pants off. *"Baby, I'm gonna fuck you so good."*

"So, um, I've, uh, I've never done this before," he told her

breathlessly, as she put a condom on him.

"Holy shit, you're a big boy, huh? Listen, I'm gonna ride your virgin cock until you cum nice and hard for me, OK?"

He nodded aggressively, mouth agape. She moaned loudly as she mounted him and did exactly what she told him she was going to, an experience he still spanked to at least once a week. He was a bit of a late bloomer, but he'd gotten a hell of a start and had more than made up for it since.

Sometimes when he was bored, he'd try to calculate his body count, though he knew it was impossible. There were far too many for which he'd been so plastered he could hardly remember. He knew it was an absurd number. If you threw in all the hookups that weren't full-on penetration, including several of his college teammates and rivals with whom he'd messed around in various states of drunkenness, then it was *well* into the hundreds. Ryan was fairly certain he wasn't gay, but he'd done his fair share of experimenting, mostly on the receiving end of blowjobs, minus a few terrible hand jobs he'd given in an attempt to be a team player.

For such a slut, he'd been really lucky. He'd gotten away with just a couple STD scares, which turned out to be nothing, and only knocked up one girl when he was 19. He'd helped her "take care of it" financially, but the anxiety, shame, and guilt that came with that experience almost killed him. He promised himself that from then on, if he didn't have protection, it wasn't happening, a promise he'd kept. He remembered that following week well; he'd spent most of it throwing up and sobbing in his brother's arms, begging him to please not tell their mom, mostly because he found out after the fact that the girl was only 16.

"I'll take this to my fucking grave, Ry. I promise you."

He rolled his eyes, disgusted with himself, as he continued his trek home. He'd lied to himself for a long time, pretended this was all fine, that this was just what hockey boys did. The truth was that he knew he didn't want this anymore; he wanted so badly for someone to love him, wanted nothing more than to feel what it was like to be in love. So many of his old friends and teammates had girlfriends, fiancés, and some were even married and had kids on the way. And he was jealous; he craved that life for himself.

But for Ryan Baylor, it was easier to hide from it because he knew deep down, in what was left of his shattered soul, he was such a scumbag that he probably didn't deserve it anyway.

A text from Luke snapped him back to the present.

L: Yo, I need details on the old broad.

R: Give me a second. We actually just finished fucking.

L: Smart ass. Seriously, how is she?

Ryan paused, as he hadn't really had time to ask or answer that question to himself yet, so he just went off instinct.

R: She's amazing, actually.

A few seconds later, his phone rang. "OK. Amazing how?"

Ryan laughed. "You really have nothing better to do right now?"

"Bro, I've eaten the same lunch for eight years. You know I live vicariously through your cock. So, amazing how?"

He hesitated; *he* wasn't even sure what he meant. "I don't know. She's like, kinda nerdy, but in a hot way, you know? And she's so easy to talk to. I can't explain it, but I feel like we've known each other for years."

"You said 'in a hot way.' So, she's hot?"

"I mean, not what I'd normally go for, but she's pretty. Very pretty. Long dark hair, a body, eyes. She definitely takes care of herself, doesn't look her age. Mid-thirties, tops."

"Wait: I'm sorry. Did my bottle-blonde addict brother just say a girl with dark hair was very pretty? Isn't that like, a cardinal sin for you stick douches?"

"Yes, but we will make exceptions in certain cases. It doesn't matter though. It's not even like that with her."

"Ryan, cut the shit. We both know what's gonna happen. And honestly, I'm here for it."

He grew agitated. "Yo: I said it's not like that with her."

"Ok, man. I'm sorry." Luke immediately backed off, knowing how pissy Ryan could get. They chatted about some random bullshit until he got back to the lobby of his apartment building.

"Hey, I gotta go. Tell Shan I said hi, and tell Mom I love her and I'll call her tomorrow." He hung up, sighed, and pressed the elevator button, as a tidal wave of anxiety suddenly overtook him.

Fuck. Here we go, he thought, hoping to God that Amara was busy so he could have a meltdown privately.

GROUNDING (6)

Amara stepped off the elevator, a hamper bag slung over her shoulder, and headed to the laundry room in the basement.

Almost 3000 bucks a month and there's no washer and dryer in the damn unit? she thought, annoyed, as she set the bag down next to a washer and tried to locate the coin slot. She scoped out a couple different machines with no luck.

Growing frustrated, she must've been muttering to herself because she heard, "It's a card, babe. You have to load it on the machine over there."

She turned to look, and an attractive younger guy was pointing at a screen in the corner. He was wearing a gray wool hat and sucking on a lollipop. "Thanks," she said, before realizing that she'd only brought quarters. "And I don't have my wallet," she said, slapping her hands against her thighs. "That's great."

He walked slowly over to where she was standing at the

washer, leaned in close to her, and held his card in front of her face with his index and middle fingers. "I got you. You can owe me one." She went to take it from him, but he wouldn't let go. She shot him a puzzled look. "Got a name, or should I just call you Beautiful?"

She blushed and pushed her hair behind her ear. "Wouldn't you like to know?"

"I mean, yeah. That's why I asked."

"Amara," she finally told him.

"Beautiful name for a beautiful woman." He smirked, finally letting go of the card so she could take it.

"Thank you. And you are?"

"Hayes," he said, extending his hand towards hers.

"Your name is Haze?" she asked curiously, grabbing his hand. "Like, H-A-Z-E?"

"My last name, yes. Like, H-A-Y-E-S." He squeezed her hand on the letter S, and then let go. "That's what everyone calls me, except my mom. I'm Tyler to her."

"Well, I'm probably old enough to be your mother, so Tyler it is."

"Yeah, I figured you must be old. I mean, don't get me wrong, you're fine as hell. It's just that you brought a bunch of fuckin' quarters to the laundry room like it's 2001. I really hate being called Tyler, by the way."

"Sorry to hear that, Tyler," she shot him a sideways look as she started loading her clothes into the washer.

"Alright, I see how it is. Amanda."

"It's Amara," she corrected him.

"I know that."

"Right," she said, pressing the button on the machine, leaning against it, and crossing her arms. "So, you actually doing any laundry down here or just searching for your next victim?"

He took the lollipop out of his mouth and pointed it toward two machines behind him. "Nine minutes, babe. That's plenty of time, don't you think?"

34

"Mmm, I'm sure it is for you, Thundercat. Well, I've got almost an hour, so I'm gonna run up and grab my wallet," she said, handing him back his card and making her way towards the door. She turned back to face him. "Thanks again. I owe you one, Tyler."

"No problem. I'm sure we can, uh, figure somethin' out." He slowly wrapped his lips around the lollipop, then pulled it out and flicked the tip of his tongue against it a few times, winking at her.

She realized her mouth was open, so she quickly closed it, shook her head, and walked out to get back on the elevator.

Holy fuck. Do only young, hot men live in this building? she thought, opening the door to her apartment.

Speaking of young, hot men: she wondered if Ryan had come back yet, but that question was confirmed quickly.

As she rounded the corner from the kitchen to the living room, she saw him lying flat on his back on the floor in the hallway that led to their bedrooms. His legs were bent at a 90-degree angle and his feet were against the wall. His hands were on his forehead, his breathing labored.

"Ryan?" she asked cautiously, standing over him. "You OK?"

"Debatable," he replied, his eyes closed.

"What's going on?"

"Just a...panic attack. Probably should've warned you about these. I tried to make it to...my room, but this is as...far as I got."

"OK. Can I help you?"

"Nope. Just gotta ride it out, focus...on my breathing. It's kinda...fucked at the moment."

She lay down on the floor next to him, bending her legs in the exact same way and putting her feet up on the wall next to his. She reached over, grabbed his right hand, and held it with both of hers. "Hey, tell me five things you can see right now."

"You. The wall. My shoes. The floor. The ceiling."

"Good. Now tell me four sounds you can hear..."

She walked him through the rest of the steps, counting down to one, and his breathing began to return to normal. He rolled his head sideways to face hers, which was already turned towards him. "You too?" he asked quietly.

"My ex. He used to get them pretty bad."

"I've been anxious for as long as I can remember, but this bullshit started when I was 17, right after my dad died. He swung his legs over and sat up. "And as quickly as they hit, they disappear. I'm sorry."

"For what?" she said, sitting up next to him. "I'm glad I could help you. Any idea what set it off?"

He closed his eyes and leaned his head onto his arms, which rested on his bent knees. He sat quietly for a bit, then lifted his head to look at her. "You know, Nick was right. You're really easy to talk to."

"I feel the same way."

"Hey, we need to get to know each other, right? So, let's play a game. We agree to share some random shit about ourselves every day. Even if it's embarrassing and completely ridiculous. OK?"

"OK," she said, unsure about where this was headed.

"Cool. I'll start. Nice to meet you, Amara. I'm 23 fucking years old and I've never even been in a real relationship. I want one, but instead of actually trying, I screw just about everything with a pulse. I immediately lose interest after, and then I hate myself. There have been two girls that I've liked even after slamming them, and both told me to fuck off. I have never been in love. Not even close, and I don't even know if it's something I'm capable of, honestly."

Amara blinked a few times. "Um, wow. You've been waiting to get that off your chest, huh? That's some heavy lifting, Baylor. OK, we're doing this, huh?" She clasped her hands and nodded. "My turn. Nice to meet you, Ryan. I'm 41, and I'm pretty sure real relationships are complete, overrated bullshit. My last 'real' relationship literally almost killed me. I probably won't ever trust anyone enough to be in another one ever again. I haven't even *seen* a dick since before my divorce, and I would love nothing more than to screw just about everything with a pulse, preferably as soon as possible."

They looked at each other, Ryan smiling. "What's that you said about heavy lifting?"

Amara shrugged. "Guess we got some shit to help each other work through, don't we?" She stood up. "Anyway, what time are we heading down tonight?"

"So, you'll come?" Ryan asked, his voice laced with mild excitement.

"Why not? Besides, maybe I'll meet something with a pulse." She winked at him.

"Yeah. Maybe," he said blankly, getting up off the ground. "Give it a few hours. I'm gonna go lay down for a bit. Shit takes a lot out of me."

She watched him walk away to his bedroom, unable to pull her eyes away from him for even a second. Everything about Ryan Baylor was beyond beautiful, and as she'd suspected would be the case, she found herself insanely attracted to him. But, having caught a glimpse of just how broken he was, she decided that, for right now at least, this one was off-limits.

Mr. Laundry Room, Tyler Hayes, however, was a completely different story.

Game on with that one.

THE TEAMMATES (7)

"Should we have brought a bottle of wine or something?" Amara asked as they got off the elevator on the fourth floor.

Ryan smirked. "You haven't spent much time around hockey players, have you?"

"None," she said. "I tended to date guys who had at least a few functioning brain cells."

He shook his head and lifted his shirt, showing off his six-pack. "Rock-hard abs plus incredible stamina equals no need for functioning brain cells."

"Aww," Amara clapped. "And you can do math? Aren't you just the whole package?"

Ryan stuck his tongue out at her, knocking on the door. A few seconds later, it opened.

"What's goin' on, Rook?"

"Hayes," Ryan leaned in and gave him a half-assed, one-handed hug. "Yo, this is Nick's cousin…"

"Shit," Hayes said, his bloodshot eyes widening, a huge smile creeping across his face. "Of course it is. Shit."

"Tyler?" Amara asked as he reached out to hug her, and they wrapped their arms around each other slowly.

"OK. So apparently *you guys* know each other." Ryan threw his hands up and watched them hug for a little bit too long before pulling away from each other. Tyler shut the door behind all of them as Osi walked over.

"Baylor. What is going on?" They hugged briefly, and Osi extended his hand towards Amara. "You are Nick's beautiful cousin? Is nice to meet you. I'm Aleksey Osinov, but everyone call me Osi."

She shook his hand. "Nice to meet you, too, Osi." Amara turned towards Ryan, who looked increasingly uncomfortable. "These the fourth-floor hotties?"

"Guilty," Hayes said, running his hands through his hair.

"Wow. Thanks for the flowers, Tyler. You're almost unrecognizable without your lil' hat and lollipop."

"Ooh, she call you Tyler. Wait, how you…" Osi stopped mid-thought and covered his mouth. "Ohhhh. She is hot cougar from laundry room?"

"Osi! The fuck?" Hayes waved him off, as Ryan shoved past them into the living room.

"Hot cougar, huh? Nice," Amara teased, punching him lightly. She went to catch up with Ryan, and Hayes followed.

There were four other very large guys and two heavily made up, scantily clad girls sitting in the living room, where a light cloud of weed smoke hung in the air and some sort of God-awful mumble rap music bumped through the speaker. Amara immediately took notice of the fact that the girls were staring at Ryan and whispering to each other.

"Boys, this is the rook, Ryan Baylor," Hayes said, as he began to point at each of them. "So, we got Kasic, Dalesy, Seggy, and Jonesy. Yo, this is Dunny's cousin, Amara. She lives with Rook. And," he turned to Amara and Ryan, "I don't know

who the fuck the birds are, to be honest. Might be Dalesy's."
He shrugged and put his arm around Ryan's shoulder. "First
things first: let's say we get you fuckin' wasted, Rook." He led
Ryan towards the kitchen, who looked back and signaled for
Amara to follow them, so she did.

"And this," Hayes said, pointing to an older guy sitting at
the kitchen counter staring at his phone, "is our resident nut
job, Rizz. Formally known as our captain, Matt Rislan."

"Nut job is a bit harsh," he said, taking a long pull off a
pen. "I'm just more awake than most."

"Yeah, if you want a good conspiracy theory, Rizz is your
guy. Flat Earth, 9/11, the *Titanic.* Fucker is straight-up insane.
Gimme that," Hayes said, grabbing the pen from him and
pulling. "Oh, and I almost forgot the best part." He exhaled the
smoke. "He'll 'read you' and let you know what kind of energy
you have." Hayes looked over at Amara and Ryan, put his finger
to his temple, and made the "crazy" motion with it.

"Crazy as it is, am I usually right?" Rizz asked, not
looking up from his phone.

"Totally. It's fuckin' terrifying, honestly," Hayes said,
lining up four disposable shot glasses and filling them with
Canadian whisky.

"Ugh, not that piss again," Rizz complained.

"Shut up and drink it." He handed them to Ryan and
Amara. He picked his up and tapped Ryan's with it. "Here's to
new friendships, and," he turned to Amara, "whatever else."

They all threw it back, and Ryan immediately reached
for the bottle, refilling his shot. He slammed that one down
too, snaked an arm around Amara's shoulder, then looked at
Hayes. "How's your girlfriend? She good?"

"Uh oh," Hayes said, throwing his hands up. "Rook's
gettin' all territorial over his roomie. Lower your leg, killer. It
was just some innocent flirting while waiting for our laundry,
that's all. Right, Amanda?" He winked at her.

"Sure," she said quietly. Sensing Ryan's uneasiness, she
changed the subject. "What else do you have to drink around

here?"

Someone called for Hayes from the living room. "Hold on, I'm comin'! Yeah, help yourself to whatever's in the fridge," Hayes said on his way out.

Amara went and grabbed a beer from the fridge, and as she walked back, Ryan was tossing back another shot of whisky. "Careful. That nasty shit sneaks up on you," Rizz warned. "You two, you're together?"

They looked at each other and smiled. "No. Just roommates. I'm Nick's cousin, actually. We...it's a long story, but we both needed a place to live, so here we are."

"That's cool. Funny how things work out sometimes. I was gonna say, there's...nah, forget it," he stopped himself, taking another pull off his pen.

"No, what? Can you seriously read people?" she asked curiously, having a seat at the counter across from him. Ryan sat down next to her, then poured and cranked back another shot. "Hey," she said to him, then mouthed, "slow down."

He rolled his eyes. "OK, Mom."

"I wouldn't call it reading. I'm just like, very in tune with other people's energies. It sounds batty, I know. My wife's more of an empath. She can feel things, but I just pick up on them very easily."

"So, what are you picking up on with us?" she asked, looking over at Ryan. "I mean, are you OK with this?"

He closed his eyes and shrugged. He grabbed her beer and took a sip. "Why not? This day can't possibly get any weirder." She noticed he was starting to slur his speech a bit.

"So, you two are interesting. You match almost completely. Your energies are nearly in total alignment."

"OK. So, what's that mean?"

"There are a few different takeaways. When did you guys first meet?"

"Um. Today, actually," Amara laughed nervously.

"Wow. No doubt you feel like you've known each other a lot longer. You guys finding you're pretty comfortable with each other?"

Ryan shot a look at Amara, then raised one eyebrow at Rizz. "You guys fuckin' with me? What kinda wizardry is this?"

He laughed and shrugged. "It's a gift, man. Saved me a lot of heartbreak, that's for sure. Most likely, you were previously connected somehow. I mean, I don't know how much you guys believe in that past-life stuff, but that's my gut feeling. You guys do need to be careful though."

"What do you mean?" Amara asked, completely rapt, as she leaned in towards him.

"You know the saying 'opposites attract,' right? Energy matches have the strong potential to clash. Fights will get ugly, and any jealousy can get out of control. Just be mindful and try to avoid all that shit. You both feel things deeply, and there's a lot of pain that you're both working through right now. That's coming through loud and clear. Be supportive, but just be aware that your feelings can very easily attach to each other's feelings, which can get messy."

Ryan got up. "Ok. I'm officially freaked the fuck out. Have fun with that shit." He saluted Rizz and made an exit to the living room.

Amara sat, mouth agape, and grabbed the whisky bottle for a refill. "Holy shit," she said, before knocking another one back. She leaned in. "I had this feeling that I was, like, way too comfortable with him, and you just said all that." She shook her head.

"And, uh, sex will really complicate things between you two. Just a PSA."

"No, we're not…it's not…we're…" Amara stammered.

"He doesn't take his eyes off you."

Amara blushed. "You're older than these boys."

"Oh yeah, I'm the team fossil at the ripe old age of 36. Got a 15-year-old son, if you can believe that. He was an oops, but he's the best fuckin' thing that's ever happened to me." He showed her a picture on his phone. "That's him, Logan, and my wife, Lindsey."

"Rizz, he's so handsome. And your wife: wow."

"Thanks. Yeah, I'm really just here to babysit these assholes, make sure no one does anything too stupid. You know what they say: young, dumb, and full of cum. So, what about you? You've gotta be close to my age. I don't mean that disrespectfully. You just seem a little, well, more mature than what normally crawls around at these parties."

"I...am 41, and it doesn't get any easier to say that out loud."

"Well, you look great."

"Thanks. So, what's Tyler like?" Amara blurted out, then tried to cover her interest. "I mean, I don't know much about him, but he seems...interesting. What's his deal?"

"Ah, Hayes? Hayes is harmless. He comes off a little rough at first, but he's actually got a big heart. And he's incredibly sensitive to others' needs, especially those he really cares about. Bit of a troubled past, but he's really grown up a lot over this last year with us. Still an absolute dumbass sometimes, but what 20-year-old kid isn't?"

Amara almost spat out her beer. "I'm sorry, you said 20? Hayes is 20?"

"Yeah, why?"

"Um, no reason. He just seems older is all. "

"Hayes has...he's been through a lot. Grew up kinda quick."

Amara frowned. "Well, anyway, I thought maybe I sensed a little bit of tension between him and Ryan."

"Oh, for sure. There's gonna be a huge power struggle there. Ryan's very insecure and Hayes is the dictionary definition of an alpha. Hayes's mouth gets him into a lot of trouble. Ryan's just gotta try not to get sucked into it, though it's gonna be hard for him since he's easily flustered." He smirked. "Sorry, I can't help myself sometimes."

"Are you kidding? This is amazing. Where the hell were you when I met my ex-husband?" She got up from her stool. "Well, I'm gonna go check on Baylor. Nice talking to you, Rizz."

"Likewise."

She grabbed her beer and moseyed into the living room, where it had gotten progressively louder, and the conversation was getting pretty rowdy amongst all the guys. There was also no sign of Ryan, and one of Dalesy's girls was missing.

"Oh, you wanna go there with me, Hayes? Question my relationship decisions?" Dalesy snickered. "OK, bitch. Who's the one who got the boot from two different billet families at 16 for fuckin' both his moms, eh?"

"Oh, shit. No, he did not go there!" Osi said, his face a bit panic-stricken.

"Dude, are you serious? Both?" one of the other guys asked.

"Listen, listen!" Hayes clapped. "This is fake news. I did not fuck both of them. I fucked *one* of them. The other one was blowin' me in her minivan and her husband caught us."

"Yeah, 'cause that's any better."

"You at least get to finish?"

"Yup. Came down her throat right as we got caught. It was kinda hot."

"There's something not right with you, Hayes. It's amazing he didn't cave your face in. The fact that you made it here is beyond me. How'd you even recover from that shit show?"

"My juniors coach took me in. Had no choice. He saw my talent. I mean, I was the fastest skater, the top scorer, and had a straight beast of a clapper, but the program refused to house me with another family. Obviously."

"Obviously," Dalesy echoed. "Because you're a filthy gutter slut."

"Yo, dude literally pulled me aside outside his house, bags still in my hands, and said to me, I'll never forget it as long as I live: 'Kid, I have a shotgun and a boat. No one will even miss you. You're here to play hockey, and unless you wanna die, you will keep your fuckin' hands, eyes, and all other body parts to yourself.' And guess what? I fuckin' did."

Troubled past is right, Amara thought sadly, immediately regretting having heard that conversation. She decided to go out onto the balcony for some air, wondering briefly where Ryan had wandered off to, though she had a pretty good idea that wherever it was, the missing girl from the living room was there, too.

✻ ✻ ✻

She wasn't sure how long she'd been outside, but it'd been a while. She'd been staring at the bustling city below, wondering what all those people were up to, where they were headed, when she heard the patio door slide open. She looked, saw it was Tyler, and turned back toward the railing. He came and stood next to her, just close enough so their elbows touched. She dramatically scooted over a smidge so they weren't.

"What's that all about?" he asked.

"You have a girlfriend, and you behave the way you did with me earlier? Do you know I'm 41 years old? Why the hell didn't you tell me you're only 20?"

"Wait: so, you're pissed at me because I have a girlfriend, or because my parents had sex 21 years after yours did? I don't follow."

"What was that shit today in the laundry room, Tyler?"

"That was called flirting. And as I recall, you were pretty into it."

"*That* was flirting?" She shook her head. "Man, I've really been out of the game for too long."

"Why, what'd you think it was?" He gasped, then smiled. "Oooh. You've been thinkin' about me, haven't you? What'd we do? Was it good?"

She made a face. "Eww. No."

"Then what's it matter if I have a girlfriend?"

"It doesn't. Considering you're practically a child."

He laughed. "Farthest thing from it, babe." He inched back over so their elbows touched again. This time, she didn't move. "So, what's up? You bangin' Rook? What's your story?"

"It doesn't matter."

"Come on, you just heard some of my greatest hits in there."

"Yeah. I really didn't need to hear all that. Forgive me if I'm not really into celebrating someone's adolescent sexual abuse."

"Nah, come on. It wasn't even like that. For one, the consent age in Canada is 16, not to mention I initiated it with both of them, so if anyone's the creep, it's me. Trust me, I fuckin' wanted it."

"You're tellin' me that at 16, you had the balls to initiate sex with not one, but two much older, married women?"

"That's exactly what I'm tellin' you, babe. What can I say?" He turned to face her. "Older women do it for me."

She turned towards him. "Your girlfriend should do it for you."

"She does."

"Then what are you doing out here with me?"

He smiled and rolled his eyes. "Amara, Amara. Clearly, you've gotten," he cocked his head sideways and leaned into her face, his lips brushing ever-so-slightly against hers, "the wrong impression of me." She felt him breathing against her lips and closed her eyes. Despite how wrong this all was, she bit her bottom lip, waiting and wanting so badly for him to kiss her. Instead, he pulled away suddenly. "No worries. I'll leave you alone if that's what you want."

Making his way back over to the sliding glass door, he opened it and turned to face her. "But we both know you'll still be thinkin' about me. Oh, you should probably check on your boyfriend. He's been in my bedroom with that bird for a bit now. I sure hope everything is OK." He shrugged and stepped inside.

"He's not my boyfriend!" she yelled, as he shut the door.

She took a deep breath, grabbed onto the railing to steady herself, and crossed her legs. *How the fuck is that fucker only 20?* she thought, hoping she'd remembered to charge her vibrator recently.

She'd definitely be using it later.

When she finally got herself together and came inside, the other girl was back in the living room, straddling Dalesy's lap and kissing his neck, but there was no sign of Ryan. Amara peeked into the kitchen, but nothing, so she made her way to the hallway that led to the bedrooms. As she rounded the corner, she saw him come stumbling out of what she assumed was Tyler's room.

"Amara!" he yelled, stretching his arms out to hug her as she approached him. "There you are!" She could see in his eyes that he was hammered. "Yo," he whispered, leaning half on her, half on the wall. "That girl just totally blew me. I don't even know her name. She just told me to follow her and started taking my pants off. We didn't even kiss. I blew a huge load all over Hayes's sheets though."

"That's…wow, that's such a great story, Ryan. I think it's time we get you back upstairs, OK?" He slumped against the wall and slid slowly until his ass hit the floor, just as Tyler showed up.

"Havin' fun, Rook?"

"Amara, should I tell him about his sheets?"

"The fuck you do to my sheets?"

"Ryan, be quiet. Tyler, help me get him back upstairs and into a bed, please."

They managed to scoop him up and get him out the door and down the hall to the elevator. As they waited for it, each of his arms draped around their shoulders, he began rambling. "You know what, Hayes? Fuckin', I don't think I like you."

"Is that right?"

"Yeah. You're kind of a douche."

Amara stifled a laugh.

"That's OK, Rook. Amara likes me, isn't that right, babe?"

"Tyler…"

"You like this douche?"

"Yeah, she does. We had a fun little conversation out on the balcony tonight. She's actually kinda horny for me."

"Tyler!"

"What?" he asked. "You gonna pretend you're not?"

"You're horny for *this* douche?" Ryan yelled, right as the door opened, where an older couple, probably in their late 70's, stood there staring at them.

"Going up?" the woman asked.

The three awkwardly waddled their way inside. "Six, please," Amara said, mortified.

"Apparently *this one*," Ryan patted Amara's shoulder, "wants to go *down*. On this douche." He patted Tyler's shoulder, as he turned to the older man. "Bro, you believe that shit?"

"It happens sometimes, son," the man replied with a shrug.

Hayes almost doubled over with laughter. "Holy shit!" he squeaked. "Rook's a fuckin' riot when he's wasted!"

"Oh my God. Will you both please shut up?"

They got off on the sixth floor and managed to get Ryan to the apartment door as Amara unlocked it. Hayes tried to come in, but Amara strong-armed him. "Nope. I've got it from here, Kindercare."

"You sure about that, babe?" She turned around, and he was sliding down the wall again. "It would appear Rook can't handle his liquor, eh?"

"Shit. Alright, help me get him into his bed." They dragged him down the hallway and maneuvered him inside his room, where he flopped onto his bed, face down, both of them just staring at him for a bit.

"You gonna puke, Rook?"

He shook his head no.

"Tyler, I'll walk you out. I'll be right back, Ryan. Don't move."

Amara followed Tyler to the door, reaching to open it for

48

him, but he blocked her hand, intertwining his fingers with hers. "I mean, if you asked me to stay right now, I would. You know, for moral support. Your new roommate is blackout drunk, you're all alone in this strange new apartment..."

"Tyler? Go home." She pulled her hand away from his.

"Fine. You're welcome, by the way," he said, opening the door and adjusting the front of his pants.

"Thank you, Tyler."

"You know," he leaned in towards her, "I don't quite understand it, but something about the way you call me 'Tyler' gets me fuckin' rock hard."

"Ok, we're done here!" She slammed the door and locked it.

"You know where to find me!" he said through the door, as she turned to go attend to her drunk-ass roommate.

She walked into Ryan's room, where he was still face down and now snoring. She tried pulling each of his shoes off gently, but he woke up as she got to the second, rolled over, and sat up, obviously disoriented. He reached down and tried to yank his shirt over his head, but it got stuck, so she helped him pull it the rest of the way off. "OK, oh wow," she said, staring at his shirtless body. The kid's abs were so perfectly defined that he didn't even look real.

He flopped onto his back and started unbuttoning his pants, finally getting them open, and tried to wiggle them down his legs. "And there go the pants. Here, hold on," she said, grabbing them at his thighs and fighting with them before finally pulling them off. As he lay there in nothing but his boxers and socks, she tried not to stare, but it was impossible. He had the best male body she'd ever seen in person; there literally wasn't an ounce of fat on him, just pure muscle. She reached for the sheet at the end of the unmade bed and covered him with it, primarily to maintain her own sanity.

"Thank you," he mumbled, his eyes closed. She reached over and ran her fingers through his hair. He moaned. "Thafeels nice."

"You need to sleep, Drunkie. I'll be in my room if you need me."

"Stay?" he yawned, holding the sheet open. "We'll cuddle."

"That's not happening."

"Come on. Two girls sucked my dick today. Make it three?"

"You know, wow, as tempting as that sounds, that'd be the worst idea possibly ever. And kinda gross."

"I know, I know. I'm just kidding." He was snoring again before she could even say anything else, so she figured this was a good time to make an exit.

What a fucking day, she thought, unable to remember not only a time when she'd had so much excitement, but a time when she'd felt so free, to just be herself and do whatever she wanted to do without having to answer to anyone. And as clearly fucked-up as these guys were, she enjoyed being around them and certainly didn't mind the attention they gave her.

She knew this was going to be one hell of a ride, but she felt a curious excitement to see just where it would take her.

FOR THE LOVE OF THE GAME (8)

"Baylor, what the actual fuck was that? Are you even watching what's going on?"

He skated back towards the bench, where the defensive coach was screaming at him. "Sorry, Coach Reilly. I guess I hesitated."

"Yeah, you're damn right you did. Did you even see the two guys who blew right past you? Where's your head at, kid? That was a game, that'd be another minus. That what you want? You wanna be the d-man who racks up minuses?"

"No, Coach."

"Well, that's what you are right now. You need to move your fucking feet and get after it! Now get back out there and run that shit again. Hayes, Segorsky, Dales: go again with

Rislan and Baylor."

Ryan skated back out towards center ice, banging his stick in frustration. The season-opening away game was tomorrow night, and he'd been completely sucking ass for the past two weeks. This certainly wasn't who he normally was on the ice. He'd been tried with just about every other defenseman on the team, but for some reason, there just wasn't that chemistry he was used to. He did not want to end up a rotating defenseman, but it wasn't looking too promising at the moment. Rislan was who he'd mostly been paired with, and he'd been great about giving him pointers.

"You've got the size, man. You gotta throw that body around, make 'em hurt," Rizz had told him. "They need to be terrified to come across that blue line when they see your big ass."

The two biggest criticisms from his coaches were that he didn't play physically enough for his size and that he was too slow, nothing he hadn't heard before. At the end of all three preseason games, he was at minus five. He could tell his teammates were getting frustrated with him, though they were nice about it, with him being the newbie.

Most of them were nice, anyway.

"Yo, Rook: you do know that on D, your job is to stop the other team from scoring, right? I can't do my fuckin' job plus yours. Get your shit together. This ain't the NCAA. And for Christ's sake, learn to fuckin' skate, eh? I'll fuckin' pay for some lessons!"

Hayes had been absolutely brutal. He was Bridgeport's star player, and he and everyone else knew it. He'd come right from the OHL and was on year two of his two-way, three-year entry-level contract with the New York Islanders, but had landed in Bridgeport having just barely missed the roster out of camp last summer.

He'd had an unbelievable rookie season in the AHL; he'd made the All-Star team and led the Isles in goals and points, until the end of March. During a game against Wilkes-Barre/

Scranton, he was cross-checked into the boards shoulder-first, a dirty hit that landed the other guy a three-game suspension. He ended up with a grade four AC separation that resulted in him needing surgery, which had pretty much laid him up for most of the summer. He'd started skating again just three weeks ago, and it had been decided that he'd start the year with Bridgeport, even though everyone fully expected him to join the big club at some point sooner than later.

When practice was over, Nick grabbed Ryan as he came off the ice. "Baylor, I wanna check out that knee again, ice it a bit before you head out. Meet me in a few."

Ryan had gotten into a collision in the last game and twisted his left knee pretty good. It was still bothering him a bit, but he taped it up and pushed through. He kept telling Nick he was fine, but considering it was literally Nick's job to assess and treat injuries, he insisted.

"It's definitely looking better, and you were skating much better, too. Let's ice it for about 20 minutes, and I want you on wall squats and hamstring curls before tomorrow's practice and before the game tomorrow night, work on that mobility." He wrapped the ice pack around Ryan's leg on the table and set a timer. "So, how's my cousin? You kill her yet?"

Ryan smiled. "Not yet. Nah, she's good. Nick, thank you. I literally couldn't have asked for a better roommate."

"What'd I tell you? I knew you two would hit it off. How's her new bartending job? I gotta call her."

"She seems to like it, I guess. She's been working a lot of nights lately, just finished training. We haven't..." he paused. "We haven't seen each other much. She's been busy with her writing, too. I think we're supposed to hang out tonight."

Ryan would choose death by wood-chipper before he admitted it to another soul, but he knew a big part of his problem on the ice was because of Amara. They'd been living together for almost a month now, and it couldn't have been going any better.

Like Rizz had said that first night, their energies were

completely in sync. They just naturally gravitated towards each other and had developed their own little routines: certain shows they'd watch, who would cook dinner when, and he always looked forward to when she'd read to him some of the freelance writing she was working on to get his opinion on it. His opinion was always that, though the subject matter was usually boring as shit and he didn't understand a word of it, he was in awe of her writing ability.

"It amazes me how smart you are," he told her, smiling at the way she'd blush when he said that.

To any outsider, this seemed like it was perfect, and it was. But the part that was fucking with Ryan's head was that he wasn't interested in being her roommate or her friend anymore. Despite all odds, mainly the 18-year-wide canyon that separated them, he'd managed to fall so fucking hard for her that it was all but making him physically ill.

Besides hockey, the only thoughts he had from the minute he woke up to the minute he fell asleep were of Amara: the way she would rest her legs across his lap when they watched TV, the way she snorted when she laughed really hard, the way she'd always cover him with a blanket when he dipped out on the couch, the smell of her body when she'd return from a workout. His existence was completely consumed by her.

He just couldn't tell her that.

He wanted to, more than anything, but there were too many variables in this complicated equation.

One, he knew she didn't want a serious relationship. She'd made that very clear. He didn't know if she'd been sleeping around like she'd initially told him she wanted to, but he damn sure wasn't about to ask. It was also a very real possibility that she just saw him as a friend.

Two, there was the fact that Ryan Baylor couldn't keep his dick in his pants if someone held a gun to his head. He was still banging random girls several times a week, though it'd recently gotten to the point where he couldn't even cum anymore unless he thought about her. Not to mention, though it was highly unlikely: what if, once they had sex, he lost interest? Then what?

Three, she was old enough to be his mother. The age difference didn't really bother him, but he was aware that it would always be front and center and that people would judge. Having kids would be out of the question; he wouldn't be ready any time soon. And how would he explain to his mom that he was dating a woman only seven years younger than her? He knew his mom, and she would flip shit for sure.

Last, but certainly not least, there was Tyler fucking Hayes.

Ever since the party, Hayes had latched onto Amara like a leech. Much to Ryan's disappointment, they'd grown close as well. He'd backed off the hyper-sexualized flirting after she sat him down and told him that it wasn't fair to his girlfriend, and he agreed to chill.

But they spent a lot of time together. He'd show up randomly at their apartment for dinner or to hang out, they'd go grocery shopping, and go for runs or work out together. It didn't sit right with Ryan; it was a weird dynamic that he didn't completely understand. He'd mentioned something to her about it once, and she'd gotten defensive.

"What, so I'm not allowed to be friends with anyone but you?"

"That's not what I said. But seriously, what can you two possibly have in common? Kid's 20 years old."

"My bad, Grandpa Time. You're so much more venerable and wiser at the ripe old age of 23."

"He just wants to fuck you. You know that, right? If his girlfriend died right now, he'd be at our door in five minutes with his cock out."

"And? He knows where I stand with that. It's not gonna happen. Tyler and I are just good friends. For some odd reason, we…just seem to get each other."

"Right."

"What's that supposed to mean?"

"Nothing. It's just...you know I don't like him."

"Well, maybe you should start. He's your teammate. Have you ever tried talking to him? Do you even know anything about him, where he's from, some of the shit he's been through?"

"I kinda don't really care. I know enough about him to know I don't like him. And maybe I just don't get why you do."

"There's nothing for you to get. Do me a favor and back the fuck up about it. I can handle my own shit, and I suggest you do the same."

The timer beeped, and Nick came back over to remove the ice pack, with Hayes following behind him.

"Good, ice that bitch. Maybe you'll actually move at a decent pace now, you fuckin' hoser." Hayes winked at him, sitting down as Ryan got up.

"It'd be such a shame if you reinjured that shoulder and had to spend the rest of the season in the press box," he spat back.

"Oh, you're a fuckin' tough guy, eh?" Hayes started to stand up, with Nick stepping in between them and pushing him back down. "Learn how to fuckin' play D, then maybe you get to run your mouth."

"Yo, boys. Baylor? Outta here. Hayes? Shut the hell up, for once in your goddamn life, please!"

"Piece of shit," Ryan muttered, walking into the locker room to grab his things from his stall. He started to feel a wave of anxiety coming over him, and he sat down for a moment, leaning his head back and closing his eyes.

After a few minutes, a voice snapped him back to reality. "Baylor, can we talk for a sec? I know you're on your way out."

He leaned forward and opened his eyes. "What's up, Cap?" Although, he already knew what was coming.

"One, just breathe through it, brother." It was literally impossible to hide anything from Rizz, who sat down next to him and patted him on the leg. "Two, I need you to make more of an effort with Hayes, guy. Coach is kinda pissed and asked me to talk to you. I can't have you two chirpin' at each other constantly. It's gettin' old."

"He started it."

"And he always will start it. That's what Hayes does. But he's earned his spot, proven himself. You're the newbie, OK? And as much as I like you, this negative energy isn't helping the team right now. This is our job, Baylor. Whatever shit's going on outside of here, you gotta leave it outside of here. You know exactly what and who I'm talking about."

Ryan sighed. "I know."

"Seriously, you need to check your personal shit at the door. This is a team, and I need you to act like you wanna be a part of it. I love you to death, kid, but don't fuck this up." Rizz got up and reached out to shake his hand. "Bus leaves at 9:00 a.m. tomorrow. Go home and get your head right."

Get my head right? Ok, Ryan thought, fully aware that there was nothing even remotely right about his head.

FINALLY (9)

"So, I don't even know what I'm supposed to do now. Do I ignore him, do I call the cops?" Amara was venting to Ryan about a customer at the bar who wouldn't leave her alone tonight. "Hello?" She waved her hand in front of Ryan's face, and he snapped back to it.

"Sorry. I zoned out. Listen, it happens again, you call me. Me and the boys will come down there and handle it. But don't walk home by yourself again. That was stupid."

"I know. I should've called you."

He was already dreading tomorrow's road trip to Lehigh Valley. It was three hours away, but since they had a home game the following night, they weren't staying over, so he'd be getting home super late. He hadn't been away from her since they met, and it was not something he wanted to do, especially not right now.

"Ok. What's the plan for tonight? It's been a while. Next

episode of *Stranger Things*? Start a movie? What are you in the mood for?" She'd just showered, and the smell of her freshly washed wet hair permeated the air; it was driving him insane. She sat on the couch next to him in shorts that had no business being so short and one of his college hoodies. She was sans makeup, and her smooth, bare legs, like always, rested across his lap.

What he was in the mood for was *her*, and he knew that if he didn't do something about it soon, he'd be on the verge of another mental break.

He sighed. "I don't know. The bus leaves at 9:00 a.m. tomorrow, and it's already after 10. I probably shouldn't stay up too late. And I still have to pack. This sucks." He placed a slightly trembling hand on her thigh and decided that, despite all his reservations, now was as good a time as any to make his move. "We haven't played that game where we share some random thing about ourselves in a while."

"Oh, you're right. We've been slacking. You wanna go first? I gotta think of something good."

"Um...yeah, I'll go. I kinda have something in mind."

"No more pants-shitting stories though, OK? That night was just ridiculous. I don't think I've ever laughed so hard in my life."

"Got it." He took a deep breath. "OK. Nice to meet you, Amara." He pushed her legs off his lap, forcing her to sit up next to him. He moved in close to her. "So, I've kinda got a problem." He stopped.

"What's wrong?" she asked, concerned. "You OK?"

"Yeah, I'm good. It's just that," he spoke slowly, "I literally cannot stop thinking about you. From the minute I wake up until my head hits the pillow, you and hockey are the only things on my mind."

"Ryan?"

"And I don't know how to say this, because this hardly ever happens to me, but I think I really like you. I like how close we've gotten, and I can't stop thinking about us. And I don't know what that means or what I should even do about it. I feel like maybe you feel it, too." He palmed his forehead, frustrated. "Oh my God, I suck at this shit. All I know is that I don't wanna just be your friend, Amara. It's not enough for me anymore."

She backed away from him cautiously, sat up straight, and leaned forward onto her lap. She was silent for a while.

"Can you please say something?" he pleaded.

"This isn't how this game is supposed to go, Ryan."

"Wow, Ryan Baylor fucked something up. That never happens. Anyway, it's your turn. Tell me something. Anything. Tell me to fuck off if you want. I'm used to that. But for God's sake, say something."

She looked at him. "OK, fine. Nice to meet you, Ryan," she finally said, grabbing one of his hands; she could feel him shaking. "You're *the* most beautiful human being I've ever seen, and I constantly have to stop myself from telling you that. I know I've been distant lately. And if I'm being honest, I've been trying to keep away from you, as hard as it's been. You're just…Ryan, you're way too young for me. There's no workaround. And we both know that realistically, there is no possible scenario where this ever works out…"

"I don't know that," he interrupted. "You don't know that, either."

"Stop. We both know that."

"You don't know that, Amara."

"This isn't a fucking romance novel, Ryan. No matter what we do, the only possible way anything between me and you ends is in heartbreak, and I can't handle another one."

"I won't break your heart."

"Please, Ryan. You don't even know how to be in a relationship."

He shrugged. "You're right. But I know I won't break your heart."

"Ryan, stop. You wanted me to say something, right? Then let me say it. I'm not ready for it, and neither are you. This isn't gonna happen, this can't happen, and knowing that?

60

The fact that I *still* feel the way I do about you is becoming a real problem for me. I don't...I don't trust myself around you, Ry."

"So, you feel it, too? This isn't me just making shit up in my head? You feel it, too?"

She nodded.

He scooted closer to her, reached the hand she was holding up to her face, and slid it slowly around the back of her neck, pulling her forehead to his. "I want you so bad," he whispered. "You want me too, don't you?"

"Ryan...this can't happen."

"Yes, it can. Show me how bad you want me," he demanded, as his other hand joined the one already on the back of her neck. Instinctively, she moved one leg across his lap, straddling him. Feeling how hard he was between her legs, she slid her hands up the front of his shirt and ran her fingertips across his abs. "Your fucking *body*, Ryan. My God."

"You want it? It's all yours, baby. I'll take you to my bedroom right now and fuck you 'til you can't move. But I wanna hear you admit that you want this."

Their foreheads still pressed together, their lips were getting dangerously close. She knew damn well that if they did this, there was no going back. This would complicate everything between them, just like Rizz had warned. He started slowly rocking his hips upwards into hers, and she responded by pressing hers down and grinding herself all over his lap. "Fuck, that feels so good, baby."

"Ryan. We can't...do this," she moaned, knowing her protest was beyond useless at this point.

This was happening.

"Then fucking stop me." His hands aggressively made their way up the front of the hoodie she had on, and right as he grabbed her tits, his tongue slid inside her mouth. She immediately met it with her own. He broke the kiss so he could yank the hoodie up over her head. She grabbed the bottom of his shirt and pulled it off, instantly returning her mouth to his.

They kissed like their mouths were made for each other; their tongues knew every move the other one was going to make, their lips knowing exactly when and where to suck, like they'd done this a thousand times.

"You've got me so fucking hard," he told her, as he grabbed her ass and flipped her over onto her back, pushing himself on top of her. He pressed his knee up in between her legs and she closed them tightly around it, reaching her hand between their bodies and grabbing him through his sweatpants. She was impressed with his size: decent length, but well-above-average girth. He grabbed her hand and forced it down the front of his pants, eliminating the barrier between her hand and his cock. "There we go. Fuck," he moaned, as she wrapped her fingers around him and began to jerk him off slowly.

He squeezed her small tits together and moved his mouth in between them, alternating between sucking her nipples and running his tongue in between her cleavage.

"I wanna fuck you, Ryan," she moaned.

"Say it again."

"I wanna fuck you so bad." She felt him harden even more as he pumped his hips faster, steadily fucking her hand. She was in the middle of wiggling out of her shorts with her free hand when a loud groan escaped him, and she felt his hot cum spurt all over her hand and the inside of his sweatpants. "Shit."

When he finished, neither of them moved and there was a lengthy pause, with Amara finally breaking it. "Hey, so…"

"Nope. Don't talk," he cut her off, embarrassed, his voice muffled as his face was pressed between her head and the couch. He sat up, adjusted his pants, and rolled his eyes. "That's just…fuckin' wonderful."

She sat up next to him and wrapped her arms around him. "For what it's worth: that was *the* hottest 30 seconds of my life."

He wiggled out of her grasp. "OK, you're not helping." He

stood up and yanked the front of his pants away from his body. "Ugh. Well, I'll be in my room with a plastic bag over my head if you need me."

"I'm just gonna…" She wiped her sticky hand all over the outside of his pants. "I'm assuming those are going in the wash." He looked at her, horrified. "What? Were you gonna wear them on the bus tomorrow? And don't beat yourself up. I give amazing handies." She winked at him.

"I really hate you."

"No, you don't." She stood up. "On that note: it's time for bed."

He grabbed her hand as she tried to walk past him. "Next time, I swear to you, I'm gonna blow your fuckin' back out."

"Ryan, I'm 41, so that's an actual possibility. And there's not gonna be a next time. This was a mistake. I told you, we can't do this."

"Oh, we're doing this. We can and we are."

"This is really stupid."

"Why? What's the issue?"

"Because I'm old…"

"Because you're older than me? Big deal. I lost my virginity to a woman 20 years older than me. Clearly, I'm not worried about that."

"Of course you did," she mumbled.

"Fuck's that supposed to mean?" He crossed his arms and stared at her intently.

"Nothing. It's just…" She sighed. "You're so attractive, it's sickening. I don't know if you even know how hot you actually are."

"I've heard a few things about it."

"OK, well, I've never been with anyone even close to you. You're an actual 10. And I'm not an idiot. I've seen the girls you run with, Ryan. My old crusty ass can't compete. I think this?" She circled her hands between the two of them. "It's clearly some kind of curious junk food bender you're on or something."

He uncrossed his arms and placed his hands on either of her shoulders. "One, if you ever refer to yourself as junk food again, I'll throat punch you. Two, what you just did to me on that couch, how quickly I came? That doesn't happen. Like, ever. Not a single one of those girls," he leaned in close to her and kissed her on the forehead, "has *shit* on you. I've felt sick about you for days, wondering how to talk to you about this without scaring you away. And I didn't spill my guts just to have you write me off. I'm prepared to fight for this, for you. I don't have the first fucking clue what I'm doing, and I fully expect to fuck it up, but I'm ready to go down swinging."

"We're both gonna get so hurt. You know that, right?"

He shrugged. "Just another day that ends in 'y' for me. It's a risk I'm willing to take."

"Fine, I'll make you a deal," she said. "I'm not committing to anything serious with you right now, OK? I can't. But if you wanna do *this* again, there's one condition."

"And what's that?"

"I want you to make nice with…"

"Don't say it. Don't you dare fucking say it!"

"…Tyler."

He groaned and threw his hands up. "I knew it. Really?"

"You're mean as shit to him."

"Because he's an asshole."

"No, he's really not. He's a good guy and he likes you. A lot. I want you to talk to him. You've got a long bus ride. Make friends with him, play 'Never Have I Ever' or some shit. I have to imagine this rift between you guys is carrying over to the ice as well, no?"

"Yeah. Rizz yelled at me today," he said quietly. "Said I need to make more of an effort with him. And apparently, Coach is pissed."

"See? Now you have two reasons to play nice. You make friends with Tyler, and," she ran her fingers slowly through his hair, "you'll get exactly what you want when you come back from your little road trip."

He reached up, grabbed her hand, and moved it down to his crotch. "I ain't 41. I can get goin' again right now. Let's go, woman."

"You know, I would, but neither of us has another 30 seconds to spare at the moment, stud." She started back toward her room, then turned back to face him. "I'm serious. I want some progress between you two this weekend."

"Fine," he grumbled, heading to his room, wondering how the hell he was supposed to connect with Tyler fucking Hayes. He wanted to connect with him, alright: connect a right hook with his jawline.

By the time he finished showering, packing, and laying out his suit for tomorrow, it was after 12 and he was exhausted. Before he went to sleep though, he fired off a single text message.

R: You were right. Just hooked up, and I couldn't even last 30 seconds into a hand job. I fucking can't get enough of her, Luke. I think I'm falling for her.

FIRST CONTACT (10)

"Hold up, hold up: make way for the man of the hour," Dalesy held his hands out as Ryan walked onto the bus. "This fuckin' guy right here!" The other guys were clapping and cheering for him, and he couldn't wipe the cheesy-ass grin off his face.

Ryan Baylor had just had the game of his life. With his help, the Islanders absolutely destroyed the Phantoms at their own home opener, 5-2. He'd put up two goals, including the game-winner, two assists, he was plus four, he dominated the PK, and he'd annihilated the other guy in his first-ever pro fight. He was named the first star of the game, and literally everyone had complimented him on his hustle, even Hayes.

"Now that is how you fuckin' do it, Rook!" he'd said to him, slapping his ass and shaking his shoulders as he walked into the locker room after the game. *"I knew you had it in there somewhere."*

He was on a serious high as he made his way through the bus, all the way to the second to last row, until he found what he was looking for. "Mind if I sit?"

Hayes looked up from his phone. "Go for it, stud," he said, patting the seat next to him.

He sat down and checked his messages. There were two: one was from his mom, wishing him luck in his first regular season pro game.

R: Thanks. It went amazing. Will call you tomorrow to fill you in. Love you!

The other was from Amara, asking how the game went.

R: I'm gonna need you to jerk me off before every game. I absolutely fucking killed it tonight. Fill you in later.

He hit send, then realized he had forgotten something.

R: Miss you.

She didn't respond, but he knew she was at work.

"You've got yourself quite the following already, Rook," Hayes said, showing him his phone screen. He had Instagram pulled up and was weeding through the comments under the Islanders' game post. Almost all of them were praising Ryan's performance tonight, and quite a few were comments from girls about how hot he was and if he was single. "Check your DM's. Let's bet: how many thirsty birds in there?"

He opened the app and checked. "Well, what's your guess?" he asked Hayes.

"I'm gonna go with 15."

"Close, 12." He laughed, scrolling. "Holy shit. Literally *all* of them want to meet up for sex. Every single one. They're not even trying to hide it."

"What did I tell you? Great time to be single, Rook."

He put his phone down and closed his eyes. There may have been 12 women trying to have sex with him, but there was only one he was even remotely interested in at the moment.

"What? You're not gonna set one up for later, slut? The bars should still be open for a minute when we get back. Betcha Osi will hit that shit up with you. Yo, Osi!" Hayes yelled, but Ryan waved him off. "Nah?"

"It's just, I kinda…can't. Right now."

"Ohhh," Hayes said. "That time of the month, eh? You still got a mouth, you know?"

Hayes nudged him, and he nudged him back. "Dick. I just…I kinda have something in the works right now, and I'm curious to see where it goes."

Hayes's eyes got wide, and he punched Ryan's leg. "It's that roommate of yours, isn't it? You two finally bang? About time."

Ryan blushed. "No, we didn't. We hooked up a little last night though. I don't know, man. I *really* like her, and that like, doesn't happen to me. Ever. And I…don't know why I'm telling you any of this."

"Maybe because that's what friends do, tell each other shit."

"Friends. Right."

"Look: I like you, man. I know you can't stand me…"

"That's not tru…"

"Save it, Rook. She tells me everything. I know you don't like me, but I'm hoping that'll change. What's your problem with me anyway? Secret time: let it fly."

"Fine. You're mouthy, you're cocky, you're nosy, and you're constantly busting my balls." Ryan was shocked at how quickly those words flew out of his mouth. He didn't even have time to think of a good lie.

"OK, the first three are spot on. But I bust your balls

because I know you're better than the weak-ass bullshit you've been putting out the past few weeks. Look at tonight. I'd like to think my ball-busting played a role in that."

"Of course you'd like to think that."

Hayes made a face. "What's your *real* problem with me? Come on, don't hold back. Say it out loud."

Ryan was pretty sure what he was getting at, but he didn't want to bring it up. "That about covers it."

"It wouldn't have anything to do with me and Amara, would it?"

Ryan felt himself getting agitated, but he remembered that he was supposed to make nice. He took a deep breath. "She can be friends with whoever she wants, man."

"Yeah, but you know she wants me, and that pisses you off, doesn't it?"

Ryan stood up, prepared to move his seat, but Hayes grabbed his arm and pulled him back down. "No, stop runnin' from your shit, man. Hash it out with me, quit bottling it up."

"What's there to hash out, Hayes? She wants you. Great. Am I supposed to sit and cry about it?"

"Can I say something? A lot of your problem on the ice, in the locker room, outside the rink, is that you get caught up in your own head. You don't deal with your shit."

"Yeah? Maybe that's just how I am."

"Yeah? Well, I'm a mouthy, cocky, nosy ball-buster. Maybe that's just how I am."

"Fair enough."

"So, you really like her?"

"That's what I said, isn't it?"

"Yes, it is. Asshole. Of course you like her. What's not to like? She's a little old, but she's the coolest chick I've ever met in my fuckin' life. And what I'm getting at, dick, is that she's into you, too."

"And you'd know this how?"

"Again: we talk. And the only fuckin' thing she ever talks about is some dickbag named Ryan Baylor."

Ryan smirked; he couldn't help it. "Yeah?" he asked quietly.

"She won't shut up about you. If I have to hear about your chiseled fuckin' abs one more time, I'm gonna throw up. She acts like a teenager whenever your name comes up, and she always finds ways to talk about you. I gave up a while ago."

"What do you mean you gave up?"

"So, the night of the party at my place. We were flirting and I came so close to kissing her when we were talking out on the balcony, but I stopped myself. Then when we dragged you back home, I told her I'd stay if she wanted me to. And I would've. I don't cheat, but I was tempted to that night."

"I don't understand. Why are you telling me all this?"

"Because I like you and I wanna be honest with you. There is something there with me and her. But if it's gonna be *you* and her, then it's nothing. You understand what I'm saying to you?"

"Not really."

"Jesus, you're dense, kid. I'm saying you don't have to worry about me with her, OK? I know you do, but you don't have to."

"You honestly want me to believe that you don't want her anymore? You follow her around like a lost puppy."

"I didn't say I didn't want her anymore, Rook. What I said is that if the two of you are, you know, then I won't touch her."

"You have a fucking girlfriend, Hayes. How about maybe that's why you don't touch her?"

"Yeah. I have a girlfriend who I'm pretty sure cheats on me. And who always brings up the fact that I'm not a real hockey player because I haven't made it into the NHL. And who didn't even come when I was laid up in bed after surgery. You know who took care of me? Osi."

"So why the fuck are you even with her? Don't you think you deserve a little better than that?" Ryan asked, the sudden anger in his voice surprising him.

"Amara said the exact same thing." Hayes shrugged and got quiet for a moment. "You believe in karma, Rook?"

"I guess I do. To an extent."

"Well, I've done some of the vilest shit you can imagine. I broke up two marriages, tore apart two whole families by the time I was 16 years old, man. Destroyed them. I have a feeling that life's giving me *exactly* what I deserve."

"What are you even talking about?"

"That's right, you were in my room with Dalesy's slut and missed that whole conversation."

"Damn, I forgot about that girl," Ryan said. He'd been so drunk he didn't even remember what she looked like, just that she could suck a golf ball through a garden hose.

"Yeah, well my sheets didn't forget, you fuckin' animal. Anyway, I almost didn't even get to play juniors because both times they placed me with a family, my dumb ass hooked up with the moms." He shrugged. "Within days, Rook. Both times. The fuckin' assistant coach for the Colts had to take me in. My actual mom got so pissed at me. *So* pissed, threatened to kick me out of my house, pull me from the team, she tried to press charges against both women."

"Why would she get mad at you? Shouldn't they have known better? You were just a kid, Hayes."

"I don't fuckin' know, Rook. I did what I did, and they did what they did. There was no pressure on either side. Just instant attraction that got out of hand very quickly. I can't help it. I fuckin' *love* older women. It's...a long story. But when I tell you it was a nightmare, it was a fuckin' nightmare."

"Sounds like it." Ryan debated sharing but went for it. "I lost my virginity to the mom of a kid I played against in juniors. Slipped me her hotel room number and rode me like a mechanical bull. I mean, for the like, 13 seconds I lasted. I was 18, and she was 38."

"OK, Rook! That's fuckin' baller shit right there. Anyway, enough about all that noise. So, you said you wanted to see where it goes with her." Hayes stared down at his hands in his lap. "Are you guys like, together?"

"I wanna be. But she doesn't. It's more of a situationship at the moment, as much as I hate that stupid word. She said she can't commit to a relationship. She thinks I'm too young, and she doesn't wanna get hurt again."

"Yo, I can't say I blame her after what she went through, man."

"I don't really know what she's been through. She hasn't opened up to me about it."

"It's fucked up. Like, really fucked up."

"Wait: she's talked to you about it?"

"Yeah. We talk all the time, about everything. I mean, mostly about you, but other stuff, too."

"Son of a bitch," Ryan muttered. "What happened to her?"

Hayes sighed. "Dude, don't tell her I told you this. Amara and Kevin, that's the piece of shit's name, they were like, trying forever to have kids. She really wanted to be a mom, but she could never get pregnant. I guess it was stressing them both out, causing all kinds of fights and shit. Anyway, he ended up knocking up a woman he worked with, and she decided to keep the baby. Mar suspected there was something going on with him and this bitch, too, but he kept telling her there was nothing to worry about and that she was crazy. She actually mailed Amara one of those ultrasound pictures with a note telling her she needed to talk to her husband. That's how she found out."

Ryan put his hand to his heart. "Oh my God."

"Right? Men have a reputation for being the cruel ones. Women are way more vicious, bro."

"I can't believe she never told me."

"I forget how it came up, but she cried a lot. She could barely get through the story. I feel bad for her, man. No one deserves that shit, especially not someone like her."

Ryan picked up his phone and saw that she'd texted him back.

A: Miss you, too. You making nice?

R: We actually just had a long conversation.

A: Proof or it didn't happen.

He turned his camera on and put it on selfie mode. "Yo, get in here. She doesn't believe we're playing nice."

Hayes leaned in, and just when Ryan went to snap the pic, he grabbed his face and kissed him right on his lips, lingering there for a moment. "Dude, what?" Ryan laughed, looking at it.

"That should do it," Hayes said proudly.

Ryan hit send and waited for her response.

A: Oh. My God. Why is this so hot tho?

R: Um, eww. So does this qualify?

A: You'll have to wait and see when you get home.

R: Cocktease.

A: Damn right. I'm leaving work now. No sign of the creep, but I'm Ubering just in case.

R: Good.

Ryan put his phone down and leaned his head back, exhausted. "You know," he said, eyes closed, "you're maybe not as big of a douchebag as I originally thought."

"Aww, Rook. That's the nicest thing anyone has ever said to me." Hayes reached in between them and pulled the armrest up, yawning. Then he leaned in, rested his head on Ryan's shoulder, and closed his eyes.

WELCOME HOME (11)

It was well after one in the morning when Ryan finally got home. He and Osi had ridden back to their building with Hayes in his Ford Raptor, and he tried to come in as quietly as he could, so as not to wake Amara.

Opening the door, he saw that the living room light was on. He set his keys on the counter and hung his suit jacket on the back of one of the stools, just as she came slinking around the corner towards him. Her hair was up in a high ponytail and she was wearing one of his tank tops with a pair of black lace underwear.

He stared, flustered. "Oh, uh, wow. Sorry if you were asleep. I was trying to…"

Before he could even finish his sentence, her tongue was tracing his lips and she was unbuttoning his dress shirt. She got it all the way undone, yanked it off his shoulders, and pushed it to the floor. Her hands migrated to his suit pants, unbuttoning and unzipping them. She pulled her mouth away from his.

"Hi," he panted, watching her drop to her knees in front of him. He clutched her ponytail as she immediately grabbed him and took him into her mouth. "Fuck," he moaned, as she began aggressively sucking him off. He looked down at her, and she looked up, locking eyes with him. "You're even more beautiful with my cock in your mouth." He knew if he let her keep going, he was gonna cum pretty quickly; he'd never in all his adventures been with someone who knew *exactly* how to touch him the way she did. It was like her DNA'd been programmed to get him off. "No. Fuck this." He pulled her head away.

"What's wrong?" she said, looking up at him.

He slid his hands under her arms and pulled her to her feet, kissing her, as he ran his hands all over her body: across her tits, down her sides, and over her ass. Ultimately, he kept one on her ass and moved the other between her legs, which she parted instinctively as soon as she felt him touch her there. "What's wrong," he said, rubbing her through her underwear, "is that you're not sitting on my fucking face right now." He pushed the fabric to the side, and feeling how wet she was, went for two fingers.

"Ryan," she moaned, as she wrapped both arms around his neck to steady herself, her legs almost collapsing as he moved his fingers in, out, and around inside her.

"Tell me how to make you cum. I wanna make you cum so fucking bad."

"Your bedroom, now."

He removed his hand from between her legs, grabbed onto her ass with both of his hands, and lifted her up. She wrapped her legs around his waist and kissed his neck as he carried her down the hallway, into his room, and dropped her onto his bed. Her legs hung off the edge as he stood over her. "Get on your knees," she instructed him, as she tore off the tank top she was wearing and chucked it onto the floor.

He reached up, ripped her panties off, and spread her legs, as she positioned them on top of his shoulders. She moaned loudly as she felt him run his tongue slowly along her clit, teasing her. He pushed two fingers inside of her again, before alternating between licking and sucking her clit while he finger-fucked her.

She knew it wouldn't take long; the kid knew exactly what he was doing. Still, she gave him some pointers to make it go quicker. As he continued using his fingers and mouth flawlessly in tandem, she felt herself tense up after just a few minutes. "I'm right there," she squeaked out. "Ryan, omigod!"

He removed his fingers, reached up to grab her tits, and buried his beautiful face between her legs, fucking her with his tongue as she came all over it.

She lay there, panting, as he walked over to his nightstand. "Holy shit. That felt…so good," she told him, as she watched him tear open a condom with his teeth and put it on.

Her heart was pounding out of her chest, realizing what was about to happen. She backed herself completely onto the bed, and he climbed on top of her. "You thought *that* felt good?" he asked, as he reached down, grabbed his cock, and guided it slowly inside of her. She whimpered, as her body, still sensitive from her orgasm, adjusted to his size. "Tell me how you want me to fuck you."

"Make me forget my name."

"Done."

He positioned himself over her, holding himself up on one elbow and gripping the headboard with his other hand. He started grinding his hips into hers slowly, teasing her and gauging her reaction. She reached her hands up and grabbed two fistfuls of his messy blonde hair, tugging on it as he continued to give it to her slowly, desperate to hear her beg for it.

"Faster, harder," she moaned, staring into his eyes, which were fixed on hers.

"You want it faster, harder?" he asked, continuing at the

same pace. "Beg me."

"God, please, Ryan. Faster. Harder. Please!"

He let go of the headboard and sat up, removing himself from her for a second. He grabbed both of her legs and moved them onto his shoulders. He leaned forward and pushed himself inside her again, grabbed the headboard with both hands, and proceeded to give her exactly what she wanted.

There was no kissing, no talking, nothing even remotely sweet or romantic about anything that was happening on that bed. The way he fucked her was animalistic; she'd never experienced anything like it before. She was so flustered by what his body was doing to hers that she couldn't figure out what to do with her hands. She moved frantically between pulling his hair, dragging her nails up and down his back, and grabbing his ass. She eventually reached them up above her head and grabbed onto his biceps, as he continued to annihilate her pussy with his fat cock.

Ryan fucked fast, he fucked hard, and he fucked steady. He didn't let up, not even for a second. The noises that were escaping her were foreign even to her. The position of his hips stimulated her clit, and she felt herself getting dangerously close to another orgasm. He noticed the change in the noises she was making and leaned down to her ear. "You're gonna cum again, huh? Go ahead, it's yours. Cum all over it, baby."

She moaned his name as she came again, tears involuntarily leaving her eyes as he fucked her hard and fast through the remainder of her orgasm, savoring his pulses all over his dick until he couldn't hold out anymore. He sat up, pulled out, and removed the condom, tossing it aside. "Finish me off," he demanded, grabbing her hand and placing it on his cock. She wrapped her hand around him and gave him a few hard, slow pulls. He crept up her body, squeezed her tits together, and groaned as she jerked his hot load all over them. "Fuck."

When he was done, he searched for something to clean up with. He got off the bed and grabbed the tank top she'd been wearing. He noticed she was crying, and when he was finished wiping her off, she rolled over onto her side away from him. "Hey. What's wrong?" He slid behind her, wrapping an arm around her body and pulling her close to him. "Talk to me."

She laughed awkwardly through her tears and nodded, wiping her eyes. "Sorry. It's just…a lot of emotions right now."

"Sorry I'm such a lame fuck," he teased, as she grabbed onto his hand.

"Yeah right," she said. "It's just…for one, I've literally never felt anything like that in my life. If this whole hockey thing doesn't pan out, you should get into porn. Holy shit, Ryan. That was…that was unbelievable." She rolled onto her back, and he draped his arm across her stomach.

"Thanks. I've been waiting a while to do that. It felt amazing for me, too, believe me." He rested his head against hers, and they lay there, naked and silent, for a bit.

She was the first to break the silence. "Also, that's the first sex I've had since my ex."

Ha! His heart jumped. *So she hasn't been sleeping around, and she hasn't done Hayes.* "Really?" he said, trying to cover his excitement. "I guess it's weird?"

"Very," she replied quickly. "When you've been with someone for 11 years, it's so strange. I'm so glad it was with you though, you fucking stud."

"Me too."

"Seriously, that was…" She shook her head. "I've never cum just from sex before like that. You fuck entirely too well." She hovered her arm to show him. "Look, I'm still shaking."

"Well, I'm available anytime. You're not so bad yourself. I was about to cum when you were going down on me in the kitchen. We have a good chemistry, you and me."

She rolled over to face him. "That we do, Baylor. Ugh, I should probably get to bed. It's late, and you've gotta pa…" She started to move, but he stopped her.

"Stay with me?" he asked quietly. "Let me fall asleep next to you."

"Ryan, I can't…"

He sat up, frustrated. "Of course you can't." He sighed, preparing to ask her the question that so many girls before had asked him. "So, like, what even is this?"

"It's…just sex, Ryan." She sat up next to him. "Let's not complicate it."

"Is it, though?" He reached a hand up to the side of her face and pulled her in for a long, slow kiss. She kissed him back and ran her fingers through his hair. He sucked on and bit her bottom lip before ending the kiss. "Please?"

She noticed the desperation and sadness in his eyes, and against her better judgment, agreed to stay. "Maybe just for a little bit."

"I'll take that." He reached to the end of the bed and pulled his blanket up. "You cold? Here." He covered their legs as they both lay down on their backs. He folded his hands behind his head, and she turned into him, resting her head and a hand on his chest.

"Your heart is racing," she observed. "You good?"

"Very."

What the hell are you doing with this boy? she thought, as she lay there listening to his heartbeat. She could feel her own beginning to match the pace of his.

"You nervous, too?" he asked.

"Very."

Neither of them said anything for a few minutes, just listened to the other one breathing. Finally, Ryan said, "So, secret time: I told Hayes about us tonight on the bus ride."

The mention of Ty's name sent a shock wave through her body, as she hadn't expected to hear it at that moment. "Oh?" she responded. "And what'd he have to say about it?"

"He said it's about time. He also said that all you do when you're with him is talk about me."

Amara lifted her head up. "That little shit! Wait 'til I see him."

"So, is that true? That you talk about me all the time?"

"I can neither confirm nor deny these accusations against me."

He reached up to where her hand rested on his chest and intertwined his fingers with hers. "Hey: all I do is think about you."

"Ryan, don't..."

"No, don't 'shush' me. Let me talk, OK? I've never felt this way about anyone before. I don't understand why you're so hell-bent on fighting this. We're compatible emotionally, we're ridiculously compatible physically. What else do you need?"

"I need to heal, Ryan!" She raised her voice, startling him. "I'm sorry. I don't mean to yell. But that's what I need. I have good moments, this being one of them, but my heart is still very much broken. I know you don't understand that, but it's so beyond broken. And I honestly don't know if it will ever not be."

"Maybe there's a reason I don't understand it, Amara. You've never told me about it."

"Because I don't like to talk about it, Ryan. That's why."

"Funny. You had no problem talking to Hayes about it."

"Oh my God. I'm gonna kick his ass!" she groaned.

"Hey, you wanted us to talk, so we talked. Boys gossip way worse than girls do. Especially hockey boys. We're the worst."

"Apparently. So, he told you?"

"Yes. And Amara, you didn't deserve that. I'm so sorry that happened to you." He kissed the top of her head. "Why won't you open up to me?"

"Because I don't want you to judge me."

"As if I'm in a position to judge *anyone*."

"Stop. I'm serious. Do you have any idea how embarrassing it is to be cheated on, especially after you've taken marriage vows? When you think you're gonna spend the rest of your life with someone, and the next thing you know, you're selling all your shit and paying for a divorce lawyer? You spend every waking moment blaming yourself, wondering what you could've done differently, what you did to cause it."

"It's not your fault, Amara. He was a piece of shit who didn't deserve you. You've gotta know that."

"He really *wasn't* though. That's the worst part. I'm angry and I'm hurt, but he wasn't a bad man. He just...he fucked up, and unfortunately, some mistakes are more costly than others. The worst part is how stupid I feel for thinking I'd found 'the one', like that's even a real thing. I just thought at this point in my life, I'd be a mom, I'd have this perfect, happy little life, maybe driving the kids to soccer practice or some shit. Not lying naked after getting railed by some gorgeous 23-year-old hockey player whose cock is a heat-seeking missile for my G-spot. No offense."

"Yeah, none taken."

"And it's sucked, but I've come to grips with the fact that the life I planned for myself? It's never," she stopped, getting choked up. "It's never gonna happen. My entire world was taken from me, all of it, in an instant. Me and him? We had our problems like everyone else, but we made plans for the long haul, and one instant killed all of it. All I've ever wanted was to be a mom, Ryan, and I'll never get to have that now. Trust me, I want nothing more than to move on, but it's not that simple." She wiped her face bitterly. "And I'm just...so fucking angry. And afraid. I don't wanna get close to someone else just to have it taken away from me in an instant again."

"You think I don't understand that? My dad went out one night to pick up dinner for him and my mom and was killed by some drunk asshole who ran a red light. That happened in an instant, too. That's life, Amara. Shit happens, but you don't stop living. You can't. Certain risks," he squeezed her hand, "will always be worth taking."

"So, what is it you want from me, Ryan? This old, broken, grumpy bitch. What are you looking for with this?"

"Honestly?"

"Yes."

"I wanna be your man."

"Jesus, Ryan."

"Yeah, I know. How crazy, right? Listen, I'm sorry that all happened to you. And I'm just as broken as you, but maybe I can help you heal. You don't have to do this alone, Amara. I wanna help you, and I want you to help me. So, I'm young. Fuck all that noise. I wanna be your man. I wanna hold your hand in public. When you introduce me to people, I want you to say, 'This is my *boyfriend*, Ryan', not 'This is my *roommate*, Ryan.' That's what I want from you, from this. And you can play this little game with me all night, OK? But I know you feel it, too. And if I'm wrong? Then maybe you *should* head back to your own bed."

He reached over onto his nightstand and turned the light off, then wrapped his arms around her body, pulling her closer to him.

Where the hell did that come from? she thought, though admittedly turned on by his sudden boldness. He was sound asleep before she could even think about responding, so she gave herself permission to get comfy in his arms.

Just this once, though.

Because besides her broken heart, there was something else holding her back that she continued to keep secret from him.

She didn't know how to tell Ryan that despite all her best efforts to ignore it, she couldn't shake it anymore.

She needed to get Tyler Hayes out of her system.

SLIGHTLY INFATUATED (12)

"So, which one is he?"

The thunderous thump of a puck slapping against the boards where they were standing jolted them both. It'd come off Ryan Baylor's stick. Amara looked through the glass at him, and he sported the biggest smile she'd seen on him yet, clearly surprised to see her. "Seriously? You literally met him before!"

"I can't fucking remember. Point to him."

"That one. Number 21," she replied, gesturing towards Ryan, as she and her new friend from work stood rink-side watching Bridgeport's warmup skate.

Amara had almost forgotten what it was like to have a female companion. She'd lost touch with most of her female friends over the years, and the only ones she'd had recently bailed after the divorce.

Dani was a little younger than Amara, at 35. She was the lifeblood of The Bull, and all the patrons knew her by name. She was on the curvier side, with huge boobs and long hair that she'd let go almost completely gray, but it worked for her. She had a boisterous personality; if she thought it, she said it, no matter where she was or whether it was appropriate or not.

"*I gotta warn ya, baby girl. I ain't got no filter on this thing,*" she'd told Amara the first time they'd met.

She'd trained Amara and they'd worked nearly every shift together over the past few weeks, where they'd spent a lot of time getting to know each other. Amara had told her all about the drama with Ryan and had dabbled in a little talk of Tyler as well. Since they both had this Saturday night off, she decided to surprise the boys by showing up at tonight's home matchup against the Hershey Bears.

It'd been three weeks since the start of the regular season, and she hadn't made it to a single game. She'd been busy; between working on a long freelance article whose deadline was looming, bartending, and banging the absolute shit out of her boyfriend, free time was in short supply.

That's right.

Boyfriend.

After falling asleep and waking up in his arms after their first time together, she'd caved and reluctantly agreed to date him, even though he snored like an asthmatic grizzly bear. She had serious reservations about it, unsure if either of them was ready for it.

Amara'd consoled herself with the fact that she wasn't the first smart woman in history to make a stupid decision just because the dick was on point, and she wouldn't be the last. The next morning over coffee, she laid out some ground rules for him.

"*So, if we're gonna do this, we need to take it slow.*"

"*Um, my tongue was just in your asshole. Take it slow as in...?*"

"As in you don't post me on social media. Like, at all. I don't want the attention and scrutiny that comes with that. And I don't want our business thrown around in that locker room. Leave me out of there. Also, you're not allowed to say the 'L' word. Ever. Until I die, then if you wanna say it at my funeral, that's the only exception."

"Amara. I mean this with all due respect. You're the weirdest fucking woman I've ever met in my life."

"These are your terms and conditions. Check the 'I accept' box or hit the 'back' button on your browser, kid."

"Fine," he said, standing behind where she was seated and wrapping her in his arms. "I accept."

"And you do know that having a girlfriend means you don't get to have sex with five Instagram sluts a week anymore, right?"

He sighed. "Fine. I mean, I can try to cut it back to like, three a week if I have to. Yes, Amara. I kinda figured that."

"Just making sure. I mean, you're a bit of a whore, Ryan."

"I guess no one's ever given me a reason not to be." He reached an arm around to her face, grabbed it, leaned in, and gently turned it towards his. "Hey: I want this. I'm gonna do this. I...I can do this."

"Let's just both agree to give it our best shot, OK?" she said softly, still unsure about how all of this was going to play out, but physically unable to tell him no.

"Does this mean you'll come to a game now?"

"I don't know anything about hockey, Ry. Not a damn thing."

"So? Don't you wanna come support your man at what he does best?"

"I'm pretty sure I did that this morning. Twice, actually."

"Well, it'd mean a lot to me if you'd come support me. Us."

"If I get a night off soon, I'll come. OK?"

And tonight, she'd kept her word.

"Jesus, he's hot as hell. You get to bang him whenever you want? Fucking look at him. Shit, 21 can do sum for *me!*"

She shushed Dani as she noticed a family with small kids

85

standing next to them, the mom glaring daggers. "PG, Dan. Keep it PG."

Amara fixed her attention on Ryan, Tyler, and Osi, who were chatting at center ice. Ryan had bent down to talk to them, as they were both on all fours stretching out their hips. He pointed in her direction, and a few seconds later, both Osi and Tyler were waving to her. She waved back, and so did Dani.

"Holy crap, they're smokin' hot, too! I really gotta start watching hockey. So, uh, is one of those two the one you're secretly in love with?"

Amara started to protest, but she realized it was useless, as Dani would just call her bluff anyway. "So *that*...would be number 17. And I'm definitely not in love with him. Slightly infatuated would be a better term."

"Uh-huh. Yeah, I certainly can understand that," she said, checking him out as he skated around the boards past them, smacking the glass in front of Amara with the butt of his stick and winking as he passed by. "Damn, Mar. He's got a baby face."

"Yeah, I know. He's only 20. You'd never know it though. Kid's got some serious swag. He's...a little dangerous."

Dani fanned herself. "My God, woman. I wanna live a day in your shoes, surrounded by all these hotties. You're the luckiest goddamned bitch on Earth, you know that?"

She made a face and snickered. "Far from it."

Amara should've been watching her boyfriend, but she just couldn't seem to peel her eyes away from Tyler. A warmness overtook her as she fixated on him: skating flawlessly, tossing a few pucks over the glass for some excited kids, and running passing and shooting drills with his teammates.

His smile was downright intoxicating; this was clearly where he was happiest, not to mention meant to be. Whereas Ryan looked very serious and focused, Tyler truly looked like he was playing and having fun, and it filled her with joy to see him so happy, especially after the events that had transpired this past week.

Dani tapped her shoulder, snapping her out of her swoon fest. "You're uh, getting the death glare, 10:00," she warned, as Amara turned around and scanned the thin crowd.

"Who? Where?"

"Your man, baby girl."

She looked back at Ryan, unaware of how long she'd even been gawking at Tyler. His smile had disappeared, and his eyes had gone cold. He rolled them at her before skating around the back of the net, snatching up a puck, and proceeding to wind up and crank a clapper right in Tyler's direction before skating to the bench and exiting the ice. Tyler had had to jump to avoid being hit by it.

"Shit," she muttered, rubbing her forehead.

"He knows?" Dani asked.

"Yeah. He knows. I mean, I've never told him directly, but he knows."

"And baby face? He feels the same way about you?"

She nodded. "We're good friends, but there's a serious sexual tension there, and no matter how much I try to ignore it, try to fight it, it's not going away. We haven't done anything because of his girlfriend and now Ryan, obviously. But it's... getting progressively harder," she said, as Tyler skated over to her and mouthed, "Fuck was that?"

Amara shrugged, knowing damn well what it was.

Tyler approached the bench, leaving the ice for the locker room, and Amara turned to Dani. "Especially since he *just* broke up with his girlfriend this week."

THE BREAKUP (13)

Tyler Hayes's breakup had been a disaster of epic proportions. Jenna had cheated on him at a nightclub in Vegas with multiple dudes, and a video of her making out with all of them consecutively was broadcast all over Instagram for everyone's viewing pleasure. Jonesy was the first to peep it, as he and some of the other guys sat on the bus after an away game checking social media while waiting for the rest of the team.

"Oh fuck," he'd said, panicked. "That's gonna be a problem."

Soon after, a series of "Uh-oh's" and "Oh shit's" echoed throughout the bus. Hayes was one of the last ones to get on; he'd been giving an interview after the killer game he'd just had. When he finally walked on, everyone was silent, which was completely unexpected for someone who'd just posted four assists and scored a hat trick, including the game-winning overtime shootout goal in what had been a complete and utter gongshow.

He looked around, unwrapped a lollipop. and stuck it in his mouth. "Ok, why's everyone being so fuckin' weird, eh?"

Ryan gestured for him to come sit next to him, moving over so Hayes could sit on the inside. "What the hell's going on, Rook?"

"I hate this," Ryan said quietly, showing him his phone. "I'm sorry, man."

Hayes watched it a couple times, turned away from Ryan, and plunked his forehead against the window. He proceeded to ride the entire two hours in complete silence, minus some sniffles, with Ryan periodically rubbing his back and shoulders.

"Fuck that bitch, bro. She doesn't deserve you." A couple of the other guys had tried to come and talk to him, but Ryan just shook his head.

The next day, he didn't show up for dryland training, and knowing he was nursing a broken heart, the guys covered for him. The day after that though, he'd blown off game day practice, which was a huge no-no.

Coach Hastings banged a stick against the bench. "And where in the glittering fuck is Hayes?"

Ryan skated over. "Coach, I need to talk to you for a sec."

He had tried to explain the situation, hoping for a shred of empathy, but Coach was having none of it. "I don't give a shit. He's a key piece, and this is his fucking job. We're knotted up in the standings against Charlotte, and we need him tonight, or special teams is gonna suffer. Not to mention, you don't get promoted to the big club by sitting around crying over some whore. If he's not dead or dying in a ditch somewhere, then his ass needs to be here. You understand me? I'm gonna scratch him for pulling this shit."

Ryan shouted to Rizz that he was going to take a quick breather, ran to the locker room, and texted Amara.

R: We've got a bit of a situation.

She closed her laptop, took her glasses off, and headed down to his apartment, knocking on the door for about five minutes straight before he finally opened it, looking like an absolute bag of hell. He was shirtless, which was not a problem, but his hair was matted down to one side of his head and he was in dire need of some deodorant. His eyes were red and puffy, and as soon as he saw her, he immediately collapsed forward into her arms, sobbing like a child. She managed to get him inside and to the couch, where she held onto him as he let loose.

"It hurts. It hurts so bad."

"I know it does, baby." She ran her nails lightly up and down his back. If anyone could relate, it was Amara; knowing that, he allowed himself to be completely vulnerable with her.

"Oh my God, it's so embarrassing. Everyone saw it. *Everyone*. My family, all my friends. The comments are out of control, blaming me like it's somehow my fuckin' fault." He fell onto her shoulder again and wrapped his arms around her back. "I didn't do anything wrong. I never once stepped out on her, not once. You know that, Amara."

"Ty, I know you didn't."

But you would've.

"She told me she couldn't do the long-distance thing anymore. Had no problem traveling to Vegas to fuck a bunch of other guys though, did she?" He burst into tears again. "Oh my God. How do I recover from this, Mar?"

Amara had figured it out. It wasn't as much about the actual breakup for him as much as it was about the damage to his image.

Either way, she knew it sucked.

"You recover one God-awful day at a time. It'll get better, Ty. I promise."

90

She sat holding him for a good hour, as he alternated between nodding off and crying, until she really had to pee. "I'll be right back," she told him, but while she was gone, he'd dragged himself to his bedroom, crawled back into his bed, and tried to disappear under the covers.

"Nope. We're not doing this." She flung his door open, stormed over to his bed, and ripped the covers off him. He groaned in protest. "Get up."

"I can't."

"Tyler, Ryan texted me. Coach is ready to sit you out tonight. She isn't worth it."

"I love her."

"Well, she obviously doesn't love you. I understand how hard it is to hear that, but you deserve better than some trifling-ass, cheating skank who puts you down and treats you like shit. Now, you're gonna get your ass up outta this bed, get in the shower, please, for the love of God, and get your shit together for tonight's game. Let's go: up!"

He rolled his eyes, but he did as he was told. On the way to the bathroom, he stopped and hugged her, resting his head on her shoulder. "I don't know where you came from, woman, but you're one of the best things that ever happened to me."

"Likewise, Tyler." She ran her fingers through his hair until they got stuck in a mat. "Ugh, go condition those locks, please. Good God." She shook her hand like she was shaking something off it.

"Rook is so lucky. I hope he knows better than to fuck this up with you."

"Yeah, me too." She felt her heart start to race, and she pulled away from him, pointing towards the bathroom door. "Shower. Shampoo. Now."

He'd managed to get to the arena on time, avoiding the scratch after some serious ass-kissing, and proceeded to have his most amazing game of the season so far. It was so clutch that the rumors about him being called up to New York had begun to circulate over social media, quickly replacing all talks of the cheating scandal.

She'd been at work when he'd texted her after the game.

T: Thanks for getting my head on straight today.

A: You know I'll always have your back.

T: I know. That's why I love you.

T: I mean that, Amara. I love you.

She quickly put her phone away but continued to pull it out periodically throughout her shift to stare at it.

On about the tenth view, she took a deep breath and pulled the trigger on the words she hadn't even exchanged with Ryan.

A: I love you. too, Tyler.

REALITY CHECK (14)

"So, Tyler Hayes, amazing game tonight. You posted two goals, three assists, seven shots on goal, just incredible hustle out there. That makes quite a few impressive games for you in a row now. You know, there have been lots of rumors flying lately about how you might get the call up to New York sooner than later. What are your thoughts on that?"

"Listen, you know, I'm just happy to be playing. It's, uh, been a rough year with my recovery and, uh, I'm just grateful to have the opportunity to play. This is a great bunch of guys, and you know, I'm just lucky to be here and hopefully I can, uh, stay healthy."

"Well, best of luck to you, Tyler. Thanks for your time."

"Thanks."

He hated giving interviews, but he understood that it was part of the deal. Hayes was many things, but articulate wasn't one of them. He pulled off his helmet, signed a few quick autographs on his way down the tunnel, and headed into the locker room, where 80's music was blasting. "Fuck, they got Rizz on aux again?" he bitched, having a seat at his stall and loosening his skates.

"You know you love the old shit, kid!" Rizz yelled from across the room.

"Yeah, apparently he's not the only one who loves the old shit," Seggy chimed in, pointing at Ryan's stall. Ryan wasn't there; he'd already made his way into the shower.

"Yoooo. That's messed up," Kasic said. "At least she's hot though."

"Eh, leave Rook alone. He's just trying to get his senior discount," Dalesy added.

"You know, Hayes, you hang out with her an awful lot." Seggy threw a roll of tape at him. "You blowin' those old ass hips out too? You better be careful, man. Brittle bones on those older broads."

"The fuck you goin' on about now?" Hayes replied, chucking the tape back at him and beginning to remove the rest of his gear.

"I just don't know why you guys are wasting your time with some old ass bitch when there's plenty of young, hot talent in need of proper defiling."

"Hey, Segorsky: that 'old ass bitch' is my cousin, so how 'bout we calm down with that shit?" Nick yelled, as he came into the locker room and went straight over to Hayes's stall. "I need to work on your shoulder for a bit."

"Tonight?" he whined.

"Yes, tonight. They're really looking at you, kid. We gotta make sure you're in prime condition. Let's go."

He followed Nick into the training room. "We'll do some external rotation stretches, some pendulums, and then you're free, OK? Lie down." He lifted Hayes's arm up and rotated it, holding it in place. "So: what's this about you hanging out with my cousin?"

"I, uh, it's not...I mean, it's not...like that," Hayes

stammered.

"Calm down, I'm messing with you. I know you guys are friends. She tells me all the damn time."

"She talks about me?"

"All. The. Damn. Time. She loves you. Says you guys have fun together. Now, I'm not too happy about her and Baylor dating, but she's a big girl, I guess."

Even though Hayes knew they were dating, for some reason, every time he heard it, it was like a punch in the balls. "Why? You have an issue with Rook?" he fished.

Nick returned his arm to the resting position before rotating it again. "Any pain?"

"None."

"Good. That's a fantastic sign. Yeah, no issue with Baylor at all. Just don't think she's mentally ready for a relationship right now is all, not to mention, he's a bit more of a playboy than I realized. It's just, I'd hate to see either of them get hurt. She's always been able to, uh, how do I say it nicely? Persuade guys. They've always just kinda fallen at her feet. As soon as one would leave, another one was right there waiting."

"I can see that," Tyler said without thinking. "She's a cool chick, I mean."

"She is. But she doesn't always think things through all the way. Likes to rush into things with high hopes and doesn't always realize that decisions have consequences until it's too late. Hence: her marriage. Everyone told her not to marry him. You can't tell her anything though. And of course, there's the age difference. I just…didn't see it coming is all. In hindsight, probably should've. But, whatever. They're both adults." He helped Hayes sit up. "Make you a deal: we can skip the pendulums if you promise to hit them first thing at dryland tomorrow."

"Works for me."

"How you feeling, Hayes?"

"Great, man. Like I said, no pain whatsoever."

"That's not what I meant."

"Oh. Right. Um, OK. Good moments and bad moments, you know? Fuckin' way she goes." He shrugged. "You know, your cousin really helped me. I was in kind of a bad place and she pulled me out of it."

"Well, I did the same for her, so I'm glad to hear she's paying it forward. She's a little broken, but she's got a good heart."

"Man, I'm slowly finding out that we're *all* a little broken."

"That we are, Hayes. Hey: see you tomorrow."

"Later, Dunny."

Hayes went back to the locker room, fully expecting to take a shower in peace; instead, he arrived to all hell breaking loose.

"I just don't get it is all."

"There's nothing for you to get, man. I like her, and she likes me. What's the fuckin' problem?"

"The problem?" Seggy stood up and inched slowly towards Ryan. "The problem is that ever since you've been fuckin' with that bitch, you've been shit on the ice and a locker room cancer, bud."

"Don't call her a bitch, man," Ryan warned, stepping closer to him. "Don't."

"Or what, pussy? Everyone's been real patient with you, but the truth is that you're a waste of cap space. You're inconsistent as fuck, and you suck on D. Probably suck the D, too."

"I'm not your mom."

Rizz came out of nowhere, wearing only a towel, and stepped between them. "Yo, boys. Calm down. Let's just calm down now, eh?"

"And maybe if you could hit that shit right, she wouldn't be all over Hayes's jock. Don't think we didn't all see that shit tonight during warmup. She was eye-fuckin' him so hard, I got half a chub just watching it."

"How the actual fuck did I get dragged into this shit?"

Hayes came over, down to nothing but his hip pads, and stood next to Ryan, facing Seggy.

"Because everyone knows you're bangin' her, too. Probably why your girl cheated. She's about the same age as those billet moms were, eh? Seems right up your alley, you little fuckin' home wrecker."

Ryan made a sudden move towards Seggy, but Hayes held him back. "Nah, fuck this washed-up piece of shit, man. He's not worth it. AHL contract with no hopes of ever movin' up to the show, and a mediocre wife who's probably on my jock, too. Just jealous is all."

Seggy let loose an exaggerated laugh. "Yeah. That's it, Hayes. She prefers *men*, not little boys."

"Yeah, I heard she does prefer men. Lots of 'em, all at once." He made a train horn motion with his arm. "All aboard the bukkake express, boys."

Seggy stepped towards him. "You're a mouthy little shit!"

"Do somethin' about it then," Hayes said calmly, his arms up and starting towards him. Now it was Ryan holding Hayes back. Osi had since wandered over and latched onto the back of Hayes's hip pads to keep him put. Hayes grabbed his crotch. "And 'little boy' nothin'. Everyone here's seen it. Biggest one in the whole locker room, bitch."

"Yeah, your fuckin' mouth, maybe."

"Hayes. Enough," Osi said, yanking him backward. "Is not worth it." Osi looked terrified; he was predominantly a peacekeeper but would jump in to defend Hayes in a millisecond.

"You're a little bitch, Hayes. You and your boyfriend Baylor."

"Yeah? Let your wife know we'll tag her any time!" he shot back as Osi and Ryan dragged him off to the showers.

Ryan turned around and wanted to say something, but seeing as he was already under such scrutiny, he decided against it. Instead, he turned to Hayes and said softly, "I don't...

I don't wanna tag his wife, man."

"Jesus, how dense are you, Rook? It was just chirps."

"I knew that."

* * *

The ride home is Hayes's truck was silent at first. Osi had gone out to hit the bars with some of the other guys. Ryan had been invited to go, but he wasn't in the mood. He kept staring at the messages Amara sent him throughout the night, none of which he'd responded to.

A: I'm sorry.

A: You played amazing. I mean, I have no clue what's going on, but lots of chatter about you in the stands.

A: Somewhere I can meet you afterward?

A: Guessing you're pissed. I'll just see you when you come home. I'm sorry.

"You should've met up with her," Hayes finally lectured. "She came out. It's the least you could've done for her."

"Hayes, don't," Ryan warned, putting his phone down and running his fingers through his hair.

"Yes, God forbid someone tries to give the almighty Ryan Baylor some constructive criticism."

"Maybe I don't want criticism from the guy who wants to fuck my girlfriend, OK?" he snapped.

"This shit again?" Hayes looked at him. "I thought I told you nothing's gonna happen between us."

"There's no girlfriend stopping you now, is there?"

"Nope. Thanks for bringing that up though," Hayes said quietly, checking the text message he'd just gotten.

A: He's pissed at me, isn't he?

"I'm sorry, man," Ryan said, his breathing labored. "I just...this shit is messing...with my head...so bad." His breathing sped up and it hit him out of nowhere. He reached between the seat and the door and hit the button, reclining his seat back. "Fuck."

"Yo, Rook. What's the matter? Shit, you havin' one of those attacks?" Hayes asked, concerned.

Ryan nodded rapidly.

"OK, shit. What'd she tell me to do?" He pulled the truck off to the side of the road and put it in park. "OK, um...oh, right. OK. Five things you can see right now, Rook."

"The dashboard. The seatbelt. The center console. My phone. Some asshole that wants...to fuck my girl." Ryan smirked, then closed his eyes.

"Yo, not the time for jokes, bitch. Um, what was...oh, four things you can hear right now?"

Hayes got him through the rest of the steps, all the way down to one, and his breathing almost returned to normal. He moved the seat back into the upright position and looked over at Hayes, who looked like he'd seen a ghost. "You good, man?" Ryan asked as if he'd been the one who's just had an issue.

"Yeah, I mean. Wow, it just hits you like that, out of nowhere?"

"Yep." He took a deep breath. "Not fun."

"That was freaky as shit. I've never seen anything like that before."

"How'd you know what to do?"

"She gave me the run-down, made me practice what to do 40 fuckin' times like it was some kind of CPR certification course." He sighed. "That woman? Cares about you so much, it's disgusting."

"Yeah? Well, she feels the same way about you, Hayes," Ryan said. "And if I'm being honest? I fucking hate it."

"Why? We're friends. Good friends."

"Because I'm...ugh, God!" He leaned forward and buried his head in his hands. "Because I'm..."

"You're what, man?"

"Because I'm fucking jealous of you, alright? Shit!"

"Jealous? Of me?" Hayes laughed. "That's funny."

"And why is that funny?"

Hayes put the truck in drive, pulling off. "Because maybe I'm a little jealous of you, man. Ever think of that?"

"That's absurd," Ryan scoffed. "Jealous of what?"

"We really fuckin' doin' this Rook? Like a couple of drunk high school bitches comparin' titties?"

"Yes. Because I don't believe you."

"Nah, fuck that. You brought it up. You go first."

"Fine. For one, you're a much better hockey player than me. There, I said it. You're gonna go to the show any minute, and God knows how long I'll be stuck in this shit league. Two, you trash talk better than anyone I've ever met before. It's seriously impressive how good you are. Three, you're insanely confident, probably because you've got like, an eight-foot cock. And mostly it's because I see the way she looks at you, man. I fuckin'...I know it's not your fault, but I can't stand it, Hayes."

"That why you tried to take me out in the warmup tonight?"

"I fucked up. I'm sorry."

"You're lucky you didn't get scratched for that shit. Everyone saw it, and I could've been a real dick. So, what do you want from me anyway? You want me to stop hangin' out with her?"

"Would you, if I said yes?"

100

"Nah."

Ryan nodded.

"How would that be fair to her? You're gonna have to get over it, Rook. You either trust your girl or you don't."

"I just...it's the way she looks at you."

"Do you even see the way she looks at *you*, Rook?"

Ryan shook his head.

"Nah, of course you don't. Always too busy focusing on the negative shit. You're one of the most negative people I've ever met."

"That's kinda my MO if you haven't noticed. Anyway. Your turn."

"Oh, I was just messin' with you. Why the fuck would I be jealous of *you*?" Hayes waited for his sour reaction, which didn't disappoint. "Look at you, man. Your face, your hair, your body. Shit, I could work out six hours a day and eat nothing but ice and I wouldn't be half as yoked as you. You've got no body hair, no body fat. All the birds sweat you. You're fuckin' hot as hell."

"And? What else?"

"What else? Sorry, didn't know I needed to rattle off a laundry list for you."

"Are you jealous because of her? Just be honest and tell me."

"Tell you what, Rook? That if I knew for a fact that no one would get hurt or find out, I'd fuck her? Is that what you want me to say?"

"Is that the truth?"

"Alternate universe scenario. Impossible to answer."

"Tell me this: is it just sexual, or is there more to it?"

Hayes sighed. "Rook, I don't fuckin' know. I just...wanna smash her, man. That's all I know. I really wish I didn't."

Ryan crossed his arms. "So do I."

They rode the rest of the way to the apartment, walked through the parking garage, and rode the elevator in deafening silence. There was so much those two boys needed to say, wanted to say to each other, but it all remained unspoken for the moment.

When the elevator stopped on the fourth floor, Hayes got out. He turned back towards Ryan and held his hand out to stop the doors from closing. "Yo: please don't take it out on her. Hate me if you want, crank a hundred pucks at my face, whatever you gotta do. But don't take it out on her. She's been through the fuckin' wringer. Just let her feel what she feels, man."

Hayes pulled his arm back and let the door close.

On the walk to his apartment, he was looking at his phone, so he didn't see until he got there that she was sitting on the floor outside of his door. "Fuck. Here we go," he muttered, putting his phone in his pocket and reaching a hand down to help her up.

"Hey. Can we talk?" she asked nervously, tightening her grip on his hand. "Is, uh, Osi here?"

"Nah. Bar hoppin' with the guys." He locked eyes with her, which was always a mistake. They were glassy; that either meant she was drunk, had been crying, or possibly both.

"We should," she snaked a hand around his waist, "go inside. To talk."

"Hey. Maybe it's not the best idea for you to come over right now, Mar."

She grabbed the collar of his dress shirt with both hands, pulled him close to her, and stopped mere inches from his lips. "I want you so bad," she whispered. He smelled some sort of alcohol on her breath. "I'll let you do whatever you want to me, Tyler."

Both of their breathing was spiraling out of control, but he made damn sure their lips didn't touch. "Come on. You can't say shit...like that to me." He reached up, removed her hands from his collar, and gently pushed her away from him. "Mar, I need you to leave." There was an urgency in his voice that she'd never heard before. "I don't want you to, I *need* you to. You understand me? We can talk later, OK?"

She nodded, turned around, and walked back towards the elevator.

He watched her walk completely out of sight, making sure she didn't return.

"Don't say I never fuckin' did anything for you, Rook," he said aloud, unlocking the door and pounding it twice with the bottom of his fist before going inside and slamming it behind him.

BOUNDARIES (15)

When she made her way back through the apartment door, Ryan was standing there waiting for her. "Hey," he said. "Where were you?"

She didn't respond.

"Listen, I'm sorry I didn't..."

She put her hand up and waved him off. "Don't. I don't care." She stormed off toward her bedroom, with him in tow.

"Can we talk for a minute? Look, I screwed up tonight, OK? I was angry and I took it out on you. I should've responded and met up with you and your friend afterward. I'm sorry."

She spun around to face him as she got to her door. "What you should've done was gone out with the guys and met up with some of your little Instagram slut following."

"What are you talking about?"

"Save it. I have internet access. I see all the comments. I see the list of who you're still following on there. Out of 800,

750 are fake blondes with huge tits and OnlyFans links. I knew this would never work, that I couldn't compete. And the worst part?" She threw her hands up. "I'm not even that upset about it."

"Well, you sure *seem* upset. So, I haven't cleaned up my follows. But Amara, it's not even like that. Do you think I'm screwing around? Because for the three weeks we've been together, you're the only girl I've touched. The. Only. Girl."

"Wow, you made it a whole three weeks!" She clapped sarcastically in his face. "Congratu-fucking-lations!"

"What...where is this coming from?"

She flung the door to her room open and tried to shut it behind her, but he pushed it back open and followed her inside. She pulled her phone from her back pocket and typed furiously for a few seconds. He instantly got a notification, which when opened, was a link to the Bridgeport Islanders subreddit.

"Happy reading. I think you'll find some of it very interesting. I know I did, especially the post *'Ryan Baylor Is Straight-Up Trash.'* Here, you like it when I read to you, right?" She clicked a few things on her phone. "Now, I can't take credit for writing this one, but regardless, I think you'll enjoy it."

Fuck.

"Mar, don't do this."

"I'm so glad Dani showed me this on Reddit. I had no clue, but, wow, what a goldmine. So, this is dated exactly two weeks ago: *'Ryan Baylor Is Straight-Up Trash: Don't bother with this douche. He claims to have a girlfriend, but he's all over my Insta DM's, likes all my stories and pictures. He'll get a little raunchy with his flirting if you push him or send him a sexy pic, but if you try to meet up, he ghosts you. I have a friend who got with him about a month ago and said he fucks like an absolute porn star, but I've gotten nowhere. I feel bad for his girlfriend. She probably has no clue that he's such a piece of shit.'* Wow, Ry."

"Um..."

"Oh wait, there's more. Someone replied: *'Agreed. Total trash bag. Like, how can you claim to have a girlfriend in one* sentence and then tell me you just jerked off to my tits in the next? If she was smart, she'd get the fuck away from him. He's clearly got issues.' This is just...I don't have words."

He sat down on the edge of her bed. "So, I'm guessing online flirting is frowned upon?"

She looked at him, wide-eyed. "Are you a complete fucking moron?"

"Yes!" he yelled, throwing his hands in the air. "I told you I've never done this before! I don't...it's just social media. Is this a big deal? It's not like I'm meeting up with any of these girls. Amara: I'm *not* meeting up with any of them, I swear to God."

It was times like this that snapped her back to the reality she'd often avoided confronting: he was young and clueless, not to mention a sex addict.

"Ryan, that's still technically cheating!"

"It *is*?"

She put her hands over her face. "Oh my God. I know you're young, but please tell me you're not this stupid."

"No, I'm definitely this stupid. That's cheating? Liking someone's stories and some playful flirting?"

"If I told another guy I just got myself off to a picture of his cock, would you consider that 'playful flirting'?"

"Fuck." He rested his forehead on his hands. "Oh, I'm *such* an asshole."

She sat down next to him on the bed and put a hand on his lower back. "And this," she said softly, "is one of the main reasons why I didn't wanna commit to anything serious with you. Despite the fact that I'm not ready, Ryan, *you're* not ready. Someone like you can't just change overnight."

He snickered, not lifting his head. "Someone like me, huh? Let me guess, I'm not 'boyfriend material', right?"

"Perhaps those girls were onto something. Ryan, before we got together, how many chicks were you hooking up with a week?"

"Usually two, maybe three on a good week."

"The first day I met you, you got sucked off by two

106

different girls within like a 10-hour period. Tell me your body count."

He lifted his head up and looked at her. "Impossible."

"I'm at 12, 13 including you. And that includes all the dicks, even the ones I just sucked. There. So what number am I?"

"I don't..."

"Listen, I don't actually give a shit. I just wanna see if you're gonna start being honest with me at some point, or with yourself. That'd be a start."

"I, um, don't...know. I was blackout for a ton of them."

"Ballpark it."

"Um. Somewhere around...wait, oral shit too, or just sex?" She rolled her eyes, and he took the hint. "OK, oral shit included? Probably somewhere in the ballpark of, and I'm estimating here: five...maybe five hundred-ish, maybe?"

She got up off the bed and put a hand over her mouth. "Wow. OK. I was not expecting that. Oh my God. Yeah, that's just not normal behavior. Over how many years?"

He held up five fingers.

"That's almost 100 girls a year, Ryan."

"Not exactly."

"Huh?"

"Guys, too."

"Jesus Christ, Ryan!"

"You think I'm proud of this?" He got up from the bed. "I'm sorry. I fucking hate me. So much."

She reached out and grabbed his hand, noticing the tears welling up in his eyes. "I kinda feel bad for you, Ryan. You're clearly searching for...something."

"Yeah. She's standing right in front of me. You hate me, too, don't you?"

She shook her head. "No, Ryan. I don't hate you. Am I disappointed in your behavior? Yeah. But I think you and I just have to...if we're gonna do this, we may have to rethink things a bit."

"So, you're not done with me?"

"Ryan, this is the most fucked-up relationship I've ever been in. And I'm divorced from a man who got his coworker pregnant. It's obvious neither of us knows what the hell we're doing here. A conventional relationship isn't gonna cut it for us. Nothing about us is conventional. We just might need to, I don't know, play around with some other options."

"I don't follow."

"What if we try an open relationship?"

He made a face. "Explain it to me like I'm an idiot. Because clearly, I'm an idiot."

"It's where we're 'together', but not limited to just each other." She could see the wheels turning pretty hard. "Ryan, it's where we can both fuck other people but still come home to each other. I've always thought I'd be up for it with the right person. Looking back, my ex apparently thought we were already in one."

"Um, Amara? I kinda don't want you fucking other guys."

"Yeah, well I'm not crazy about you fucking other girls either, Ryan."

She saw the sadness in his eyes. "What if I just try harder?" he said softly.

"It's not that easy. You're not gonna be able to keep it in your pants, and maybe…I shouldn't ask you to."

"I kept it in my pants for three weeks. Just worth noting again. Yes, there was some inappropriate online activity, but I kept it in my pants. I mean, I may have smacked it a few times…"

"Ryan?" she interrupted.

"Yeah?"

"Stop talking."

"Got it."

"Great. So, you didn't fuck someone else for a whole three weeks. But it was a struggle. With this? It doesn't have to be."

"Amara, two of my strongest personality traits are jealous and anxious. You know that. Like, if you're off with other guys, there's no question I'm gonna lose my fucking mind."

"It's not a free-for-all. We have to establish ground rules. Boundaries. Certain acts might be off-limits, or we have to clear it with the other person before going for it, or maybe we do threesomes or group stuff instead of going off one-on-one."

"You into girls?"

"I can be. I'm into experimenting with you if that's what it takes."

He ran his hands through his hair. "You're blowing my mind right now."

"And apparently you're into guys, so it could work."

"I'm not..." He paused, shaking his head. "I mean, I'm not *into* guys. Willing to experiment is a better way to put it."

"Same difference. Think about it, OK? Anyway, you should head back to your room. I wanna sleep alone tonight."

He walked over to her, wrapped his arms around her upper back, and squeezed. "I'm sorry I'm so broken. I don't know why, but you need to know that the way I feel about you isn't bullshit. I meant every word of everything I said to you. Amara," his voice cracked, "I'd take a fucking bullet for you. I'm not real good at sorting out my feelings, but I know I still want this. Whatever we decide to do, whatever happens, you're my number one and that's not ever going to change. *Ever*. I just... needed you to hear that."

"The only reason I'm even suggesting this is because it's this or I lose you. And Ryan, losing you isn't an option."

✻ ✻ ✻

You'd have thought Ryan Baylor was cramming for the most important final exam of his life. He'd stayed up into the wee hours of the morning researching 'open relationships' and came to the kitchen for coffee in the morning as prepared as he'd ever been for anything.

Amara walked in, stretching her arms over her head, as he sat at the counter glancing at his phone and scribbling something in a notebook. "Hey," she yawned, grabbing a mug out of the cabinet. "Are you...are you taking notes?"

"So, I haven't really slept that much, but I thought about what you said last night. I've been doing a ton of reading, and I think I have some ideas."

"Wow. Seriously?"

"Yes, seriously. Look: I'm not gonna fuck this up, too. But if this is how you wanna move forward, we have to be on the same page with some things."

She sat down across from him and took a sip. "OK, fine. This should be interesting. Let's hear it."

"So first," he started, looking back through his notes, "it's important that we're upfront and honest with whoever we decide to, you know. They have to know what they're getting into. And I think for us, threesomes, or like, group stuff might be the way to go."

"Oh, do you, now?" she smiled. "And why's that?"

"Because Amara, the thought of you getting off on another guy without me makes me wanna kill myself. And I know I wouldn't feel comfortable getting off on another girl without you. At least if I'm there and I *see* it, that might cut down on some of the jealousy for me. It's gonna be really weird, but I don't know, I'm trying to keep an open mind here. Like, it might suck, but maybe...it might be kinda hot, too."

"Agreed. So, what else?"

"Both of us need to agree on the person. If one of us is uncomfortable, for any reason, it doesn't happen." He turned back a page in his notebook. "Another thing: if either of us catches feelings for someone else, that needs to be brought to the other one's attention immediately. Don't hide it. This would obviously apply mostly to you since I can't see myself ever catching feelings for anyone but you, like, ever."

"That'll change."

"No, it won't. Oh, and so before we get into any situation, we pull each other aside and set some quick ground rules. If there are certain things we don't want the other one doing with a certain person, that needs to be laid out very clearly before anything goes down."

"Wow, you've really put a lot of thought into this. Impressive."

"Check out my Instagram follows when you get a chance. Down to under 350, thank you very much."

"Weeded through the 'spank bank' follows, did you?"

"Yep. I'm not making excuses, but most of them were left over from juniors and college. I couldn't even tell you the last time I followed some random girl. It definitely hasn't been since we met. But I still deleted them all. All of them. Gone."

She looked at him; he seemed so proud of himself. "I underestimated you, Baylor. And nice work on the notes. I wasn't sure if you'd be on board with this or run screaming."

"If it's what you want, then it's what I want. You said it: losing you isn't an option. I'll do whatever I have to do to keep you."

She reached across the counter and grabbed his hand. "Anything else you wanna add?"

He glanced at the microwave clock. "I've gotta head out for dryland in a few. It's gonna suck so bad. I got like, no sleep. But there's one more boundary, and I don't think you're gonna like it."

"And what's that?" she asked.

"We both have to approve of the other person, right? Amara, this arrangement doesn't include Hayes."

She let go of his hand. "How'd I know that was coming?"

"I just can't. I went back and forth about this for hours, but I just can't. Amara, if I had to watch you with him…" his voice trailed off.

"You're afraid you might like it?" she finished for him. "You know, Ryan, if I didn't know any better, I'd *swear* you had a thing for him."

He furrowed his brow. "Amara, no Hayes. That's a boundary I won't budge on. I...I just can't." He got up, gave her a quick kiss on the top of the head, and went to get ready.

"Yeah, well. We'll see about that one," she said quietly to herself, finishing her coffee.

EXCEL (16)

"Wow. Amara. I mean, wow," Ryan swooned, as she walked out into the living room wearing an extremely short, tight red dress, cut low enough to reveal some cleavage, as much as her push-up bra could muster for her small chest. Her long, dark hair was pulled into a low ponytail that draped over her right shoulder, and her lips matched the color of her dress. She had on black heels that were sexy but also padded with memory foam because after all the years she'd spent beating the shit out of her feet, she just couldn't handle the full-on "fuck me shoes" anymore.

"Thanks. You don't look so bad yourself." She looked him up and down, appreciating the white dress shirt and incredibly form-fitting black pants that hugged his thick ass and thighs to perfection. His usually messy blonde hair was perfectly styled, and the combination of his deodorant and cologne was a scent she'd have found a way to fuck if it was humanly possible.

They were headed out to Excel, Bridgeport's newest and hottest nightclub, with a few of the guys and some of their significant others. They were looking forward to a night out together since they hung out at home most of the time, but they also decided that it was a prime opportunity to try out their new arrangement.

"So, how are we gonna do this?" she asked him quietly in the backseat of the Uber. It was close enough to the apartment that they could've walked, but it was just too damn Connecticut cold outside. Osi was sitting in the front seat attempting to carry on a conversation with the driver, and she didn't want to air out their business.

"Here, look," he showed her his Instagram on his phone, making sure she didn't think he was hiding anything. "Don't laugh, but this is called a 'pussy flare,' as horrendous as that sounds."

"I'm sorry. A *what* now?"

He smirked and snapped a quick selfie of just him, remembering that she'd asked to be kept off his social. "I post a pic, tag it with Excel, and add some text about how we're headed there." He closed the app.

"And then?"

"And then you wait. Girls will view it, and either like it or comment about how they'll be there and want to meet up."

"And this works?"

"Every single time. How do you think I met all the chicks I used to fuck with? This streamlines the process because A, you can see what they look like and pick the ones you want, and B, you know they're down to fuck, so you don't waste 75 bucks on drinks just for them to tell you they're going home to their boring-ass husbands at the end of the night."

She smirked at his detailed description of the positives of the 'pussy flare.' The kid was ridiculous. Sometimes, he could be the most clueless idiot on Earth, and other times, he could rival Einstein with his infinite wisdom. There was no rhyme or reason to it, but it was one of her favorite things about him. "You never cease to amaze me, Baylor." She shook her head. "How long do you wait?"

"Oh, they're already there." He opened the app, a mere two minutes later, and clicked on his messages. "It's at 103 views and six girls have commented so far. Here." He handed her his phone. "Scroll through and see if you like any of them. I'll work it out."

"So, this is great for girls, but what about guys?"

"That poses a bit more of a challenge, but, uh, you'd be surprised," he said with a shy smile. "Hockey boys have a reputation for being pretty...open-minded."

"Really?"

"Oh yeah. I mean, we don't go around advertising it, but in juniors and especially college because we're drunk all the time? Every guy I've ever messed around with was a teammate of mine or an opponent. It happens a lot more than you'd think."

"Why though?"

He shrugged. "Most hockey boys are unapologetic sluts. I don't know why. Probably has something to do with leaving home so young, being naked around other guys all the time. I'm not really sure, to be honest with you."

"Shit. So how far did you go? Like, did you ever..."

"No, never. A couple of guys tried, but I said no. A lot of kissing. So much kissing. Touching, hand jobs, a few BJ's. No, I never gave one."

"I bet you'd be really good at it. I mean, your lips. And that tongue of yours."

"Don't get any ideas."

"So have you...with anyone recently?"

"Nah. Not since college."

"And is there, um, anyone who you'd maybe wanna..."

"Amara? Hayes still isn't happening."

"Damn." She shrugged. "Worth a shot."

Ryan nudged her, pointed to the front seat, and giggled

as he overheard Osi arguing with the driver about something. "Oh, everyone say is best show ever, but this is number one bullshit!"

"I like that. 'Number one bullshit.' I'm definitely adding that into the rotation," she laughed.

"He says that all the time. It's hilarious. He gets pissed on the ice? 'This is number one bullshit!' So funny. Hey, can I ask you something?" Ryan interrupted Amara's scrolling through the story comments, which were up to 13 now.

"What's up?"

"So, what exactly is it about Hayes that does it for you?"

She exaggerated disgust. "Tyler doesn't *do* anything for me."

"Hey: we said we were gonna be honest with each other, right?"

"Fine. Honestly? I don't wanna talk to you about this."

"Come on. I need to know why you look at him the way you do. It's not for me. It's for my anxiety. Please?" He feigned puppy eyes.

"Man, you really love talking about him, don't you?" She sighed, fidgeting with her clutch in her lap. "Fine. Since we're being honest: I think it's his confidence. He is so fucking confident, especially for someone his age. He seems like he could really take control of...things. What do you guys call it, BDE? And he's beautiful. Not perfect like you, but beautiful in his own way. He's brutally honest and doesn't sugarcoat anything, which is kinda hot. And..."

"Alright, OK, stop. Sorry I asked." Ryan waved his hands uncomfortably. "Have you done *anything* with him, Amara? Even before we started dating. Anything at all?"

She shook her head intently. "Absolutely not. Tyler Hayes is a perfect gentleman if you must know," she lamented, thinking about how she'd come on to him the other night at his front door after finding the subreddit post, and how he'd sent her home. "He really is."

He grabbed her hand as the Uber pulled up to the

club's entrance. "Hey. Let's just enjoy ourselves tonight. OK? If it works out, we'll deal with it." He raised her hand to his lips, kissing it gently and squeezing. "But let's just have fun together. I wanna have a good time with you."

She smiled. "OK."

* * *

"You get used to it!"

Amara could barely hear herself think over the excruciatingly loud EDM pumping to the point that she could feel it in her bones.

A younger, very attractive blonde woman wearing way too much makeup had taken a seat next to her at the bar, where Amara had gone for a break after dancing nonstop with Ryan for the last hour or so. Memory foam or not, her feet were literally about to die.

"I'm sorry?" she shouted to the woman, taking another sip of her third whiskey on the rocks.

The woman leaned in right up against her ear. She still had to yell, but not as loud. "I see you staring at him, all those girls all over him. You just have to change your mindset." She reached a hand out. "I'm Natasha. Conner Dales's fiancé. Dalesy?"

"Oh. Hi," she shouted, shaking her hand. She thought back to the party at Tyler's apartment, and this wasn't either of the girls Dalesy had brought. It especially wasn't the girl who was sitting on his lap kissing his neck in the living room after blowing Ryan and God knows who else.

"You're Baylor's girlfriend, right? He's super-hot. Girls aren't gonna leave him alone. Literally, the minute you walk away, they'll be all over him."

"Yeah. I've kinda noticed."

"Come with me!" She grabbed Amara's arm and led her across the club, eventually to an outside area illuminated by hanging string lights, fireplaces, and propane heaters, where a bunch of people sat smoking and vaping. They found a couple of chairs near one of the firepits and took a seat. "Ah, that's better! I can actually hear myself think again. Amanda, right?" Natasha pulled out a pen, pulled, and offered it to Amara. "You want? Might help take the edge off."

"No thanks." She held up her whiskey. "I'm good. And it's Amara."

"Amara. That's pretty. So, you guys have a bit of a May-December thing going on, huh? What's he, 20 years younger than you?" She took another pull. "I'm sorry. That sounded bitchy. I didn't mean it like that. You're stunning, seriously. The other guys are jealous as shit. They talk about Baylor's cougar all the time. Especially Seggy, Jamie Segorsky? He'd fuck you in a heartbeat. Don't waste your time though. He's the absolute worst in bed. Great dick, but so selfish."

She smiled awkwardly. "Wow, OK. Yeah, Ry's 18 years younger than me." She made a face as she said it aloud. "And I probably belong in prison."

"Nah. I mean, that's an insane gap, but I guess it works for you guys, huh? Conn's 8 years older than me. Anyway, I noticed you staring at him, surrounded by all those girls. Listen, you'll get used to it."

"I wasn't...I mean, it's...fine." She wasn't gonna tell her that they were fishing for one to take home and share.

"I used to get so jealous when Conn would have chicks all over him, but I learned that you have to focus on the bigger picture." She flashed her gigantic engagement ring, her earrings, her expensive purse, and pointed to her shoes. "These? Cost $3000. When he gets called up to the NHL, the amount of money coming in is going to blow your mind, plus any sponsors he gets. It makes it a lot easier to look the other way if you get my drift." She took another pull; Amara noticed her eyes, though bloodshot, were stone cold. "I know he cheats. Trust me, I'm no saint either. I've run through half that locker room. Actively trying to get my hands on Hayes, but he just won't bite. Rumor has it he's got a gorgeous cock."

Amara's hackles were raised at the mention of his name. "I'm actually pretty close with Tyler myself," she said matter-of-factly.

"Oh, OK then. So, is it true? Is he hung like they say he is?"

"Wouldn't know. We're just friends."

"Well, that's no fun. Hey, you'll have to put in a good word for me."

"Right."

Natasha continued. "There's a dark side to all of this, a seedy underbelly, if you will, that so many girls can't handle because they go into it with this delusion that it's about love. It's not. Most of these guys have been so used and abused that they aren't even capable of love. It's about financial stability, comfort, convenience. Listen, I didn't sign a prenup. When I decide I've had enough, and I will, I'm set. You have to look away sometimes and remember that you're the one he's going home with. Make sure he gets tested, make sure he doesn't knock anyone up, or if he does, he makes her terminate it, and make friends with some of the other guys on the team. It, uh, helps."

"Uh huh. Thanks for the advice. Listen, I'm gonna go find a bathroom…"

"Hey, ladies. Mind if we join you?" Two younger guys came and sat down in the empty seats next to Natasha.

"Absolutely, gentlemen," she crooned, as Amara watched her deftly remove her engagement ring and sneak it into her purse.

Amara stood up. "I'm actually gonna head in. Nice talking to you," she said, turning and walking back towards the bar. The better looking of the guys got up and followed her.

"Hey. I didn't get your name." He reached out and touched her shoulder, so she pivoted to face him. "I'm Evan."

"Amara," she responded without thinking. "But I was just on my way to find a bathroom."

"Don't go back in. Little known secret, but there are bathrooms out here, just around that corner. Much cleaner and pretty quiet. I can take you over there if you want. The handicap stall in the women's room is my favorite." He whipped out a condom and held it in front of her face. "Wanna check it out with me, maybe let me pull that dress up and have an orgasm between those beautiful legs?"

She laughed, taken aback. "Wow. A man that gets right to the point. I'm good though, thanks."

"Is it because I'm younger? I'm 28, but I promise I'll make it worth your time."

"Sorry, baby. But 28 is just *entirely* too young for me. Hey, good luck though!"

"Whatever. Bitch," he mumbled, as he turned to head back towards Natasha.

Amara smirked, heading back inside the club so she could pee and get a status update from her boyfriend. She could feel the whiskey starting to do its thing.

She pushed her way through the crowd on the way out of the bathroom and finally located Ryan standing near the bar, a drink in one hand and the other resting on the shoulder of a beautiful, young blonde who was seated there.

"There you are!" she yelled, approaching him, downing the rest of her whiskey, and slamming the empty on the bar in front of the babe.

"Hey." He immediately moved his hand from the blonde's shoulder and put his arm around his girlfriend.

"I was out back with Dalesy's fiancé. Man, talk about a vile human being. Oh, and some dude asked me to fuck him in the bathroom. He literally waved a condom in front of my face."

Ryan raised an eyebrow. "That's lovely. Anyway. So, Kaylie, this is my girlfriend, Amara."

"Nice to meet you!" Amara shook her hand, staring at her huge tits that were barely covered by her bright yellow halter top.

"She's, uh, down, if you wanna get out of here," Ryan told Amara, then leaned into her ear. "You still wanna do this with me? You can say no."

"Nah, I'm good. So, it worked? The pussy flare?"

"Yep. Told you. Like a charm."

Kaylie tapped Ryan's shoulder, and he leaned down. "She's gorgeous. I wanna watch you two together."

"That's not a problem, but you're gonna spend some time on my cock, too," he responded, signaling the bartender. "Hey, can I close out? Mar, wanna get us an Uber? I'm gonna text Osi so he knows we're leaving."

EXPERIMENT #1 (17)

The ride home in the Uber was quiet, minus the smooth jazz playing on the radio. The three of them sat crammed together in the backseat of the Chevy Equinox, with Ryan in the middle. He made sure to put his arm around Amara, while Kaylie's hand rested in his lap, toying with his inner thigh.

Amara stared at the girl's hand, and she could see Ryan's cock thickening. Unsure if it was the liquid courage awakened by three glasses of straight Tennessee whiskey or what, she grabbed Kaylie's hand and placed it on Ryan's growing hard-on. "Kiss her," she whispered into his ear.

He immediately turned his head towards Kaylie and began to make out with her. Amara watched him suck and bite her bottom lip, the same way he did when they made out.

She couldn't process the sudden, foreign feeling that came over her as she watched him kiss this woman who was so much younger and more beautiful than herself. It was an intense anger coupled with an intense sexual desire, and the two battled furiously for her attention. Her hand wandered down to Ryan's lap, where Kaylie had begun jerking him off through his pants. She grabbed onto his dick to help, and a loud moan escaped him when he felt her join in.

The fun, however, was quickly halted. "Uh uh, honey! No love stains up in this car. Save that shit for when y'all get home!"

"I'm sorry, Letitia!" Ryan called out to her. He'd had her so many times as a driver that they were on a first-name basis. "You forgive me?"

"Ryan, Imma whoop your damn ass. You cute, but you ain't that cute. Hands to your damn selves, ladies. Y'all almost home."

She let them off at the door of the apartment building. "Y'all have fun!" she said, as they piled out. "You better wrap that shit up, Ryan!"

"I will. Bye, Letitia!"

The three wandered into the building and waited for the elevator, which was down on the basement floor. When it made its way up to the lobby and opened, there stood Hayes in a wool hat, t-shirt, and sweatpants, with a laundry bag next to him, as the three of them got on. "Well, well, well. The fuck do we have here?"

"Just got back from Excel," Ryan exhaled, as Kaylie ran one hand through his hair and felt up his abs with the other. "It was a good time."

"Apparently. Yo, Mar, you OK?" he asked, as he noticed her leaning her head back against the elevator wall, eyes closed.

"She's fine," Ryan responded.

"I didn't ask you. Mar, you good?"

The elevator hit the fourth floor and opened. "I'm fine, Tyler," she said, not moving or opening her eyes.

"Right. That's convincing. Well, have fun with... whatever the fuck this is." He stepped out, and as Amara opened her eyes, she saw him hyper-focused on her. He mouthed the words "Text me" just as the doors closed.

When they got off on the sixth floor, Ryan put an arm around each of their waists as they walked to their apartment. Once inside, Ryan turned to Amara. "Wait here," he told her, as he escorted Kaylie to his bedroom and quickly returned. He grabbed her face with both hands and pulled her in for a kiss. "Hey? She's just a toy for us to play with for a little bit, OK? She means absolutely nothing to me."

Amara nodded. "She's so much prettier than me."

"Not even close. In fact, she told me how gorgeous you were at the bar and that she wanted to watch us. It's not a competition. We're all playing for the same team here, OK?"

"You've done this before? With more than one girl?"

"Uh, yeah."

"Of course you have."

"Stop it. This is about us right now. So, what are the rules? Anything I need to know?"

"Don't fall in love with her."

"That's not gonna happen, Amara. Seriously, what's off-limits?"

"Nothing. Just please don't ignore me."

"Have you seen yourself in this fucking dress? I couldn't ignore you if I wanted to." He grabbed her hand and led her to the bedroom, stopping outside to kiss her one more time. "Just. A. Toy. You understand?"

Amara nodded obediently, following him inside and closing the door behind her.

Kaylie sat on the bed, down to nothing but her red panties, back against the headboard, gripping it, with her knees bent. Ryan crawled onto the bed in front of her, and she instinctively spread her legs for him, as he crept up her body, squeezed her tits together, and buried his tongue in between them. Amara just stood there, frozen, watching her boyfriend suck on another woman's tits for a few seconds. He stopped and looked up at Kaylie. "My girlfriend's never been with another woman before. Think you can help her out?"

"Of course," she said, beckoning Amara with one finger to come join them, as she and Ryan began kissing. Amara made her way to the side of the bed, grabbed the hem of her dress, and pulled it up over her head. Kaylie reached an arm out, grabbed her ass, and pulled her down onto the bed next to them. "She's got such a beautiful body, Ryan."

"Doesn't she? She's perfect." He leaned over and kissed Amara, then kissed Kaylie again, finally bringing Amara over so that the three of their tongues met simultaneously.. Though it was awkward, Amara had never been so turned on in her life. Ryan pulled away, leaving only her and Kaylie kissing, and he exited the bed to go get a condom.

Amara was on top of Kaylie, lying between her legs, her small tits pressed against Kaylie's huge, fake ones, when she felt Ryan unhook her bra and grab her hips from behind. Kaylie pulled off the bra as Amara arched her back and moaned at the feeling of Ryan moving her panties aside and pushing inside of her.

"Fuck her real good for me, baby," Kaylie moaned, making eye contact with Ryan as Amara leaned down and sucked on her nipples. Having never done this before, she just did what she liked to have done to her, and based on the noises Kaylie was making, it seemed to be working.

It'd only been maybe a minute or so when he pulled out. Kaylie cupped Amara's face, bringing it up to hers. "Do you mind if I eat you out while he fucks me for a bit?"

Before she could answer, Ryan flipped her over so she was lying on her back. Kaylie crawled between her legs and arched back, whimpering as Ryan shoved his cock inside her. Amara locked eyes with Ryan as Kaylie began licking slowly between her legs, and within seconds, actual seconds, of watching him fuck her, she came all over Kaylie's tongue. "Oh fuck! Fuck!" It was an orgasm much more intense and wetter than her usual ones.

"Mmm...you didn't tell me...she was a squirter," Kaylie

moaned, moving her hands up Amara's body and kissing her stomach while Ryan continued to rail her from behind. Not long after, Amara watched as he pulled out, ripped the condom off, and jerked himself off all over her back.

Amara lay there, panting, as Ryan got up to get a towel for Kaylie's back. He immediately gathered her clothes off the floor and gave them to her, pulled his boxers on, and threw one of his t-shirts to Amara. "So, did you want me to call you an Uber, or will you get one for yourself?" He seemed really eager to get her out of there.

She began putting her clothes back on. "I'll take care of it. Don't worry, I wasn't gonna try to sleep over or anything." She winked at Amara, finished getting dressed, and messed around on her phone for a bit. "All set. He'll be here in 10 minutes."

"I can walk you down and wait with you, just let me throw on some shorts."

"It's OK. I'm a big girl." She looked at Amara. "Hey, thanks for the good time, beautiful. Take care of him."

"Let me walk you out," Ryan said, following her out of the bedroom.

A sudden feeling rushed over Amara, and she wasn't sure how to interpret it. It was a mixture of fear coupled with some panic, a smidge of regret, and a whole lot of shame. She practically ran to her bedroom, slammed the door behind her, and immediately turned the shower in her bathroom to as hot as she could stand it.

Don't you dare cry. This was your brilliant idea, she thought bitterly, but it was too late.

The tears crept down her face as she peeled off his t-shirt, opened the sliding glass door, and positioned herself under the stream, hoping it would rinse away this new, unwanted feeling that permeated her soul at the moment.

She wasn't sure how long she'd been standing motionless under the water before Ryan came in and joined her. He didn't speak a word, just stood behind her and wrapped her in his arms. She couldn't help the tears and hoped the water would hide them from him.

But he knew her a little better than that. "You're upset," he finally said. "Talk to me."

"I'm fine," she barely squeaked out.

"Don't lie to me."

"It's...just leftover insecurity from his cheating. I'm sorry."

"Don't ever apologize for feeling what you feel."

"It felt better with her than with me, didn't it?"

"Nothing on Earth feels better than with you, Amara."

"You finished with her though."

"Because I watched you cum and couldn't hold it anymore. That's just where I happened to be when it was go time."

"I didn't like that. I wanted you to finish with me."

"Then it doesn't happen again."

"I was so turned on watching you fuck her, but so jealous and angry, too. I don't know which emotion to give control to."

"That's normal. I'm sure I'll feel the same way watching you with another guy."

"Do you think less of me now?"

"Absolutely not. If anything, this makes me feel even closer to you. Like I said, she was a toy for us to play with. That's it. Did you see how quickly I got rid of her?"

"She was young. And really beautiful."

"Yeah, she was. But so what? Lots of girls are beautiful. And all she kept telling me was how beautiful *you* were. No one compares to you. No one. You're the most beautiful woman I've ever known. Not girl. *Woman*."

He reached a hand up to the fogged-up glass door, took his finger, and wrote "Ryan", drew a heart with an "'s" below it, and wrote "Amara" below that. "I know I'm not supposed to say it, but you never said I couldn't write it on the shower door. You know what? Fuck it. Amara, I love you. I'm not gonna stand here and pretend I don't. I love you."

"You say you love me, but you just did what you did with

her. I'm having a hard time understanding that."

"Because Amara, I don't associate sex with love. I never have. They exist in two separate realms for me. I can have sex with someone and feel absolutely nothing."

"And you think that's normal?"

"I never said that. But it's the way I operate. The fact that I also get to have sex with someone I love is like, a bonus for me."

"Well, I can't say it back. I'm sorry."

"And you don't have to. Doesn't change how I feel."

She turned the water off, and they both stepped out. He grabbed a towel and took his time as he slowly, gently dried off her entire body, all the way from her hair down to her toes. As he finished and began to dry himself off, she lay down on the bathroom floor mat. Unsure whether it was all the whiskey or the stress of the range of emotions she was experiencing, she didn't feel right. He curled up behind her, grabbing a dry towel from the rack and throwing it over them.

"You don't have to stay here," she said softly. "I just need a minute."

"Listen, I'm falling asleep holding you tonight, so if that's on a bathroom floor, then that's what it is."

And that's what it was.

OTHER OPTIONS (18)

"So which one: the red one or the black one?" She held up both dresses on hangers as she finished getting packed for Nick's wedding, which was in a few hours at a hotel on Long Island.

"What's it fuckin' matter? You could wear a plastic bag and you'd still be a smoke," Tyler told her, as he lay on her bed scrolling through his phone. "But you better pick one because we need to grab Osi and get going. The traffic's a real bitch over there."

The team had gotten a rare break in their schedule from the previous Sunday to the upcoming Sunday, so Nick planned a small wedding for that Friday. A few of the players who hadn't decided to go home or take a quick vacation would be in attendance.

Osi and Tyler would.

Ryan would not.

"I hate that I won't be able to come with you," he'd told Amara. *"But you understand that I have to go, right?"*

"I know. I totally get it. I was just looking forward to another night out with you."

Luke had called him Tuesday morning to say that their mom had ended up in the hospital after passing out. It didn't appear too serious, but they were running a bunch of tests because they couldn't figure out what had caused it. Ryan decided that he needed to be there and had flown out to Minnesota that day.

"Amara? Behave," he'd told her, before leaving for his Uber and after pulling her in for a long, slow kiss.

"I'm gonna go with the black one," she said aloud, folding it and placing it inside her suitcase. "I just have to grab my makeup and hair stuff and then we can head out."

"So, hey: I never got to ask you," Tyler said, putting his phone down. "The fuck was goin' on the other night with you guys?"

"What do you mean?" She played dumb, as she went into the bathroom.

He followed her, leaning against the door frame with one arm above his head. "You know exactly what I'm talking about. The super-hot, stacked blonde who was molestin' Rook in the elevator."

"Oh. That? Umm, nothing. We're just...trying out something different. It's fine. Ugh, where the fuck is my foundation brush?" she whined, moving things around wildly on her vanity.

"Is it fine?"

"Yes! God, where is it?"

"Why are you so flustered right now, Mar?"

"I'm not flustered!" she yelled. "There it is." She snatched the brush, stuffing it into her toiletries bag and zipping it aggressively. She grabbed the bag off the counter, pushed by him, and went back into her room to get her suitcase. "Come on, we need to go. Text Osi."

"He's got you fucking other girls with him? Already? And you're cool with that?"

"Tyler," she warned. "Back off."

"You get to play around with other dudes, or does this arrangement just benefit him?"

"That's none of your business, OK?"

He took her suitcase from her and set it down. "If you're upset, it's very much my fuckin' business. And you're upset. So, you better talk to me."

She immediately let herself fall apart in front of him, collapsing onto his shoulder while he ran his hand up and down her back. "Yeah, that's exactly what I fuckin' thought."

She pulled away after a few seconds and wiped her eyes. "It was me. I suggested we try an open relationship. That was our first time, and it was hot, but I kinda regret it." She sat down on the edge of her bed, wiping her eyes.

"I bet you do. Why the fuck would you even suggest some shit like that?" he asked, sitting next to her.

"Because he's...who he is. I don't know if Ry's even wired for monogamy. And I don't wanna get cheated on again. I won't survive it."

"No man is wired for monogamy, Mar. If you care about someone, you work at it. Amara, did he cheat on you? I swear to God, I'll fuckin' beat his face in."

"No. I just found some stuff online...that's what I was trying to talk to you about that night I was outside your door and you made me leave."

"Because you smelled like alcohol and were coming on to me like a horny prom date. What kinda stuff online?"

"It was the Islanders subreddit."

"The *what*?"

"It's a forum where people can post about different topics. Bridgeport has one, and girls didn't have a lot of nice things to say about him."

"Like?"

"They said he told them he had a girlfriend and that he

wouldn't meet up with them for sex."

"And that upset you? Sorry, I don't follow."

"No, it's..." She pulled her hair back and let it fall again. "But he said all that while he was still flirting with them online, making sexual comments, telling them he jerked off to their pictures, liking all their stories and shit. And then when they'd try to meet up, he'd ghost them, basically leading them on."

"This is after you two agreed to date?"

"Yes."

"Wow. What a piece of garbage."

"I just don't know if it's fair for me to ask him to..."

"Ask him to what, act like your boyfriend? The boyfriend he basically pressured you into having? He doesn't get to have it both ways, Amara."

"It's just...he's still young."

"Bullshit! He's fuckin' three years older than me, and I have no problem tellin' a bitch to go home."

"Shit. I always forget how young you are, Tyler."

"Yeah? And I always forget that you belong in a nursing home, Grandma."

She elbowed him. "Dick."

"So, what'd those hoes have to say about me?"

She laughed. "There's been nothing posted since your breakup, but before? That you don't cheat, that you won't cheat, that you don't respond to messages, and to not even waste your time. Every single one of them."

He flexed. "Boom. See that? That's how it's done." He looked down at the floor. "It's not that complicated to be a real man, Amara. You wanna screw around, you don't get into a relationship. You wanna be in a relationship with someone, you make sacrifices."

"Coming from the guy who ruined two marriages," she replied, instantly regretting it when she saw the hurt that crept across his face.

"That's fucked up. I made mistakes, OK? Big, heavy

mistakes that I have to carry around daily, that haunt me nonstop. But that's not an excuse not to change. I'm not that 16-year-old lost kid anymore, Mar."

"I'm sorry. I had no right to say that."

"No, you didn't. But you're hot, so I'll let it slide."

She changed the subject. "Back to what I was saying. As far as making sacrifices, with this...arrangement, we kinda don't have to."

"You gonna come cry on my shoulder every time he fucks another younger, hotter girl and your old ass feels insecure?"

"Will you let me?"

"You know I will."

"I mean, I had some fun with her, too. And it was kinda hot watching him do his thing with someone else. I just have to force myself to get used to it is all. Besides, I have some other options of my own I'd like to explore."

"Well, for the record, I know you both pretty well, and I think this is a real fuckin' stupid idea."

"I don't remember asking what you think," she spat back.

"So, uh, you never answered my question." He snuck an arm around her waist and scooted her closer to him, so their hips touched. He reached his other hand around the back of her head, pulling her forehead to his.

"What are you doing?" she asked, running a hand across his chest.

"Do you get to play, too? You allowed to explore those other options?"

"Yes."

"Really?"

"Uh huh," she panted.

"Well? Go on, then."

"Ty." Her heartbeat thumped uncontrollably in her ears as his lips *finally* pressed against hers, followed quickly by his tongue. She met it briefly with her own, which sent a shock wave through her entire body, before pulling back abruptly and pushing him away.

"Jesus, Amara, come on!" he whined. "How long are we gonna fuckin' do this?"

"Yes, I do get to play, too. But it has to be threesomes or group stuff, no going off one-on-one. And I can't play with... *you*, Tyler. That's his main boundary."

"Of course it is!" He stood up abruptly, adjusted the front of his pants, and shook his head as he grabbed her suitcase again. "Fuck. Just...get the rest of your shit. We gotta go!" he snapped. "You're fuckin' unbelievable!"

"Tyler..."

"I don't wanna hear it. Let's go." He got to the front door, stopped, threw her suitcase to the ground, and whipped around to face her. "Nah, fuck this! You had no issue tellin' me how you felt about my ex-girlfriend when we were together, so now it's my turn. If you wanna bang other people, and if he wants to bang other people? Break it off with him!" he shouted, startling her. "You're not this stupid, Amara. You know he's using you, right?"

"No, he's not," she protested. "He's not."

"Yes, he is! He's using you to fill some void in his stupid, fucked-up brain. You provide this part-time girlfriend experience while he gets to continue being a full-time sloppy whore. He's controlling you. You don't see it?"

"No, he's not."

"Stop making excuses for him. What, just because he makes you cum hard? Plenty of other guys can do the same, minus the mind games. He's controlling you, Mar!" He got right up in her face and jammed a finger into her chest. "And you're *lettin'* him! You're fuckin' lettin' him. You know, I'm disappointed in you. I really thought you were smarter and stronger than this." He picked her suitcase back up and walked out.

"So did I," she said softly, following Hayes out the door.

THE WEDDING (19)

She twisted the last curl into her hair, sprayed it a final time, and did one more makeup check in the mirror of the hotel bathroom. It was the room with a single king-sized bed that she and Ryan were supposed to be sharing for the evening, but where she'd now be spending the night alone.

The ceremony was starting downstairs in about 20 minutes, and just as she finished checking her outfit in the full-length mirror, there was a knock at the door.

"You ready?" Tyler said, standing there with Osi. They both looked incredibly handsome, but especially Tyler. His hair was actually styled for once and not crammed inside a wool cap, and the blue plaid suit he was wearing complemented his dark green eyes flawlessly. He'd been letting a bit of facial hair grow in, which for Tyler took about 10 seconds, but he'd trimmed it up neatly for the occasion.

"Ty, you look really nice," she told him, as he avoided eye

contact with her.

"Yeah, thanks. We should go."

He was being short with her, which meant he was still pissed off from earlier. The drive didn't help things; they'd bickered nearly the entire ride, speaking in code so as not to reveal too much to Osi.

"You can't have two sets of rules for the same fuckin' game. That's not fair."

"When you're the one making up the game and the rules, you can do whatever you want."

"How is that fair? The expectation is that there's some sort of end goal, right? How can one person be playing by one set of rules and the other by a different one? Get the fuck outta the left lane, jackass!" Tyler honked the horn and abruptly swerved the truck into the middle lane.

"I don't understand why you care so much. If all the players in the game are aware of the different sets of rules, and they agree to them, what's it matter?"

"Did they agree to them? Or did some of the other players pressure them into accepting rules that maybe they didn't want to? And now they're stuck with a disadvantage, while others play to win every time. Move, fucker! I hate the fuckin' Belt Parkway! This is literally what hell must be like."

"Maybe it's a necessary disadvantage."

"Oh, is that right? A necessary disadvantage. Maybe some other players wanna join the game but can't because of these fucked-up sets of rules for the different players already in the game. It's like hockey. You can't blow offsides for one team and let the other just skate right the fuck on in without the puck. It's not the same game."

"You know I don't understand hockey."

"You don't understand a lot of things. For someone so smart, you're really stupid sometimes."

"Piss off, Hayes." She never called him 'Hayes' unless she was annoyed with him.

There was a silence, which Osi finally broke. *"Is not the*

same game."

"*What?*" Amara and Tyler asked in unison.

"*Two sets of rules for same game no work. If two sets of rules for same game, is not the same game. Is two separate games.*"

"*Thank you, Osi!*" Tyler yelled, slapping the steering wheel. "*Thank you.*"

"*By the way: is very obvious neither of you is talking about actual game.*"

The three of them walked down the hall to the elevator, got on, and Osi hit the button for the lobby, which was on the same floor as the ceremony and reception. As they got off, Amara spotted Nick standing there and shuffled over to him, giving him a huge hug. "Congratulations! I'm so glad this is finally happening for you. You nervous?"

"Nah, not really. Just happy for this day to be here. You know he's been driving me nuts. Hey: I appreciate you being here. I know weddings aren't the easiest for you. Thank you." He kissed the top of her head.

"I wouldn't miss it for anything. Gonna go grab my seat. Good luck!" She blew him a kiss, went into the ceremony room, and sat in the seat Tyler had saved for her.

He leaned over and whispered in her ear. "I mean, I guess I get it, but this wedding is an absolute fuckin' sausage party. Christ. I've never seen so much dick."

She giggled and smacked him on the arm. "Stop it."

"I was kinda hoping to get laid here tonight. Guess that ain't happening."

"Don't all you hockey boys play both sides anyway?"

He blushed, smirking. "Nah."

"Never?"

"Not...in a very long time." He immediately changed the subject. "Anyway, I forgot to tell you, but you look real pretty. I'm just gonna tell everyone that you're my date tonight, OK?" She spoke fluent Tylerese, and that roughly translated to, "Sorry I was such a dick earlier."

"OK," she said, shifting in her seat as she thought about

their brief kiss from earlier, how much the thought of his tongue turned her on, and how much she desperately wanted to pick up where they left off.

"Any word on Rook's mom?" he asked.

"Not sure. Last we talked, she was home and doing fine, but I haven't...I actually haven't heard from him at all today," she said, checking to make sure she'd put her phone on silent.

"There's a surprise," Tyler mumbled.

"Don't start."

"You know I don't sugarcoat shit, babe. You need to ditch his dusty ass before you get hurt again."

"He's not going to hurt me."

"He already did, Mar. Did you forget you were cryin' in my arms earlier today?"

"No, I remember. And just so you know, that wasn't because of him. That was my own insecurity messing with my head."

"Do you remember kissin' me?"

"Tyler!" They'd been whispering loudly, but she raised her voice, causing people to turn and look. "Stop it. Now."

He leaned over to her ear. "Because I haven't stopped thinkin' about it for even a second."

She closed her eyes. "Please, not right now."

The ceremony started, and he finally backed off. When he heard her sniffling during the exchanging of vows, he grabbed her hand, brought it to his lips, and kissed it.

He didn't bother to let it go, nor did she bother to pull it away.

* * *

"Holy shit!" Tyler plopped down at the table, where Amara had been engaged in small talk with a few of Mark's coworkers. He was feeling no pain, having downed about his sixth Jack and Coke. Amara had started the night grabbing them for him, but they quickly realized no one was checking ID. He'd spent the last half-hour tearing up the dance floor, which amused Amara to no end, seeing as he couldn't dance to save his life.

"Having fun out there, Dancing Queen?" she teased, watching him slam the nearest glass of water and wipe his face with his arm.

"Yeah, but I'm sweatin' like a whore in church." The jacket and tie had come off and his shirt was halfway unbuttoned.

"Lettin' all that luxurious chest hair fly free tonight?" She grabbed onto his collar with one hand and tugged it lightly.

"Respect the chest lettuce, eh? You know you think it's sexy."

"Perhaps a little."

"It's so hot in here. Come on," he said, grabbing her by the arm and standing up. "Come get some air with me."

They made their way back into the lobby and headed out a side door, which led to an outdoor sitting area, where the firepits were roaring since it was a cold, New York November night. They found a couple of chairs and Amara sat down, immediately rubbing up and down her arms. "We can't stay out here long. It's freezing."

"You kidding? This feels like Heaven!" She felt him put his jacket around her shoulders before sitting down next to her. "I got you. Grabbed it for you on the way out, since I know your old ass is always cold."

"Thank you." She pulled it tightly around the front of her. It smelled like him, and she closed her eyes, inhaling deeply.

"So, talk to me."

She sighed. "What do you wanna talk about, Tyler?"

"This little arrangement between you and Rook..."

"Jesus, Ty. You don't quit."

"What's the end game, Mar?"

"What do you mean?"

"I mean, where's it headed with him? I don't know if you know this, but I spend a considerable amount of fuckin' time worryin' about you."

"Now why would you go and do a thing like that?"

"Because!" He stood up dramatically and threw his hands up. "You've been through hell. You...you should be out here havin' the time of your life, doin' whatever you want. You meet a guy at work, you wanna go home with him? You should go home with him. Meet a hot, young stud in the laundry room you wanna bang? You should bang him."

"Provided he doesn't have a girlfriend at the time," she reminded him. "Or believe me, I would've."

"Duly noted. Anyway, you shouldn't be tied down right now, especially not with someone as fuckin' needy as Rook. You know he's impossible, Mar."

"I am very capable of making my own decisions, Tyler."

"Are you though?"

"This is exhausting. I really don't wanna do this with you anymore."

"Good!" he yelled. "Because I don't wanna do this anymore with you either. Jesus, Amara. I've been walking around with a raging hard-on for you for two months. I had a girlfriend, then you had a boyfriend, now I don't have a girlfriend, and you and your boyfriend have an actual agreement to bang other people, which somehow, I got excluded from. What the fuck are we supposed to do? Ignorin' it clearly isn't workin' anymore."

"I don't know, Ty. I wish I did."

"Well, here goes nothin'." He dropped down to one knee in front of her, reached into the pocket of his jacket, pretended to have a ring box, and pretended to open it in front of her. "I have a question to ask you. Amara, will you..." He clasped his hands together on her lap, shook them back and forth, and pretended to cry. "Will you *please* let this happen? I'm begging you! We kissed for half a second today and I've already jerked off twice in my hotel room. *Twice.* I can't smack it to you

140

anymore, woman. My dick is legit gonna fall off. Please?" He looked up at her, with slightly drunk eyes and the stupidest grin plastered across his face.

"Get. The fuck. Up!" she laughed, kicking him, as he stood up and sat back down next to her.

"You like that?" He nudged her. "You got a 20-year-old begging you for it. Literally begging. You better knock it off with that insecurity shit, woman. There's not a man alive you couldn't fuck if you wanted to."

"So, secret time? Our little kiss today did things to me."

"Yeah?"

"Yeah. Like, I felt it in parts of my body I didn't even know I had. I can't stop thinking about it."

"I really thought that was it, that I was gonna fuck you right there on your bed today. You know it's gonna happen, right?"

She exhaled. "I know."

He leaned over, nuzzling his head into the crook of her neck, and placed a hand on her leg. "Come on, let's just get it out of our systems tonight. He's not here. What are you gonna do in that huge bed all by yourself? He doesn't ever have to know it happened, Amara. It can be our little secret." She felt his hand creeping up her thigh, a finger toying with the hem of her dress. "I'll have you grippin' those sheets harder than he does, I fuckin' promise you that."

"Ty, stop." She pushed him away gently and stood up, though she was seriously considering his offer. Maybe if they just pulled the trigger, their feelings would fade and they could move forward as friends, or...something. "Come on, let's go back inside. It's too cold out here."

As they walked back into the reception, she took off his jacket, handed it back to him, and he tossed it over his shoulder. "I gotta rock a piss. Get us more drinks." He disappeared to the bathroom as Amara headed to the bar.

"One Jack and Coke, and a whiskey on the rocks, please," she told the bartender, after waiting in line for a bit.

"Make that two whiskeys."

Her eyes widened. She flipped around and found herself face to face with Ryan Baylor, looking sexy as ever in a tailored black suit with white pinstripes, a black tie, and a white dress shirt. "Oh my...hi! How? What?"' She threw her arms around him and kissed him. "Hi!"

"I wanted to surprise you. That's why I didn't text you at all today. Surprise!" He smiled at her. "I called Nick earlier to make sure it was cool if I crashed. Flight was delayed or I'd have been here sooner. So, you look like a goddess. Who's the other drink for?"

Shit.

Shit, shit, shit.

"Yo, some dude is launching' over that bath..." Tyler's face sank as he returned to the bar, where Amara was now standing next to her boyfriend. "Where the fuck did this kid come from, eh?" He wrapped an arm around Ryan's shoulder and gave him a quick, little-too-hard squeeze before grabbing his drink from Amara. She could tell he was pissed but trying to hide it.

"Thought I'd surprise my girlfriend and come home early. I paid for the room. It'd be a shame not to get any use out of it." He winked at her, looked Tyler dead in the eyes, and took a sip of his drink. "Don't you think?"

"Totally. I'll, uh, see you guys in there." He turned and walked away. Amara's eyes followed him until he was out of sight, then landed back on Ryan, who was finishing his first whiskey and asking the bartender for another. He grabbed it and threw about half of it back, which Amara knew meant that he intended to get drunk. "Come on, I wanna dance with my girl for a bit," he said, leading her back into the reception hall.

Shit.

THE ULTIMATE COMPROMISE (20)

"Yo: Rook's toasted again," Tyler pointed to where he was dancing completely alone on the floor to Madonna. He was a little better of a dancer than Tyler, but that wasn't really saying much.

Amara had tapped out a while ago and joined Tyler at the table. Osi has since retired to their room with a girl he'd met up with on Tinder and had informed Tyler he'd text him when it was safe to come up.

"You've got room to talk. You can't even open your eyes all the way," Amara said, staring at him slumped over in his chair.

"I may have partaken in some herbal enhancements as well," he said, waving his pen and sticking it back in his pocket.

"That explains it. You're supposed to be quitting,

remember?"

"Yeah, well, I don't want to right now," he replied petulantly, sticking his tongue out at her and checking his phone again. "Guess I'm the designated homeless tonight." He tossed it on the table and folded his arms.

"Nothing yet? I'm sure he'll be done soon. He has to be. They've been up there for over an hour."

"Osi isn't a sprinter. That Russian motherfucker is a marathon runner. It could be another two hours. Kid fucks for days at a time."

"Wow, who'd have thought? Good for him though!"

"Good for who?" Ryan yelled, grabbing her shoulders from behind and startling her. "Sorry, that was loud. Good for who?"

"Osi. He's been up in their room for over an hour with some Tinder chick and he's not responding to any of Ty's messages."

"Ooh, you don't think she killed him, do you?" Ryan asked, sitting down and stuffing an entire cookie in his mouth.

"I hope not, or we're all gettin' called in for questioning," Tyler said. "Anyway, that was the last song. Apparently, the DJ quit after watching this dickbag try to dance." He pointed at Ryan, who promptly flipped him off. "I'm gonna go find Nick and say goodbye, and then go sleep in my fuckin' truck, I guess."

Ryan leaned over to Amara after Hayes had walked away. "You look smokin' tonight. Did I tell you that yet?"

"About eight times," she laughed, grabbing his hand. "Thank you, again."

He sat back in his chair. "I'm just so lucky. I can't stop thinking about the other night and how hot it was sharing you with someone else but knowing that you're still all mine after."

Judging by the slight slurring, she assumed he was caught in the middle of a whiskey-fueled ramble, so she indulged him. "Yeah, it was pretty hot. She was...talented."

"I wasn't sure how I'd feel about it, but I fuckin' loved it."

"Yeah, it was kinda fun. I guess."

"You know, I've had a few drinks."

"You don't say, Ry?" He was definitely drunk, but not sloppy, slide-down-the-wall drunk, for which Amara was eternally grateful.

"And," he leaned in and whispered into her ear, "I'm feeling pretty generous again right now."

"OK. Well, in case you haven't done a once-over, it's slim pickin's around here. Hardly any women, and the guys that are here wouldn't really be barking up *this* tree if you catch my drift." She grabbed her phone and stuck it in her purse. "Wanna head up to the room?"

Ryan motioned over to where Hayes was standing and talking to Mark and Nick.

"Yeah, we'll stop and say goodbye on the way out."

"No, Amara. I mean, Hayes?"

"Yes, Ryan. That's Tyler Hayes, your teammate."

"No, I mean…you know. *Hayes*?"

"I'm not picking up what you're putting down, stud."

"Did you wanna maybe, I don't know…invite him up to our room and play around with him a little."

She rolled her eyes. "You're hilarious. Really. Come on, let's head up."

"Amara, I'm not kidding."

"Thought our little arrangement didn't include him?"

"It didn't. But you look hot. He looks hot. I'm drunk. And I want…I mean, I know *you* want him. You should get what you want."

"What's the catch? You wake up tomorrow regretting it, blame me, and I've gotta find a new home? No thanks, Ry. I've seen how your brain works." She stood up.

"Well, that's a lie, because my brain *doesn't* work." He stood up and put his arm around her. "Come on, let's go talk to him."

"Ryan, are you positive? I mean positive, because if this gets chucked back in my face, or if this is some kind of test that

I'm supposed to pass…"

"Amara?" he brought a finger to her lips to "shush" her, then whispered in her ear. "Do you wanna ride his cock tonight or not?"

She felt her heart begin to race and her legs turn to gelatin. "Yes," she said quietly, biting her bottom lip.

"That's what I thought. So, let's go talk to him."

"It has to come from you," she told him.

"And why's that?"

"Because I sorta filled him in on everything today, and he already knows he's persona non grata."

Ryan exhaled, annoyed. "You really do tell that little fucker everything, don't you?"

"Yeah. I mean, he's kinda…my best friend."

"Welp, let's go toss a wrench into those spokes, shall we?"

They approached Nick and Mark, said their goodbyes, and the newlyweds soon wandered off to some of the other guests who were leaving as well. That left Ryan and Amara standing with Hayes, who was checking his phone again.

"Nothing yet?" she asked.

"Nope."

"Man, that's crazy. Ryan?" she nudged him in the ribs. "Did you have something…"

"Oh, right. So, did you wanna come upstairs and help me fuck the shit out of my girlfriend?"

Amara and Hayes shot each other a look, both of their eyes practically bulging out of their skulls. They turned back towards Ryan, who shrugged.

"What, Amara? You said you thought it was hot when Hayes didn't sugarcoat things, right? So, I'm giving it a shot. Why play games? That's the plan, Hayes. You down for a little two-on-one scrimmage? Couple of sticks, one net?"

"Who the fuck *are* you right now?" she asked Ryan, staring at him and running her fingertips up his arm, decidedly turned on by his boldness.

"Whoever you want me to be," he responded, staring directly at Hayes. "Come on, kid. You like to make all that noise all the time, so here it is. You DTF or what?"

He shoved his phone in his back pocket and shrugged. "Alright. Let's fuckin' go then."

"Super," Ryan said, as he led the trek to the elevator, with Hayes and Amara in tow.

"What the fuck happened?" Hayes mouthed to Amara as they followed Ryan.

"I have no idea," she mouthed back. "It was totally his idea though. Are you OK with this?" she whispered.

"Um. What the *fuck* do you think? Do you remember me literally begging you earlier?"

"Even with him there?"

"I can handle Rook, don't you worry. Oh, he's gonna regret this shit. He's about to see how his girlfriend is supposed to get fucked."

"You better watch yourself," she warned him. "Don't sleep on him. Ryan's a fucking dynamo. He's the best I've ever had."

"Yeah. That's about to change."

EXPERIMENT #2 (21)

The three of them stepped off the elevator and made their way to the room. Amara opened the door with the key card, and as they all got inside, she kicked off her heels and threw her purse on the dresser. In seconds, she felt Ryan's hands sliding up the sides of her body as he grabbed her and pulled her close to him.

He leaned in and kissed her neck, moving his lips to her ear. "You can do whatever you want with him. Nothing is off-limits." He gripped the side of her neck firmly. "Just don't go falling in love with him. You're not his and he's not yours. You understand me?"

"Yes," she moaned. "You know I'm all yours, baby."

"Good girl."

He turned to Hayes, who was emptying his pockets onto the dresser. "Here. Why don't you get her outta that little black dress for us?"

Ryan shoved Amara in his direction, and Tyler put his hands up to stop her from stumbling into him.

"Why don't you fuckin' take it easy, Rook?" he said, moving his hands slowly around her waist and leaning into her face. "You OK?"

Amara fisted his hair with both hands and pulled. "Shut the fuck up and kiss me again." She immediately pushed her lips into his, her hands grabbing wildly at the buttons on his dress shirt and pulling them apart. Their tongues found each other again, and they kissed slowly, deeply, intently. Both could feel the other one smiling, relieved at finally being able to experience this long-awaited feeling. His hands crept to the hem of her dress, and he pulled it up over her ass as Ryan watched them make out.

"Jesus. Either of you gonna come up for air?"

She jumped up and wrapped her legs around Tyler's waist as she yanked his dress shirt over his shoulders and pushed it to the floor. He grabbed her ass and backed up until his knees hit the edge of the bed, falling backward and pulling her on top of him. He broke the kiss as his hands snaked up her sides, ripping the dress off over her head and leaving her straddling his lap in only her bra and thong.

"I want you to make such a fuckin' mess on my lap, babe." He grabbed her hips and steadied them against his, which he'd begun thrusting upwards.

"Tyler," she moaned. "Tyler. Fuck."

She felt Ryan unhook her bra from behind, pull it off, and cup her tits with both hands, pushing them together. "Is he a good kisser?" Ryan whispered into her ear.

"Yes. God yes."

"Better than me?"

"Wouldn't you like to know?"

He snatched her off Tyler's lap and tossed her onto the bed, face up. He'd since removed his dress shirt and slid up next to her on the opposite side of Tyler, who'd rolled over and positioned himself next to her in the same way. Ignoring her boyfriend, her face immediately turned back to Tyler's, their tongues playing sloppily outside of their mouths.

Ryan hovered over them, slipped a hand in between their faces, and forced her toward him. She opened her mouth for Ryan but reached around the back of Tyler's head, inviting him to join their kiss.

She arched her back and let out a small squeak as she felt both boys' tongues inside her mouth, unable to tell whose was whose. Deciding to play a little, she pulled away from them, and to her surprise, they kept right on kissing each other.

"Oh my God," Amara moaned. "That's the hottest thing I've ever seen." She stared, amazed, watching them slowly take each other's tongues into their mouths without even so much as a slight hesitation.

And they didn't stop.

She watched as Ryan brought a hand to the back of Tyler's head, with him doing the same, as they pulled each other in closer, deeper, like she wasn't even there. They kissed like it was something each of them needed.

Not wanted.

Needed.

They kept at it for awhile, tugging on each other's hair, as Amara swore she heard little moans escaping from one of them.

Ryan broke the kiss first. "You like watching us suck on each other's tongues, don't you?" he asked her, removing Tyler's hand from the back of his head and pushing it between Amara's legs.

"God yes. It's so...fucking hot, Ry," she whimpered, staring at Tyler's hand in her lap, beyond desperate for him to use it.

"You know, I don't believe you. Tell me if she likes it, Hayes," he ordered, pulling her thong down to the middle of her thighs. Tyler slowly pushed his middle finger inside her pussy, smiling at how wet she'd gotten for them.

"Oh yeah. She loves it, Rook. Like a fuckin' Slip and Slide

150

down there."

"Guess we should keep going for her then, huh?" Ryan pressed his palm flush against Tyler's, pushing his own middle finger inside of Amara as he crashed his lips into his teammate's again.

She was tempted to close her eyes, but she couldn't stop watching them kiss as they finger-fucked her simultaneously. She wiggled her thong the rest of the way down her legs and kicked it off so she could spread her legs wider for them. "You two...fucking *shit*," she moaned, bucking her hips in an attempt to get both boys' fingers as deep inside her as they could go. "I've never wanted anything...as bas as I want this."

Again, Ryan pulled away first, leaving Tyler with his mouth open and looking a little disappointed.

"Enough of this high school shit." Ryan leaned into Amara's ear. "I wanna see you ride his cock."

"Whatever you want, baby," she panted.

They both removed their fingers and Ryan pulled her up to sitting. He ran the finger that'd just been inside her over Tyler's lips, and he immediately opened his mouth to suck it. "She tastes good, doesn't she?" Ryan asked.

"Fuck yeah, she does."

Amara dropped to her knees in front of Ryan and worked to undo his pants as Tyler stood up and worked feverishly to undo his own. When she'd gotten Ryan's pants off, she crawled to Tyler. "Sit next to him," she instructed, which he did, their thighs touching.

"Wow," she said aloud, admiring both of their naked bodies, but focusing on Tyler. Though different from Ryan's nearly-perfect, flawless physique, he was incredibly sexy in his own right. He didn't have abs like Ryan, but he was slim and toned. His arms and chest were well-toned, and though he sported some body hair, she found it to be a turn-on. His thighs were small but solid, and most importantly, he had a huge dick. "You have a permit for that fucking cannon?" she joked, running a hand up each of their thighs.

"You're gonna take every inch of him," Ryan ordered. "And you're gonna take it like a good girl."

"Can I suck it for a little bit first, baby? It's so gorgeous, just begging to be sucked."

"If you want, but don't get him off. I need to watch you fuck him."

"Fuck, Rook. Who even *are* you?" Tyler asked, as Amara positioned herself in front of him, reached up, and wrapped a hand around the base of his cock. He grabbed the sides of her head and stared her down as she took as much of his eight inches into her mouth as she could and jerked the rest. "That feels fuckin' amazing, babe."

"She sucks a good cock, huh?" Ryan asked. She looked over to see if he was watching her, but his eyes were dead focused on his teammate's face as she pleasured him.

"Too good," he moaned, closing his eyes, throwing his head back, and pulling her hair. "Mar, you gotta stop or...I'm gonna go."

"Stop," Ryan ordered, then turned to Tyler. "Lay on the bed so she can get on top of you." He motioned with one finger for Amara to get up, so she obeyed and stood in front of him. He grabbed her ass with both hands and pulled her towards him. "I want you to make him cum hard. Harder than he's ever fucking cum before."

"That's not gonna be a fuckin' problem," Tyler said, as Amara crawled up his body and straddled his waist. "God, I've fuckin' wanted this forever." She positioned herself and slid down slowly onto him, both of them moaning loudly at the feeling they'd waited two months for. "Can you take it all?" he asked, gripping her hips. "Most girls can't."

"I'm not most girls," she said, sliding the rest of the way, taking all of him completely inside of her and beginning to grind her hips slowly back and forth. "Fuck, Ty. Your huge cock, omigod. I could...cum like this. You're gonna make me cum."

"Better than him?" he moaned, pushing and pulling her

hips as she rode him slowly but steadily. "Do I fuck better than he does, babe?" He looked over at Ryan, who stood at the end of the bed jerking off slowly as he watched his girlfriend grind herself all over Tyler.

"No, he's pretty good. But I'm gonna...holy shit, I'm fucking...gonna cum, Ty!"

She let out a series of loud half-moans, half-whimpers as she came with his cock stuffed completely inside her.

"Well, that was quick," Ryan observed, speeding up his pace as he watched his girlfriend get off all over his teammate's cock.

"Get on top and fucking rail the shit outta her. She likes that after she cums."

"I bet she does." He flipped her over, removing himself from her temporarily as she spread her legs and he positioned himself on top of her. He leaned down to her ear. "Is it OK that we're not using anything?" he asked quietly.

"I don't care. Just fuck me," she panted, turning her head to the side of the bed where Ryan was standing. She reached over, taking his cock from his hand and guiding it into her mouth right as Tyler pushed himself inside her. She moaned loudly as he grabbed her tits with both hands and fucked her steady, hard, and fast while she sucked Ryan off in tandem with Tyler's rhythm.

"You look pretty with his cock in your mouth," he told her, his eyes fixated on Ryan, who grabbed the back of her head aggressively as he fucked her face.

Ryan was fixated on Tyler as well, and it wasn't long before the sight of his teammate fucking his girlfriend had him on the verge of exploding. "Tell me where to cum," he told him.

"Down her fuckin' throat."

He groaned, pushed himself in as far as he could, and held her head in place as he came, staring directly at Tyler through his entire orgasm.

Ryan pulled out and Tyler continued to fuck her. "You

liked watching me swallow his load, didn't you?" she asked.

"A lot more than I thought I would. I'm gettin' so close, babe. Where do you want me to go?" he asked, nearly out of breath. Ryan had since sat down on the opposite side of the bed, no longer interested in what they were doing.

She reached up, grabbed his hair, and yanked his head down to hers. "Cum inside me, Ty. I wanna feel you."

"You sure?"

"Yes. Go ahead, baby. You feel so fucking good!" She whimpered, as she felt him release his load deep inside of her. He was so big and hard that she could feel every powerful spurt. She shoved her hips upward into his and lifted her lips to kiss him, forcing him to taste Ryan on her as he emptied himself inside her while moaning into her mouth.

He lay there motionless on top of her for a few moments before he started laughing.

"What's funny?" she asked, as he ran his fingers through her hair and kissed her forehead.

"That's such a load off my shoulders, babe."

"No pun intended."

"You have no clue how fuckin' much I wanted that to happen."

"I think I might have an idea," she said, running her fingertips up and down his back. He stayed for a few seconds before getting up and pulling out of her.

"Uh, let me go get a towel," he said, noticing the mess between her legs.

He got off the bed, grabbed his boxers, and pulled them on as he went to the bathroom. She sat up, and a box of tissues came flying at her and whacked her in the arm.

"What the..." She turned to look at Ryan, who was still sitting on the opposite end of the bed. "Thanks?"

"Did you just let him nut inside you?"

"Yeah, it just..."

"That's really fucking irresponsible. Clean yourself up, slut."

"Whoa, what?" He grabbed a pair of shorts, threw them on over his boxers, and pulled on a tank top. He slipped on his dress shoes and headed to the door, looking like a complete hobo.

"Where are you going?"

"For a walk."

"No, you need to talk to me."

"Nothing to talk about."

"This was your idea!"

"Amara, I'm just going for a walk."

"Ryan, don't do this to me."

"Every-fucking-thing's not about you!" he yelled, as he stormed out of the hotel room.

Tyler came out of the bathroom and shook his head, handing her the towel. "Can't say I didn't see this coming. Where are your pajamas?" he asked, rooting through the contents of her suitcase until he found her a T-shirt and a pair of shorts.

As he tossed them to her and she put them on, he noticed the tears welling up in her eyes. "Goddamn it. No. Don't you dare waste any more tears on him. All you fuckin' do is cry over him. Aren't you tired of feeling like this yet?"

"Apparently not," she said, wiping her face. "He's such an enigma."

"Yeah, that's one word to describe him. I have a few other choice words." He pulled back the covers and patted the bed. "Well, Osi hasn't texted me back yet, so come on." He held up the covers for her, and she crawled under them, feeling him slide behind and wrap an arm around her. "He wants to act like a piece of shit? Then fall asleep with me. We'll use the shit outta this bed. Fuck him."

She grabbed onto his hand, squeezed it, and closed her eyes, hoping that maybe she'd wake up and this would all just be some sort of fucked-up dream. "Do you feel any different?" she asked him quietly after a few minutes had passed.

"Huh? What?" He'd started to drift off to sleep, and her

voice startled him.

"Do you feel any different? Now that we finally did it."

"I mean, my balls are about 10 pounds lighter. You're gonna have my DNA drippin' outta you for a month."

"That's...not what I meant, Ty. About me. Do you feel any different about me? Like, we did this and now you're gonna start ignoring my texts and avoiding me."

"Totally. In fact, who are you again?" He kissed the back of her head. "Don't be a fuckin' idiot, Mar. Nothing's changed. You ain't gonna get rid of me that easily, woman."

"I don't want to. You're...kinda my best friend, Ty."

"I know. And honestly, you're probably mine, too." He brushed her hair back from her face. "But can I say that I don't wanna do it again? Nope."

"Neither can I."

SOME CLARITY (22)

"Rough night?"

Ryan nodded, having a seat at the half-full hotel bar, as people were starting to filter out. He looked about as disheveled as humanly possible, with post-sex hair, a white tank top, neon green basketball shorts that literally came to his knees, and black dress shoes with no socks.

"What are you drinkin'?" the bartender asked him.

He patted his shorts and sighed. "Water, I guess. Left my wallet in the room."

"I got you," the bartender told him. "Whatever you want. You look like you need it."

"Uh, thanks. Whiskey on the rocks, please."

"Wow, OK. Wouldn't have pegged Ryan Baylor for a straight whiskey guy." Ryan shot him a puzzled look. "Yeah, I know who you are. Grew up a huge Isles fan. My wife and I take our kids to Bridgeport games all the time. Much cheaper. I'm

Chris."

Ryan shook his hand and examined him. He was probably about Amara's age, a decent-looking guy with a few stray grays peppering his dark black hair. He poured himself a shot, handed Ryan the whiskey, and lifted for a toast. "To an NHL call-up sooner than later."

Ryan clinked his glass. "I'll drink to that!" He sipped, realizing he probably should have been drinking water, but deciding at this point, it didn't really matter.

"Wanna talk about it?"

"Talk about what?"

"You look like hell, kid. What happened?"

He took another sip. "You good at keeping secrets?"

"It's literally the most important part of a bartender's job. Hang on." He went to grab a drink order from another customer, as Ryan debated just how much he was willing to divulge. Chris returned. "So, what's going on?"

"You know what? Fuck it. All my personal business is apparently all over the internet already anyway. So here goes: I'm in an open relationship with my much older roommate and we just banged out a threesome with another guy, which I knew I couldn't handle, but agreed to anyway because I wanna make her happy. But the thing is: there's no making this woman happy. Everything I do seems to piss her off or upset her."

Chris stood there for a moment, wide-eyed, before shaking his head. "Yeah, that's some pile of shit, bud. How much older we talking?"

"She's 18 years older than me."

"Wow. That's a hell of a gap. So, she's about my age then. I'm 43."

"She's 41. I'm...hopelessly fucking in love with her, but I can't seem to do anything right."

"Welcome to women. Especially at this age? She's finding herself, bud. The whole 'midlife crisis' thing that guys go through? Women hit it about this age, start questioning all their life decisions, trying to rediscover themselves, figure out who they are. My wife's going through the same. I mean, we're not in an open relationship though. That just seems like an unnecessary added layer to this shit cake."

"It's…a long story. But she recently got out of a divorce, coupled with the fact that I'm kind of a sex addict, so when she pitched it to me, I figured, 'Fuck it, why not?' And it's turning out to be an absolute nightmare. Oh, and the guy we just hooked up with? It's her best friend, who also happens to be one of my teammates."

"Ryan Baylor, Ryan Baylor," he said, pouring himself another shot and topping Ryan off. "I hear a lot of things as a bartender. But that? Wow." He threw back the shot as Ryan took another sip. "I don't think I've ever heard anything quite like that."

"Yeah. In about a month of dating, we've somehow managed to completely fuck things up with each other. We were friends. Almost wish we'd just kept it at that."

"It sounds to me like you're trying to make something work that isn't gonna. That gap, man. You guys essentially speak two different languages. There's an entire generation between you. Anyway, you're young, hot, soon to be loaded. Why aren't you just out there having a good time?"

"Because," he said sadly. "I can't even picture my life without her anymore. She's…an amazing woman. She's so patient with me. Yes, I piss her off, but she's so supportive."

"My hot take, for what it's worth? She's too old for you, Ryan. Especially coming off a divorce like that. She doesn't know who she is or what she wants. And when she finally figures it out, it's gonna be different from what you want. You guys might play well together, but where's it gonna go long term?"

Ryan sighed. "I don't know. I just know I love her. So much."

"I understand that. But sometimes that just isn't enough." He grabbed a rag and wiped down the bar. "I don't suppose you'd tell me which teammate it is?"

Ryan shook his head. "I gotta keep *some* secrets."

"Fair enough. It, uh, wouldn't happen to be Tyler Hayes, would it?"

Ryan was dumbfounded. "How the…?"

Chris pointed over to the entrance of the bar, where Hayes stood, head on a swivel.

"Shit," Ryan dropped his head into his hand before looking back at Chris. "Hey: secrets," he reminded him, polishing off the rest of his drink and putting his fist out.

Chris bumped it with his. "No clue what you're talking about. Ryan, good luck with…everything."

"Thanks, man."

He walked up to Hayes. "Hey."

"Oh my God. The fuck you doin' out in public right now lookin' like someone trash-picked you?" Hayes pointed to his outfit. "Are you kidding me with this shit, Rook? Have people been throwin' spare change at you?"

Ryan shrugged. "I needed to get away for a minute."

"Well, it's been more than a minute. She was worried, asked me to come look for you."

"And you always do whatever she wants you to, don't you? Like a good little lap dog."

Hayes threw his hands up. "The fuck you want from me, Rook? Huh?"

"Can we talk?" Ryan asked seriously. "I think…I think we should talk."

"Fine," he muttered, turning and heading back inside. The lobby was practically empty, so he motioned to a couple of somewhat secluded couches, where they each took a seat on a separate one. Hayes crossed his arms. "So? Talk."

"I feel like there's a lot we need to say to each other."

"Like?"

"OK, well first, you should've used protection with her, or at the very least, pulled out. That's just stupid, Hayes. I've been responsible for…" he paused, looked around, and lowered his voice. "For an abortion, and I wouldn't wish it on my worst enemy."

"Don't worry, we already talked. Hittin' up a CVS on the ride home. Last thing the world needs right now is a little mini-Hayes runnin' fuckin' amuck, eh?" His attempt to make Ryan smile flopped, so he continued. "For what it's worth, she asked me to do it."

"I don't care. You know better."

"You're right."

"And just for the record, I...wait. Did you just say I'm right?"

"Yeah. See, you got this whole fuckin' speech prepared, but you don't even listen. It was dumb. I got caught up in the moment, and it won't happen again."

"Uh, *this* won't happen again, Hayes. I never wanted this to happen in the first place, OK?"

"So why did it then?"

"Alcohol and testosterone."

"You think either of those things are goin' away anytime soon?"

"I knew how bad she wanted it, and I just wanted to make her happy, but...she's never happy."

"Rook, do you even know your own girlfriend, man? She's a lot of great and wonderful things, but happy?" He laughed. "Happy isn't one of them."

Ryan rubbed his forehead. "Why do I feel like you know her so much better than I do?"

"Because I do. We *talk*, Rook. We open up to each other about shit. She's pretty much my fuckin' therapist. Do you guys talk about stuff, the hard stuff? The painful stuff?"

"Not really. Well, like, sometimes."

"Rook, can I say something?"

"You're gonna say it anyway, so go ahead."

"I don't know what you're doin' with her. Like, what's the goal? You forced her into a relationship when neither of you was ready. Now, a month into it, you're having fuckin'

161

threesomes because she's scared to death you'll cheat if she doesn't do it with you. Do you know I held her today as she bawled? Bawled, man. Broke down in my fuckin' arms because of what happened the other night with that girl. She might've cum, but she was *not* OK with it." He looked at Ryan, who had tears streaming down his face. "And now look at *you*. What the actual fuck are you guys doing to each other?"

Ryan wiped his eyes. "I don't know. I just can't lose her. I can't."

"You're not gonna lose her. That woman would walk across fire to the ends of the goddamn Earth for your pathetic ass. But she isn't ready to be your girlfriend. And frankly? You're not ready to be her boyfriend. She deserves a little better than you. Sorry."

"And you saying all this has nothing to do with what just happened?"

"Fuck no. You think I wanna date her? You out of your mind? Amara and I would kill each other. We're friends, I guess now with benefits. But that's it. I could fuck her a million times and it wouldn't change a damn thing because Amara and I understand each other. I don't feel like you guys understand each other at all, and honestly, I don't know if it's your fault or hers."

"So fine, let's say we stay friends. What happens when she finds someone else? How do I deal with that?"

"What happens when *you* find someone else, Rook? You think you guys are gonna last? She's almost your fuckin' mom's age, bro."

"I love her," he said softly. "She's the first and only woman I ever felt this way about."

"You probably always will. And that's fine. But she'll always be the one that got away because it's just not gonna last. You have to know that. And it's no one's fault. Just shitty timing is all. You guys can be friends, but you gotta form an actual friendship with her first. You guys jumped into this shit way too fuckin' fast. You fucked her one time and, boom! You were dating. You know I'm gonna tell you like it is. This is how it is."

"God, Hayes," Ryan said. "I wanna hate you so bad, but I don't. Not even close."

A few moments of silence passed. "So, what else did we need to talk about? You said we had a bunch of shit to say to each other."

"Well," Ryan sighed. "I can't believe I'm saying this out loud, but...I *really* liked kissing you, and I have no fucking idea what to do about it. So, there's that."

"Yeah, well. Guess what? I *really* liked kissin' you, too. But why does somethin' have to be done about it? You're always trying to put everything neatly into a fuckin' box. Why is that?"

"My anxiety. It doesn't really like when things are messy."

"Life is messy, Rook. You can't plan everything out. You'll drive yourself crazy. Learn to just let things be what they are, man."

"So, like, back to us. How do I just let that be?"

"Again: just let things be what they are. There is no 'us.' We had a threesome, we were drunk and horny as fuck, and we made out a little. You're not gonna sit there and try to tell me you've never hooked up with other guys before, are you?"

"No, I have."

"And did you fall deeply in love with any of them?"

"No."

"There you go. We kissed, and it felt good. I'm not tryin' to date you. We end up drunk and horny in a hotel room on the road? I don't know, maybe I'll suck your dick. Rook, your problem is you overthink shit to the point of exhaustion. You stress yourself out. You gotta stop that shit."

Ryan looked at Hayes and was in absolute awe of him. "You're probably one of the smartest fucking people I've ever met, you know that?"

"Fuckin' right I am."

"Where'd all this infinite wisdom come from at 20 years old?"

He shrugged and ran a hand through his hair. "Been through my fair share of shit, Rook. I just see things clearly for what they are."

"It's a gift."

"I guess. Listen, we can't sit here all night. It's already after one, and we gotta leave early so we get back for practice tomorrow. You need to go upstairs and get some sleep, but first, you better apologize to her for callin' her a slut. That wasn't cool and you're lucky I don't knock your fuckin' ass out. She's not a slut, not even close."

"I know. And I will. Speaking of sluts, is Osi done?"

"At this point, I don't give a fuck. I'm goin' in. Maybe I'll hit up a second threesome, eh?" He nudged Ryan as they got up to walk to the elevator.

"Hayes?"

"Yeah, Rook?"

"Would you really suck my dick?" Ryan smiled and winked at him.

"Not if you keep your shit up, I won't."

"Hey, seriously. Thanks for talkin' to me, man. I feel better."

"I got you."

* * *

He'd planned to open the door as quietly as possible but was forced to knock at the realization that he'd forgotten his key card.

On the third knock, she opened the door only a crack, having latched the slide lock. "Password?"

"I'm the biggest fucking dick that ever lived and I don't deserve you."

She shut the door, removed the lock, and opened it all

the way. "I'll accept that."

"Hey, sit down with me?" he asked, reaching for her hand. "I just have a few things I need to say."

"Yeah, I have a few things to say too, and I'll start with this: why do you even own those shorts? You're way too sexy to own those shorts, Ry."

He laughed, as they sat down on the edge of the bed together. "They were literally the only bum shorts I had clean, and I had to pack in a hurry to get here on time." He looked away from her and clasped his hands in his lap. "First, I'm sorry I called you a slut. You're not."

"Thank you. That really hurt."

"I know. And I'm sorry, Amara. So, I had a chat with Hayes, and...I think I may have pressured you into being my girlfriend. I'm not sure we really know each other like we think we do. He knows you so much better than I do, and I feel like maybe we need to make more of an effort to build a friendship."

"So, what are you saying?"

"Amara, you know how I feel about you. And I'd love it if we stayed together and tried to build that friendship at the same time. But if you want your space, your freedom, then you should have it. You deserve that after what you've been through."

"Again: what are you saying?"

"I'm leaving it up to you..."

"No, Ryan! You don't get to do that. If you wanna break up, then nut up and say it."

"Amara, I don't wanna break up with you. But I have a question for you. Do *you* wanna break up with *me*?"

She didn't answer.

"Amara, do you wanna break up with me?"

"Yes."

He nodded. "OK."

"I'm sorry. I can't do the open relationship thing with you. I thought I could, but I can't. It's not working. I care about you too much."

"Interesting timing," Ryan mumbled.

"Excuse me?"

"Well, it's just funny you say that right after fucking Hayes. That's all."

"And you fucked your little fake blonde Barbie doll, so what the hell do you care?"

"Stop!" He waved his hands in front of him. "This is... we're going backward. Alright, so we're breaking up. What's that mean?"

"It means you're not my boyfriend anymore, Ryan. You're free to date and fuck whoever you want. But it also means that I am, too."

"Are we gonna try to build up our friendship, or do you wanna just end it all and be done with me?"

"Ryan, I'm never gonna be *done* with you. It'll just be like it was before we started dating. We hang out, we talk, we continue to get to know each other."

"The problem is that the whole time we were doing that, I was falling in love with you."

"We'll figure it out. We're gonna be living together. It's not like we can avoid each other. I wouldn't want to anyway. I like you, Ryan. I really do. But this, like I said from the start, was over before it even began. We will never work."

"What about hooking up?"

She sighed. "We shouldn't. But I think we both know we will. You're the best I've ever had, Ryan. And yes, you're better than Hayes."

"Seriously? Because you came after being on his dick for like, 10 seconds."

"Just because of his size. Had nothing to do with his skill. I mean, I did all the work myself. Your skill level is unmatched."

"I mean, is it OK if we still hook up?"

"Probably not. But this is our game. We get to make the rules. And if one of us starts seeing someone else seriously, then it has to end."

"I really don't wanna lose you."

"And I understand that. But you can't waste your time with me, because your life? It's out there waiting for you somewhere. Ryan, you're so young and you've got so many good things coming your way. Your career is just taking off. You're gonna be an amazing hockey player, score all...the... fuckin' goals or whatever it is you hockey boys do. You're gonna be even more famous than you are right now, and you're gonna be rich. Like, private jet lifestyle rich. You're not even gonna remember the early days when you had to split an apartment with some old, grumpy divorced bitch."

"That old, grumpy divorced bitch is one of the best things that ever happened to me."

Noticing he was crying, she grabbed his hand. "Maybe that's true up to this point in your life, but someday I'll just be a memory."

"Never."

"Yes. I will. I'm learning more and more that people come into your life for a variety of reasons and they don't all stay. Believe me, someday, when you least expect it, you're gonna meet the absolute person of your dreams. You're gonna propose with probably the biggest rock ever and get married. You're gonna stay faithful because you're gonna go to therapy for your sex addiction, and you're going to be the most amazing husband and father, Ryan. You really are. Your life is out there. It's not here. As much as I hate that it's not, it's not. We're just two people whose paths happened to cross at this particular moment in time for whatever reason. And honestly? I'm glad they did."

"And you?" he asked sadly. "Where do you end up?"

She shrugged. "Wherever I'm supposed to. You know, I think a lot about what Rizz said the first night we met, how you and I probably had some connection in a past life. I'd like to think that those two foregone versions of us? Maybe they...I'd like to think maybe they made it."

"Yeah well, I'd like to think that, too, but based upon this shit show, they probably went down together on the fucking

Titanic."

"Yup," she laughed, wiping her eyes. "I probably pushed your big ass right off that door, too, and watched you sink to the bottom of the ocean."

"Yeah, and then fucked Hayes on top of it afterward."

"You are such a dick." She smacked his arm.

"I know," he said. "Guess I should get some sleep. Hey, I can feel my anxiety creeping up, and it's *bad*. Can you lay with me, at least until I fall asleep? Please?"

She couldn't have said no to him even if she'd wanted to. Which she didn't.

THE TRANSITION (23)

"So? How's it going?" Dani asked as she cut fruit for the upcoming night shift. "I haven't seen you since everything went down. You holdin' up OK?"

"Yeah, I mean, it's totally fine. It really was for the best."

"And what the fuck is that Miss America answer? This ain't a beauty pageant, bitch. It's me. And I can smell a lie like a fart in an elevator, so you better fess up!"

Amara finished pouring a beer and set it down at the server pick-up before standing next to Dani. "Fine. It sucks. Is that what you wanna hear? It fucking sucks, Dan. We went from friends to lovers to almost complete strangers. Aside from having sex once, we've barely spoken a word to each other. He's in his room most of the time, and I'm in mine. It fucking sucks."

It'd been two weeks since the breakup, and things hadn't been going as Amara had hoped. The ride home from the wedding in Tyler's truck was awkward and mostly silent, aside from getting some of the dirty details of Osi's Tinder sex marathon.

"I am sorry for you to hear this, Amara. Forgive me."

"I'm sure she's got some stories of her own. Care to share any, babe? Got anything that could rival that?"

"Shut it, Tyler."

"Seriously, I should not talk this way in front of your girlfriend. I am sorry."

"Go for it. She's not my girlfriend anymore."

"Wait, what?" Hayes had asked, shocked.

"You heard me. We broke up last night. It's over."

Ryan had practically gone into hiding around the apartment. He'd leave his room to grab food, to use the bathroom, or go to practice or his games. Amara had knocked on his door one night in an attempt to open a dialogue with him. When he answered, he was shirtless, and instead of making words, she reached out and ran her hand up his abs, resulting in them clawing at each other furiously, and ultimately with Ryan fucking her raw against the inside of the door frame.

When it was over, Amara had tried to talk to him.

"I'm worried about you."

"Don't be."

"You can't stay holed up in your room like this."

"Watch me."

"Are we just not gonna talk ever again?"

He'd shrugged.

"So, about what just happened..."

"Don't read too much into it. I can have sex with someone and feel nothing. Remember?" He kicked her clothes into the hallway and slammed his bedroom door in her face.

"And it's not that I don't want to talk to him, Dan. I just

don't know what to say."

"Nothin' you can say, baby. You broke his heart. You know better than anyone that takes time." She finished stocking glasses in the freezer. "So, uh, what's baby face got to say about all this?"

"Said Ry's really struggling. On-ice performance is suffering big time, and he's worried they might send him down to the Railers."

"The *who*?"

"It's the Islanders' other minor league team, one step below Bridgeport."

"What a fuckin' team name! Kinda suits him well, no?"

Amara half-smiled. "I know Ry, and that would destroy him."

"You and baby face hooked up again since the wedding?" Dani shook her head, shuddering. "I still hate you, by the way. I can't believe you had them both at the same time and lived to tell about it. My heart would've given out. I'd have legit fucking died."

"It was, uh…it was somethin' alright. But no. We agreed that now isn't really the best timing."

"But you're gonna again, right?"

"Uh, yeah," Amara said quickly. "Honestly, I can't stop thinking about it. About him. I thought I'd get him out of my system and we could move on. Instead, he's like a fucking drug, and I'm itchin' for my next hit."

"Big cock?"

Amara gasped. "Dani!" She gestured to a couple of men sitting at the end of the bar.

"Please, baby. Everyone here knows I'm straight trash. So, is it?"

"Huge," Amara said, smirking. "And his lips, his tongue…ugh. He's *such* a good kisser. It still blows my mind that he's so young."

"And did he use that tongue anywhere else?"

"OK, no more!" She whipped her lightly with the rag

she'd been using to wipe down the bottles. "We're gonna lose business if you scare all the customers away."

"Baby girl, we're not scaring anyone away. Especially not that one," she said, pointing to one of the men wearing a backward New York Giants hat. "He's been staring into your soul for the last half-hour. Hey!" she yelled to him. "What's your name, baby?"

He pointed to himself, and she confirmed. "Jake!" he yelled back.

Dani grabbed Amara from behind by her shoulders and pushed her down to the end of the bar where he was seated. "Jake, this is Amara. She's very single. Stop staring at her and talk to her."

"I, uh, I wasn't..."

"Bullshit."

He smiled. "OK, you caught me. Amara, that's a beautiful name. I'm..."

"Jake," she finished for him, shaking his hand. She sized him up: probably late thirties or early forties, with sharp features, a full beard and mustache, piercing blue eyes, and jacked arms that looked like they were about to bust through his T-shirt sleeves. "It's nice to meet you...Jake."

"You too...Amara."

❋ ❋ ❋

"You wanna run some over-speed drills with me?" Hayes grabbed a towel and wiped himself off. They'd just finished their conditioning workout at the arena gym and had a few hours to spare before tonight's game. Hayes knew Ryan didn't want to go home.

"Yeah, I guess." Hayes offered his hand and pulled Ryan up off the floor as they headed to the locker room to suit up.

"We gotta work on your speed, man. That's one of the things they're most concerned about with you. You're like a drugged-up turtle out there, man."

"I know. Been hearing it my whole life. I'm not a fast skater. And it doesn't help that I don't have a whole lot in the tank right now."

"Then you gotta fuckin' fill that shit back up, Rook. They're...they're talkin' about the Railers, man. Overheard the coaches sayin' they're gonna be making some moves this week. You do not want that."

"Maybe I should just go. I fucking suck here. It's not like I'm moving up anytime soon. It might be nice to be two hours away from her, anyway." He finished lacing up his second skate and stood up.

"Don't say that. It's gonna get better, man. It's a fresh wound right now. You just gotta lick it and move on."

"I fucked her two nights ago."

"That's...not what I meant by lick it, Rook." Hayes finished lacing up his skates, then they grabbed a couple of sticks and headed down the tunnel. "She initiate it?"

"It just happened. She knocked on my door, and I answered shirtless. The rest is history."

"Well, that explains it. I'm about 90 percent sure that woman probably flicks her shit thinkin' about your abs. You knew what you were doing."

"Maybe a little." He skated over to the bench and dumped a bucket of pucks onto the ice.

"You guys still not talking?"

He snatched a puck and dragged it back and forth on the ice in front of him. "We haven't really, just small talk. But I avoid that too, if I can. I've been...I've been doing some writing, actually."

"Yeah?" Hayes stole the puck from Ryan and took off with it, running the first drill. He waited for Ryan to skate in a circle, then moved the puck out to the face-off dot, and transitioned backward while maintaining control. He passed it to Ryan, who took crossovers to the blue line, inside to outside, working his lateral movement, and then cranked it at the net.

"Not bad, but try to keep your feet movin'. You hesitated. You gotta speed up, fast as you can. Push past your comfort zone. Let's go again."

They ran it two more times and skated over to the bench for some water. "So, what've you been writing about? I didn't even know you *could* write."

Ryan squirted him in the face with his bottle. "Dick."

"You've been writing about *dick*? Is it one of those smutty hockey romances? Some of that shit's actually pretty good."

"I don't even wanna know *why* you know that. Nah. Just...my thoughts, getting everything down that I'm thinking. How I'm feeling, what's been triggering my panic attacks. It's...my therapist recommended it, and it's kinda, what's the word? Cathesis? Carthetic?"

Hayes stared at him blankly. "I look like a fuckin' dictionary to you? So, a therapist, huh?"

"Yeah, she's...I meet with her twice a week, all online. I'm learning a lot about myself. I'm mostly doing it for my anxiety, but we talk a lot about the sex stuff, too."

"Oh, you mean how you'll fuck literally anything that isn't nailed to the floor?"

"And some things that are, if the mood strikes just right."

"There's my Rook!" Hayes hugged him. "I like hearin' you joke around again, man. So, what's she have to say about it?"

"It's a direct result of my anxiety. I can't control that, I couldn't control my dad's death, but sex and how I react to it is something I can control. The fact that I write girls off after I fuck 'em is me trying to get control of something because I feel like I don't have control over anything else in my life."

"Well, that's fuckin' depressing, eh? Hey, at least it's not just because you're a filthy piece of street trash."

"Yeah, at least. She also suggested I apologize to as many of them as I can. Not sure where I'd even start. I mean, we're talking hundreds, and way too many that I don't even

174

remember."

"Hundreds? I'm sorry, did you say hundreds?"

"Hookups included? I'm in the fives, no doubt."

"Oh, Rook. You really are a disgusting whore."

"I know. It's not something I'm proud of. I'm working on it."

"Rook. *Hundreds*?"

"Why? Is it that bad? What's your body count?"

"Let me think." Hayes paused for a minute. "I think I'm at 43."

"Get the fuck outta here!"

"Or it's...44, now."

"Yeah. Let's not talk about that one," Ryan skated away, and Hayes followed him. Ryan flipped around backward with the puck as Hayes tried to steal it.

"I think you should talk to her, Rook."

"Why? There's nothing to say."

"Because you're supposed to be workin' on your friendship. Wasn't that the agreement?"

"I don't think I can do it. I'm not strong enough."

Ryan stopped skating near the net, and Hayes snowed him. "You don't think you can do what?"

"Be friends with her. I'm thinking...I might need to find a new place to live."

"Jesus. You're gonna break her fuckin' heart, Rook. She's already a mess."

"That makes two of us."

"If you guys would just talk to each other. You can't just cut her off completely. You have to try."

"I can't, man."

"Why not?"

"Because I can't."

"Why the fuck not?"

"Because it fucking hurts!" Ryan yelled, gutturally, his voice echoing throughout the empty arena. "It fucking...hurts. What, so I'm gonna sit around and watch her date other guys, bring them home and listen to her fuck them? And don't even get me started on you and her."

"Here we fuckin' go with this shit again! We haven't done shit since that night, man. Not even a hug."

"Give it time. I heard the way she moaned for you. I watched the way you guys kissed. I'm not a fucking idiot, Hayes."

"It's just sex, Rook. That's all. I fuckin' promise."

"It's never 'just sex', Hayes. Not with her." He played with a puck as he talked, passing it from the front of his stick to the back, before winding up and cranking it into the boards.

"I'm heading back in. Don't tell her about our conversation today. I don't want her to know about the therapy, or…anything else. Understood?"

"I can't do that, Rook. I can't keep shit like that from her. Make you a deal though. I'll keep quiet if you have this same conversation with her. She's working tonight and we've got games today and tomorrow. So, I'll give you until Sunday, or I'm singin'. Deal?"

Ryan rolled his eyes. "Fine. Deal."

ROOKIE LAP (24)

"So."

"So."

Amara and Ryan sat across from each other in a booth at Rocco's, their favorite pizza place, which was about a 10-minute walk from their apartment. It was Sunday, the deadline Hayes had given Ryan before he would spill the beans to Amara. He'd approached her and asked if they could talk, which caught her off-guard, seeing as he'd been all but missing for the past few days.

She agreed but suggested that it be in public so that A, the conversation didn't get too heated, and B, they didn't end up horizontal.

"What'd you wanna talk about?" she asked quietly, playing with the straw in her Diet Coke.

"A few things. This first one, I really don't wanna tell you. Honestly, I don't really wanna tell you either, but Hayes threatened that if I don't tell you, he will."

"Ry? You're freaking me out right now. Can you just get on with it?"

"Fine. So, I know I've been holed up in my room, as you called it. But there's a reason. I'm…I started seeing a therapist, online, twice a week."

"Ryan, that's amazing!" she exclaimed, genuinely excited for him.

"Yeah. We're weeding through a lot of my issues, like the anxiety and my panic attacks. But she's working with me on my sex addiction as well, helping me get to the root causes and whatnot. I'm…kinda meeting myself for the first time ever. It's weird, but it turns out, I don't really know me."

"You have no idea how proud of you I am for confronting this. Honestly. I don't have words. You've grown a lot in the few months I've known you."

"Thank you." He picked up his straw paper and twisted it into a ball. "So, one of the things she has me doing is writing. I've been writing a lot, about my feelings, my thoughts, anxiety triggers, etcetera. Just so you know, I'm not sitting in my room crying over you the entire time. I just needed you to know that."

"Well, I'm glad to hear that. Writing can be so cathartic."

"Cathartic! That's the word!" he yelled, startling her, then lowered his voice. "I was trying to remember it the other day." The waitress brought over the two slices they ordered and set them down. "Thank you, sweetie," Ryan said.

"Of course," she replied with a wink.

"So that's one thing. The other thing," he said, picking at some cheese that had slid off his slice, "is that I'm in a pretty good amount of pain, Amara. I have this giant pit in my stomach and no matter what I do, how much I try to ignore it, it won't go away. The only thing that gives me any relief at all is seeing you, but even that's temporary because as quickly as I feel better, I instantly remember that it's over and it starts to hurt all over again."

She picked at the crust on her slice; neither of them had eaten a thing. "I understand that. I've wanted to talk to you, Ry, but I don't exactly know what to say."

"Let's start with this. Do you miss me?" he asked, staring down at his plate.

"I do."

"I miss you, too. So much. But Mar, being around you is breaking me down. I'm total shit on the ice, I'm shit off the ice, and I don't know how to fix it. The only thing I can think of is that maybe…I might need to find somewhere else to live."

She snickered, pushing her plate away from her. "So much for being friends and getting to know each other better, huh?"

He reached across the table and grabbed her hand. "Then please, tell me what to do, Amara," he begged in a low voice. "Tell me how I'm supposed to get up, see you every day, knowing that we can never be more than friends, knowing that'll never be enough for me, and keep my shit together. I'm all ears."

She stared at her hand in his. "I don't know, Ryan."

His eyes filled with tears, and he let go of her hand. "God, why can't this just fucking *work*?"

"I don't want you to leave, Ryan. I want you to stay."

"Amara, I don't want to leave either. I just don't know if I'm strong enough to stay."

"Remember that game we used to play, where we'd tell each other random, embarrassing shit about ourselves?"

"Yeah?"

"I miss that. It's stuff like that, Ryan. Before our feelings got in the way, we really did have a connection. And I wish…I wish we could have that again."

"I do, too."

"Then stay. Please? I don't want you to leave. Let's hang out tonight, do something fun. As friends."

"What'd you have in mind?"

At that moment, they both got notifications on their

phones at the same time. She reached for hers first. "Oh my God!" she gasped, as Ryan checked his phone and read the same message:

T: Just got the call. I'm going to the fucking Isles, baby!!! Come to the game tonight. 6:05 start.

"Oh my God. He's going. Holy shit. Well, guess I know what we're doing tonight."

"This is amazing," she said, looking at Ryan. She knew he was happy for Tyler in his heart, but the look on his face told a different story. She reached over and touched his hand. "Hey? Your time is coming."

"Yeah," he said blankly. "Guess we should go get ready if we're gonna get to the game on time."

❊ ❊ ❊

"So how's it work?" Amara asked Ryan, as the two headed into UBS Arena after taking the Bridgeport Ferry to the LIRR, which let them right off at the venue.

"There's a whole section they designate for players' families and friends. Each player on the roster gets two tickets per game to give to family or whoever. Ty wanted us to have his."

"Aww. So do we have to pick them up at will call?"

He just looked at her. "No, Grandma. They're on my phone."

"Shut it. So, is Osi coming? I would've thought for sure he'd be here."

"Nah. Apparently, he's been barfing with a fever for two days. Couple of the other guys were sick last week, too. Hope it's not gonna run through the locker room. He said to text him

180

updates."

They went through security, scanned the tickets, and entered the arena just in time for the warm-up.

"Come on." He grabbed her hand and hurried her to the stairs that led down to the glass. "Our seats are second level, but I wanna get down to watch the warm-up. He's gonna take his rookie lap."

"What's that?"

"When a player makes his NHL debut, he skates a lap or two by himself during the warm-up, before all the other players join him. It's tradition. I don't wanna miss it."

"Aww," she put her hand on his shoulder. "That's literally the cutest thing I've ever heard."

"I'm just really proud of him, you know? Kid works his ass off. No one...no one deserves this more than Hayes."

She didn't tell him, but she could see that the therapy was working already. The Ryan Baylor of a month ago wouldn't even be here, and now here he was, rushing to the glass, excited to support his friend.

They made their way down to the boards, which were packed, but they managed to squeeze into a primo spot when some fans recognized Ryan, he signed some autographs, and Amara took some pics of him with them.

The pucks dumped out onto the ice, a cleaned-up version of "Stay Fly" by Three 6 Marfia began blaring through the sound system, and then Hayes took to the ice alone. The crowd went absolutely crazy for him, amid the sounds of the other players banging their sticks against the bench and in the tunnel.

He'd never looked more alive, more at home, than he did at that very moment. It was quick, as the other guys joined him on the ice shortly after, but he owned every second of it like the absolute fucking boss he was.

Amara looked up at Ryan after she'd heard him sniffing. "Ryan Baylor, are you crying?"

"No!" he scoffed, attempting to cover it up. "But you are."

"Duh," she laughed, wiping her eyes with the back of her hand. On about his fourth lap around, Hayes spotted them and skated over to where they stood. The smile he flashed them was the biggest she'd ever seen. "Thank you," he mouthed. Amara made a heart with her fingers, holding it up to the glass, and Ryan gave him a nod.

Someone tapped Ryan on the shoulder, and he turned around. "Yo, Baylor. When are we gonna see you out there?"

"I don't know, man. I'm working on it. Hopefully soon."

Ryan continued to make small talk with some of the fans, and even though she'd seen it before, it was always surreal to her that people knew him and wanted his picture and autograph. She just saw him as her pain-in-the-ass roommate and ex-boyfriend, but to many others, he was so many other things: a hero, a role model, a fantasy.

To her, he was just Ryan.

When he'd finished chatting, after drawing a small crowd that included a few pre-teen girls who had literally cried as they took a picture with him, they grabbed a few beers and headed up to their seats in the second level.

"Twenty-eight dollars for two beers should be a fucking crime," Amara complained, as they shimmied down the row across laps and sat down.

"Well, they gotta fund these overpaid assholes' salaries somehow," Ryan joked, winking at her.

"This is a really nice place," Amara observed, looking around. "Much nicer than Total Mortgage Arena." She took a sip, and as she viewed about three rows in front of them and about 10 seats to the left, she damn near choked on her beer. She coughed, trying not to spit everywhere, as she grabbed Ryan's arm and squeezed it hard. "Holy...shit!"

"What? What's wrong?"

"That's fucking *Jenna!*"

Ryan looked, and sure enough, there she was, posing as another girl took pictures of her, complete with a portable ring light.

"That fucking *skank!*" Amara growled.

"Why the hell would she be here?"

"Good question. I would love to get up and beat that bitch's ass right now."

"Calm down, Conor McGregor. I'm being heavily scrutinized at the moment, so you better fucking behave yourself. I can see the headlines now: *'Ryan Baylor tossed from Islanders game, as girlfriend arrested for assault.'*" He paused, sipped his beer, and corrected himself. "Ex-girlfriend, I meant."

"Let's see, shall we?" Amara pulled out her phone and opened Instagram. "Help my fuck, no she did not!" Jenna had posted a perfectly posed and lighted picture of herself at the game with the caption, *"Ty finally making his NHL debut. So proud of you, Hay Hay! Always your number one fan."*

"Hay Hay?" Amara put her finger in her mouth and pretended to vomit.

Ryan looked at the picture, taking Amara's phone and zooming in on her face. "So, I think I...yeah, I may have smashed her. I didn't think so at first, but I think I did."

Amara just looked at him. "I'm actually surprised your dick hasn't fallen off yet."

"So am I, to be perfectly honest."

"While she was dating Ty?"

"No! God no, I would never! Party at my college, like sophomore year. Think me and a few of the boys may have... never mind. It's not important."

"Baylor? You're an absolute hoe." She chugged the rest of her beer, reached a hand over to his lap, and ran her fingers slowly up the inside of his thigh, stopping just shy of his crotch. "And I kinda love it."

"Yeah?" he asked, his voice laced with surprise and a bit of excitement.

"Yeah."

"Did you maybe wanna, um, go get another beer with me or something?" he asked, staring at her hand in his lap.

"Yup."

"OK then." He got up, and she followed, shimmying down the aisle again. They walked down to the second-level concourse, which wasn't as crowded as the one on the first level. He began playing mental chess, trying to figure out the best, most inconspicuous place for them to go. Grabbing her by the hand, he pulled her behind him as he spotted and headed towards a family restroom. "Knock and make sure it's empty," he told her, looking around to make sure no one was staring.

"Empty," she said, holding it open. He gave one final once-over and quickly pushed her inside, locking the door behind them.

He turned to her and reached a hand up to her throat, squeezing gently, and leaned into her ear. "You want me to fuck you in this bathroom right now?"

"Yes! God yes!" she moaned, running her hands up the front of his shirt. His hand still around her throat, he pushed her back against the wall, kissing her, as her hands moved to his belt. She finally got it undone after fumbling with the buckle for a bit.

He reached down to the waistband of her jeans, unbuttoning them, unzipping them, and ripping them and her thong down to her ankles. He took a brief inventory of his options: sink, toilet, changing table, or wall. "Bend your ass over and grab onto that sink," he instructed, as he positioned himself behind her. "And try to be quiet." She let out a loud moan as she felt him push his fat cock inside her. "That's not being quiet!"

"I'm sorry. It's impossible to be quiet with you and that fucking thing."

He grabbed her hips and thrust inside her, able to go deeper because of the angle. She bent over even further and arched her back into his thrusts.

"You love gettin' fucked by me, don't you?"

"Yes. God, yes. Yes!" she whimpered, as quietly as she could while he railed her from behind.

"See? You can break up with me, but we both know

you're not going anywhere. You'd miss this cock too much."

"I'm not going anywhere, baby. I'm in love with your cock." She felt him speed up and knew he was about to go. "Cum for me, baby. Cum nice and hard."

He groaned loudly, pulled out, panicked for a moment, and moved her out of the way. "Oh shit...fuck," he laughed, as he jacked his load into the sink of the family bathroom at UBS Arena.

Amara pulled her pants up and giggled at the absurdity of what had just happened. "I'm willing to bet that's a first." She rinsed the sink, making sure to wash away all the evidence, then looked over at Ryan, who was fastening his belt. "You OK?"

"Yeah, I'm fine," he said quietly. "Come on, let's get back."

She cracked the door, and of course, there was a mom with two little kids waiting outside. She opened it all the way and walked out. The woman started towards the door but backed up quickly as she saw Ryan follow. "Sorry. I had... emergency," he said, trying to cover his face as he passed her.

Amara had taken off, so he ran to catch up with her. "Oh, no you don't!" he yelled, wrapping both of his arms around her from behind and pulling her towards him. "Leaving me to deal with that shit."

He pressed the side of his face against the side of hers, and she grabbed onto his hands that were around her chest. "Sorry, I panicked."

"I miss this," he whispered, turning his head to kiss her cheek.

"I miss this, too," she said softly. "Now get me another beer so I can pretend I know what's going on with this game."

WHEN WORLDS COLLIDE (25)

"You're sure it's OK if I come?" Amara asked as they headed down to the lower-level entrance that led to the players' locker room and family lounge.

"You're with me. It's fine."

The game ended with the Islanders beating the Leafs 3-1. Tyler had held his own. He didn't score, but he put up two assists and was a plus three for the night, which wasn't bad for only getting in 16 minutes of playing time. Ryan was just happy to see the game end so he didn't have to answer any more questions from Amara.

"You know in Star Wars *when Yoda just dies because he's just done with answering Luke's questions?"*

"No, because I'm not a fucking nerd."

"Anyway, I feel that on a spiritual level after watching a hockey game with you. Read an article, woman. It's really not that complicated."

They approached the security in front of the family lounge, where Ryan showed his Bridgeport badge, and they were quickly let in. Many of the guys' wives and kids were there waiting, and the players were starting to filter out of the locker room one by one, as the game had ended about a half hour ago.

"Ryan fucking Baylor!" A tall, extremely handsome guy approached him and extended his hand.

"Hughesy, what's up?" Ryan shook his hand and gave him a quick hug.

"You here for Hayes, I'm guessing? This his mom?" he asked, pointing to Amara, who made a face.

"There it is," she said, nodding slowly and smirking.

"Uh, yes and no. This is my roommate, Amara McDonough. Dunny's cousin."

"Oh, my bad, bro. I was gonna say, Hayes's mom is an absolute smoke." He winked at Amara. "So, what's up? How's it going over in Bridgeport, man? I was hoping I'd see you here by now."

"Baylor, holy shit!" Another guy made his way over to them, and Amara figured this would be a good time to just go have a seat and wait for Hayes, saving Ryan the trouble of having to explain to anyone else that she was not, in fact, Tyler Hayes's mother.

There were a series of couches and comfy chairs next to the private concession stand and bar, so Amara had a seat on an empty couch. She watched a couple of the players' young kids playing with their toys nearby as they waited for their daddies. She did her best to ignore the unexpected sadness that immediately overtook her, as she thought about the fact that someday, one of the kids waiting would be Ryan's with a woman who wouldn't be her.

Opening her phone in a futile attempt to distract herself, she felt someone sit down next to her. Looking over, she saw

Jenna primping into her phone camera, fixing her dark, wavy hair, and applying more lip gloss to her insanely large, filler-injected lips. She looked at her phone, and then lifted it to her face, speaking slowly as she recorded a voice-to-text message.

"He hasn't come out yet. Waiting in the family lounge for him. Probably hitting up a party with him later. Call you tomorrow."

Amara found herself staring at her. Though she'd clearly spent a lot of money to get there, she *was* beautiful, and it was easy to see why Hayes had fallen for her.

"Hi?" Jenna said, waving to Amara.

She snapped out of it. "Hi. I'm sorry. Jenna, right?"

"Yep, that's me. And I'm guessing *you*? Must be Amara."

She was taken aback. "Yeah. Um, how'd you know?"

"Just a feeling. You're Ryan's girlfriend, right?"

"*Ex*-girlfriend, yes. So, you and Tyler. You're back together then?"

"Wow. Don't let him hear you call him Tyler. He doesn't let *anyone* call him that. Anyway, hopefully we will be soon. We've been talking over the past two weeks, trying to work shit out. He called me today as soon as he got the call-up, and I canceled a trip to Cabo just to be here for him. Maybe this will score me some points."

Shut up.

Shut up.

Shut up.

No luck.

"You broke his heart. You know that, right?"

"Yeah, I know. I didn't mean to. It just kinda happened."

"It tore him up bad."

"Yeah, well. Shit happens, honey. He'll forgive me. Especially now that he's playing *real* hockey. He needs a hot WAG on his arm, and I could really benefit from the publicity that comes with having a professional hockey player boyfriend. We're pretty much meant to be."

"Right. Well, good luck with that. Hey, random question:

have you ever been to a party at the University of Minnesota, here in the States? Maybe like, four years ago or so?

"Umm, no. I don't think so. Never even heard of it. Why?"

"No reason."

"Right. Well, since we're asking random questions then: did you fuck Ty?"

Amara's eyes shot open, as she let out an uncomfortable laugh. "Excuse me?"

"It's just that he's super-into older women. I mean, I'm like, eight years older than him, but he likes 'em near death for some odd reason. So, did you guys fuck? I mean, I don't care. I know it would've been after we broke up. Hay Hay would've never cheated on me."

"I...wow." She thought about lying but decided to own it. "Yeah. We did."

"I figured. He's got an amazing cock, eh?"

She could feel her blood beginning to boil, knowing full well this little bitch was baiting her. "Yup. He sure does."

"So, I think it's adorable that you guys are friends or whatever, but I'm gonna have to ask you to back off, K? You had your fun with him, but he's mine. Someone like Ty doesn't end up with someone like you. Honestly, you were way outta your league with Ryan. Guys like this? Go for girls like me, not you." She shrugged. "So bitchy, I know. But sometimes the truth hurts."

"Yeah, it does. You know what else hurts? A fist across your goddamn jaw." Amara stood up, and Jenna followed, bringing them face to face. Amara lowered her voice. "For the record, not only does he *let* me call him Tyler, but he fucking loves it when I do. He tried to kiss me the very first night we met and then tried to sleep over at my apartment while Ryan was blackout drunk. As I recall, you guys were definitely together at the time. So, Botox Barbie, maybe you're not that special after all, considering I've had your 20-year-old boy toy literally on his knees *begging* for this old-ass cunt."

Jenna's face dropped as Ryan immediately swooped in, pulling Amara back and stepping in between them. "Whoa, back up. Everything OK?"

"You better control your mother here, Ryan!" Jenna yelled, turning a few heads. "Before I knock her the fuck out!"

"Mommy, are those ladies fighting?" a little girl asked.

"I'm outta here!" Amara yanked away from Ryan and took off towards the door.

"Shit!" He turned back to see if Hayes had come out yet, then chased after Amara.

She was already halfway around the empty first-level concourse when he caught up with her. "Hey! What happened?" He reached for her arm and stopped her. "What happened?"

"She started with me, so I gave it right back. Ugh!" she screeched, pulling at her hair and spinning in a half-circle. "I can't fucking believe he's talking to her again! Is he stupid? What a vapid, narcissistic piece of cheating dog shit!"

"Tell me how you really feel."

"I just don't get what he sees in her. She's so...she's so... ugh!"

"Why do you care so much, Amara?" Ryan asked quietly. "I know why. Do you?"

"Tyler...deserves better. He deserves someone who treats him better."

"You mean someone like you?"

"Ryan, stop. No, that's not what I said. It's just..."

"Goddamn it, Amara." He shook his head. "Stop it. I watched the way you two kissed, the look in your eyes. I've never seen that look before. You can both keep telling me there's nothing there, that it's just sex, but you're fucking lying. I'm not stupid. I know you think I am, but I'm not. You'll never admit it, but you and I both know he's the reason we're not together anymore."

"I don't...I don't have feelings for Tyler. We're just..."

"Friends. Right. Let me ask you a question: if he was 15

190

years older, would you date him?"

She didn't answer.

"That's what I thought."

Ryan's phone rang; it was Hayes. "Yo, man."

"Rook, what the fuck happened, man? Jenna said Mar went after her?"

"I'm not entirely sure what went down. I kinda came in at the tail end of it."

"Put her on the phone."

Ryan handed the phone to Amara. "What?" she huffed.

"Yo, what happened?"

"If you wanna talk in person, I'll talk in person. I'm not doing this over the phone."

"Where are you?"

"The main concourse. By the Central Market."

"Stay there."

"You better come alone!" she yelled, but he'd already hung up.

Within a couple minutes, he was there, wearing his wool hat and the blue plaid suit he'd worn to the wedding. He approached them and immediately hugged Ryan. "Thanks for being here, man. Means the fuckin' world that you came."

"Wouldn't miss it. You looked awesome, man."

He turned towards Amara and grabbed her hand. "Hey. Come here," he whispered, pulling her in for a hug.

"Hi," she said coldly, barely hugging him back.

"Thank you for being here."

"Yup."

"You're pissed at me. What the fuck could I have possibly done?"

Ryan walked away, giving them their space. Amara stood with her arms crossed.

"What happened?" he asked.

"She's lucky she still has teeth in her fake-ass mouth. You ran back to her? Really, Hay Hay?"

"Mar, don't."

191

"Oh, I will!" She lowered her voice, knowing they were within earshot of Ryan. "You had zero problems inserting yourself into my relationship, which, by the way, I ended on your advice. She cheated on you, and you're back with her?"

"Who the actual fuck said I'm back with her?"

"Then why's she here?"

"Because I promised her that when I got my first shot, she'd be here. And I keep my fuckin' promises, Amara. Who got my two family tickets? You and Rook, not her."

"She said some vile, vile fucking shit to me, Ty. She's a real asshole."

"I know."

"She also said you guys have been talking, trying to work things out?"

"Have I *talked* to her? Yes. But as far as trying to work things out, it ain't happenin', I can tell you that."

She stared him down. "I don't believe you."

"I'm not fuckin' askin' you to!" he yelled, causing Ryan to whip his head around. He hadn't wandered too far in case any more shit popped off.

"Well, you better go. You've got a party to hit up, right? She was telling someone all about it."

"Yeah, actually I do. And for one, she's not invited. I was, however, gonna invite you and Rook, 'til you decided to go all super-bitch on me."

"You deserve better," she said through clenched teeth. "And I don't wanna hold you while you fall apart in my arms again when she breaks your heart."

"Will you let me?"

"You know I will."

"Amara, look at me: I am not getting back together with Jenna. OK?"

"You promise?"

"Yes. I promise. Listen, come out. Hughesy's got a monster house on Gilgo Beach, right on the bay. It's about 35 minutes from here. You and Rook should come."

"Is she coming?"

"No. I'm gettin' rid of her as soon as I'm done with your crazy ass. Part of the reason I wanted her here, and it's fuckin' petty as shit, but whatever, is because I wanted her to see what she gave up. What she could've had if she didn't fuck me over. So will you come?"

She looked down at her outfit, which consisted of ripped jeans, powder blue Converse All Stars, and one of Ry's Bridgeport Islanders hoodies. "I'm not exactly dressed for the occasion. Besides, I don't need a whole night of people asking if I'm your mother. I probably should just head home."

"Please come?"

She sighed. "Fine. If Ryan wants to go, we'll go."

"Rook? Party at Hughesy's beach house. You down?" Tyler yelled over to him.

Ryan knew it was in his best interest to spend as much time with the guys in the big club as possible. Even though he wasn't really in the mood for a party, he agreed.

THE GILGO BEACH INCIDENT (26)

"You know what happened out here, right?" Amara asked Ryan as they rode to Hughesy's house in the back of an Uber. Tyler had hung around for a bit after the game to do some press, so he told them to just meet him there.

"No. What?"

"A serial killer wreaked havoc here. A few women went missing and when they started searching, they uncovered like, 10 bodies. They finally caught the guy decades later."

"You and your fucking true crime shows. Well, at least they caught him, so we won't end up numbers 11 and 12, huh?"

"Oh, FYI: Jenna said she's never even heard of the University of Minnesota."

"You actually asked her that?"

"Yeah, I needed to know. So, false alarm."

He shrugged. "Good to know. Guess she's got a twin out there somewhere. And, uh, why did you need to know?"

"I don't know."

"Couldn't stand it if you weren't the only girl in the room who's smashed both me and Hayes?" She turned away from him and folded her arms. "Hey, I'm sorry. It was just a joke."

"Yeah? And you're just an asshole."

"Well, *that's* rude."

"You said house number 130, right?" the driver asked.

Ryan checked his phone. "Yep, 130."

They pulled up, and Amara's jaw dropped as they got out. "Holy fuck."

It was an exquisite, three-story wooden mansion, right on the bay, complete with a large boathouse and a dock that moored several speedboats and jet skis. It was too cold for water sports, but the enormous house itself was the perfect party destination. They walked up the seemingly endless boardwalk that led to the front door, which was cracked, and through which they could hear music blasting and a bunch of people talking inside.

"Guess we just…go in?" Ryan asked, pushing it open.

"Hey: don't abandon me, please. I really don't wanna be here."

"Keep your phone on. I gotta socialize with these guys, you know that. If we get separated and you need me, text me, OK?"

"Right," she muttered, annoyed, pushing past him and taking off down a long hallway, leaving him in the foyer.

"Mar!" he called after her, as two chicks had already approached him, the less attractive one grabbing his arm and cozying up next to him.

"Don't worry about her. She's a big girl," the girl on his arm said, smiling.

"Baylor! I'm glad you made it. And…I see you've met

Kate," Hughesy said, making his way over and pointing to the short, chunky cute brunette with huge knockers who was hanging onto him.

"Actually, I haven't. Nice to meet you, Kate. I'm Ry..."

"I know who you are," she said with a wink. "Waiting for you to come join us over here on the Island, baby."

"Yeah, uh, me too," he replied uncomfortably.

"Jesus, Kate, give the boy some space!" the other chick said. She was an older, taller blonde who had clearly had a ton of work done on her face. She threw an arm around Hughesy. "So did I do a good job, babe?"

He kissed her. "Absolutely. That's why I married you. This is my wife, Amy. She and Kate got everything set up for tonight, so if you have any issues with the food, drinks, or anything else," he patted her on the head, "this is where to send your complaints."

"Really, Aiden?" She rolled her eyes. "Yeah, well, I plan on being way too drunk to handle any complaints, so do me a favor and just talk shit about me behind my back like a normal person!" she laughed.

"Hayes here yet?" Hughesy asked.

"Haven't seen him. He said he was hanging back to do some press and would meet us here."

"I'm sure he'll show up soon. He held his own tonight, that's for sure."

"Wanna go get a drink with me?" Kate asked Ryan.

"Um, you know, maybe in a little bit. I'm gonna go mingle for a few, but uh, I might catch up with you later." He pulled away from her gently. "Where's everyone hanging out?"

"Right down that hallway, bang a left. Most people are in there or up on the second floor. Third floor is usually for, uh, other activities. Just FYI."

"I can meet you up there later," Kate offered.

"Cool. I'm just gonna..." he pointed and headed down the hallway. He shook his head in disbelief, as it was literally getting to the point that he couldn't go anywhere without women swarming him.

And it was kind of getting old, considering there was only one woman he wanted.

* * *

"Listen, I'm not saying I don't like Gouda. All I'm saying is that it's a little overrated."

He sat back and threw his hands up, slapping his knees. "I don't understand how you can say that! The smokiness, the softness of how it nearly melts in your mouth, the way it actually melts when heated. How can you say that?"

"Hey, I said what I said, OK?" Amara took another sip of her drink, which was some sort of fruity concoction containing entirely too much alcohol. She loaded another piece of Gouda onto a cracker, stuffed it in her mouth, chewed, swallowed, and shrugged. "Overrated."

She'd been engaged in a riveting conversation about cheeses with who she assumed was one of the Islanders players, whom she'd met when he'd accidentally knocked her drink over on the kitchen island as she was loading up a plate with some snacks.

She'd been starving, realizing that aside from a few handfuls of popcorn at the game, she hadn't eaten all day, which could've been the reason that after only two drinks, she was feeling no pain. He'd helped her clean up the spill, poured her another drink, and followed her as she headed up to one of the second-floor gathering rooms, deciding that the first floor was way too people-y for her liking.

"So, who are you anyway?" he asked. "The Bridgeport hoodie tells me you're either with Baylor or Hayes."

She nodded, covering her mouth as she scarfed down another cracker. "Actually," she said, swallowing. "I'm Tyler Hayes's mother."

His face sank. "Are you serious?"

"Yeah. What, don't the guys usually invite their moms to these parties?"

"Um…not, uh, not usually. But, uh, I guess…"

"Calm down. I'm fucking with you. I'm not his mom. Everyone always thinks I am, though. We're good friends, me and Ty. I'm also…hold on, you might wanna get a pen and paper. I'm Baylor's roommate, his ex-girlfriend, and Nick McDonough's cousin."

"Wow. That's a hell of a resume."

"And yes, I'm way too old for Ryan. Hence, why we're exes. It didn't really work out."

"Nah, you're not old at all. What are you, 32, 34? Can't imagine you're that much older than me. I'm 30."

She laughed, taking another sip of her drink. "I'm 41, actually."

"Shut the fuck up!"

"Honest to God!" She put her hand up. "So, who are *you*, anyway? Based on the height and physique, I'm gonna guess you play?"

"What about my physique would make you say that, exactly?"

"Well, you're just like, solid muscle, with a ridiculously nice ass and legs." She shrugged. "Am I right?"

"Well, thank you," he said, slamming the rest of his drink. "And yes. I'm Neil Halloway. Or Neilly, as the boys call me."

"What do you do? I mean, like Ryan is defense, Hayes is… um, the other one." She saw him laughing. "Sorry. I know next to nothing about hockey."

"I'm the other one. So, you know just enough to know that you like banging the players, right?"

"Well," she said shyly. "I definitely can't say I don't. The few I've been with?" She made the chef's kiss motion. "C'est magnifique!"

"Few, eh? So, there's been more than just Baylor?"

She shrugged, tilting her head and pursing her lips.

"Guess you'll never know, will you?"

"Hey, did you want another drink?" he asked, standing up. "I'm heading back down for another, and I'll grab you one."

"If I didn't know any better, I'd say you were trying to get me drunk, Neil Halloway."

"Just being a gentleman, Mrs. Hayes."

Though she knew he was just busting her balls, her heart fluttered a little at the sound of being called "Mrs. Hayes."

Calm the fuck down, Mrs. Robinson, she thought to herself.

"Seriously though, I didn't catch your name."

"Bring the drink and," she shoved the plate towards him, "more sustenance, and maybe I'll tell you."

"Deal. Don't go anywhere, Beautiful, OK?"

She watched him walk away, staring at his amazing ass until it was no longer in view. Looking around, she noticed the room they were in was beginning to fill up as well.

Shit, she thought, wondering if there was somewhere more private they could go, having already made up her mind that she would hook up with him if it got to that point. Even though she'd already had Ryan earlier, she was definitely up for round two. She sighed and crossed her legs, thinking about how hot it'd been getting bent over a sink and taking his dick in the arena bathroom just a few hours ago. As much of a pain in the ass as he was, he was always *such* a phenomenal fuck...

"There's my girl!" she heard, quickly snapping her out of her daydream. Tyler bounded over to where she was sitting and practically fell onto the couch next to her. "How long have you been here? I just got here maybe like an hour ago, and I was looking for you and Rook, and I saw Rook downstairs hangin' with some of the other guys, and this beefy-ass brunette was hawkin' him hard as fuck, but he was having none of it."

"Tyler?" she asked cautiously. "Why are you rambling a mile a minute?"

He wiped his nose, and she noticed he had a bit of blood coming out of it. He looked down at his hand. "Oh, fuck. My bad."

She handed him her cocktail napkin, and crossed her arms, staring at him intently. "You're high."

"Whaaaat?" he asked, exaggerating his surprise.

"You're rambling, your nose is bleeding, your pupils look like dinner plates, and you're twitchy as fuck. Did you rip lines?"

"What are you talkin' about?"

"Tyler? Don't lie to me."

"Fine. I'm high as fuckin' shit right now."

"Ya think?" She rolled her eyes. "Really, Ty? Weed is one thing, but this shit can fucking kill you."

"Listen, Mom. I'm a big boy. I can take care of myself."

"Shit. You really are his mom, aren't you?" Neilly handed Amara her drink and reached out to shake his hand. "What's goin' on, Hayes?"

"Nah, she's not my mom. Just likes to think she is sometimes. It'd be weird if she was, considering I've filled two of her holes with my cock, wouldn't it, babe?"

"Tyler Hayes!" she yelled, smacking him in the chest.

"Ow," he recoiled. "Hopin' to make it into all three soon."

"Keep dreamin', Ty."

"Wow. Hayes, too?" Neilly asked, sitting down on the other side of her. "Now I'm jealous."

"Don't mind him. Apparently, he's been ripping lines of coke."

"Yo, are you tryin' to fuck Neilly? Bro, aren't you mar...?"

Neilly cleared his throat loudly and made a small cutting motion across his throat.

"Tyler? Get your silly ass away from me before I knock you out."

"Fine, whatever." He stood up and started to walk away. "I'm tellin' Rook!" he turned around and called back to her.

"This isn't over. I will deal with you later!"

"I look forward to it...Mom!"

She took a sip of her drink, setting it down on the table in front of them. "Unreal," she said, shaking her head. "You forgot the food, by the way."

"Cleaned out. Not a damn thing left down there. Sorry. Hey, don't get too mad at him. Everyone gets coked out of their minds at these things at one time or another. Enough people here to keep an eye on him. He'll be alright."

"What about drug testing? He's been trying to quit weed, but if he tests positive for coke..."

Neilly laughed. "The NHL has the laxest drug testing in professional sports. It'd shock you to find out how many guys are actual cokeheads."

"Yourself included?"

"Nah, not anymore. Used to be. Too old for that shit now. Ah, he's young, just played his first game. Let him live a little."

There was a brief silence, during which Amara slammed the rest of her drink. "Wow," she said, closing her eyes. "I am feelin' *good*."

"You ever gonna tell me your name?"

"And why do you wanna know so bad, huh?"

"Because," he said softly, leaning into her ear. "I need to know what to moan while you're sucking me off in a few minutes."

"Oh, wow. OK."

"Clearly you like fuckin' hockey players. Wanna add another one to your roster, one who actually has hair on his balls this time?"

"Sure. Somewhere we can go that's a bit more private?"

He took her by the hand and pulled her up off the couch. "Third floor. That's where everyone goes to do drugs and fuck. Come on." He led her up a spiral staircase, and she grabbed the railing to steady herself, as all the turns were messing with her equilibrium a bit.

The third floor opened to a large sitting area, where several couples were making out on the couches, and some with each other. "That's usually not a good sign. All the bedrooms might be full. But...one more place to check." He pulled her down the hallway, turned right, and checked the door handle. "Score," he said, as she followed him inside a bathroom, with him closing and locking the door behind him.

Apparently, I'm the woman who fucks hockey players in bathrooms now, she thought.

This bathroom, however, was like nothing she'd ever seen before. It was probably the size of the living room in their apartment, complete with an oversized clawfoot tub centered in between a window that overlooked the bay. It had a walk-in shower that could easily fit six people comfortably, and his and hers sinks with a lighted vanity and stool in between them. "Holy shit," she said, taking it all in.

"Welcome to NHL paychecks, Mrs. Hayes," Neilly said, as he cupped her ass, scooped her up, and set her down on the vanity, kicking the stool out of the way so he was positioned right between her legs. "Now let's say we get my dick in your mouth, eh?" He reached down to his pants and began to undo them, as she rested her arms on his shoulders and watched him work his belt loose.

He lifted his head and went in for a kiss. It was messy as hell, nothing like kissing Ryan or Ty, but she just went with it. "Come on," he said, grabbing her arms and moving them to his waist. "Take off my pants."

"Wow, in a rush, are we?" she said, as she yanked them down aggressively over his ass. Somehow, one of the pockets had flipped inside out, and she glanced down at the floor when she heard a "ping" sound, watching a silver wedding band bouncing across the tile. "Um," she said cautiously, immediately removing her hands from him and moving herself as far back against the vanity as she could. "Please tell me that's not what I think it is."

"Fuck," he muttered, staring down at it and watching it spin for a bit before coming to rest.

"So, you're married?"

"Sometimes." He leaned towards her and tried to kiss her again. "Right now isn't one of those times."

She lifted her hands and pressed them both against his chest, trying to push him away, but he wasn't budging. "Hey, I don't think I wanna do this anymore."

"Come on, it's just some drunk, sloppy head. It's not like I'll be leaving her for you."

"Neil, I'm serious. I wanna leave."

"And you can," he said, as he grabbed both of her hands and pulled them off to either side of his chest, "as soon as I nut down that pretty little throat of yours."

Smacked with a rush of adrenaline, she broke free of his grip, placing her hands against his chest again and shoving as hard as she could, causing him to stumble backward. The next thing she knew, her head whipped to the side, and she felt a sharp, intense pain against the right side of her face.

It took her a second to realize that he'd hit her. As he was fastening his belt, she took the opportunity to hop off the vanity and try to make her way towards the door, but he clutched her upper arm and pulled her back to him. "Look, I'm sorry. I got caught up. Let's just forget this happened, OK?"

She nodded, and he let her go. She stumbled toward the door, still dazed from how hard he'd hit her, tore it open, and practically ran out and down the hallway. Before she turned the corner, she tried to compose herself, but the tears had already begun. She wiped them bitterly and found the spiral staircase, heading back down to the second floor.

Pulling out her phone to text Ryan, she looked up and saw him standing and laughing with a bunch of guys near where she'd been sitting with Neil before. They made eye contact, and within seconds, he was at her side.

"Amara, hey. What happened? What's wrong?"

She just shook her head and closed her eyes, tears streaming down her cheeks.

He lifted a hand to the right side of her face, and she winced in pain. His posture stiffened. "You better fucking tell me what happened right now before I lose my shit."

"Halloway...hit me," she choked out.

203

The look that washed over his face was one she'd never seen before on a human being. The intense rage that ignited his eyes terrified her, and she grabbed onto his arm as they both spotted Neil coming down the staircase.

"Ryan, please don't!" she begged, but it was too late. Like a scene from a movie, it seemed to happen in slow motion. She watched as he marched over to him and, with deft precision, cocked his right hand back and blasted him in the jaw, knocking him backward before he'd even had a chance to react.

He proceeded to punch him two more times, taking one to his own face in the middle of it all that he didn't even seem to feel. Wrestling him to the ground, he straddled Neil's hips and continued to wallop him four more times, alternating hands, as his right knuckles were completely torn open, though he wasn't sure if the blood was his own or Neil's. Amara just watched in horror, frozen, as two other guys pulled Ryan off him and shoved him back.

As he stood over Neil, he spit onto his bloodied face. "You put your hands on my girl again and I swear to God, I *will not* stop until you're in a fucking body bag."

"Enough, Baylor. Get the fuck outta here!" one of the guys shouted, as he tended to Neil, who lay writhing in pain on the floor. A crowd had gathered around them, and he put his arm around Amara's shoulder, blood spatter on his hands and shirt.

"Uh, we need to leave. Now," he said, urgency in his voice, as they pushed through bodies and made their way downstairs and out the front door.

NO GOOD DEED (27)

Everyone was silent when Ryan walked into the arena that following Tuesday for practice, including him. He entered the locker room, made a beeline toward his stall, and began unloading his personal belongings. The eyes of the other players were fixed on him; he could feel it, but no one said a word to him. He grabbed a roll of tape and started to wrap his right hand when Nick approached him.

"Can I give you a hand with that?" he asked gently.

"Nah."

"Let me see." Nick lifted a hand to his face, and Ryan turned his head to give a better look at his swollen black eye, which hurt like a son of a bitch. "Vision's alright?"

"Yep."

"Hey. What you did for her..."

"Don't mention it," he interrupted coldly.

"They're, uh, they're gonna call a meeting with you in

a few. Just wanted to give you a heads-up. Hastings is beyond pissed."

"I figured."

"I just want you to know, you did the right thing, man. Halloway's a legit piece of shit. Always has been."

"Thanks, man," Ryan said quietly.

"Anyway, I'd wait to dress. I don't know...you might not be staying, is all." Nick patted him on the shoulder. "Whatever happens, just know you did the right thing."

Ryan had a seat at his stall, crossed his arms, and awaited his punishment, thinking back to that night and everything that had transpired.

He and Amara had practically run from Husghesy's house, fearing that someone may have called the cops. Having Ubered to a nearby hotel, she cleaned him up in the shower and washed the blood out of his shirt in the bathtub, hanging it to dry on the shower curtain rod. Afterward, they both lay in silence, each of them on a different double bed, with Ryan finally breaking it.

"What the fuck were you thinking going into a bathroom with him?"

"There it is! I was wondering how long it would take for you to blame me."

"A fucking bathroom, Mar?"

"Are you intentionally being ironic right now, or...?"

"You don't ever think, do you?"

"Ryan, all the bedrooms were full and I kinda wanted to blow him, OK? I'm single, so I really don't see the problem."

"You were just with me a few hours before that."

"And? You've never had multiple hookups in the same day? Because we both know that's a fuckin' lie."

"That's...different."

"Different. Right. So, you're the only one who gets a free pass to be a slut then. Is that it?"

"He's married, Amara. With two young kids. You're literally no better than the whore who fucked your ex."

He regretted it as soon as it'd left his lips. She'd almost been sexually assaulted and *had* been physically assaulted, both of which infuriated him. He knew neither was her fault, but he didn't have the first clue how to process the blinding rage that was slowly consuming him. He knew she didn't know he was married until she saw the ring on the floor, but his anger begged him to say something that would hurt her.

And hurt her he did; she hadn't spoken one unnecessary word to him since.

He couldn't get past the fact that she'd just been with him earlier that night and then was willing to go off with another man mere hours later. He couldn't get past the fact that other guys found her attractive and wanted to be with her. And mostly, he couldn't get past the fact that she wasn't his girl anymore but was continuing to lead him on.

He'd naïvely thought after they'd hooked up at the game and flirted a bit, maybe they could give it another shot. Instead, all the bullshit happened with Hayes and Jenna, then the party, and the night just hadn't gone the way Ryan had planned.

What he did to Neil Halloway was of course retribution for his treatment of Amara, but it was more complicated than that. The punches he'd thrown were also punches he wanted to throw at his deteriorating relationship with Amara.

They were punches he wanted to throw at Hayes for going to the show first and for whatever the fuck he and Amara had going on between them.

They were punches he wanted to throw at himself for being such a mentally unstable whore that he chased away the only woman he'd ever given half a damn about.

They were punches he wanted to throw at his shitty performance as a shitty defenseman in a shitty development league.

Most of all, they were punches he wanted to throw at the colossal fucking mess he'd managed to make of his life.

And what scared him the most is that he's pretty sure if those two guys hadn't pulled him off, he would've beaten Neil

Halloway to death.

"Baylor." Rizz called his name and snapped him back to reality. "Coach Hastings needs to see you. Come on."

He got up and they walked slowly to the conference room. "Hey, I heard what happened, and for what it's worth, you were 100 percent justified."

"Thanks, man. Think Coach will say the same?"

"I doubt that. But whatever happens, I support you, man. I just wanted you to know that."

They arrived at the door, which was cracked, so Ryan walked in. Seated at the table were Coach Hastings, Coach Reilly, who was the defensive coach, and the Bridgeport GM, a pompous ass named Tom Sellars, who Ryan had met briefly at his contract signing.

"Close the door behind you," Coach Hastings directed. Ryan did and had a seat across from them. "I'm assuming you know why we called you here."

"I do."

"As I'm sure you know, this is a professional organization, and this kind of behavior is highly frowned upon, Ryan," the GM lectured. "We've heard some things about what happened, but we wanted to give you a chance to speak to it. We'd like to hear your side of the story before we make a decision about your future here."

Ryan took a deep breath and folded his hands on the table in front of him, hoping that he'd be able to remember what he'd practiced a million times in preparation for this meeting.

He spoke slowly. "My roommate and I attended a party at Aiden Hughes's house on Gilgo Beach following the Islanders-Leafs game on Sunday night. We were at the game to support Tyler Hayes in his NHL debut." He gulped and took another deep breath, feeling his anxiety creeping up. "While at the party, my roommate entered a bathroom with Neil Halloway with the intention of engaging in sexual activity with him, and upon learning he was married, she asked him to stop. He refused, and when she tried to push him away, he hit her in the face. She has a bruise from it."

He looked across the table and noticed Sellars scribbling notes in a notebook. "Then what?"

"I met up with her shortly after, and upon learning what had happened, I retaliated against Neil Halloway for what he'd done to her."

"*Allegedly* done to her," Sellars added.

"Sir, with all due respect, that's what happened. My roommate isn't a liar."

"These are serious accusations, Ryan. Against a veteran player who's been a pivotal part of this organization for over eight years."

"I understand that, Sir. But none of the accusations are false."

"Isn't it possible that maybe it didn't go down *exactly* as she told you it did?" Hastings chimed in. "You know, maybe they were messing around, it got a little rough, she got angry after learning he was married and wanted to get back at him? Come on, man. You know how these women are."

Ryan could feel his blood beginning to boil and his face turning red. "Coach, again, with all due respect, she isn't a liar. If she told me that's what happened, then that's what happened."

"And you proceeded to beat Neil Halloway to the point of a fractured orbital and a concussion. He's out for at least four weeks. He was taken to the ER. Did you know that?"

What Ryan *wanted* to say was "Good. The pussy got what he deserved." But what he said instead was, "No, I didn't. And I'm glad he'll be OK. I was angry, and I got carried away. I should have shown more restraint."

"You should've kept your fucking hands to yourself, Baylor!" Hastings yelled, pounding the table. "Do you understand the position this puts me in? I...Jesus, kid, I *liked* you."

"You're very lucky you didn't catch an assault charge.

You could be sitting in jail right now if we hadn't done so much damage control," Coach Reilly said. "There don't seem to be any videos, thank God, but we've had to scrub this shit clean on so many levels."

"An assault charge?" Ryan asked incredulously. "I would think Halloway could've caught one as well for attempted sexual and successful physical assault against my roommate."

"*Alleged*," Sellars added again.

It was clear who was the favorite in this situation, and it wasn't Ryan Baylor.

Ryan nodded. "Yeah. Alleged. Sorry, you'll have to forgive me. I'm young and I forgot how these things work in this league for a minute."

"Excuse me, kid?" Sellars growled.

"She's gonna get the Kyle Beach treatment. Cover it up and deny it 'til you die, isn't that right? Wouldn't dare wanna risk any bad publicity or loss of ticket revenue."

"Baylor, you're way out of line!" Hastings yelled, standing up.

Ryan stood up as well. "Coach? You have two daughters. They're what, 12 and 15, is that right?"

"What's your point?"

"As a father, I'd imagine you'd want your little girls surrounded by men like me, willing to stand up for them when shit hits the fan, no? Or would you rather them be surrounded by rapey assholes like Neil Halloway?"

"This...isn't about me, and it isn't about them. This is about you and the fact that you physically assaulted a member of this organization to the point of hospitalization. Don't forget that, Baylor."

"Right," he said, pushing in his chair. "Listen, this meeting is over..."

"Sit down, kid. This meeting is over when I say it's over," Sellars ordered.

"No. It's over now. Do whatever you have to do with me. But I'm not going to sit here for another moment and have my integrity and my roommate's integrity called into question. Do whatever you have to do. Shoot me a text. I'm gonna go dress for practice." With that, he walked out of the conference room, slamming the door on the way out.

He closed his eyes and leaned back against the wall in the hallway, as the adrenaline dump caught up with him, and his legs began to shake. When he opened his eyes, to his shock, all the guys were lined up outside the door, *all* of them, Nick included, with their fists out. Thankfully, they were lined up on the left side, since his right knuckles were practically burger. He bumped them, one by one, with Seggy giving him a nod of approval, as he made his way back towards the locker room.

Rizz was the last one in line, and when Ryan got to him, he collapsed into his arms and broke down. "It's all good, brother. You're brave. Just breathe through it, OK?" Rizz said softly, running his hands up and down his back. "I'm proud of you, Baylor."

For the first time in over two months, he knew he was right where he belonged.

He just wasn't sure for how much longer.

I SUCK AT
GOODBYES (28)

Wednesday, November 24
c/o Ryan Baylor

Effective Immediately:

Please be advised that you have been reassigned to the
Worcester Railers by the Bridgeport Islanders.

You are expected to report to practice in Worcester
on Friday, November 26. Details about when and
where have been sent to your team email.

An update on your progress will be provided two
weeks from the date of this letter.

Tomas Sellars, General Manager

Amara stared in horror at the piece of paper that he'd left on the kitchen counter, as she'd just got home from picking up a few things at the grocery store. "Oh my God," she said aloud, covering her mouth and setting her bag down. She heard heavy metal music blasting from his bedroom, which meant that he wanted to be left the fuck alone.

She immediately called Tyler, but he hadn't picked up, so she shot him a quick text.

A: Call me the actual SECOND you can. We have a lot to talk about.

She couldn't help but feel like this was somehow all her fault. If they'd just gone home after the game, none of this would have happened. She hadn't even spoken to Tyler since everything went down at the party, which was not normal. She chalked it up to the fact that he was on the road with New York in Dallas and was trying her best not to read too much into it. But it'd been over two days, and she'd never gone even a day without talking to him before.

Not to mention, tomorrow was Thanksgiving, and not only would Ryan be traveling to Massachusetts, but now she'd be spending it completely alone. Nick was headed to Long Island to visit Mark's family, and of course, he'd invited her to tag along. She declined, still planning on spending the day with Ryan, even though they still hadn't talked since the hotel room.

Well, fuck. This just keeps getting better and better.

Just then, Tyler texted her back.

T: Just touched down at MacArthur. Headed back to the apartment. I'll come by in a bit if you'll be home.

A: Working tonight at 8. Biggest party night of the year. Ugh. Come by before, or I'll just call you when I'm done. Things just went from bad to worse.

About two hours passed, and Amara had just nodded off on the couch when she heard a knock at the door. She got up to answer it, and there stood Tyler, dressed in khakis, a red polo shirt, Vans, and of course, his signature wool hat. "Well, don't you look dapper?"

"Dapper? Thanks, Grandma Ethel. Got any Werther's Originals for me? Some rice pudding, perhaps?"

"Fuck off," she said, opening the door as he waltzed in, slapped her ass, and helped himself to a beer from the fridge.

"So," he said, cracking it and sitting down. "I guess we've got some shit to talk about, eh?"

"You really didn't even attempt to contact us at all, after what went down at the party? That's messed up, Ty."

"Oh, you mean after Rook got jealous seeing you with another man and decided to beat him into the fuckin' ER? By the way, what the fuck happened to *your* face? He better not have hit you, too."

She shook her head. "You have no idea what happened, do you? Guess I shouldn't be surprised, considering you were coked out of your goddamn mind."

"I was waitin' for that. You never disappoint, woman. Yes, I fuckin' got high. Ninety percent of the people there were high, OK?"

"Since when are you such a good little follower?"

"Don't be a bitch."

"Don't call me a bitch."

"Then don't fuckin' act like one."

"You didn't even call or text, Tyler. Once."

"First of all, do you know how busy I was? The NHL isn't

214

the fuckin' AHL, Amara. Between practices, appearances, press, interviews..."

"Rippin' lines of coke out of strippers' asscracks."

"OK, that's a *very* specific accusation. There was *one* trip to a strip club. There *may* have been some coked-up sex, but I assure you, no asscracks were involved."

"So proud of you, Ty. You've really made it." She rolled her eyes and walked over to the sink, distracting herself by drying dishes and putting them away.

"What's up your ass? Seriously, why are you being so cold to me?"

She slammed a mug on the counter, shattering it and startling him. "Why am I being so cold? This bruise?" she yelled, pointing to her face. "Is from Neil Halloway. When we went upstairs to hook up, I found out he was married and tried to stop it, but he wouldn't let me. I tried to fight my way out and got punched in the fucking face! That's why Ryan beat his ass, and that's why he's been reassigned to Worcester, for sticking up for me when they just wanna sweep it under the rug. All the while, my best friend, the only person in this fucking world I trust, has ghosted me for almost three days. So, forgive me for being so cold, Tyler. I was physically assaulted and nearly raped. But hey, I'm sorry for being a bitch."

He had a look of complete shock on his face, then folded his arms and dropped his head onto them against the counter.

"You better fucking say something. You've had three days to be quiet."

He picked his head up and wiped his eyes. "Amara," he said quietly. "I didn't know. I swear to God, I didn't fuckin' know."

She'd only seen him cry one other time.

"Well, now you do. And Ryan and I haven't spoken since that night. I've been...completely alone to deal with this, Ty."

He got up, walked over to her, and wrapped her in his arms. "I'm sorry. I'm a dick. And I'm sorry."

She hugged him back, melting into his arms and

inhaling his intoxicating scent deeply. She'd missed it so much.

He pulled away after a few moments. "So, when's he gotta be in Mass?"

"By Friday."

"Shit. Where is he? How is he?"

She shrugged. "I told you, we haven't talked. He left this," she said, holding up the letter, "on the counter today, and that's the only reason I know. He's been in his room all day."

"Should I try to go talk to him?"

"I mean…"

Just as she said that, his door opened, and he came down the hallway struggling with three huge bags. Tyler went over to help, grabbing one from him.

"Hayes. Back already?"

"Yep. They only wanted me to stay for two games, try me out. I may get called up again if there's an injury, but for right now, roster's full, so I'm back in Bridgeport."

"You going home?"

"Nah. We have a game Friday. Wouldn't be worth it."

"Well, I'm on my way to Worcester for at least two weeks, so hi and bye, I guess."

"That's shitty, man. Amara filled me in, and you did what you had to fuckin' do. I'm proud of you."

"Yeah, well. No good deed goes unpunished, right?" He put his two bags down on the floor. "Amara, I need to talk to you before I leave."

"You're not leaving until tomorrow, right? I thought we'd spend Thanksgiving here."

"I'm leaving right now."

"Now?" she yelled. "Ryan, you're gonna be alone for Thanksgiving?"

He shrugged. "I don't…have a whole lot to be thankful for right now anyway. Hayes? Give us a minute?"

"I got you." He walked into Amara's bedroom and closed the door, giving them some privacy.

Ryan and Amara stood face to face. "Ry, I've hated not

talking to you, but what you said really hurt me."

"I'm sorry. I was completely out of line, and I'm sorry. I'm gonna say some things and then I'm just gonna leave real quick because I suck at goodbyes."

"This isn't goodbye, Ryan."

"For now it is. Listen, I've got a rough two weeks ahead of me, and as much as it kills me to say this, Amara, I can't talk to you for these two weeks. At all. Not a text, not a phone call, not FaceTime, nothing. I want these next two weeks to be like we never even met."

"Oh. Wow. Speaking of things that hurt."

"Amara, stop. We broke up, but you keep leading me on, making me think there's hope when there's clearly not. I love you, and I'd get back together with you yesterday. But that's not what you want, so you've gotta give me some space. I'm sorry, but I have to leave now." He picked up all three of his bags and wrestled them out the door. "Tell Hayes I said bye."

The door closed, and she stood there staring at it for a few moments, hoping he'd come back in and take it all back.

But he was gone.

And as much as it hurt, she knew it was probably what was best for both of them.

"You OK, babe?" Tyler came around the corner and put a hand on her shoulder.

She nodded. "What other choice do I have?"

WRONG ROOM (29)

"Biggest party night of the year, and this is it?" Dani bitched, looking around the half-empty bar. It was already 11:30, so if it was going to get super-busy, it would've done so by now.

"Don't complain. I'd much rather it be like this than a bunch of drunken idiots falling all over the place and puking in the bathrooms."

"Yeah, but those drunken idiots are mostly hot college guys who usually end up shirtless. Oh wait, I forgot. You're too good for that. Too busy banging hockey gods." She poured a couple of beers, set them down at the end of the bar, opened a tab, and strutted back over to Amara with crossed arms. "So, you gonna tell me what happened to your face?"

"Shit," Amara said, turning to check it out in the mirror behind the bar. "My makeup didn't cover it all?"

"I mean, I'm right up on ya, so I can see it. It better not

have been one of those boys. I'll kill 'em."

"No, God no. Neither of them would ever." She let out a huge sigh and filled Dani in on the events of the past few days: Tyler's call-up, the fling in the arena bathroom, the fight with Jenna, the Gilgo Beach incident, and Ryan being sent to Worcester.

"Damn. And he said he didn't want to talk to you at all, for two weeks? That boy's heart is destroyed. Easy to understand why."

"What do you mean?"

"Baby girl, you know how he feels about you and you're still banging him? You're giving him all kinds of mixed signals."

"He was always Mr. 'I can have sex with the whole planet and not feel anything.' I just thought...I don't know what I thought."

"You're messing with his head. I know you don't wanna, but you've gotta stop banging him. He's never gonna heal if you keep leading him on. Don't you want him to move on, to find his happiness? Then you gotta let him."

"I know." She took her phone out of her pocket and checked, half-expecting to see a message from Ryan, but there was nothing.

"So, baby face is back home?"

"Yeah. He came by today for a bit, right as Ryan was leaving."

"You've got the whole apartment to yourself. Maybe you should ask him to keep you company?"

"I was actually thinking about it. I wanna get with him again so bad I can taste it."

"Why don't you see if he's around? Listen, I can handle this crowd if you wanna take off."

"You sure?"

"Please, baby girl. I could run this whole place myself. See what he's up to."

She pulled out her phone to text him but froze. "I'm

nervous."

"Nervous about what?"

"It just...it still feels like cheating on Ryan. Even though we're not together, it feels like it."

"Mar? You ain't gettin' any younger. If you wanna do something, do it. Besides, you think Ryan's not gonna slay a bunch of young, hot pussy out in Boston, or wherever the hell he's goin'?"

"He's probably doing it right now," Amara said, becoming irrationally jealous at the thought. "Fine," she said, biting the bullet.

A: Hey. Do you wanna come over tonight? I can leave work now.

T: We fuckin?

A: Yeah. I can't stop thinking about you.

T: Shit, I was just kidding. You serious?

A: Deadass. Bring condoms. Meet me at my place in about a half hour.

T: I fuckin came twice reading that last message. You're in trouble, woman.

She tucked her phone into her back pocket. "Done."

"Alright, baby girl. Here, let's split up the tips before you head out."

"Don't worry, I'll pick them up later."

"Damn. Can't wait to get at it, can ya?" Dani teased. "Have fun. And I expect a full report on Friday."

Amara grabbed her jacket, gloves, hat, and bag from the cabinet under the bar. "You got it. Have a good night."

"Not as good as yours. Fuckin' bitch."

Amara laughed, slung her bag over her shoulder, and headed towards the door.

"Hey! Don't tell me you're leaving. I was literally coming in here to see you."

Shit. Play it cool.

"Wait...Jake, right?"

"Yep. Amara. So, you're outta here?"

"Yeah, it's kinda dead, and I'm actually on my way to meet up with a friend."

"Damn. OK, well I'm just gonna go for it then. Can I take you out for coffee or something? That's way lame, I know. I just...I've kinda been thinking about you a little bit. It doesn't have to be coffee. Dinner, drinks, whatever you want."

"Um, yeah. I think...I think that would be nice."

"Yeah? Oh, good! Wow, I was so nervous you'd say no," he laughed. "What's your number? I'll send you a text so you have mine."

She told him, then checked the message he'd sent her.

J: It's a date, beautiful.

-Jake

"Well, hey. Have fun with your friend, and I'll be in touch. Happy Thanksgiving!"

"You too! See ya." She smiled as she walked away and headed towards the front door. As she stepped outside, the frigid Connecticut November air was like a punch in the stomach, and she hugged herself. She briefly wished she'd called an Uber, but decided that at this point, on the night before Thanksgiving, the walk, though freezing, would be a lot quicker.

"What the fuck took you so long? I'm out here freezin'

my balls off."

She flipped around to see Tyler standing there. "Seriously? No one told you to come pick me up."

"You didn't think I was gonna let you walk home in this shit, did you? Come on, my truck's runnin' and I'm parked illegally."

She followed him to his truck, which was double-parked about a half-block from The Bull. He opened the door for her, and she climbed inside, where she was grateful that he'd blasted the heat and turned the seat warmer on for her. He got in, and before she'd even heard his door close, his lips were on hers.

She moaned as she felt his tongue rubbing against hers slowly. He knew exactly where to put it and how to move it, which excited her. His right hand snaked around the back of her head, and his left made its way up her thigh. She grabbed the sides of his face and pulled him deeper into the kiss, unable to get enough of him into her mouth. She wasn't sure how long they'd been at it, but they only stopped because someone honked at him to move.

"Alright, dickhead! I'm goin'!" he yelled, shifting into drive and pulling off.

She looked over at him, breathless. "I haven't been able to stop thinking about you. I thought once we hooked up, we'd get it out of our systems and that'd be it."

"Nope. So many things I didn't get to do to you yet. We make it out of the parking garage without my face in your pussy, it'll be a miracle."

"Ty, I just don't want this to ruin our friendship."

"I already told you it won't."

"I don't wanna go three days without talking to you again."

"Mar, you know why. It had nothing to do with us fucking, alright? Stop being so paranoid, like I'm fuckin' goin' somewhere. I'm not."

"I'm sorry. I just...I think I may have lost Ryan, and I

don't wanna lose you, too."

"You didn't lose Rook. He's just figurin' some shit out. And you won't lose me. I promise you." He turned into the parking garage, found a spot, and turned the truck off. "Come on," he said, as they both got out. He grabbed her hand and held it as they entered the building and waited for the elevator. He was wearing sweatpants and, very clearly, nothing underneath.

"See somethin' you like?" he teased, noticing her staring.

"I see a lot of things I like," she replied, grabbing his other hand and leaning in to kiss him again. The elevator door opened, and they stepped on, continuing to kiss slowly until it reached the sixth floor, where they got off and she dragged him by the hand down the hallway toward her apartment door.

"Damn, woman. Slow down!" he laughed, trying to keep up with her.

"I'm sorry," she said, fumbling through her bag for her keys. "This is all I've thought about for weeks." She finally found them, got the door open, and dragged Tyler inside by his arm. Once the door was closed, she pushed him up against it and began kissing his neck as she tore open his jacket.

"Hold on," he said, pushing her hands away gently. "Clearly I'm gonna need some energy for you tonight." She continued to claw at him as he reached into the inside pocket of his jacket.

"Wanna slam a Red Bull? Think Ry has a few left in the fridge. He knows how much I hate those fucking things."

"Nah," he said, removing a small bag about a quarter of the way filled with white powder. Holding it open, he dipped a finger in and scooped. Before she could even say anything, he brought it to his nose, snorted, and it disappeared. He shook his head a few times and stuffed the bag back into the pocket of his jacket. "What?"

Amara crossed her arms and stared at him, as he removed his jacket and hung it over the back of one of the stools, running his fingers up and down his arms in a jerky motion. "So, you're that guy now?"

"What guy?" he said, moving close to her and reaching for her waist with twitchy hands. "If you mean the guy who's about to fuck you into a coma, then yes. I'm definitely that guy."

She blocked his hands. "You're a fucking cokehead now, Ty? This why we didn't talk for three days, because you were high outta your mind?"

He rolled his eyes, removed his hat, and tossed it onto the counter. "I really wish you'd get off my dick about it," he said, pacing in front of her. "I know what I'm doing. You don't need to act like my fuckin' mother all the time, you know."

"Do you? Because I've seen people destroy their lives because of this shit."

"Calm down! It's a little pre-sex bump. It feels amazin'. You wanna try? It's so fuckin' good, I'm tellin' you."

"Thanks, but no thanks. You know, maybe we should just call it a night," she said, tossing her hands up and making her way towards her bedroom.

Following her, he grabbed her arm and spun her around to face him. She noticed his pupils were beyond dilated. "Hey. I'm under mad stress lately. The tiniest bit takes some of the edge off, OK? I know what I'm doing. I've done it before, and I've never gotten addicted. I wouldn't lie to you, Amara. Come on, you really gonna send me home right now?" he asked, pressing her firmly against the wall. He reached for her hands, which were down at her sides, and ripped them up over her head, pinning her wrists there. His lips hovered in front of hers. "I mean, I can go home if you want."

She moved her lips forward, but he pulled back, tightening his grip on her wrists as he felt her trying to move them. "Ty," she whispered, as one hand stayed on her wrists while the other slid down the front of her body, stopping at the waist of her pants. He slipped a finger between the fabric and her skin, running it back and forth slowly as she tilted her head back and exhaled.

"What?" he asked. "Somethin' you want me to do?" He twisted his hand around so his palm was against her skin and shoved it down the front of her pants. Parting her legs instinctively for him, she felt him start to rub her through her underwear. "Why are you so wet for me, huh?" he whispered into her ear as he snaked his middle finger under her thong and pushed it inside her as far as it would go, curled it, and began rocking his hand back and forth.

"Shit," she whimpered, as he fingered her against the wall, her hands still pinned above her head.

He let go of her hands and removed his other hand from her, and she immediately went for his pants. "You missed it, didn't you?" he asked, as she flipped him around so his back was against the wall. She yanked his sweatpants down to his ankles and dropped to her knees in front of him, wrapping a hand around the base of his cock and slowly licking her way down from the tip, teasing him. "Fuck," he moaned, pressing his head back against the wall and running his fingers through her hair.

He let her lick up and down it for a little while, and as soon as she started to suck it, he pulled her away by her hair. "Get up," he instructed her, as he pulled his pants back up and she did as she was told. He reached for her hand and led her down the hallway, opening the door to Ryan's bedroom.

"Uh, wrong room, Ty," she told him, trying to move him away from the door, but he fought it.

"Nah. It's definitely the right room."

"No," she said, yanking her hand away and shaking her head. "No way!"

"Yes way. Come on, let me fuck you in his bed. You know how many times I've jerked off thinkin' about this?"

"Well, keep it in the spank bank then, because it's not happening."

"Please, babe?" he begged, wrapping his arms around her waist and leaning in to kiss her. At the same time, he quickly backed her up into Ryan's bedroom and shut the door behind them, leaving them in pitch dark.

Her other senses heightened by the loss of sight, she inhaled deeply, picking up on Ryan's scent as if he was standing right there next to them.

IT'S THAT OBVIOUS, EH? (30)

She reached over to the wall for the light switch as they kissed, flipping it up. "Why do you wanna be in here?" she asked, breaking the kiss with Tyler and looking around at the room in which she'd spent countless nights. "It's kinda fucked up."

"I have my reasons."

She noticed his nose bleeding a little, so she went over to Ryan's dresser and grabbed a tissue from the box, next to which was a framed picture of Ryan, Tyler, and her.

Osi had taken it the night of the wedding, before the threesome. In it, her arm was around Ryan, and she was kissing him on the cheek. Tyler had photobombed them by sneaking in and kissing him on his other cheek. Ryan's eyes were closed, and he had a huge smile across his face, mid-laugh, amused by Tyler's shenanigans.

Truth be told, it was a God-awful picture. There were so many other beautiful pictures of her and Ryan that he could've framed, but he'd chosen this one. She'd asked him about it the night they went to watch Ty's NHL debut, as she'd come in to borrow one of his hoodies to wear to the game.

"Why the hell did you frame that picture?" she said, picking it up and examining it. *"It's so bad."*

"Because," he said, loading his wallet and phone into the pockets of his jeans. *"It's the last time I remember being happy."*

She tipped it face down, heading over to Tyler, and wiping his nose with the tissue.

"Oh, shit. My bad," he said, grabbing it from her, finishing the job, and tossing it into a nearby trashcan. "My girl's always got my back," he said, taking her by the hand and leading her to the edge of Ryan's bed. "Now sit down," he ordered.

She sat, eyes locked with his.

"Clothes off."

Grabbing the hem of her shirt, she tore it over her head and tossed it onto the floor. She immediately moved to her pants, getting them undone and lying back on the bed as she wiggled them off and tossed them at Tyler's feet.

"Bra."

She sat up and unhooked her bra, slipping it over her shoulders and dropping it onto the bed.

He got onto his knees in front of her, running both hands up her thighs and stopping just shy. "So, we're at that point, eh? I tell you what to do and you'll just do it?"

"Tyler, we've been at that point since the laundry room. At least in my mind."

"Wow. So...you'll do whatever I want?" He wrapped his arms around her back and leaned in to kiss her stomach.

"Whatever...the fuck...you want," she panted, running her fingers through his hair as he kissed all around her belly button and worked his way down. He moved to her underwear and took them between his teeth.

"Lay down."

She lay back on the bed and he dragged her thong down as far as he could with his teeth, fighting with them a bit before losing patience and reaching up to tear it off with his hands. He positioned himself between her legs and brushed his fingers across her inner thighs, causing her to spread them apart for him. "Put your hands above your fuckin' head."

She did.

"I'm gonna eat you out 'til you cum all over my face. Then I'm gonna fuck you with my giant cock 'til you cum again. You good with all that?"

She nodded aggressively.

He moved his face down between her legs, pressing his fingertips against the area right above her clit, massaging gently as he began to lick slowly. He gauged her reaction, adjusting his speed and rhythm accordingly based on her breathing and sounds. When he felt her hips begin to shift slightly, he used both hands to spread her apart and went in super-gently with his teeth. He alternated between licking, flicking his tongue in small circles, and nipping at her clit, running his teeth against it just lightly enough to create multiple sensations and keep her guessing.

"Ty. Fuck," she moaned, grabbing two fistfuls of her hair and tugging, as he continued to eat her out. "It feels so good. Don't stop."

And he didn't.

He continued to work his tongue and teeth steadily against her until he felt her grip on his hair tighten and her hips lift off the bed. "I'm gonna cum," she squeaked out, as he licked all the way down, proceeding to tongue-fuck her as she moved her hips against his face in time with her orgasm.

When she was finished, he crawled on top of her and kissed her, forcing her to taste herself on him.

"Did you just fucking...use your teeth?" she panted,

running her hands down the sides of his body.

"Sure did. And the giant wet spot on Rook's comforter tells me you didn't mind."

"Fuck no. That was the best oral I've ever gotten."

"That's what I wanna hear," he said, moving his lips to her neck and licking down to her tits. Grabbing them and pushing them together, he sucked in between them, flicking his tongue against each of her nipples.

"Sorry. There's not much to work with," she said, causing him to bite down. "Ow! No!"

"Then don't talk shit on your body. It's fuckin' perfect. Everything *about* you is perfect, babe."

He sat up, straddling her hips, and she ran her fingers down his chest and stomach. "Sorry I don't have abs like Rook," he said, causing her to punch him lightly in the stomach. "What? I know that's your thing."

"*You're* my thing, Tyler," she immediately replied without thinking.

"Is that right?"

"You get me so hot. You have since the first day I met you." She reached down to the massive hard-on in his sweatpants and grabbed it. "Besides, I'll take *this* any day over abs."

"Oh, you're gonna take it, alright," he said, lifting his hips up to remove his pants and then palming his face. "Shit! The condoms are still in my fuckin' truck."

"Just use one of Ry's. He keeps them in his nightstand, second drawer."

"I'm, uh, not sure we use the same size, babe."

"Calm down, tiger. You see the girth on that thing? He uses the ones for big boys, too."

"Wasn't really starin' at it that night, but I'll take your word for it." Tyler got up and rooted through the second drawer, then closed it. "Sure it's the second drawer?"

"I think I would know," she said defensively, getting up and checking again. "Hmm. That's weird. Unless he moved them?" She checked the top drawer, and they weren't there either.

"Looks like Rook's plannin' on gettin' busy out in Mass, eh?" He sat back down on the bed.

"Of course he is," she mumbled, straddling his lap and wrapping her arms around the back of his neck.

"Hey," he said quietly. "Why do you care? You're here with me, in his fuckin' bed, no less. What's it matter what he does?"

"It...totally doesn't," she shrugged. "It's whatever."

"Wow. That's convincing," he teased, laying back and pulling her down on top of him. "So how we doin' this? You came quick and hard as fuck on top last time. You wanna do that again?"

"Listen. What I don't wanna do is take any more Plan B pills, Ty. I spent years of my life trying *to* get pregnant, and between you and Ryan lately, I've been eating them by the handful like they're Skittles."

"So you're still fuckin' him?"

"I mean, yeah. But only a few times. We actually..." She smirked. "We did it in the family bathroom at UBS the other night."

"And do you think that's smart?"

"Probably not. But we didn't get caught. Almost did, but we didn't."

"That's not what I mean, Mar."

"Then what *do* you mean, Ty?" She climbed off his lap, becoming increasingly irritated with his line of questioning, and sat next to him on the bed.

"You broke up with him, something he's struggling with big time. Maybe you should back off the sex with him."

"Oh, really? What happened to I should just do whatever I want? 'Meet a guy at work? Bang him!' Remember that speech?"

"Rook's not just some guy at work, though. He's...my friend and you're kinda fuckin' with his head, for real."

231

"Wow. That's rich, coming from the guy who just ate his ex-girlfriend's pussy in his bed."

"Don't make this about us. This isn't about what you do with me. This is about what you do with him, and sex shouldn't be it. He can't handle it, Amara. He acts like he can, but he clearly can't."

"How about you worry about yourself and let me worry about myself, OK?"

"Fine. Then I don't wanna hear another fuckin' word about me gettin' high. But just for the record, it ain't you that I'm worried about. It's him, and I'm not OK with you hurting him. You broke up with him for a reason..."

"Yeah, because *you* told me to. Just a reminder," she interrupted.

"Whatever the reason was. You're hurting him, and it's not cool."

"And you think he'd approve of this activity right here, do you?"

"Totally different. He'll never find out this even went down unless you tell him."

She sighed, growing frustrated with him, as she'd found herself doing more and more lately. "Are we still doing this? Because if not, I'm going to bed."

He pushed her backward onto the bed and slid up next to her, hand around her throat. "Oh, we're still fuckin' doin' this. Now what are my options? Seeing as we don't have any protection and you don't wanna take a Plan B. Can I pull out?"

She shook her head. "Nope. Don't trust it."

"Well, I don't want a blowjob. I wanna fuck. Want me to run down to the truck? I really don't want to, but I will if it gets me inside you." He shrugged. "Or, you know, I can just put it in your ass."

There was a pause. "I'm not opposed to that," she finally said softly.

His eyes got huge. "You're not fuckin' with me? You're serious?"

"Yeah, why not? I've never done it before though, so you gotta go slow. Especially since you're packing that fucking howitzer."

"I've never done it before either. Girls are always too scared. Yo, I'm so fuckin' excited right now." He pointed at his dick, which had become fully erect again. "Look at that shit!"

"Yes, Ty. It's glorious." She rolled her eyes. "Yeah, I'm excited too. I'm about to lose my ass virginity to someone who can't even legally drink a beer yet. I'm pretty sure this qualifies me to be put on some sort of list."

"Oh, you definitely belong on a list," he teased.

"Fuck off," she said, smacking him lightly. She got up off the bed. "Be right back."

In about 30 seconds, she returned with a bottle of lube from her room and tossed it at him. "It ain't happening without this. And lots of it." She climbed onto the bed next to him. "I'm serious. Can you please go slow?" she asked nervously.

"Yes. If you're uncomfortable with any of it, it stops. You just gotta let me know."

She flipped herself over onto her knees, and pressed her ass back towards him, arching her back and stretching her arms out in front of her, bringing her chest flush against the mattress.

He took the bottle and coated one of his fingers, pressing it gently against her asshole. "So you really never did this with Rook?"

She whipped her head back to look at him. "Are you seriously talking about him *right* now?"

"What? I just thought…"

"No. I wanted to, but he said he's not really into it. Now can you shut up about him, please? My God, you two have the weirdest fucking relationship I've ever seen."

He slipped his finger slowly inside of her, moaning at how tight the initial feeling was. She whimpered a little. "You OK?" he asked, waiting for her nod before starting to move his finger in and out. He felt her body adjust to it, and soon after, she began rocking her hips backward.

He removed it, grabbed the lube, and slathered nearly half the bottle all over his cock, rubbing some onto her, all while making an absolute mess of Ryan's comforter. "Whoops. Hope this shit doesn't stain," he said, as he grabbed onto her hip with one hand, using the other to line himself up behind her.

He began to push himself inside gently and slowly, getting about a quarter of the way in, and she whimpered again, but louder this time. "Feel OK?" he moaned, his eyes closed and his other hand moving to her opposite hip.

"Yes. It's just...weird. Good weird, though. Keep going." He kept pushing himself in, now a bit more than halfway inside. "I don't think I can take it all. Just keep it like, right there."

"Got it," he said, as he began to thrust in and out, careful not to go too deep. "Fuck, it feels fuckin' good," he moaned, his fingertips gripping her hips for dear life. "You like it?"

"Yeah, it's...different. Don't stop."

He stared at her body, sprawled across his teammate's bed for him, while he carefully pulled back and pushed inside her tight ass, quickening his pace a bit to see if she protested. She didn't and started to push her hips back against him. He went in a little deeper each time, and each time, she met him with her hips until his entire eight inches was inside her. "Yeah, that's right. Take it all. Fuck."

"Faster," she told him, moving her hips in a circle. "Fuck me faster."

He pulled himself almost completely out, then pushed all the way back inside, faster as she requested, but there was no chance he was gonna last long. She was moaning his name loudly and looked so good from this angle, as her tight ass took his entire huge cock, that he couldn't hold on anymore. "Fuck, I'm gonna go." He pulled himself out, grabbing her ass with one hand as he jerked himself off all over it with the other. "Oh shit."

He knelt there, dazed, admiring his handy work, before she snapped him back to reality. "Can I get a cleanup on aisle three over here, man? Or is this where I live now?"

"Shit, sorry," he apologized, getting up to grab the box of tissues from Ryan's dresser. He started to wipe her up. "Wow. That is *so* much cum."

"That's lovely. Can you please hurry this up?"

He finished, and they both visited the bathrooms to clean themselves up a bit. When she was done, she'd thrown on some dry underwear and a t-shirt and came back into Ryan's room, where Ty was lying naked on his back in the middle of the bed. She picked up his sweatpants and chucked them at him.

"What? I can jizz all over your ass, but my naked body's where you draw the line?"

She rolled her eyes, lying down next to him. "Ty, lie there naked then. I don't give a shit. Just thought maybe you wanted your pants back on."

"If I wanted them back on, don't you think I'd have grabbed them?"

"Are you intentionally trying to be annoying lately, or is it just happening by chance?"

"Why? Does it turn you on?" he teased, pulling his pants back on and draping an arm across her stomach. She grabbed his hand and held it.

"Kinda."

"So, let me ask you somethin'…"

"Ugh. Nothing good has ever followed that sentence starter."

"It's truth time. Ready?"

"Oh, here we go," she mumbled. "Do I get one next?"

"Sure. You know I'm an open book, babe. But you can't lie, OK? You gotta tell me the truth, even if it sucks and you don't wanna."

"I don't lie to you, Tyler. I have zero reason to."

"Alright then. Truth time: what's your ideal situation look like?"

She made a face. "I'm not sure I understand the question."

He turned over towards her, propping himself up on one elbow. His other hand still draped across her stomach, he dragged his fingertips lightly in circles around her hip. "I mean, with me, with Rook, with whoever else. If you could build the perfect situation for yourself, what's it look like?"

She shook her head. "I still don't follow."

"Jesus, sometimes you're just as dense as he is!" he complained. He reached his hand up to her face, forcing eye contact. "Is this just sex, or do you maybe feel something else?"

She looked away, letting go of his hand. "I can't answer that..."

"Uh uh. Nope. You agreed to tell me the truth."

"Then I decline to answer. Lying by omission..."

"Is still lying!" he interrupted. "Spill it, woman."

"Fine. Ugh, I hate you. Fuck. My ideal situation? You're about 10 years older, and I'm about 10 years younger. OK? But since that's impossible, then yes, this is just sex. Really, really hot sex." She shook her head. "But that's all this can ever be."

"I keep tellin' him it's just sex with you. And I know it is because that's what it has to be. It's just, sometimes, I don't know, I like to think about if things were different."

"But they're not, Ty."

"I'm not him, you know. Maybe me and you..."

She sat up abruptly, running her fingers through her hair. "Don't. Don't even finish that sentence. You're 20 goddamn years old."

"Be 21 in two weeks."

"Yeah? And I'm twice your age. Just...don't even go there."

"Fine," he grumbled, turning onto his back and folding his hands behind his head.

"So, alright. Truth time? There's one more part to it.

236

Ry's older, too, and it's...perfect situation? Alternate universe scenario? It'd be the three of us. No jealousy, no drama. I'd sleep every night between both of you if it was possible. But it's not, so it doesn't matter."

He nodded, then went silent for a bit. "So what's your question for me? Truth time."

She looked up at the ceiling fan, turning slowly and humming. "You have to answer honestly."

"I know that."

She took a deep breath through her nose and asked him the question to which she was pretty sure she already knew the answer. "Ty? Do you maybe have some feelings for Ryan that go beyond just friendship?"

He smiled, shook his head, and sat up next to her. His smile faded, and he stared down at his hands in his lap. "It's that obvious, eh?"

"Totally. For what it's worth, I'm...pretty sure it's not one-sided, Ty."

He sighed. "Been fightin' with this since I met him. Especially since that night at the wedding. I don't know what it is, exactly. I'm not like, in love with him or anything. He's just...he's..."

"I know. Believe me, I know."

"I kinda like your idea, about the three of us. But..."

"...it can't happen," she finished quietly, crossing her arms.

NOT YET (31)

Fifty-seven miles.

That's how far Ryan had gotten into his 115-mile drive to Worcester before having to pull over the Hyundai Tucson he'd rented.

Luckily, there was a rest stop nearby as soon as he felt it coming on, so he quickly exited the highway, found a secluded spot, and reclined his seat back. Trying some of the new techniques he'd gone over with Dr. Gephart, his therapist, he took a few deep breaths and repeated, "This is going to pass. This is going to pass."

But it wasn't passing.

"*You can also focus on your happy place,*" she'd told him. "*Think about where you feel most relaxed, most calm.*"

He closed his eyes, picturing himself on the ice as a kid. Growing up in Minnesota, his dad flooded the backyard every winter so he had a place to practice, and when he thought about his happiness, that's where it was: the silent, frozen world where he was still the star, where his dad was still alive, where hockey was still fun, and where his heart was still intact. This used to be his happy place.

But it wasn't anymore.

He couldn't get his breathing to slow down, and he'd begun to sweat through his shirt. Unbuckling his seatbelt, he tore his jacket off and tossed it onto the passenger seat. He reached into the cup holder for his phone, and his first instinct was to call her.

But he knew he couldn't.

The next option was Luke, who picked up on the third ring.

"What's goin' on, Ry?"

"Luke? I...fucked up. I really...fucked up!" he cried into the phone.

"Are you OK? Where are you?"

"Um..." He looked around. "Somewhere near...Hartford, I think."

"What's wrong? You having a panic attack?"

"Yes."

"Put me on speaker." Luke walked him through the grounding steps, and as he'd gotten down to one, he felt his breathing begin to return to normal. "How you feeling?"

"Better," he said quietly, putting his seat back up and running his hands through his sweat-soaked hair. "I'm OK now."

"So what's goin' on?"

Ryan told him *everything* he'd purposely kept a secret the last few times they'd spoken: the failed open relationship, the threesomes with Kaylie and Hayes, the breakup, the therapy, Hayes's NHL debut, the fight, and his reassignment to the Railers. "In like, two months, I've somehow managed to completely fuck up every aspect of my *entire* life, Luke. And I don't have the first clue how to fix any of it."

"Ry, sometimes you can't fix it. Sometimes you have to

just play the hand you've been dealt and move forward. Look at Mom. Think she ever thought she'd be a widow in her early 40's? She didn't fix that, but she's moving forward."

"I don't understand how I can love her so much when there's nothing we can do to make it work. And I hate that she's so close to him. It makes me sick."

Luke exhaled. "How sure are you that you love her? Are you sure you're not just infatuated with her? You don't...no offense, Ry, but you don't have a whole lot of experience in this field."

He didn't really have a good answer. "I just know."

"Maybe this two-week break from her is a good thing. See if you still feel the same way after not talking to her at all."

"I wanna call her," he said, hanging his head. "I know I shouldn't, I know I said I wouldn't, but I want to."

"Don't do that, man. You have to give yourself some space."

"I know what's gonna happen. She's gonna be with Hayes this whole time I'm away, and the thought of it is driving me fucking insane."

"Then don't think about it. Seriously. You're going to a new city, you're single. You'll find plenty to keep yourself busy."

"My therapist said I need to stop banging around so much."

"Yeah? Your therapist also said not to bang Amara anymore, and clearly, you didn't listen to that. You just need something to get your mind off it all, man. The only advice I can give you is to just take these next two weeks to focus on yourself. Put in the work in Worcester, and hopefully, that'll be it and you'll get back to Bridgeport."

"Thanks for talking to me. I appreciate it. I should probably get back on the road."

"Hey, can I ask you something without you getting all pissy with me?"

"Sure."

"You sure this is just about her?"

"I don't understand."

"You...Ry, you talk about her, but you talk about *him* just as much." He paused. "Probably more. Do you know that?"

"I don't...no. It's only because of her and him...no." He laughed uncomfortably, then paused. "Luke: I'm not...no."

"I mean, it's OK, Ryan. I wouldn't care, Mom wouldn't care. You...you know that, right?"

Ryan was silent.

"You know that, right?"

"Yes," he whispered.

"And if you ever wanna talk to me, about anything, you can. I mean it. *Anything*. You got it? I'm always here for you. Nothing you tell me could change that."

"I know that, too, Luke."

"Just making sure. Anyway, what are you doing for Thanksgiving?"

"Probably sitting in a hotel room by myself." He snickered. "How pathetic is that?"

"It's not pathetic at all. You're an athlete who has to travel for his job. Happens all the time, man. Listen, Mom and I will FaceTime you tomorrow, OK? Seriously: focus on you. Try not to think about her, try not to think about him, and just focus on doing whatever you gotta do to get your ass the fuck back to Bridgeport. I love you, Ry."

"Love you too, Luke."

He hung up, composed himself, and put the car in drive, trying his best to ignore the part of the conversation he'd just had with Luke: the part he wasn't ready to face just yet.

He distracted himself with his Spotify "Fuck Everything: Part 2" playlist, alternating between screaming the lyrics and wondering what fresh hell awaited him a mere 57 more miles away.

* * *

241

"Check in for Baylor," he told the woman at the front desk of the Hilton at which he'd booked a room for the next two weeks. He thanked God the league was picking up the tab for it; otherwise, at 325 bucks a night, he'd be staying in a tent on the sidewalk.

"You're all set. It's been paid for, you just need to sign here."

"Thank you," he said, grabbing his key card and pushing his baggage cart down the hall towards the elevator. Mentally exhausted, he checked the time on his phone.

6:47 p.m.

"That's it?" he asked incredulously, feeling like it must've been at least midnight. All he wanted to do was get into his room and sleep, preferably straight through tomorrow, and wake up just in time for his first practice with the Railers on Friday.

The fucking ECHL.

Just when he thought things couldn't get any worse, here he was in the lowest possible position he could be within the Islanders' organization. Though hard to show it, he was incredibly grateful that he hadn't been traded. The feeling he got was that while the coaching staff didn't think he really did anything wrong, there was pressure from above to "punish" him for daring to question them.

"Dude, you put in your two weeks, and they'll reassign you. Don't even sweat it. Same shit happened to me last year," Kasic had assured him before he'd left practice on Wednesday morning when he'd received the letter. *"You'll be back in no time."*

Once he'd unloaded all his bags in his room, he decided he'd return the luggage cart to the lobby before settling in for the night. As he stepped off the elevator and made his way to the front vestibule, he noticed a tiny blonde woman outside sitting on the wall along the hotel's drop-off and loading zone. She was wearing a short, tight red dress, just like the one

Amara had worn to Excel, and she appeared to be upset.

Mind your fucking business, Baylor, he thought. *You've got enough on your own plate at the moment.*

But the dress had brought back so many intense feelings of their night together after they'd left Excel, resulting in a sudden, unexpected hard-on. Before he knew it, he was outside and making his way over to her. She was slumped over onto her hands, which rested on her knees, and crying.

"Hey," he said cautiously. "Is everything OK?"

"Fucking asshole!" she yelled, popping her head up and pounding her hands against the wall on either side of her hips.

He backed away slowly. "Sorry, my bad."

"No, I didn't...not you. My husband. My stupid fucking husband. You know, we came out here from Boston to spend Thanksgiving with my family, got all ready to go out for the night, and, of course, he starts a huge fucking fight. He left. Took his shit, took the car, and left me here. Told me to find my own ride home and won't pick up the phone. So, yeah." She wiped her eyes with the backs of her hands and looked at Ryan, who was staring blankly at her. "Sorry. You didn't need my whole life story."

"Nah, it's all good," he said, sitting down next to her. "That's kinda shitty."

"Ya think?" she laughed. "So, what's your deal, gorgeous?"

He snickered, shaking his head. "It'd take me the next two days to explain it. But I'm...not here because I wanna be, let's just say that much."

Don't do it.

Don't do it.

Don't do it.

Don't do it.

"Did you wanna, maybe..." he motioned towards the inside. "Grab a drink at the bar? You can vent more if you want. I'm a pretty good listener."

Fuck, Baylor.

"No," she replied quickly.

Taken aback, he got up. "Oh, OK then. Listen, have a good..."

"I don't want a drink, and I don't wanna vent," she said, getting up with him. "I'll go to your room with you, though."

"Yeah, let's go," he said without hesitation, turning to walk back inside.

She followed him to the elevator, where he pressed the button and they both stood awkwardly, waiting. "So what's your name?" he asked her.

"Does it really matter?" she asked, as the elevator doors opened and she stepped in, motioning for him to come inside. As the doors closed behind him, she leaned on the back of the elevator and he moved in, placing a palm above her head flat against the wall, and snaking the other around the back of her head as he brought his lips to meet hers. They kissed for a few seconds, and he could immediately taste the alcohol on her breath when the elevator hit the third floor and opened.

As he pulled away, he got a good look at her; she was cute, but he could tell she was older, probably about Amara's age. He grabbed her by the hand and pulled her down the hallway to his room.

"You sure you wanna do this?" she asked. "I'm probably old enough to be your mother. What are you, 25?"

He laughed, sliding his key card into the door, pushing it open, and extending his arm inside. "I'm 23. And yeah. I'm fucking sure."

"Good. I want you to destroy me, gorgeous."

"That won't be a problem."

She walked in, and he closed the door, locking all his thoughts of Amara and Hayes out in the hallway, if only for a little while.

THERE IT WAS (32)

Just as Kasic had promised, the two-week punishment in Worcester had been just that, and before Ryan knew it, he was packing his bags up to head back to Bridgeport. When the text and email had come through late that Thursday evening that he'd been reassigned to Bridgeport, he made sure everything was ready to go for him to roll out early the next morning.

Ryan Baylor had fucking done it.

He'd gone two whole weeks without talking to her, though he did check in with Hayes periodically just to make sure everything was OK and to get updates on the Isles. He'd also made it two whole weeks without a random hookup, minus the sad wife in the red dress on the night of his arrival.

After he'd finished having sex with her, he immediately felt like the biggest piece of shit on Earth, and he'd reached out to Dr. Gephart, who'd talked him down from the ledge.

"Ryan, you have to understand that you're going to mess up.

And when you do, you have to forgive yourself and move on. You can't dwell on it."

"I don't know why I did it. I wasn't even that attracted to her. It was like I just couldn't stop myself from it. I even told myself not to do it the entire time I was doing it."

"That's what sex addiction looks like, Ryan," she'd told him. "For the rest of this week, here's what I want from you: whenever you think about hooking up with some random person, I want you to stop what you're doing and write down everything you're feeling at that exact moment. But I want to seriously challenge you to not hook up with anyone else for the duration of your stay in Worcester, OK? Let's see where we sit in about two weeks, unless you need me before then, in which case, you can always reach out."

Ryan had taken her advice and had ended up with 46 pages of a Word document by the time he'd packed his bags the night before his departure.

Forty. Six. Fucking. Pages

But: he'd done it, and the feeling of accomplishment was like nothing he'd ever known. For the first time in a very long time, he knew he was going to beat this.

Additionally impressive, Ryan hadn't had a panic attack since the day before Thanksgiving, when he'd spoken to Luke on the drive out. There were so many things that should've triggered one for him: being in Worcester; the fling with the sad wife in the red dress; the fact that he'd spent Thanksgiving alone in his hotel room eating a shitty gas station sandwich and watching *ALF* reruns; and the fact that he'd only *practiced* with the Railers, having been named a healthy scratch for all five of the games they'd played in those two weeks.

"Don't take it personally, Baylor. We all know why you're here, and it's bullshit. You're too good to be here anyway, kid," the defensive coach for the Railers had told him, sensing his frustration at not being able to play.

Every single one of these shit scenarios should have sent him into an anxiety-fueled tizzy.

Instead, he'd managed to handle all of them.

He'd even read and finished an entire book, taking the opportunity to read one of those smutty hockey romances Hayes had gone on about. To his surprise, it was *actually* pretty good; it was about this goalie who had an anonymous one-night stand with some chick at a costume party, and she ended up being his teammate's sister and ultimately his roommate. He was a slow-ass reader, which wasn't helped by the fact that he had to stop at several choice scenes to smack off, but he'd actually finished an entire book, something he hadn't done since probably middle school.

Friday morning, he arrived at the rental car building to return the Tucson at about 11:00 and waited outside for the ride he'd arranged back to his apartment.

"This fuckin' guy!" Hayes yelled out the window of his truck, pulling into the parking lot and honking at him. He screeched tires into a space, parked crooked as hell, jumped out after barely having turned it off, left the door wide open, and ran over to where Ryan was standing on the curb with his bags. "What's good, Rook?" he said, throwing his arms around him, with Ryan doing the same.

"Everything, now that I'm back home," he said, squeezing Hayes before they let go of each other.

"Fuck, I missed your dumb ass. So much, kid." He swung one of Ryan's bags over his shoulder as they headed towards the truck. He tossed it into the bed, with Ryan doing the same before hopping into the cab. "You ready to go home?"

"Fuck yeah, I am." Ryan leaned his head back against the seat. "So? What'd I miss?"

"Yo: last night, after practice? Dalesy found out his fiancé has been fuckin' Seggy again and he flipped the fuck out, bro. Threw a chair at him, and it caught him square in the face. Ended up with six stitches. It was insanity. I don't know how Hastings hasn't had a fuckin' heart attack yet."

"Holy hell. Betcha he didn't get sent to Worcester," Ryan complained. "Why do I miss all the good shit?"

"I don't know, man. All I know? His fiancé is for the streets. She's tried to get me to fuck her so many times. I can't even be near her. Shit makes me uncomfortable as hell."

"Mar said something about that when we went to Excel…" He stopped himself.

There it was.

Ryan took a deep breath.

"She's OK, man. She's really happy you're coming home, no lie. We both missed you. A lot."

"I missed you guys, too. And I think we're gonna be OK, me and her. I've kinda accepted that we're not together anymore, and I just wanna focus on building up a friendship with her. I think I might be ready for that."

"That's good, Rook." Hayes paused, debating whether or not to let him know, and finally deciding that it wouldn't be fair not to. "Hey, so, there's something you should probably know."

"Yeah? What's that? You two run off and get married while I was gone?"

"Nah. Thought about it, but we ultimately decided against it." For now, he thought it best to fast-forward through the part about him pounding her in the ass on his bed, along with the four other times they'd had sex while he was gone: twice in his truck, once on Amara and Ryan's kitchen countertop, and once in the laundry room of the apartment building, just to bring everything full-circle. "Seriously, you guys aren't together anymore, so it really isn't a big deal, but…"

"But what, Hayes? Spill the tea already."

"Alright. She's kinda datin' a guy she met at The Bull. They're not like, together, and I don't think they're fuckin'. But she's been out with him a couple times for coffee, and I think she really likes him."

There it was.

Ryan leaned forward, resting his head in his hands and exhaling loudly.

"Rook, you g…"

"Gimme a minute," Ryan interrupted. "Just gimme…a minute." He felt his heart beginning to race, but he began to reason with his anxiety.

She isn't your girlfriend anymore. She deserves to be happy, just like you deserve to be happy. You should be happy for her. She's your friend, and friends support each other.

Employing another successful technique that Dr. Gephart had shared with him, he felt his heart rate start to return to normal. "You meet him?" Ryan finally asked.

"Nah," Hayes replied. "But I've seen him."

"And?"

"It's bad, Rook."

"Oh God. Bad as in what?"

"He's older, probably her age, which I think will be really good for her. But he's jacked. Like, jacked. Arms like fuckin' cannons. And he looks just like Seguin, bro."

"Fuck," Ryan ran his fingers through his hair and looked at Hayes. "Seguin? Fuck. I want her to be happy, but is it too much to ask for her to be happy with someone who doesn't look like the literal hottest man alive?"

"I just wanted to give you a heads-up. I wouldn't bring it up to her, but if it does come up, I didn't want you to be blindsided."

"Thanks, man." He sighed. "Well, I *was* over her."

"Stop it. Anyway, guess what?"

"What?"

"It's my birthday, bitch!"

"Oh shit. Finally legal!"

"Damn straight. And after the game tonight, we're all going out to celebrate. So make sure you bring your clothes with you to the arena because we're leaving right after."

"Happy birthday, Hayes. I'm glad we can finally party together."

"Me too."

Hayes cast a sideways glance at Ryan, remembering the "truth time" conversation he'd had with Amara the night they'd spent together in Ryan's room.

"It's that obvious, eh?"

"Totally. For what it's worth, I'm...pretty sure it's not one-sided, Ty."

Hands gripping the wheel, he battled with the overwhelming urge to ask him if he felt the same, ultimately deciding that now wasn't the appropriate time.

But he knew that at some point, he'd have to bite the bullet.

Hayes helped Ryan carry his bags up to the apartment and into Ryan's room. He peeped the comforter quickly, making sure Amara had gotten rid of all the evidence, which she had. "We'll head out around 3:00. Come get us. We'll Uber over so no one has to drive home tonight," he said, leaving Ryan to reunite with Amara in private, even though he really wanted to stay just to make sure it didn't go south.

Ryan looked around his room, thinking about how much he'd missed being here. Glancing at his dresser, he noticed the picture of him, Amara, and Hayes had been flipped on its face, which he thought was strange. He walked over and flipped it back up, smiling at it. They'd both become two of his absolute favorite people in the world in such a short amount of time. Sure, he had his issues with both of them, but what friendship didn't have its issues?

One thing he knew for certain, deep down in the darkest parts of his soul, is that no matter what, either of them would go to bat for him in a second. He remembered telling Amara before he left that he didn't have a whole lot to be thankful for, but he regretted having said that. Those two alone filled his heart with gratitude.

"Knock knock," she said, tapping against the doorframe, startling him. "Sorry. Didn't mean to scare you."

As hard as he tried to fight it, the sight of her standing there brought him immediately to tears.

"No, please don't cry. Then I'm gonna cry, too." She moved quickly to where he met her halfway, and wrapped her arms around him, melting into his embrace. He dropped his head onto her shoulder and sobbed as she ran her nails back and forth across his scalp. "Hi," she said softly.

He picked his head up. "Hi."

"I missed you. A lot. This place just isn't the same without you leaving your shit all over for me to clean up."

He laughed, wiping his eyes and brushing the shoulder of her shirt. "Sorry, I think I got snot all over your shirt."

"I'll let it slide."

"Being away from you sucked," he told her matter-of-factly. "I hated every second of it. But you'd be so proud of me, Mar. I've been taking my therapist's advice, and for the most part, I was able to keep things under control while I was out there. I only had one panic attack, and," he bragged, holding up his index finger, "only *one* hookup."

"*You* had only one hookup?"

"Uh huh. And I read an entire book. The whole thing."

"Look at you, Baylor. Almost unrecognizable!" She punched him lightly in the arm. "So glad you're doing well. Not texting you for two weeks wasn't easy, but I wanted to respect you. And it sounds like it was for the best. You look a hell of a lot better than the last time I saw you, that's for sure."

"I feel better, too."

"Good."

"So how've you been?" he sat down, patting the edge of the bed for her to sit.

She started to, but after a brief flashback to what Tyler had done to her there, she decided against it. Not to mention, they had a track record of ending up naked and on top of each other in situations such as this. She leaned against the dresser. "Think I'll stay over here."

"Mar, I'm not gonna..."

"I know that."

"Then come sit. Please? Here," he scooted all the way to the end. "Sit at the other end then."

Getting as far away from him as she could without

falling off, she sat down. "I've been...good. Working a lot, writing a ton. Just finished a huge freelance job that paid incredibly well. Treated myself to a nice dinner and some new clothes." She tucked her hair behind her ear and shrugged. "It's been good."

"I'm glad." He smiled at her, wondering if she would tell him about the new guy she'd been seeing, but nothing. "So how'd you spend Thanksgiving? I betcha it wasn't as awesome as mine. Nice to meet you, Amara. I spent Thanksgiving alone in a hotel room. I ate a gas station sandwich, watched reruns of this ridiculously dumbass show called *ALF* that I could not seem to turn off for some reason, and read some of a hockey smut novel."

"That? Sounds awesome, actually. *ALF* was the shit back in the day, by the way. Nice to meet you, Ryan. I begrudgingly went with Tyler and Osi over to Dalesy's, where they were doing a sort of 'misfit Friendsgiving' for anyone who didn't go home. A few of the other guys showed up, actually. There were probably about 25 people there, which is way too many for my liking. Headed out early, 'cause Ty couldn't stand Dalesy's fiancé coming onto him anymore." She gasped. "Yo, did he tell you about the chair?"

"He did. That's fucking insane."

"Right? So after that, we came back to Tyler's, smoked a bowl, and killed an entire pumpkin pie. One of those giant-ass Costco ones. Fell asleep watching *Gremlins*." She shrugged. "It wasn't bad."

"That also sounds awesome."

"Would've been better if you were there though."

"Yeah," he sighed, looking down at his hands. "Hey, you comin' out for Hayes's birthday tonight?"

"Of course. Wouldn't miss it. And what I mean by 'wouldn't miss it' is that if I *did* miss it, Ty would never, ever shut up about it. So, yup. Already mentally preparing for it." She got up from the bed. "I'll see you later then?"

"Yeah, definitely." As he watched her walk out of his

room, he realized there wasn't a chance in hell he would ever fully get over that woman.

Not a fucking chance in hell.

He was certain it wouldn't be with her, but he knew right then and there that no matter who he eventually ended up with, she would always be his gold standard.

TY'S 21ST BIRTHDAY (33)

"So, where we going, anyway?" Ryan asked, having just gotten out of the showers and beginning to get dressed at his stall. Even though they'd lost, it'd been a great welcome-back game for him: plus four, no stupid penalties, and Coach Reilly complimented him on his speed, on which he'd been working to improve to the point of exhaustion.

"Hayes wants to check out Excel," Kasic told him.

Ryan gulped. "Great."

"What? Not a fan?"

"It's...fine. Just some memories there I'd rather not have."

"Well, that's where the birthday boy picked. Hey, you looked great tonight, man. You've been working on your speed, eh? Definitely shows, kid."

"Thanks. Had nothing but time out in Worcester. You know they scratched me every single game? Such bullshit."

"Oh, tell me about it. I told you, happened to me, too. Sellars is a fuckin' dickhead, for real. 'Jonathan,'" he began in a mocking tone, "'this is a professional organization, and this type of behavior is highly frowned upon.' Yeah? How 'bout you frown upon deez nuts?"

"That's actually pretty spot on, man. So, why'd you get sent?" Ryan asked, then realized maybe he was overstepping. "I mean, you don't have to tell me."

"Nah, it's good." He looked around, making sure no one was within earshot, then leaned into Ryan and spoke softly. "It's not, like, common knowledge, so just keep it on the DL. But you know how Nick's the athletic trainer?"

"Yeah?"

"Well, he's new. The old one quit halfway through the season last year after finding out that I banged his daughter and her friend at a party. They told me they were 21. Turns out, they were more like 17. He had a fuckin' fit, understandably, and came after me. I tried reasoning with him, apologizing, but he wouldn't stop. So, I ended up beating the shit outta him. Only a few of the other guys know about it." He shook his head, sitting down to put on his shoes. "It's always somethin' in this locker room, Baylor. You'll figure that out if you haven't already. Hastings is a saint, for real. I'd have fuckin' murdered us all, hid the bodies, and started over by now."

At that moment, Hayes came bounding through, a bottle of Canadian whisky in one hand and one of the coaches' bullhorns in the other. "Bus leaves in 10 minutes, bitches!" he yelled.

"You don't need to yell into a bullhorn, you fuckin' idiot," Seggy complained.

"And you," Hayes spoke into it in a normal tone, "don't need to fuck your teammates' fiancés."

"If it wasn't your birthday, I'd kick your ass, you mouthy

little shit!"

"You ain't gonna do shit, bitch!" Hayes turned the bullhorn off and put it down next to Ryan's stall. "You ready, Rook? Gonna be a wild fuckin' night. Got a party bus, reserved a spot in the VIP lounge with full bottle service."

"Damn. Went all out, huh?"

"Yup. Figured what better way to spend those paychecks from the two NHL games. I mean, that and payin' my mom's mortgage for three months."

Ryan smiled. "You're a good dude, Hayes."

"Fuckin' right I am. Can't take it with you when you're dead, eh?" He took a swig out of the bottle and pulled out his phone. "So, Mar's gonna meet us there. I think she's bringin'..."

Ryan had an instant hot flash.

"...that chick Dani from her work. The gray-haired bitch with the huge cans? I swear, I'd hook up with her just to get my face in between those fuckin' things." Hayes offered the bottle to Ryan, who took it and immediately began chugging. "Yo, slow down, killer," Hayes said, snatching it back. "This is *my* night to get carried back to my apartment, not yours. Come on, let's get outta here."

* * *

Amara approached the VIP entrance to Excel cautiously, as memories of her and Ryan's night here crept across her consciousness and parked themselves at the forefront of her thoughts.

It's not gonna happen again. It was one time, and it's done and over with, she told herself, wrapping her arms around her body in an attempt to stay warm. December in Connecticut was no joke, nothing like Seattle. Even with the absurdly thick puffer jacket she had on, she was pretty sure her eyeballs were going to freeze if she didn't get inside soon.

"Um, I think you *might* be in the wrong line."

Amara turned around to find two younger girls, wearing next to nothing and shaking like crazy from the cold, staring at her. "This is the VIP entrance. The regular one is," one of them said, pointing, "over there."

She rolled her eyes and turned back around, moving up towards the bouncers. "Amara Hayes. Here for my...son Tyler," she told them, certain she knew him well enough to know that his smart ass had listed her as his mother. They quickly scanned the list, placed a pink wristband on her arm, and let her through. "Goddamn. Welcome, Mama Hayes!"

She turned to the two girls, stuck her tongue out, and flipped a gloved middle finger before turning and heading inside. After checking her coat, she headed upstairs into the VIP section and scanned the crowd for anyone she knew. The music was so loud she could feel it in her bones, and she was pretty sure it was still the same exact garbage song that had just been playing on repeat since the last time she was here.

Her hair twisted into a high bun and wearing a blue, long-sleeved, knee-length bandage dress paired with silver heels, she stepped over to the railing that overlooked the dance floor. She immediately spotted a crowd of about eight blondes, and sure as shit, there was Ryan, smack-dab in the middle of them with his shirt completely unbuttoned and attempting to dance. "Of course," she said aloud, shaking her head, and watching them take turns pawing at his abs.

Dani had bailed at the last minute, which was a bummer. One of her kids was sick and her husband got called into work. "*Trust me,*" she'd told her on the phone. "*If there was any other option, I'd take it. Sorry, baby girl. Have so much fun!*"

Though she tried to deny it occasionally, she knew she was way too old for this shit, for this scene, and times like this reminded her of it. The boys were young and could hang. They drank too much? A good puke, nap, Red Bull, shit, and a BLT later, they were back to almost 100 percent. She drank too much? The next three days were like tiptoeing through a fog-covered alternate reality. She'd much rather be out on one of her coffee dates with Jake than here.

Jake.

She'd been seeing him for about two weeks, having had their first coffee date on the Friday after Thanksgiving, when he'd picked her up after her shift at The Bull. He was 47, divorced, gorgeous, and the partial owner of a construction company with a few friends of his. They hadn't had sex yet, but they'd made out a little outside her apartment door after their second date. He'd ridden the elevator with her after she'd invited him up, but to her surprise, he'd quickly put a stop to it.

"What's wrong?" she'd asked, as he'd pulled away from her.

"Nothing. It's just, I don't meet many women I like, Amara. And I'm really enjoying getting to know you. I think it'd be better if we just took things kinda slow. That's all. In my experience, sex kinda...complicates things."

"Tell me about it," she'd added.

"So, let's behave then, OK? There's no rush." He'd kissed her on the forehead and promised to call her the next day, which he did.

She'd gone inside, half-grateful that he was such a gentleman, but also half-annoyed because she'd really wanted it. As much as she enjoyed being with both Ryan and Tyler, there was something about a good-looking older man's swag with which they just couldn't compete.

She'd started towards her room when there was a knock at the door; figuring it was him having changed his mind, she opened it without looking.

"Oooh, I saw that."

"Ugh, you're a literal stalker." She'd opened the door and Tyler had followed her inside, closing it behind him.

"What? I was comin' by to see how your little date went. Lemme guess: more coffee? Riveting conversations about your favorite color?"

"You know, there's this little thing called a phone," she'd teased, leaning against the counter and crossing her arms.

"You could've just texted me."

"Guessing it didn't go well since you're in here with me instead of blowin' him right now, eh?" he'd said, helping himself to a glass of water from the fridge.

"No, it went really well, actually. He just wants to wait to have sex, that's all. I'm pretty sure that's called being a gentleman."

"Well," he'd said, finishing the water, setting the glass down next to the sink, and approaching her. *"I wouldn't know the first fuckin' thing about that. You all torqued up from kissin' him?"* He'd backed her up against the counter and reached for the waistband of her pants, unbuttoning them.

Impulsively, she helped him get them off, as he'd scooped her up by her ass and set her on the countertop. *"Hey,"* she'd told him, running her hands up his chest and across his shoulders. *"I really like him, so this? Might have to stop soon."*

"I get that," he'd said, shedding his pants and kicking them off. *"But soon ain't right now. So shut the fuck up, kiss me, and let's get some cum all over this countertop."*

She grabbed the railing and leaned back a little, closing her eyes. She'd fucked Tyler three more times over the past two weeks, but she knew it had to stop, with both him *and* Ryan. She hadn't expected to find someone else by whom she was so intrigued, but life, as it had a habit of doing, had made other plans for her.

Either way, she really didn't wanna screw things up with Jake.

A hand on her shoulder snapped her back to the present, and she spun around to see Ty with a drink in his other hand. "It's Jack. That alright?" he yelled over the music.

She smiled. "Of course. Thanks." It was *his* birthday, and he showed up by her side immediately with a drink for her. He was way more of a gentleman than he even realized.

He handed it to her and leaned in for a quick kiss. "Thanks for comin', Mom," he teased, as the super-hot cocktail waitress came by and asked him if they needed anything.

"Nah, we're good, Heather. Thanks, baby."

He and Amara both turned back towards the railing and focused their attention on the dance floor.

"You hammered yet?" she asked him, taking a few quick sips of her drink, hoping to get there soon herself.

"Yep. Slowin' down for a bit. Been rippin' whisky since the arena. Not tryin' to be a fuckin' hot mess just yet."

"Too late for that," she teased, looking over at him, but his eyes didn't budge. He was still hyper-focused on the dance floor. She leaned over to his ear so she didn't have to yell as loud. "You should just go for it with him."

He shot her a look like she was crazy, pointing down at him. "Yeah, well. He's a little preoccupied at the moment." A few other guys had joined him and distracted some of the girls, but he had begun grinding with two of them, one in front of him and one behind him, and their hands were exploring *all* of his body.

"You know he's an attention whore. I'm telling you, he feels it, too."

Ty leaned into her ear. "And so, what? I just go down there, grab him, and start makin' out with him in the middle of a crowded club in front of our entire fuckin' team? That'll go over real well."

"That's not what I said. But if you invite him over later tonight, I guarantee you he shows up."

"Alright, fuck this," he said, turning away from the railing and grabbing her by the hand. "I'm ready to be a hot mess. Shots?" he asked, leading her back towards their table and sitting area in the lounge. They sat down together and he flagged Heather, ordering two shots of Jaegermeister, which arrived within a minute.

"Oh my God," she complained, picking it up and sniffing it. "People are still drinking this? You know how many nights this shit had me on my literal deathbed?"

"Oh, suck it up," he said, clinking her glass and throwing it back. A couple of the other guys waved Hayes over to where they were standing. "Hey, I'll be back, OK? Anything you want, let Heather know. It's all paid for, babe."

She watched him walk away, slammed the shot, and sucked down the rest of her Jack, promptly ordering another when Heather came around again. She was starting to feel pretty good, but, as usually happened at these things, she found herself alone again. Since the outside sitting area was closed due to the weather, she grabbed her phone from her clutch and decided maybe it'd be fun to send Jake a few flirty texts.

A: What are you up to, sexy?

J: Lying here, thinking about you, actually.

A: Good to know. Thinking about you, too.

J: Can't wait to see you again.

A: Out with some friends right now. What if I swing by afterwards? We can, you know...talk. Or something.

J: Was trying to be a good boy, but you're making it really hard. In more ways than one.

J: Text me when you're on your way.

She'd just finished her drink when Ty came back over, grabbed her hand, and pulled her up. "Come on, let's go dance. I know I'm fuckin' terrible, but it's my birthday, so you can't say no."

"Ugh, fine," she complained, following him as he led her towards the stairs and stopped at the top of them.

"Maybe you should take the lead," he slurred, swaying a bit.

"Hey: no coke tonight?" she asked.

He shook his head no.

"Good. Keep it that way."

"Yes, Mom."

She pulled his hand and led him down the stairs to the first floor of the club. When they got there, he sauntered behind her with his hands around her waist, and she noticed a lot of eyes following them as they made their way out onto the dance floor. They carved out a little spot for themselves and he immediately grabbed her, pulling her hips into his and moving them against her in time with the music. Her hands wrapped around the back of his neck, and she pressed her forehead against his chest, looking up at him periodically.

"So, how's your little boy toy? You guys fuck yet?" he yelled into her ear.

"First of all, my little boy toy would be *you*, considering Jake's almost 50. And second, wouldn't you like to know?"

"You like him, eh?"

She nodded. "I do. A lot."

"So, soon I'm not gonna be able to do this anymore, right?" He reached a hand down under her chin, forced her face upwards to meet his, leaned down, and kissed her. She knew a lot of people were watching, but she didn't care; she ran her hands up his arms, through his hair, and kissed him back.

For a while.

"Maybe you won't want to anymore if things work out with a certain someone," she said after he'd finally broken the kiss.

"I'll never not want to. But I'll do whatever I gotta do if it means you're gonna be happy."

She blushed, pulling his ear down to her mouth. "You do know there's a ridiculously tiny part of me that's madly in love with a ridiculously tiny part of you, right?"

He nodded. "Same."

"Just making sure."

"So, you really think I should go for it with Rook?"

She nodded vigorously. "You two are seriously hot together. I could watch you guys kiss forever."

262

"What if he's not feelin' it?"

"He's feelin' it, Ty."

"But what if he's not?"

"One way to find out, right?"

They danced for a little while longer, when Tyler decided he wanted to go back upstairs because he could no longer see straight. The two of them held hands as she led him off the floor and towards the stairs. She happened to look up at where they'd been standing against the railing earlier and locked eyes with Ryan. She wasn't sure how long he'd been watching them, but he nodded slowly, then shook his head.

"Shit." She could sense he was pissed. She snagged Osi, who happened to be passing by at that moment. "Hey," she called, grabbing him and giving him Ty's hand. "Get him back upstairs, OK? He's ripped up." She kissed Tyler quickly on the cheek. "Happy birthday, you fucking stud. I gotta go."

She made her way quickly towards the coat check, threw it on, left the club, and prepared for the freezing, 15-minute trek back to the apartment. She'd seen that look in Ryan's eyes before, and it meant he was prepared to start some shit. Knowing he would follow her out of there, she left, ensuring that he wouldn't stay and fuck up Tyler's birthday. She tried to get just enough ahead of him that he didn't catch up to her so they could hash it out at home instead of outside in the freezing cold.

No such luck.

"Hey, wait up!" he called, jogging to catch up with her. "Um, so what the hell was that tonight? Still just friends?"

Here we go.

THE END OF THE BEGINNING (34)

He reached a hand up to her throat. Squeezing gently, he moved his other hand between her legs, then whispered into her ear, "You know you're always gonna end up right back here with me."

As he leaned in to kiss her, feeling her hands begin working his belt loose, he suddenly felt sick to his stomach.

This wasn't what healing looked like for either of them.

If there was even a shred of hope that they could salvage a friendship and both move on with their lives, then there couldn't be any more excuses; this *had* to come to an end.

"Hey." He broke the kiss and sat up, moving to the edge of her bed. "Amara, we can't do this anymore."

She crawled behind him, running her hands across his shoulders and down his chest. "Then why are we? Why did you come to my room?"

He slid himself over and away from her grip. "I don't

264

know how not to. What I do know? Mar, this is toxic and destroying us. It's definitely destroying me." He ran his fingers through his hair. "I saw you leave the club and I had to follow you. I don't wanna be away from you, but being near you is killing me." He turned around to look at her. "What the fuck am I supposed to do, Amara? I saw you kissing Hayes tonight and…"

She scooted to the edge of the bed, sitting next to him. "Ry? Let's talk about that."

"OK. It enraged me, seeing you all over him like that."

"Why?"

"Because…" He stopped.

"Because you wanted it to be you."

"I always want it to be me with you, Amara."

"No, Ry. You wanted it to be you with *him*."

He exhaled and shot up off the edge of the bed. "Why… you know, Luke said the same thing the other day. Why does everyone think I've got a thing for him?"

"Because you do, Ry."

"No, I don't. I…don't."

"Ryan?" she asked cautiously.

He paced back and forth.

She continued. "We're friends, right? Yeah, it's a little fucked-up right now, but you can be honest with me. I've known you've had a thing for him for a long time, Ryan."

"I'm not like, in love with him or anything," he said quietly. "I don't know what it is."

"And there's nothing wrong with that. At all."

"Um, there's a fucking lot wrong with that, Mar." He continued pacing. "He's my teammate. I can't…we can't. They won't understand. And I'm not…I mean, I fucking love hooking up with girls, you know that."

"You don't have to stick a label on yourself, Ry. Did you know that Mark's the only guy Nick ever dated? He had a different girl every other week before Mark. And now they're married."

"I'm not marrying Hayes."

She laughed. "I didn't say you were. But what I'm saying is that maybe you should just talk to him."

"And say what?"

"You tell me."

He sat down on the floor in front of her dresser, leaning back against it. "What if he doesn't feel the same way?"

"He does."

"How do you..."

"Trust me, he does. Talk to him. OK?"

Ryan looked at her. "Tomorrow's road trip should be interesting. And what am I supposed to do about you?"

"What about me?"

"Tell me how to get over you. Every time I think I'm fine, we end up fucking, and I'm right back where I started. I wanna move on from you, Amara. My head knows this is never gonna happen, but my stupid heart is clinging to this hope that it might. Help me. Please."

"Ry, I've been irresponsible with you, and I'm sorry. What happened at UBS should have never happened, and tonight shouldn't have happened, either. I'm glad you stopped it."

"It's not because I wanted to, believe me. I had to."

"Either way, it shows a lot of growth on your part."

"Hey," he said, leaning forward toward where she was sitting on the edge of the bed. "I said some wicked shit to you tonight, and I'm sorry."

"I wasn't too nice to you either, so let's call it even. We know how ugly our fights can get. Rizz tried to warn us that first night we met, but we didn't listen. Neither one of us ever listens. To shit."

"The last thing I ever want to do is hurt you, Amara. When I get angry, I say things, horrible things, that I don't mean. I've done it a few times to you now, and I'm really sorry."

"It's OK. I know your heart. None of what you say in those moments ever comes from there."

They sat quietly for a few minutes, with Amara finally speaking. "Ryan, I don't know how to say this, so I'm just gonna say it and hope that maybe it will help you. I'm dating someone. I have been for almost two weeks, and I...really like him."

"I know," he replied calmly. "Hayes told me. And I hope he gets hit by a bus...I mean, I hope he makes you happy." He smiled at her, but she didn't smile back. "Terrible joke. Sorry. Listen," he said, reaching up to where she was sitting and taking her hand. "You deserve happiness. And I hope I can meet him someday, you know, when doing so won't rip my worthless heart out of my actual asshole." He got up from the floor with her help, stretched his arms over his head, and yawned. "I should get some sleep. Bus leaves at 9:00 a.m. That should be a fun ride. Everyone's gonna be tore up."

He headed towards her door, put one hand on the doorframe, then turned around to face her. "Hey, um. So now that you've got yourself a man, you gonna stop bangin' around with Hayes?"

She nodded. "You gonna start?"

He smiled, blushing. "Maybe."

"For what it's worth, I am 100 percent here for Ryler."

"Ryler?" he laughed. "Oh, that's so bad."

"You kidding? It's literally perfect. I tried Bayes, Haylor, and Tylan, but Ryler is where it's at."

"You've thought about this a lot, haven't you?"

"Yes. And Ryan, I'm serious: talk to him. OK? There's no shame in it. And just so you know? If everyone else in the goddamn world turns their back on you, I won't. Ever. We have our shit to wade through like everyone else, but I'm here for you. I just needed you to hear that."

He winked at her and tapped the doorframe twice. "Samesies. Hey: I'm glad we talked. Night, Amara."

"Night, Ryan."

Closing the door and starting down the hall, he heard her yell, "Ryler is happening!"

He smirked, then had a moment of sheer panic, wondering if this next chapter he was about to open would hurt as much as the one he'd just closed.

One way to find out, right?

RYLER HAPPENS (35)

The Bridgeport Islanders' bus looked as though someone had dug up a bunch of corpses, dressed them up in suits, and propped them up in its seats. With the exception of Rizz and a handful of other guys who hadn't come, *everyone* was either half-dead or still drunk from Hayes's birthday bash.

Ryan had ended up driving the Raptor to the arena, as he was the least banged up out of the trio. When he'd got down to the fourth floor, Osi answered. *"Is not good here. So much vomit, all night long. Is like hospital ward."*

Hayes had shuffled over to the door wearing sunglasses, holding his travel bag in one hand and a garbage bag in the other. *"I'm never gonna stop pukin', Rook. I think I'm dyin'."*

"You'll live. You can sleep on the bus ride."

They pulled into the arena and parked in the underground lot. Ryan grabbed Hayes's bag from him and set it down, as he immediately leaned his back against the truck upon getting out. "Rook," he whimpered. "I'm gonna die."

Ryan examined his friend, who looked like he'd gotten

dressed while blindfolded with one hand tied behind his back. "No you're not. Come here," he said, as he grabbed the bottom of Hayes's dress shirt and tucked it slowly and neatly into his pants, moving his hands up his chest to fix all the buttons, which he'd fastened in the wrong holes. "You're such a mess right now." He patted his shoulders, grabbed both of their bags, and led him by the arm to the bus.

They made their way to the back, passing by several guys who were already slumped over against the windows or onto each other and snoring. Taking the next to last row, Ryan grabbed the window seat, leaned his back against the glass, and bent one leg up on the cushion. He motioned for Hayes to sit between his legs, laying with his back pressed against Ryan's chest, his head resting on his shoulder, and both of his knees bent with his feet up on the cushion. Ryan draped his arms across the front of Hayes's body.

"Get some rest. It's a good three-hour ride," Ryan told him. "Let me know if you're gonna puke, OK?"

"I love you, man," Hayes mumbled, closing his eyes and settling in.

"Damn. You're still at the 'I love you, man' level of fucked up? Ooh, it's gonna be a long day," Ryan joked, running his fingertips slowly across Hayes's chest, but then stopping when he realized where he was and what he was doing.

"Where'd you disappear to last night, anyway? You go home with one of those birds who was molestin' you on the dance floor? Shit was like a fuckin' porno, man."

Ryan laughed. "Nah, I wish. Mar and I...we had a misunderstanding. We hashed it out. We're all good now."

"You and that woman are constantly fightin', man. What the fuck you beefin' about now?"

"Actually, it was about...you."

"Me?" he asked, trying to sit up, but Ryan gently pushed him back down. "It was my birthday. Fuck did I do?"

"Speaking of pornos, do you remember making out with her in the middle of the dance floor?"

"Did we make out? Shit. You know how many people actually thought she was my mother? Did we make out in front of everyone?"

"In front of everyone. For like, five minutes straight."

"Wow. Nope, don't remember that."

Ryan sighed. "I followed her home and we kinda got into it. We almost had sex again, but I stopped it. It was a long night."

"Christ, Rook. You two need to stop bangin' already. Every time you do it's like you open a hidden portal to another undiscovered dimension of Hell. Don't worry, I laid into her last week about it, too. It's not healthy. You two just need to stay friends and leave it at that."

"I think we may have gotten to that point last night. I don't know. It's...hard with her."

"She tell you about her new man?"

"Yeah. Listen, I don't really wanna talk about that. Why don't you get some rest?" Ryan brought a hand up to Hayes's head and ran his fingers through his hair, Hayes moaning slightly at his touch.

He grabbed Ryan's other hand and held it, proceeding to pass out cold for the remainder of the bus ride.

And Ryan could not have been happier.

❉ ❉ ❉

If the bus ride wasn't bad enough, practice was a shit show of epic proportions. Between the number of guys who had to stop and throw up and the fact that no one could move, it was a miracle Hastings didn't trade the entire team right then and there.

"Hayes? Why the fuck would you plan this shit the night before a game? Do you have any brain cells in your fuckin' head, kid?"

"Sir, no sir," Hayes groaned, lying down on the bench, having just yakked into a nearby trash can in the tunnel.

"Well, guess what? I'm not scratching your sorry ass. You're gonna get out here, play like shit, let anyone scouting from the big club see you play like shit, and maybe you'll learn your lesson. None of you are getting scratched. So suck it up, idiots. There's literally no point in this practice. Go back to the hotel, take naps, and attempt to get your shit together for tonight. Jesus tap dancing Christ!" he yelled, kicking a Gatorade bottle and taking out an entire rack of twigs on the way back to the locker room. "Pick that shit up, Hayes!" he yelled from inside the tunnel, and it echoed throughout the arena.

Hayes crawled over to where the sticks were, starting to pick them up one by one and load them back onto the rack.

Ryan came over to help him. "I'm pretty sure we're just gonna find him dead in his office someday. That man's blood pressure has to be through the roof. This team is a fucking mess, man."

"How the fuck am I supposed to play tonight? I can barely move."

"You'll figure it out. We'll go back to the hotel and you can sleep for a bit more, maybe take a hot shower."

They headed back into the locker room and Hayes plopped down onto the bench in front of his stall. He leaned his head back and closed his eyes when he felt someone beginning to untie his skates and take them off.

"Don't say I never did anything for you," Ryan teased, a look of sheer disgust washing over his face as Hayes looked down at him. "Yo, your feet need an exorcism, man. My God."

"Yeah, they're brutal." He leaned back again, but Ryan grabbed his hands and pulled him forward.

"Nope. Let's get the rest of your gear off."

"Can't I just wear it back to the hotel?" he whined. "It's literally across the street."

"No, Hayes. You cannot leave the hockey arena drunk, wearing all your stank-ass gear back to the hotel. Can you imagine those social media posts? Come on now, get up."

"Ugh!" Hayes stood up, stumbled, and attempted to pull his jersey up over his head. Ryan had gotten down to just his hip and shoulder pads in the time it'd taken Hayes to finally get the jersey off. Shaking his head, Ryan took off the rest of his gear and pulled on his sweatpants.

"Come here." He grabbed Hayes and helped him remove the rest of his gear while he slumped over like a dead fish. It took about 10 minutes, but he managed to get all of it off and get him dressed, too.

"Get some rest, boys," Rizz ordered, coming through the locker room. "You guys looked like total shit out there."

And rest they did.

But it didn't help much.

That night's 7:05 p.m. game against Wilkes-Barre/

Scranton was, as expected, a complete blowout. Most of the guys had sobered up, Hayes included, but were exhausted from being so hungover all day. Many of them weren't able to even make it through their 45-second shifts, and the number of penalties they'd taken, including offsides and icing, made the game go on forever. Regulation had ended at an unheard-of 10:10 p.m., with most of the fans having bounced early, knowing that at 7-3, there was zero chance of a Bridgeport comeback.

Hastings hadn't even bothered to address them afterward; he just left for the hotel, leaving Rizz to deal with the team.

"Boys, that was the worst game any team has ever played in the history of professional hockey. I'm embarrassed to call myself a part of this team tonight. And, for the record." He got right in Hayes's face. "This shit does not happen the night before a game, ever again. Are we fucking clear?"

"Yes, Cap."

"And none of you better even think about going anywhere but to your hotel rooms to go to sleep." With that, he stormed off to the showers.

"I think I might just shower back at the hotel," Hayes told Ryan. "I just wanna get the fuck outta here, man."

"That's fine. I'll meet you back at the room then. I'm way too gross to even think about putting my suit back on right now." He wrapped a towel around his waist, having taken off all his gear.

"I don't even fuckin' care. See you over there."

Heading into the shower, Ryan closed his eyes, leaned his head back, and let the water run over him for a good five minutes while he tried to calm the anxiety he felt beginning to creep up. Not only had he just skated in the shittiest hockey game ever played, but he was about to head back to a hotel room with Hayes, and he couldn't decide whether or not he should go for it.

He couldn't deny it anymore; there was something there between them, though he didn't really understand what it was. He'd hooked up with other guys before, but he'd never really been *attracted* to one the way he was to Hayes, even having jerked off to him several times over the past few weeks. Ryan tried to remember when he first felt it and decided it may have been the night they first talked on the bus ride home from Lehigh Valley when Hayes had fallen asleep with his head on his shoulder.

Thinking back to all the issues he had with Amara and Hayes, he realized that, despite what he'd told himself, the jealousy he'd felt hadn't been solely about Amara. He rinsed the soap off his body, wondering if it was even possible to have feelings for two people at the same time, which he deemed a valid concern, considering Ryan Baylor hardly ever felt anything for anyone.

He finished showering, dried off, got dressed, and gathered up his belongings from his stall.

"Baylor!" Rizz yelled, just as he was heading out the door. "Hang on."

Great. Here we go.

"What's up, Cap?"

"You carried this shit show tonight. I wanted you to hear it. Your feet are finally moving, man. It's incredible. Team played like ass tonight, but you held it down." He held out his hand, and Ryan shook it.

"Wow. Thanks, man. I appreciate that."

"Do me a favor? When you get back to your room, bitchslap Hayes for me. I love him, but kid's a total dumbass sometimes."

"Will do," he said, making his way out of the locker room, to the arena's exit, and ultimately across the street to the hotel.

When he'd gotten up to their room, he went to put the key card in the door and froze. Soon, he found himself pacing back and forth outside the door, in much the same way he had before losing his virginity to his rival's hot mom in juniors.

There's nothing to be worried about. Just go in there, act normal, and if something happens, it happens, he reasoned with his thoughts.

"Fuck you doin', Baylor?" a voice said, startling him. He jumped and saw Seggy coming down the hall with a bucket of ice.

"I, uh, I just forgot my key card...oh wait, there it is," he replied awkwardly, fumbling in his pocket as it dropped onto the floor.

Seggy just looked at him and shook his head as he

walked by. "You're an odd fuckin' duck, Baylor. You know that?"

"That's the word on the street," he said, picking up the key card, biting the bullet, taking a few deep breaths, and opening the door.

The fuck?

He looked around and realized Hayes wasn't even there. "Where the hell did he go?" Ryan said aloud, emptying his pockets and beginning to take off his suit. He'd gotten down to his boxers and began rooting around in his overnight bag for a pair of shorts when he heard the door beep and then open. Hayes came in, giggling like a little girl and carrying a plate with several slices of pizza heaped onto it.

"I definitely just took like, what was left of Dalesy's pizza while he went to go…well, hey there. Didn't know it was gonna be this kinda party," Hayes joked, catching a glimpse of Ryan standing there in his underwear. He tossed the plate down onto the table in front of Ryan, picked up a slice, and shoved it in his mouth. "I literally just knocked on doors until I found food. I had to eat somethin'. I'm fuckin' starving. Take what you want."

"Nah, I'm good. Not really hungry."

Hayes shot him a dejected look and stopped chewing. "Do you know," he began, his mouth full, "what kinda hoops I had to jump through to get that shit for you?"

Ryan rolled his eyes and smiled. "Fine," he said, grabbing a piece, biting it, and putting it back down. "Thank you."

"You're welcome." Hayes finished the slice he was eating, scarfed down another one, and flopped backwards onto one of the beds. "I will be so glad when this night is over." He pulled off his T-shirt and laid there in his sweatpants, as Ryan threw on a pair of shorts over his boxers. Hayes gave the thumbs-down. "Boo! I was enjoying the view. Just don't cover up those sexy ass abs."

"Oh, I was just about to get dressed and suggest we head down to the bar, do some Jaegerbombs. No?"

Hayes sat up, put his hand over his mouth, and shook his head slowly. "Dude, don't even joke. Don't. Even. Joke."

"Sorry," Ryan said, as he had a seat on the other bed. "So what do you think practice is gonna look like on Monday?"

"I don't even wanna think about it, man. We're in so

274

much trouble. I'm guessin' suicide drills until someone vomits. And I love how I'm gettin' all the blame. I didn't hold a gun to anyone's head and make them get fucked up."

"Yeah, but you paid for it all, so you might as well have."

"Whatever. Everyone had a good time. At least I think they did. I don't have a clue what the fuck happened. I'm lucky I didn't wake up in a ditch. Thank God Osi's always got my back, since my two other besties pretty much left me for dead."

"Oh, you are the most dramatic motherfucker I've ever met."

"And you wouldn't have it any other way, Rook."

"So is Osi pissed you weren't rooming with him this trip? You guys always room together. Why'd it change?" Ryan fished, lying down on his side and propping himself up on one elbow, facing Hayes.

Hayes rolled over on his bed to face Ryan, propping himself up the same way. "Dunno," he shrugged, smirking. "Maybe he's sick of me and needed a break."

"Maybe."

Hayes moved, and a sharp pain shot through his shoulder. He winced, grabbing it and sitting up.

"What's wrong?" Ryan asked, sitting up as well.

"That fucking hit I took in the second. Got my shoulder good. I didn't say anything to Nick because he's a fuckin' spaz and would've pulled me, but it's killin' me."

"Your bad shoulder?"

"Yep. It's…fine. I'm fine."

"Here," Ryan said, getting up and moving over to Hayes's bed, sitting down next to him. "Lemme work it a bit. I've got Biofreeze if you want." Ryan brought both of his hands to his teammate's shoulder and began to rub lightly, Hayes leaning his head forward. "Is that good?"

"Perfect. Yo, you're spoilin' the shit outta me today, eh? Got me undressed, geared up, outta my gear, dressed again, now this?"

"What can I say? I have a soft spot for your stupid ass, Hayes." He continued rubbing his shoulder, and he felt his heart start to race. "Maybe someday you'll return the favor. Karma, right?"

Ryan continued for about a minute. "Still good?" he checked in.

275

"Actually, could you go a little lower?"

Ryan moved his fingers down a bit. "Like there?"

"Nah, lower."

"There?"

"Lower."

Ryan gulped, dragging his fingertips down to the middle of his back. "There?"

"Lower."

Closing his eyes, he moved his hands onto either of Hayes's hips. "There?" he asked softly.

"Gettin' closer." Hayes placed his hands on top of Ryan's and pulled them around onto his stomach. He tried to push them lower, but sensing Ryan's apprehension, he turned around to face him instead. "So, I know we're not drunk, but we are in a hotel room on the road, and I did make you an offer if you remember." He brought his hands up to Ryan's shoulders and leaned into his face, just inches from his lips. "Do you remember?"

Ryan nodded, trembling.

"You want it?"

"So fucking bad."

Hayes pushed him back onto the bed and crawled on top of him, hovering over him on one elbow and running his other hand through Ryan's hair as he bent down to kiss him. Ryan brought his hands to the back of Hayes's head, pulling him deeper into the kiss, bending his left leg, causing Hayes's hips to fall directly on top of his.

"I've...wanted this," Hayes said in between kissing him, "for a really...long...fuckin' time." He kissed his way down to Ryan's neck, biting softly and bringing his hand slowly down the front of his body, across his chest, and stopping on his abs.

"Me too," Ryan panted, keeping his hands on the back of Hayes's head.

"Put your fuckin' hands on me then."

"I can't. I'm...so nervous," he whispered, his heartbeat thumping in his ears.

"There's nothin' to be nervous about. It's just us. Here," he said, sitting up, straddling his legs, and reaching a hand to the waistband of Ryan's shorts. "Let's relax you a little, eh?"

"Fuck," Ryan moaned, as Hayes grabbed both his shorts and boxers and slid them off, Ryan lifting his hips to help him.

Hayes got up, and Ryan took notice of his massive hard-on as he pulled him to the edge of the bed and got down onto the floor between his legs. He looked up at Ryan seductively, like he was about to say the sexiest shit ever, and hit him with, "I've never sucked a dick before, FYI. So if it's garbage, my bad."

Ryan immediately began to laugh. "Head's like pizza. Even when it's bad, it's still alright."

"Reassuring," Hayes mumbled, wrapping a hand around the base of Ryan's cock. "Rook, I don't know what to do with my other hand," he said, waving it around.

"Seriously? Just...fuckin' put it somewhere," Ryan bitched, grabbing it and placing it on his abs.

"Wow, this is going well. We should start a fuckin' OnlyFans, eh?"

"Will you shut up and suck it already?"

And he did.

Hayes took him all the way into his mouth with zero hesitation, wrapping his lips around him, working his tongue and his hand all at the same time. Ryan couldn't even think about closing his eyes; they were fixed on his teammate, on his knees on a hotel room floor, sucking on his cock. He grabbed the back of Hayes's head, steadying him as he began to thrust his hips forward gently. "Turns out that big ass mouth of yours...is good for something besides talking shit after all."

Ryan knew he wouldn't last too much longer, which was probably a good thing, as he felt Hayes beginning to gas out. He stood up, took both of Hayes's hands, and put them on his ass, returning his hands to the back of his head and thrusting quick and hard. "I'm gonna cum. You swallowing me?"

Hayes nodded, and Ryan let out a loud groan as he nutted into his teammate's mouth. When he'd stopped moving his hips, Hayes pulled away, wiped his mouth, and stood up, smirking. "Betcha never thought you'd blow a load down my throat when you first met me, eh?"

"That felt so fuckin' good. Seriously. You've never done that before?"

"Nope," he said, approaching Ryan, gently pushing him back onto the bed and taking off his own pants. He crawled on top of him and kissed him, inviting Ryan to taste himself on his lips while he grabbed Ryan's hand and moved it towards his cock. Ryan barely touched it, instead moving his hands to

Hayes's back and running them up and down it.

"You can touch me too, you know."

"I know. I'm just..."

"Let me fuck you, Rook," he whispered into his ear. "I wanna fuck you so bad right now."

Ryan brought his hands around to Hayes's chest and pushed him gently up and off him. "I can't do that."

Hayes sighed, rolling his eyes. "You won't touch me, you won't let me fuck you. What *can* I do?"

"I'm...sorry. I'm just really nervous about...all this, Hayes."

"Fine. Well," he said, getting onto his knees on the bed next to Ryan. He grabbed his cock in one hand and ran his fingers all over Ryan's abs with the other. "Guess I'll just take care of it myself." Ryan watched him as he jerked himself off while touching and staring at him. "Your fuckin' body, Rook. Fuck. It's perfect." He gave himself a few quick tugs, pressed his cock against Ryan's abs, and moaned loudly as he shot off all over his stomach.

Without a word, Hayes went to the bathroom and came back with a towel. He chucked it at Ryan, who cleaned himself up as Hayes pulled his boxers and sweatpants back on.

"Never think of this when you're drying your face with a hotel towel, do you?" Ryan joked, but Hayes didn't respond. He climbed into the other bed, pulled the covers over him, and turned his back towards Ryan. "Hayes? I'm sorry..."

"It's fine, man," he interrupted. "I'm just tired. Long day. Get the light."

Ryan turned the light off and lay there staring at the ceiling. He knew he fucked up; he wanted so badly to play with Hayes more, but he got inside his own head. For God's sake, the kid had sucked his dick and he couldn't even help him out with a hand job?

Way to go, Baylor.

He couldn't fall asleep; he just kept tossing and turning, thinking about how he'd messed up. Unable to take it anymore, he got up and stood between the beds, trying to work up the nerve to climb in next to him. He found himself pacing again, frustratedly running his fingers through his hair.

Finally, he heard, "Rook, stop bein' a twat and get in the fuckin' bed already."

Hayes lifted the covers and Ryan slid in behind him, pressing his chest against his back. He wrapped an arm around the front of him and swung his leg over Hayes's legs, with Hayes immediately resting his hand on top of it. He leaned forward and gave him a few quick kisses on the shoulder. "I like this, Hayes. I like being with you like this."

"Me too, Rook." He sighed loudly. "Will anyone else though?"

NUMBER 47 (36)

Christmas.

Christmas was in three days.

This year was flying by, and Ryan could hardly process all that'd happened in the past few months.

For one, there was Amara and Jake. The two of them were spending an absurd amount of time together, and there had been several nights that she hadn't come home, about which Ryan confronted her.

"Listen, could you give me a heads-up if you're staying out?" he'd asked her one night as they sat eating dinner together at the dining room table.

"Yes, Dad. I'm sorry."

"Stop it. I worry about you, and I wait up for you. If I don't hear you come home, I can't sleep. And I don't wanna start blowing up your phone while you're...you know." He pushed his food around on his plate with his fork. *"Just please shoot me a quick text if you're staying out, OK?"*

"I can do that."

Things had *somewhat* returned to normal between them since their talk on the night of Hayes's birthday in the sense that they hadn't had sex or fought, both of which were praise-worthy accomplishments for the doomed duo. It wasn't that he was over her; hell, he'd probably never be. They were just distracted from one another, as both their attentions were currently focused elsewhere, with hers on Jake and his on Hayes.

Hayes.

That was another story altogether. After they spent the night together in the hotel room, things had been tumultuous, to say the least. Ryan woke up alone the next morning, with Hayes having moved to the other bed at some point during the night.

"Mar wasn't playin'. Like, are you OK? I don't think a human being should snore like that, man," Hayes had told him when he'd asked why he moved. *"Thank God I had a fuckin' old pair of earplugs in my bag or I'd have choked you unconscious."*

Ryan knew there was more to it than that, but he didn't press the issue. In the two weeks that had passed, there were no discussions of "What is this?" or "What are we?" They'd since hooked up a handful of times more, each time with Hayes pressing Ryan to fuck, and each time with Ryan completely punking out.

"You know, for such a sex god, you're awfully shy around me," Hayes had said, zipping up his pants after they'd jerked each other off in the back seat of Hayes's truck. He'd reached over and grabbed Ryan's hand. *"Rook, do you even like hookin' up with me?"*

Ryan reached his other hand to his face, kissing him gently. *"Yes. God, yes. It's all I think about. You...I'm just really nervous when it comes to you, and I don't know why."*

Truth be told, Ryan knew exactly why. Only Amara knew about them; Hayes hadn't even told Osi, and he told Osi *everything*. Even though they weren't really "dating," so to speak, whatever they *were* doing wasn't something either of them felt comfortable advertising just yet.

They'd nearly gotten busted once in the Bridgeport Islanders' training room after finishing a workout together. Hayes had hit him up for some tips on how to shred his abs, so Ryan had put together a stabilization routine for him that included an obscene number of planks, both regular and side.

"*I can't fuckin' hold it. I'm gonna die!*" Hayes complained, shaking like crazy as he fought his way through another one-minute plank.

"*You wanted to shred, right?*" Ryan said, on his knees in front of Hayes. "*This is how you shred. Hold it, hold it, come on, you got it!*" He'd slapped the ground and counted him down for his last few seconds. "*Come on: three, two, one, done!*"

Hayes fell face down onto the mat below him, groaning and panting. But he'd done it. "*My core is worthless, man.*"

"*Get into a cobra. That'll help.*"

"*The fuck's that?*"

"*Here.*" Ryan demonstrated it in front of where Hayes was lying. "*Pop your chest up, but roll your shoulders back, and keep your hips flat against the mat.*"

Hayes copied it, face-to-face with Ryan. "*Like this?*"

"*Almost. Just gotta...*" Ryan leaned forward, pressing his lips against Hayes's. He smiled and reached an arm up to Ryan's shoulder, playfully knocking him over so that he ended up lying on his back, upside down, with Hayes moving his arms on either side of his face.

"*That's better.*" He leaned down and stuck his tongue in Ryan's mouth, as the two began to suck face on the floor of the training room. They quickly pulled away from each other as they heard the door open, Ryan grabbing a nearby towel and Hayes standing up as Kasic and Dalesy walked in.

"*Jesus, Hayes. You're gonna knock someone out with that fuckin' thing,*" Kasic teased, pointing at the massive hard-on he was sporting. "*Can't blame you, though. Baylor in a compression tee and tights is bone-worthy, for sure.*" He walked by and punched Ryan lightly in the shoulder.

They'd driven back to the apartment parking garage in silence. Hayes parked the truck and finally said, "*We gotta be fuckin' careful, man. We can't do that shit anymore.*"

Ryan agreed, and then they proceeded to hop in the backseat and dry hump each other, rubbing their cocks together until they both came in their pants.

"Hey," Ryan said, knocking on Amara's slightly opened bedroom door. "Can I come in?"

"Of course." She opened it for him, and he entered, got a running start, and flung himself onto her bed, accidentally knocking over the suitcase she'd just spent 45 minutes meticulously packing. "Baylor!" she yelled, annoyed. "With your big ass."

"Sorry," he said, getting up to help pick it up, but she pushed him back down.

"I got it."

"So, you guys leave tonight?" he asked, grabbing one of her throw pillows, squeezing it, and tossing it up in the air.

"Yes. He's picking me up in a few minutes."

"Turks and Caicos, huh? Fancy way to spend Christmas."

"Yeah, well. He knows I hate Christmas, so I guess this is his attempt to try and cheer me up. And just so you know, I didn't let him pay for me. I paid for my half."

"That's...really none of my business, Amara. And who the hell hates Christmas? What are you, the fucking Grinch?"

"The woman who opened what she thought was a Christmas card last year, and it ended up being a sonogram of her husband's baby with another woman." She slammed the lid to her suitcase and smacked it. "That's who hates Christmas."

"I suppose that's warranted."

"Why are you all mopey, anyway? When are you leaving for Minnesota?"

"Tomorrow morning. I mean, I'm excited to go home, but I'm gonna miss you, and...him."

"Things any better?"

He sighed. "Nope. I don't know why I can't just let loose with him. I know it's frustrating the shit out of him. It's frustrating me, too."

"Anyone else know?"

He shook his head. "Just you."

"You guys'll figure it out. It's all new to you, Ry. You hated him, then became friends with him, then shared him with your ex-girlfriend, and now you're dating. It's a very confusing dynamic."

"We're *not* dating," Ryan corrected her.

"OK," she said sarcastically. "Keep telling yourself that."

"Speaking of dating," Ryan said, sitting up. "Since he's picking you up, can I meet him?"

"I...well, he's not coming up. I'm meeting him in the lobby." She gathered her suitcase and carry-on and brought them both over by the door.

He got up and followed her, still holding the throw pillow. "Then I'll walk you down, carry your bags for you. I wanna...I wanna meet him, Amara."

"Why?"

"I'm not sure."

"Listen, you will. I just...not yet, OK?"

They looked at each other. "Does he know about me? About us?"

She looked away. "He knows...that I have a male roommate. He doesn't know you're a 23-year-old smokeshow, doesn't know you're a professional hockey player, and he doesn't know we dated or slept together."

"I wouldn't really call what we did sleeping." He winked and threw the pillow at her, but she didn't react. "So that'd be a no then. Does he know about Hayes?"

"*Fuck* no, he doesn't know about Tyler. Are you insane? What happened with me and Tyler is the kind of shit a girl takes to her grave."

"You ever gonna tell him about either of us? I mean, we're a part of your life, Amara."

"Yeah, a part that I'm not ready to share with him just yet."

"From a guy's perspective? The longer you hide it, the more pissed he'll be."

"From a *jealous* guy's perspective, you mean. Jake's...he's not like that."

"Mar, you've known him for like, five minutes. You have no idea what kind of crazy he is."

"Well, some people don't air out their crazy right out of the gate like you did, Baylor."

He rolled his eyes. "You know what? Have a good trip," he mumbled, pushing his way past her and out the door.

She followed him. "Ry, wait!" She pulled the back of his shirt to stop him. "I'm sorry."

He turned around. "Don't be. You're right. I'm crazy." He threw his hands up in the air and let them fall. "I'm anxious, I'm a...what'd you call me? Oh, a pathetic slut, and apparently I'm fucking gay now, too. I'm such a horrible person that you won't even let your new boyfriend know I exist. I get it. There's nothing to be sorry for, Amara. I'm a fucking piece of shit, and you never miss an opportunity to remind me of it." He walked down the hall towards his room. "Don't follow me!" he called, slamming his door.

She stood there, motionless, as she got a notification on her phone.

J: I'm downstairs, beautiful.

Grabbing her bags and starting towards the front door, she turned and looked back at his room, wanting to say goodbye.

Instead, she just left.

❊ ❊ ❊

Ryan had just gotten out of the shower and was preparing to pack his bags for his trip out to Minnesota tomorrow morning when he heard a knock at the door. He threw on a pair of shorts and went to answer it.

"You really never wear a fuckin' shirt, do you?" Hayes asked, pushing past him while carrying a couple of wrapped presents. "Not that I'm complainin' or anything." He set the presents down on the counter and looked around. "Mar here?"

"Nope. Left with *Jake* for Turks and Caicos." Ryan mockingly said Jake's name.

"That old bitch didn't even say goodbye to me? Eww. Fuck this, I'm takin' her present back."

"She was upset when she left, so that's probably why."

Hayes rolled his eyes. "Lemme guess: you two fightin' again?"

"Not really. I mean, I called her out on something, and she wasn't trying to hear it. You know how she is. You can't tell her anything."

"Hmm. Sounds vaguely familiar," Hayes joked. "What happened?"

"I just asked if I could meet him real quick, and she said no. You know she hasn't even told him about either of us?"

"And this somehow surprises you?"

"Kinda, yeah."

"Rook, come on. You're not this dumb, man. Put it into perspective. You're 41, comin' off a horrible divorce, just puttin' yourself back out there, and you finally meet someone your own age that you can actually stomach. You gonna bring up the fact that you had flings and a fuckin' threesome with two well-endowed hockey players in their early 20s? That one fuckin' railed you senseless while you had the other one's dick in your mouth? Really think about that shit for a second, man. What dude is stickin' around after that revelation?"

"I never thought of what I had with her as a fling, Hayes. Not once."

"Well, Rook." He shrugged. "Unfortunately, that's what it was to her, man."

"Talk about a fucking gut punch."

"You gotta let her go. Ramara is not gonna happen." He grabbed Ryan's hand and dragged him over to the couch. "Now sit down so I can give you your present. I gotta head out early as shit tomorrow morning. Flight's at 6:00 a.m."

"Damn. You going to your mom's?"

"Yup," he said, grabbing the larger present from the counter and bringing it over to the couch. "Hopefully she won't be too wasted the whole time."

Ryan watched Hayes's face drop. He'd mentioned before that his mom was an alcoholic, but he hadn't really talked about it that much, so Ryan didn't push it, figuring he'd open up to him about it when he was ready.

"Anyway, so this," Hayes said, proudly handing the box to Ryan, "is for you."

"Wow, I…Hayes, I'm actually…I'm terrified to open this," Ryan teased.

"Oh, piss off. You're gonna regret that." He had a seat next to Ryan as he began to open it.

Ryan pulled back the lid to the box, moved the tissue paper, saw the royal blue, and stopped. "No. Hayes, I can't…"

"There's no one else I'd want to have it."

Ryan looked at him. "Are you sure?"

Hayes nodded. "Absolutely."

He reached into the box, carefully lifted it out, and held it up: the New York Islanders jersey Hayes had worn in his NHL debut game. He flipped it around, staring at his name and the number 47, which was his assigned number with the big club.

"I had it cleaned 'cause it fuckin' reeked like ass. But I wanted you to have it. I think...I *know* you're a big part of why I got there this year. Besides, your face was the only one I was lookin' for in the crowd that night, anyway."

Ryan put it down on the end table, leaned over to Hayes, and wrapped his arms around him, with Hayes doing the same. "I'll take good care of it, man."

"Fuckin' right you will."

Ryan pulled away from the hug, but Hayes kept a hold of his hand. Ryan checked the clock on the cable box.

9:07 p.m.

"So, I'm guessing you wanna call it an early night then?" Ryan asked, standing up from the couch and pulling Hayes up with him.

"I mean, you kickin' me out?"

"No. I just," Ryan said softly, running a hand down the front of his chest, "had a little something I wanted to give you, too."

Hayes stared at his hand, which began making its way to the waistband of his pants. "Is that right?"

"Yeah. Come on," Ryan pulled him gently by his waistband towards his bedroom. Once inside, Ryan shut the door behind them, leading Hayes to the edge of the bed, where he sat and watched Ryan remove his shorts. Hayes reached down and lifted his shirt over his head, tossing it aside, as Ryan straddled him, pushing him backwards onto the bed. Their lips met immediately, followed by their tongues, as they kissed fast and sloppily, hands greedily running up and down each other's bodies.

"Hey," Ryan moaned, grabbing Hayes and rolling over so he was underneath him. "I want you to fuck me."

"And you're sure?"

"Yeah. I'm sure."

"Hollup," Hayes said, climbing off Ryan and heading towards the door. "Be right back."

Perplexed, Ryan figured he knew what he was doing, and took the opportunity to get up and grab a condom from his nightstand. He heard Amara's door open and then close a few seconds later.

Hayes returned with a bottle of lube and tossed it onto the bed next to Ryan.

"Is that...from *her* room?" Ryan asked, shaking his head. "Never mind. I probably don't wanna know."

"No, you definitely don't," he said, removing the rest of his clothes, climbing back onto the bed, and sliding up next to Ryan, who began to flip himself face down, but Hayes stopped him. "Nah. I wanna look at you, and I want you to look at me."

"OK," Ryan said quietly, grabbing the condom and tearing it open with his teeth as Hayes straddled him.

"Um, you know I can't knock you up, right?"

"No shit," he laughed, as he rolled the condom onto Hayes's cock, bending both of his legs and moving his own cock up onto his stomach and out of the way. "It can get a little...I'd just feel more comfortable."

"That's cool." Hayes dumped the other half of the bottle onto himself, making an absolute mess of Ryan's comforter for the second time. "Dammit."

He lined himself up, as Ryan grabbed onto his shoulder with one hand, the other wrapped around his own cock. "Go slow, OK?" he whispered.

Hayes nodded, and pushed himself slowly inside, allowing Ryan's body to adjust to him. "You good, Rook?"

Ryan nodded, squeezing his eyes shut and biting down on his bottom lip, as Hayes went a bit further. It was a little uncomfortable, but he was determined for this to happen. "Keep going," he told him, starting to jerk himself off. "I want it all, baby."

"Don't gotta tell me twice." He pushed himself all the way inside, Ryan taking all of him, and began to thrust himself in time with Ryan's strokes. "Fuck," he panted, as Ryan opened his eyes and the two of them stared at each other. "You like that?" Hayes asked.

"Yeah. Oddly...fuckin' good."

"Good."

"You?"

"Oh my fuck, yeah."

They didn't take their eyes off each other for a second, Hayes leaning back onto his calves and grabbing Ryan's knees, continuing to fuck him steadily from a different angle as he watched him caress his own cock.

They didn't say a word. There was no need or desire for dirty talk; just the feeling of each other's bodies and the look in each other's eyes was sufficient for this moment they shared together, a first for both of them.

Hayes could tell by the increased pitch of Ryan's moans that he was about to cum, so he quickened his pace a bit. Ryan reached his free hand up to Hayes's face, pulling it down to his own, and shoved his tongue into his mouth. He whimpered onto his teammate's lips as he came all over his own stomach, with Hayes coming inside him just a few seconds later while moaning Ryan's *actual* name. Hayes pulled out and collapsed next to him, and they both lay there, silent, except for their heavy breathing.

Ryan reached a hand up to Hayes's hair and tugged lightly. "Hey. That's the first time you've ever called me Ryan and not Rook."

Hayes shrugged. "I got caught up in the moment, man."

"Does this mean I can call you Tyler now?"

"Do you wanna fuckin' die?"

"If I had to die, I can't think of a better place to do it than lying naked next to you on my bed...Tyler."

"Oh, for fuck's sake, piss off with the sappy shit, eh?" Hayes got up, off the bed and went across the hall to the bathroom, before coming back, handing some tissues to Ryan and putting his boxers and pants back on. "I'm gonna head out. I still gotta pack."

"Fuck me and run, huh? After all we've been through?" Ryan teased, cleaning himself off and pulling his shorts back on.

"Yeah, that's it. I have no more use for you now that I've massacred your tight, virgin asshole."

"That was way harsh, Ty," Ryan said, getting up from the bed and following Hayes to the front door, bummed that he didn't pick up on his perfectly timed *Clueless* reference. "Seriously? Nothing?"

"Hey. I'm gonna miss you," Hayes said softly, grabbing his hand. "I already can't wait to get back to you."

"Me too. I mean, I'm gonna miss you, not me. Unfortunately for me, I'm stuck with me."

"When you coming back?"

"When's the first practice?"

"The 29th, I think."

"Probably the 28th then."

"That's what I was thinkin', too." Hayes opened the door, kissed Ryan, and stepped out into the hallway. "Have fun at home, and I'll see you soon. Number 47." He winked at Ryan.

"I don't follow. Aren't you number 47?"

"Yeah, but so are you. The jersey? That's kinda the other reason I wanted to give it to you. You're…number 47 for me."

Ryan furrowed his brow. "I thought you said you were at 44 after Mar?"

"I was. And then there was a stripper out in Dallas…"

"Oh, Hayes. You banged a stripper?"

"What? You never banged a stripper, Mr. 500-Plus?"

"I have not."

"'Bout the only thing you haven't banged then. And there was a chick at Hughesy's beach house. So, numbers 45, 46, and," he said, poking Ryan's chest. "Number 47."

"But how did you know we would…"

Hayes smirked.

Ryan nodded.

"Merry Christmas…Ryan."

"Merry Christmas…Tyler."

HAPPY DAY, ALEX AND DAVIS (37)

"What time did you want me to order the food?" Amara asked, stocking the fridge with beers.

"Um, whenever. I think everyone's coming over around 6, so maybe like, right before then?"

"OK, so I think I've got everything covered. Beer's in the fridge, food, plates and shit." She wandered around the kitchen aimlessly, with Ryan eventually putting a hand on her shoulder.

"Hey. Stop stressing. It's gonna be fine," he told her, as she slumped down onto one of the stools.

"I can't help it. I'm so nervous."

"You guys really like each other, right?"

"At this point, I'd say that."

"Then you have nothing to worry about. If he likes you, he's not gonna care."

Amara sighed.

Tonight was the night she was finally going to introduce Jake to the two parts of her life she'd successfully squelched for nearly two months. It was January 16th, and also Ryan's 24th birthday. Having learned his lesson from the Hayes birthday debacle, when Amara asked what he wanted to do, he'd opted for a quiet night at the apartment with some of the guys, some Chel, and some food and beers. She planned and picked up everything, except the cake, which she left in the hands of Ryan's boyfriend.

That's right.

Boyfriend.

Having fought it as hard as he had, there was nothing else Ryan could call Hayes at this point, as nearly everyone knew what was going on between them.

When Ryan had gone home for Christmas, he sat with his mom, Luke, and Shannon at the kitchen table the first night, just drinking, shooting the shit, and catching up. A lot of things had come up during the course of the conversation, and then it happened.

"So, stud. You got a girlfriend out there yet, or you still 'Bang 'Em and Bolt Baylor'?" Shannon had asked him.

He felt himself getting nervous, but he figured these were the people, besides Amara and Hayes, with whom he could be the most honest. *"Dude, my mom's right there!"* he joked, taking a deep breath. *"And, uh, actually, I am...seeing someone."*

"That's awesome, honey. What's her name?"

Ryan looked at Luke, who gave him a nod. *"So, um, well... his name is Tyler, or Hayes, as I call him. And he's...my teammate."*

He'd waited for the shocked looks, the disappointed faces, the inappropriate comments, but they hadn't come. Everyone had just started asking questions about how long they'd been dating and what he was like, much to Ryan's pleasant surprise. Although, explaining what Hayes was like to anyone who'd never met him was always a challenge in and of itself.

He'd been getting ready to go to sleep that night when his mom knocked on the door of his childhood bedroom.

"Hey, Mom," he said, opening it for her. *"What's up?"*

"I just wanted to let you know, about what you said tonight..."

292

"Are you disappointed in me, Mom?" he interrupted sadly, fighting back tears.

"Oh, Ryan. I've never been disappointed in you a day in my life," she said, hugging him, as he fell apart in her arms.

He pulled away from her after a bit, wiping his eyes. "I didn't mean for this to happen. I'm so sorry."

"For what, falling in love? Ryan, I'm your mother. You don't think I already knew? All those girls, but somehow, none of them ever made the cut? Listen, take it from me. Life's too short and unpredictable to worry about what anyone else thinks. The only thing I want for my son is for him to be happy. Does this Hayes make you happy?"

He nodded. "Very."

"Then I hope to meet him sometime soon. I love you, Ryan. Not a damn thing could change that."

"Would Dad have said the same?"

"Of course he would have. He loved you more than anything. He'd be so proud of you."

The teammates were surprisingly accepting, as well. Hayes and Ryan had gone on somewhat of a "just wanted to let you know we're dating" locker room tour, starting first with Osi.

"You think I didn't know this? Has been weird shit going on with you two and Nick's hot cousin for long time now. Gay, bi, I don't care. You're happy? All that matters to me."

Kasic and Dalesy acted like they'd solved the final puzzle on Wheel of Fortune and won a trip to Tahiti.

"Fucking, I knew it!" Kasic yelled, punching Dalesy in the arm. "Yo, remember that day we showed up to train and Hayes popped up off the floor with that giant boner?

"Oh my God, yes! I forgot about that boner. Ha! You two? Duh!"

Nick was, of course, supportive, having first made sure Amara was OK with everything and that nothing was being done behind her back.

"Dunny, you'd fuckin' shit yourself if you knew half of what went down between the three of us," Hayes had told him. "But I assure you, she's fine with this. She's…kinda the one that pushed us to go for it. She sniffed it out long before we ever did."

And then?

There was Hastings.

They'd nervously knocked on his office door after practice one afternoon, sat down, and filled him in.

"So, do you two just wake up in the morning and say to yourselves, 'How can we fuck up Hastings's blood pressure today?' Do you? Is that what you two do?"

They looked at each other, then back at Hastings. *"No, Coach, that's not..."*

"Do you think I fucking care where either of you is sticking your cock? Knock yourselves out, boys. Have at it. But I'll tell you the same thing I tell everyone else: your personal life stays off the ice and it stays out of my fucking locker room. Last thing we need is any more flying chairs. Understood?"

"Yes, Coach."

They'd both walked out, giggling. *"That kinda went better than I expected,"* Ryan said.

"I don't know how he hasn't fuckin' quit yet. For real."

"So, I have a favor to ask you," Amara said, snapping Ryan back to the present.

"Anything."

"As far as he knows, you and Tyler are in a gay relationship."

He feigned shock. *"Are* we in a gay relationship? So *that's* why he's always trying to suck my dick." He clapped his hands together and pointed at her. "Mystery solved!"

"Ryan, he doesn't know about anything else. He doesn't know we dated or fucked, he doesn't know I fucked around with Ty, and he doesn't know about the threesome. And that's how I'm gonna need it to stay. You understand?"

"Fine," he agreed reluctantly. "But I still think it's bad practice to start a relationship by hiding a bunch of key things from the other person."

"Well, thank you, Dr. Phil. You get a boyfriend and all of a sudden you're a self-proclaimed love guru."

"Amara, chill. I'm not gonna say anything."

"I'm gonna go get ready." She got up and headed towards her room, passing by him on the way. She stopped and leaned in, kissing him on the cheek. "Ryan, I'm serious. Please don't fuck this up for me. For once since I came to Connecticut, I'm *actually* happy."

"I won't," he said softly, hoping he'd hidden the fact that her words felt like a straight kick to the nuts with a steel-toed boot.

"I tried to make you happy, Amara," he said quietly when he heard her door close. "I really did."

* * *

"You're fucking kidding me, right? You had one job, Ty. One job."

Amara stared at the cake in horror. "Who the hell are Alex and Davis? 'Happy Day, Alex and Davis'? Did you get the wrong cake?"

Tyler cracked up, bending over and smacking the countertop a few times. "Holy shit," he squeaked. "Your face!"

"What the fuck is this, Ty?"

"Relax. It's from *Schitt's Creek.* We watch it all the time. He'll get it. You're lucky. It was between this and 'Congrats, Mafuckas.' Hopin' I made the right call."

Tyler slapped her ass and went to the fridge, grabbing a beer. "I know, I know. I can't slap your ass anymore. Sorry. Old habits."

"Get it out of your system before Jake shows up. And you're getting the same speech your boyfriend got. He doesn't know about...anything. He knows you two are together, and that's it."

"Aww, you didn't tell him about how just a bit ago, you were all, 'Oh, Ty, I'm such a slut for your cock!'? Didn't mention that, babe?"

"Tyler! I'm not kidding. Not a fucking word."

"Hey," he said, hugging her. "I'm not gonna say anything. I wouldn't do somethin' like that to you."

"Promise?"

"Promise. But, um, there is something you should probably be aware of."

"And what's that?"

"Rook ate half an edible."

"I'm sorry? I'm sorry," she laughed. "I *thought* you just said Ryan ate half an edible right before the party where he's supposed to meet my boyfriend. Tell me I heard you wrong."

Ty shrugged.

"How long ago?"

"'Bout..." He checked his phone. "Almost an hour ago. Should hit him in the next hour, hour and a half."

Amara looked at the clock.

5:46 p.m.

Fuck.

She threw her hands up. "That's it. You're only job tonight, the only reason you exist on this planet right now is to babysit him and make sure he doesn't do anything stupid. You understand me?"

Tyler nodded. "I'll do my best. But, um, there's something else you should probably be aware of."

She buried her hands in her face. "Oh God. What now?"

"I, uh, ate the other half." He smiled, waving at her. "I'll probably be fine, but just wanted to forewarn you."

"Tyler Hayes. I'm going to fucking murder you."

❋ ❋ ❋

Things had gone well for a bit. People showed up, and the Chel tournament taking place in the living room was becoming quite the spectacle.

"Boom, motherfucker! That's how it's done! Just like real life, ain't one of you got *shit* on me!"

"Shut the fuck up, you cocky little bastard."

"Yeah? Your mom didn't seem to mind last night."

"Wait, you fuckin' pole-smoker. Don't you mean my dad?"

"Shit, I'll take 'em both on at once, you dusty fuckin' queef."

Amara snickered, listening to Tyler run his mouth to Seggy as she straightened up what she imagined it'd have looked like if a pack of ravenous wolves had raided her kitchen. "Fucking hockey players," she muttered, as 20 minutes after a metric shit ton of food had arrived, there was literally *nothing* left. "How the hell did they rip through all this food already?"

Thankfully, she'd caught Jake before he left.

A: Can you bring 8 pizzas? I'll explain later
J: Seriously?

J: You're lucky you're hot.

As Amara poured herself a glass of wine, taking a quick break, Ryan wandered into the kitchen.

"Hey, stud. How you feelin'?" she asked cautiously.

He stared at her blankly, his eyes barely opened, then busted out giggling. "I can't...I can't feel my arms!"

"Jesus, Ry. Well, look," she said, grabbing one and shaking it, then the other. "They're both right here. Why the hell would you...never mind. Because you're an idiot. That's why."

"Are you mad at me?" he whined, throwing his arms around her and leaning on her, damn near knocking her over. "It's my birthday. You can't be mad at me on my birthday."

"Tyler!" she yelled. "Come get your sloppy boyfriend before I knock him out!"

"Play for me, sweetie," he said, tossing the X-box controller to the chick Osi had brought.

"Wait, I have no idea what I'm doing!" she laughed.

"Figure it out!" he called back to her as he rounded the corner to find Ryan slumping over onto Amara. "Yup. He's fucked up."

"Yeah, no shit. And you?"

"Please, babe. It's gonna take more than half an edible to take me down."

"I'm not fucked up. I just can't feel my arms."

"Yeah, that'd be fucked up, Rook," Tyler said, pulling him off Amara and getting him over to one of the stools at the counter.

Just then, she heard a knock at the door, and she shot them both a death glare, pointing at them. "I watch nothing but murder shows. If you screw this up, I swear to everything holy, no one will ever find either of you. You understand me?"

She opened the door, and there stood who she assumed was Jake, unable to see his face behind the mountain of pizza boxes he was holding. "Can you help me please? My arms are literally on fire."

She grabbed five of them, holding the door open with her foot for him as he walked into the kitchen and set them down on the stovetop. She set hers down on the counter and turned towards him, wrapping her arms around his neck and leaning in for a quick kiss. "Thank you. You know, I, uh, don't have any money though," she teased, dragging a hand down the front of her chest slowly and licking her lips. "Think we can work out some sort of other method of payment?"

"You're sick," he said, kissing her again. "And I love it."

Before she could even introduce him to the boys, six more giant men rolled through the kitchen and started ransacking the pizza, acknowledging Jake in passing.

"Sup, man?"

"What's good, bro?"

"Good lord. Are you feeding an entire football team?" he joked, watching them load up, grab beers, and disappear back to the living room.

"Sorta. Hockey, actually. So, Jake. This, um…these…" she looked at Ryan and Tyler. "This is my…roommate, Ryan Baylor, and his boyfriend, Tyler Hayes."

"Um, OK. Wow," Jake said, blinking a few times and reaching his hand out to shake Ryan's. "It's nice to meet you, Ryan."

"I'd shake your hand, man, but I did an edible and can't feel my arms."

Tyler took over, shaking Jake's hand. "Don't mind him. It's nice to finally meet you, man. Mar's told us all about you. All good things."

She stared at Tyler, dumbfounded. His entire demeanor and tone had changed, and he'd actually strung together consecutive sentences without dropping a single f-bomb. He winked at her, nudging Ryan and walking him into the living room, leaving the two of them alone.

"You want a glass of wine?" she asked, taking a sip of her own.

"Yeah, why not?" He sat down on the stool where Ryan had just been. "So, he's younger than I expected. Wow."

"Yeah, he's 23, well, 24 now." She handed him the wine glass. "He's a professional hockey player for the Bridgeport Islanders. Ever heard of them?"

"I think so. Minor leagues, right?"

"Yeah, they're the AHL affiliate for the New York Islanders. Fun fact: they used to be called the Soundtigers," she said proudly, amazed at herself for having learned *something* about hockey. "Tyler and most of the other guys here are part of the team, too. Hence, the need for more pizza. These guys literally never stop eating." She took another sip of her wine. "I know I didn't tell you, but I didn't want you to feel weird about it, with him being so young. It's a long story how I ended up here, but he's a good guy. He and Tyler are...both really good friends of mine. I'm glad you finally got to meet them."

"I'm not gonna lie. It's a little weird, but I mean, whatever." He took a sip of his wine. "An older, hot divorced woman and two young hockey studs? Has all the makings of a horrible porn. Hey," he said, raising his glass to clink hers, "good thing they're gay, or I'd be worried about you with them."

"Yeah," she smiled awkwardly, clinking his glass and chugging the rest of her wine. "Good thing."

NEVER HAVE I EVER (38)

"Is this ever not gonna be weird?" Jonesy asked, walking by where Hayes and Ryan sat on the floor and mussing up Ryan's hair before taking a seat on the floor next to them.

Hayes's back was pressed against the wall, legs spread and knees bent, with Ryan seated between them. His arms were wrapped around Ryan's chest, with Ryan holding onto his forearms.

It was around 11:00 p.m., and only a handful of guys who were too drunk to drive remained: Jonesy, and Dalesy and Kasic, who were both sprawled out and taking up the entire sectional.

"Aww, do the big bad gay boys make you uncomfortable?" Hayes joked, reaching up to Ryan's face, twisting it to meet his, and shoving his tongue into Ryan's mouth. They kissed for a bit, then Hayes pulled away. "How about that? That better?"

"It's all good, man. It's just weird seeing your teammates hangin' all over each other, that's all," Jonesy said. "Especially when they were just bangin' the same chick like, a week ago."

"Uh uh," Hayes said, clearing his throat and making the slashing motion across his neck as Amara stumbled into the living room, having been in her bedroom with Jake for about the last hour or so.

"You guys are still hanging?" she asked, slightly slurring her words and sitting down near Hayes and Ryan. "Can you feel your arms yet, stud?" she asked Ryan, shoving him lightly.

"Yup." He waved them around. "You done fucking him? Pretty sure the whole sixth floor heard you two going at it."

"Jealous?" she said, to which Ryan rolled his eyes.

From the couch, Dalesy announced, "We were just about to play 'Never Have I Ever.' You old heads wanna get in on it?"

"Nope. No, we weren't," Hayes cut in. "We were not about to do *that*."

"Aww, why not?" Jake came in, having refilled both his and Amara's wine glasses and handing one to her before having a seat on the floor.

"Bro, you know you look just like Tyler Seguin?" Kasic chimed in.

"No. Who's that?" Jake asked, confused.

The guys groaned in disbelief.

"Plays for Dallas. He's only like, the hottest man that's ever played hockey and possibly lived," Ryan replied, leaning his head back onto Hayes's shoulder and looking at him. "No offense."

"He's actually not even that hot in person," Hayes added.

"You're a terrible liar."

Jake shrugged. "So, I guess that's a good thing?"

"Uh, yeah," Dalesy added. "You got those rock-hard abs like him, too?"

"Nah, I'm too old and I like carbs too much. Used to, though."

"Yeah, but look at your fuckin' arms, man. What do you bench?"

"Eh, I can put up 350, no problem. I can deadlift almost 500, though."

"Shit. Amara's out here dating the fuckin' Terminator," Kasic joked. "Quite an upgrade from this asshole." He pointed to Ryan.

"Uh uh," Hayes warned, giving him the death glare. "Nope."

"Upgrade?" Jake asked, turning toward Amara, who sipped her wine and made bug eyes at Kasic.

"Just...because they're always together, you know because they're roommates. That's all."

Jonesy changed the subject. "So, who's going first? Everyone got a drink?"

Amara started to get up. "Maybe we should just head back to my room," she began, but Jake held onto her arm and gently kept her in place.

"Nah, we can hang with these little boys. Besides, maybe we'll learn something new about each other."

"Yeah, why *don't* you stay and play, Mar?" Ryan suggested coldly. "I'm sure it'll get real interesting."

"Mar?" Hayes warned. "You don't have to play if you don't wanna."

"No, it's...fine. Fuck it, I can handle it," she said, taking a huge gulp of her wine. "Let's go then. I'll go first. Never have I ever hooked up with one of my teammates, current or past." She watched all five Bridgeport boys take a drink. "Mmhmm." She turned to Jake. "It turns out *all* hockey boys are a little gay."

"Apparently," he said.

"OK. My turn," Jonesy started. "Never have I ever hooked up with more than one person sitting in this room right now." He looked at Amara, who looked at Ryan and Hayes.

Ryan went to lift his beer, but Hayes pushed his hand down. Neither he nor Amara drank.

"Mmhmm," Jonesy grunted.

"My turn," said Kasic. "Never have I ever sucked Baylor's dick."

Hayes took a sip.

Amara didn't.

"We sure that's everyone?" Kasic asked. "No one else's gotten down on that sausage?"

"I'll go next. Never have I ever," Dalesy began, "made out with Hayes in the middle of the dance floor in a crowded club."

Everyone looked at Amara. She didn't drink.

Jake leaned into her ear. "Why do I feel like these are very pointed questions?"

302

"My turn," Ryan said, staring at Amara and sitting up and away from Hayes. "Never have I ever broken someone's heart."

Everyone except Ryan drank.

"I go again since everyone drank but me."

"Those aren't the rules," Amara protested.

"I make the rules," Ryan spat, continuing. "Never have I ever lied to someone about how I felt about them, making them think they were special when they were really just a selfish distraction from my fucked-up past."

Everyone except Ryan drank again.

"Guess I'll just keep going."

"Rook? That's enough." Hayes pulled him back toward him, but he pushed him off.

"Nope, we're just getting started."

"Nah, fuck it. It's my turn," Amara cut in. "Never have I ever treated someone like absolute shit simply because they didn't feel the same way I did about them and I was too goddamn immature to handle it."

"Aaaand, here we go," Hayes mumbled.

Ryan nodded, chugging. "OK. Never have I ever lied to someone I was dating about my *real* relationship with my roommate and his boyfriend because I'm so goddamn desperate to move on from it that I just don't give a fuck who I hurt in the process!"

Amara snickered, throwing back her entire glass of wine and chucking the empty glass against the wall, shattering it. "Fuck off, Baylor!" she yelled, popping up from the floor and storming off toward the front door.

The room went silent, as the front door slammed. Ryan got up to go after her, but Jake strong-armed him. "Leave her, man. I got her."

"The fuck you do, bro!" Ryan snapped, pushing his arm away, as they both got up off the floor and headed towards the door, with Hayes scrambling right behind them.

"Fuckin' ay!" Hayes bitched, flipping off the other three guys in the living room on his way out. "Great idea, you fuckin' twatwaffles. Really. Top fuckin' notch."

The four of them exited the apartment, leaving Dalesy, Kasic, and Jonesy alone.

No one said anything for a while until Dalesy sliced

through the silence with, "Never have I ever blasted a fart while getting head."

"I think the game's done, man," Jonesy replied, as he watched Kasic slowly raise his beer and take a sip. "Oh, you filthy bitch."

✳ ✳ ✳

"Hey!" Ryan called, jogging after her down the hallway. "Hey!"

She didn't turn around.

Hayes and Jake followed them as they headed towards the elevator. "You wanna be with her, man? You better get used to this shit."

She pressed the button for the elevator, as Ryan came up behind her. "And where do you think you're gonna go right now?"

"Someplace where you're not!" she spat back. The door opened, and she tried to get in, but Ryan reached out and grabbed her arm, pulling her back. "Don't fucking touch me, Ryan Baylor!"

Jake made a move like he was going to step in, but Hayes held him back lightly. "Relax. She can handle herself." Hayes pointed to the ground and took a seat so he could keep an eye on their argument, beckoning Jake to do the same. "This? Is what Rook and Mar do."

"Why the hell's it so contentious between them?"

Hayes snickered. "I wouldn't even know where to start. I will say this though: a huge part of the problem? They're the same exact fuckin' person. One just has a dick. Frick and fuckin' frack, those two."

She let the door close without getting on, and Ryan let go of her. "I asked you to please not fuck this up for me, Ryan."

"*You* fucked this up for you, Amara. Not me!" he yelled. "You ever gonna start taking responsibility for anything that happens in your fucking life, or you just gonna live forever as a victim?"

"Rook, it's late and we're in the hallway. Keep it down," Hayes warned.

"Oh, you've got some fucking nerve, kid! Those

questions? What the hell was all that?"

"Why won't you just be honest with him?" Ryan asked, motioning towards Jake. "He seems like a good enough guy, probably too good for you..."

"Oh, really? Well, everyone knows Tyler is entirely too good for you!"

Hayes shrugged, leaning over to Jake. "Can't fuckin' argue there."

They bickered back and forth while Jake and Hayes watched rapt, like it was an episode of *The Real Housewives of Bridgeport*. "What is it I need to know here, man?" Jake finally asked Hayes.

"Listen, whatever you need to know? Needs to come from her. Rook's immature as fuck, but he's got a point. You two need to have a talk."

They turned their attention back to Ryan and Amara, who were both using their hands like a couple of Italian grandmothers as they argued.

"I don't understand why you had to start your shit, Baylor. You're with Ty now, and I'm with Jake. Why is that not enough for you?"

"Because I'm still fucking in love with you!" he yelled, dropping to his knees and burying his face in his hands. "And I don't *wanna* be anymore," he whimpered, looking up at her.

"Ryan, *I'm* not in love with *you*. I never was, and I never will be. I love you, you're one of my best friends. But I'm not in love with you."

"I know that. That's why it hurts so fucking bad."

"You? Have to get over me, Ry. It's not fair to Ty. You have to."

Jake looked over at Hayes, surprised, expecting him to react. "Um, wow. And this is fine with you?"

"Listen, man. It's not a secret. I know he's stuck on her. He has been since the day he met her. I was for a long time, too. But what am I gonna do, get mad at him for feelin' what he feels? I don't love it, but I love him."

Jake shook his head and exhaled. "You're a much better man than I am. So you and her? You had a thing, too?"

"Like I said, man," Ty said, checking his phone. "Talk to her. You need to talk to her."

"This is all..." He stood up, shaking his head again. "This

is too much. I think I'm gonna take off."

The doomed duo was now both on the floor across from each other, seated directly in front of the elevator doors. Jake approached them cautiously, but neither of them even took notice of him.

"Do not lie to me: did you stop your therapy, Ry?"

He nodded slowly, avoiding eye contact.

"Why would you do that? It was helping. You were doing so well."

"I thought I was better," he said softly. "And I thought I was strong enough to do it on my own. I wanna be strong enough to do this on my own."

"Ryan, it can take years to get to the point where you're 'better.' It doesn't mean you're not strong. You're one of the strongest people I know. But you don't stop just because you think you're better. You need to see it through to the end."

"Hey, sorry to interrupt...whatever *this* is, but I'm gonna head out. I'll Uber home and come back for my car tomorrow. This is just...clearly, there's a lot going on here, and I'm in the way, so..."

Amara jumped up and tried to put her arms around him. "Listen, we should probably..." He pushed her away lightly. "So, that's it?"

"I don't know, Amara. All I know is that this? There's some weird shit going on here, and I don't really know if I wanna be a part of it." He pressed the button on the elevator and waited, as Ryan got up off the floor and backed away, giving them their space.

"So, that's it?" she repeated, tears welling up, as the door opened and he stepped on.

"Maybe we can talk about this later. Or maybe not. I just...right now, I need to go."

She watched the door close and stood there staring at it for a moment.

"Amara?" Ryan asked, but she turned away without a word and headed back down the hallway to the apartment, with Hayes following behind her.

Ryan caught up with him and attempted to grab his hand, but he pulled away and just kept walking. "Hayes? I'm sorry..."

Turning around, he shrugged his shoulders. "This

is...just a giant fuckin' mess." Ryan leaned forward and Hayes immediately put his arms out, pulling him in for a hug.

"I'm sorry," Ryan whispered. "I really like you. I'm just...I'm not over her, man."

Hayes broke the hug. "You *like* me? Aww, isn't that cute?" he said disappointedly.

"Hayes, that's not...I meant..."

"You meant what? You have no problem telling her you love her. Do you love me? Because I love you, Ryan. A fuckin' lot, actually."

"I think so."

"You think so?" He nodded. "Well, listen, I'm goin' home. This night needs to end. Do me a favor: let me know when you know for sure so I don't waste any more of my precious fuckin' time with you."

"Hayes, you're not wasting your time with me. Don't ever think that."

He changed course and started walking back towards the elevator, then flipped around to face Ryan. "You wanna continue this shit? Then a few things have to happen, Rook. For one, get your fuckin' ass back to therapy. Clearly, you need it. Two, you *have* to get over her. I don't know how many times you need to hear it from me, from her, but it is not gonna happen with you two. You know I love Mar to death, but I refuse to live in *anyone's* shadow, man. As much as I've always wanted it to be the three of us? It's not gonna. You have to let her go, for you, for me, and for her. And three?" He pressed the elevator button and it opened. He stepped in and turned to face Ryan. "You're gonna fix this shit with her and Jake."

The door started to close, but Ryan blocked it with his arm. "He needed to hear the truth."

"That wasn't your decision to make, Rook. That was hers, and you stole that from her. I don't agree with her hidin' it, and you might not either, but it wasn't your call. You're gonna fix it. I don't know how but figure it the fuck out."

Ryan moved his arm and watched the elevator door close.

"Happy fucking birthday to me," he mumbled, trudging back towards the apartment.

TRUTH HURTS (39)

It'd been almost two weeks.

Amara and Jake hadn't spoken at all. When she'd reached out to him the following day, he let her know that he needed some time to process all that had happened. She'd even offered to tell him everything, but he wasn't having any part of it.

"I like you, Amara. I really do. A lot. But whatever you have going on with those young boys? I don't want any part of that shit."

Once again, in an instant, she'd found herself in the same place she'd been when her ex-husband had cheated and after her divorce: lying in her bed, wishing death would swallow her whole. There was a small portion of it that was because of Jake, as she really did like him, but it was mostly a resurgence of excruciating memories that she had hoped never to revisit again.

She'd thought a lot about what Ryan had said to her that night in the hallway.

"You ever gonna start taking responsibility for anything that happens in your fucking life, or you just gonna live forever as

a victim?"

As much as it killed her to admit it, he was right.

None of this would have ever happened if she'd just been able to keep her hormones under control. Sure, she'd wanted to play around after her divorce, but never at the expense of those two beautiful boys' feelings.

For her to keep pretending this was all Ryan's fault was completely ludicrous. She'd taken him for all he was worth, knowing full well from the day they'd met that he wasn't a man who was mentally prepared to handle any of this. And truth be told, she'd done him dirty: she'd dated him when she didn't want to, she'd enabled his sex addiction by coaxing him into an open relationship, and she'd led him on after dumping him literal minutes after fucking his teammate in front of him.

She'd *broken* him.

And then there was Tyler, who she'd used for sex on multiple occasions just because she could, knowing damn well that as much as he tried to play it off, he had feelings for her, too. She had no right to lead either of them on the way she had, and despite all of it, both had stuck by her side, having taken care of her over the past couple weeks.

"Hey."

Ryan had knocked on her door on day two of her hibernation with a plate in his hand and a bottle of water under his arm. *"Can I come in for a sec? I just brought you something to eat. You need to eat, Mar."* He'd set the peanut butter and jelly sandwich, which looked like a blind, one-armed toddler had made it, and the water on her nightstand as she'd pulled the covers up over her head and rolled away from him.

"I guess you're still mad at me. I'll leave. Just wanted to make sure you had something to eat."

If she'd had any balls, she'd have told him the truth: she wasn't mad at him at all. She was furious with herself for the damage she'd done to him. He wasn't the same man she'd met in September, and she knew it was all her fault.

By the third day, when every single one of his texts had gone unanswered, Tyler's grace period had expired, and he arrived at her bedroom door. He'd come in without knocking, sat down on the bed next to her, and reached a hand up to her face, stroking her cheek.

"Why don't you shower? You'll feel better, and it's pretty fuckin' obvious you haven't." He waved his hand in front of his nose in a futile attempt to get her to smile, then pulled back the covers, slipped his hands under her arms, and helped her get up. He led her to her bathroom, set the water for her, and helped her get undressed, keeping his eyes squeezed shut the entire time.

"It's nothing you haven't seen before," she mumbled, stepping into the shower and closing the door behind her.

"I know. But I'm a fuckin' gentleman."

"You really are, Ty."

He'd gathered up some clothes for her, laid them on the bathroom sink, and waited in her room until she finished and re-emerged. *"Wanna go for a ride somewhere? Anywhere you wanna go. Ice cream, pick up some hookers. It's your world, babe."*

She shook her head no and climbed back into her bed, with him sitting next to her and resting an arm across her body.

"You and Ry OK?" she asked quietly, remembering how Ryan had told her he was still in love with her in front of Tyler, which she was pretty sure hadn't felt good.

"Yeah, we're fine. He's been suckin' my dick like, three times a day since that night, so I mean, I guess I should thank you. I think my balls are goin' numb."

"I'm sorry, Ty. I really am."

"Don't be. He gives a badass BJ. Like, the best head I've ever gotten. Good way to shut his whiny ass up, too."

"No, I mean I'm sorry for...everything. Everything that happened with Ryan, everything that happened with you. I used both of you guys. I didn't intend to, but I did. And I have an insane amount of guilt about it."

"Hey?" He ran a hand through her hair. *"I have zero regrets about anything that happened with you. We fuckin' had fun, Amara, and you led me and Rook to each other. Neither one of our stubborn asses would've ever acted on our feelings if you hadn't encouraged us."*

"I hurt him, Ty. I hate myself for it. He didn't deserve that."

"Nah, you both hurt each other. He wasn't innocent either. And not for nothin', but Ryan Baylor's been hurtin' girls his whole life. There's only so much shit you can throw at the world before it gets fed up and tosses some back at you." He patted her arm and

leaned in to kiss her on her forehead. *"You don't need to worry about Rook. I'm gonna take care of him, OK?"*

"You love him?"

Tyler nodded. *"So fuckin' much it terrifies me."* He got up from the bed and headed towards her door. *"I'll check in with you later, OK? If you need anything, you know where to find me."* He closed her door and left, and though she'd never been more grateful for another human being, it was time.

She knew exactly what she needed to do.

*   *   *

Ryan paced nervously outside the restaurant and checked his phone.

3:56 p.m.

He wanted to go inside, but he was too anxious. Going inside would make it real; at least out here, he could pretend he was doing something else entirely.

He'd been back to therapy twice since his birthday, explaining to Dr. Gephart everything that had gone down with Hayes and with Amara and Jake.

"I don't believe you're in love with her, Ryan. What I believe is that she's the first woman who's ever given you a run for your money. You're used to calling the shots, throwing girls away when you decide you're done with them, controlling who gets to come close to you. She came in and took that ability away from you. I don't deny that there's love between the two of you, but you're not in love with her, Ryan."

"Why does it hurt so bad then?"

"Sometimes our most painful experiences end up being those that we create within our minds."

"Hey," a voice said, and Ryan turned around to see Jake. "Why didn't you wait inside? Aren't you freezing?"

"I'm fine. Thanks for agreeing to meet with me."

"Yeah, no problem."

They headed inside, opting for a high top in the bar area. The waitress had immediately come over, they'd ordered a couple of beers and made some small talk until their drinks arrived at the table.

"So? I guess you're wondering why I wanted to meet up

with you," Ryan began.

"I think I have a pretty good idea, but let's hear it."

"I wanted to…" He took a deep breath and closed his eyes. "Sorry. I'm getting anxious. Give me a sec."

You need to explain things to him and fix things for her. She didn't deserve what you did to her and neither did he. He deserves to hear the truth, just like you deserve to hear the truth. You can do this.

He opened his eyes. "OK. I'm good. I wanted to let you know why all of that happened, and I'm hopeful you can work things out with her because she really likes you, man."

"I really like her, too," he said. "But Ryan? I'm almost 50 years old. I don't have time or patience for this bullshit. Especially coming off a divorce recently? I don't need any more drama."

"I can understand that. So, here's the deal: we ended up as roommates by chance. I needed someone to split rent with, and she needed a place to live. Her cousin is my athletic trainer and he arranged it. From the minute we met, there was an instant connection, and we began hooking up within a few weeks. I'm pretty sure I misinterpreted my attraction to her as love. I'm…kind of a whore, so I figured if we hooked up and I didn't wanna immediately forget she existed, it must be love, right? Anyway, she never wanted to date me. Amara is incredibly smart. She knew this shit would never work, but I kept pushing, and for whatever reason, she finally agreed. It… all got real messy after that."

Jake stared blankly at him for a few moments. "And where's your boyfriend fit into this equation?"

"They had a flirt fest in the laundry room the day she moved in, and they wanted each other ever since. Hayes could flirt his way into *anyone's* pants, clearly. He had a girlfriend at the time, though, so she wouldn't touch him. We eventually… shit," he paused. "We eventually had a threesome and she immediately broke up with me. We kept hooking up, but she was hooking up with him, too."

"Jesus," he muttered, looking away. "Is there anyone else? Do I need to get myself tested?"

"Trust me, I know this all sounds awful, but if you know anything about her, she's…she's been through hell. Has she told you what happened with her ex?"

"Yes, Ryan. We talk. I know a lot about her."

"Then you know what an amazing person she is. The first day I met her? I had a major panic attack, and she got down on the floor with me and walked me through it, didn't even hesitate. She's caring, she's nurturing, she's patient, she's…she's…"

He snickered. "She's banging a bunch of dudes half her age, too."

"Two. Not a bunch," Ryan corrected. "And she *was*. She isn't anymore. I haven't been with her since before Thanksgiving, and she and Hayes stopped as soon as you two got serious."

Sighing and taking a sip of his beer, Jake looked away. "I don't know, man. I don't know if I can get past all this. Oh, and side note: how the hell did *you* end up with Hayes?"

"Because of her. She knew we had feelings for each other before we even did. She encouraged us to go for it, and I'm so grateful she did because as it turns out, I'm…very much in love with him."

"You ever worry about getting traded? That happens all the time in pro sports, doesn't it?"

"Thanks, man. Didn't have enough to be anxious about already," Ryan teased, earning half a smile from Jake. "We would deal with it. The good news is that the paychecks are fat, so traveling to see each other won't be an issue, you know?" Ryan shrugged. "I'll make it work for him. I'll do anything I have to do for Tyler Hayes. But back to her: I know you're gonna do what you want, but I think you should give her another chance, man."

"You just turned 24. Hayes, what, just turned 21? So, she was banging him when he was 20? She's 41, Ryan. That's… fuckin' weird."

"You do any wild shit following your divorce?" Ryan asked, staring at him intently.

Jake laughed. "Touché."

"People do weird shit after divorces, man. She was cheated on and she wanted attention, wanted to feel beautiful, desired. We gave that to her, and she ate it up. Don't hold that against her. What woman doesn't want that?"

Leaning back in his seat and crossing his arms, Jake nodded slowly. "I gotta hand it to you, Baylor. It's obvious you really care about her, you and Hayes. It's not like you guys just used her."

"Against all possible odds, the three of us are incredibly close. We fight constantly, we get on each other's nerves, and we've all fucked each other. But no matter what bullshit shows up, we find a way to get through it. She's one of the best friends I've ever had."

"And you plan on keeping that friendship with her?"

Ryan leaned down and in towards Jake, lowered his voice, and said, "Not keeping it? Isn't even an option. You want her? You get me and Hayes, too."

"You trying to be a tough guy?"

Ryan laughed, throwing his hands up. "Yeah, was it at least sort of intimidating? I mean, you could literally bench press me, so."

"Not intimidating at all."

"Dammit. Honestly though: everyone comes with a story. And a story isn't just a single, straight line, right? It's a series of ups and downs, highs and lows. Don't judge someone's story solely based on one or two scenes or chapters you didn't like. It's..." Ryan stopped, then nodded. "It's a *really* good book."

SHE'S GONE (40)

Three days after his talk with Jake, Ryan had just returned to the apartment from the team's road trip to Charlotte, and he couldn't have been happier to be back home.

While there, the guys had all gone out after the game to one of the local spots, and a few of the Charlotte players were there. Hayes had gotten separated from Ryan for a bit, and when he'd finally reunited with him, he found him getting a little too cozy for his liking with one of the Charlotte defensemen out on the back patio. The other guy's arm was around Ryan, and while to any outsider, it looked like just two drunk guys chatting it up, Hayes knew better.

He approached them from behind, tapping Ryan aggressively on the shoulder. *"Just thought you should know I'm headin' back to the hotel."* He immediately turned to walk away, with Ryan calling after him.

"Wait, Hayes. I wanted to introduce you. This is Mike Kane. I played juniors with him. Mike, this is my boyfriend I was just telling you about." Hayes stopped and came back towards them,

Ryan reaching his hand out and pulling him over to where they were sitting. *"Come sit. We were literally just talking about you."*

Mike scooted over, and Hayes sat down in between them, with Ryan mouthing, *"It's OK."*

"Nice to meet you, man. Baylor hasn't shut up about you for like, 20 minutes straight. I'm glad to see all our intuitions were spot on."

"Yeah, it turns out, everyone knew I was gay but me."

Hayes had taken a deep breath, grabbed Ryan's hand, and the three of them shot the shit for a bit until Ryan decided it was time for them to call it a night.

Riding in silence for the entire trip back to the hotel, Hayes finally broke it when they were both in the bathroom, having just finished brushing their teeth.

"Rook?" he asked, palms pressed against the countertop and staring at Ryan in the mirror.

"Yeah?"

"You ever hook up with him?

"Does it matter?"

"No," He paused, then asked, *"Do I have to worry about you?"*

Ryan set his toothbrush down, wrapped his arms around his chest from behind, and stared at his beautiful boyfriend in the mirror. *"No. I love you. Tyler? I love you."*

"Will you tell me if you, you know..."

"No. Because it won't happen."

"I wanna believe that."

"Is there any reason not to?"

Hayes snickered, making a face at Ryan in the mirror. *"Have you met you?"*

"Yes, I have. Just recently, as a matter of fact. And you know what? For the first time ever, I kinda like myself. I'm in therapy, I'm working through the issues I've struggled with my whole life, and I'm in love with an amazing guy." He kissed Hayes on the cheek and let go of him. *"But I deserve your trust. And if you can't give it to me, then that's something you need to work on, not me."*

He left the bathroom, and Hayes followed him. *"I trust you, Rook."*

"Good. Because you have absolutely no reason not to. Your past doesn't define you, and my past doesn't define me." Ryan grabbed his hands, which were trembling. *"Our present and our*

future? Those are what define us. OK?"

Hayes nodded. *"OK."*

Ryan knew he'd never admit it to him, but Hayes was terrified.

And truth be told, so was Ryan. But he knew one thing: he was more terrified of a life without Hayes in it than anything else, and he wasn't going to fuck this up, too.

As he waited for Hayes to come up, having stopped at his apartment to drop his things off and grab some clothes, he went into his room and set his travel bag down next to his dresser. Glancing at the picture of him, Amara, and Hayes out of habit, he noticed there was an envelope propped against it with his name on it. Confused, he picked it up, opened it, and began reading.

> **Ryan,**
>
> **There are no excuses for what I've done to you. I was reckless in my treatment of you, something you didn't deserve.**
>
> **There is so much more I have to say to you in person, and someday, I will.**
>
> **For now, I've paid the remainder of my portion of the lease, and I truly hope you can understand why I couldn't stay.**
>
> **You did everything right, Ryan. I'm sorry I didn't.**
>
> **Amara**

On about the fifth read-through, he rushed over to her room, thinking maybe she was playing a cruel prank.

All her things were gone off the dressers.

Out of the bathroom.

Out of the closet.

Ryan stood there, lost in his own thoughts, and hadn't heard Hayes come into the apartment. "Rook, what are you doin' in here, man?"

He turned and handed the letter to him, watching his face sink as he read it. "What the..."

"She's gone, Hayes. She moved out."

"Fuck."

"Did you know about this?"

"Swear to God, Rook. I had no fuckin' idea."

Ryan shook his head. "She's gone."

"It was just a matter of time, man. Honestly? It's probably for the best."

* * *

"So, what is it you wanted to talk about?" Amara asked Jake, as the two went for a stroll along the marina after enjoying an entirely-too-expensive dinner.

Being mid-March now, the weather wasn't as excruciatingly cold as it had been the past few months, though it was still a bit windy. There was enough she loved about Bridgeport, but Connecticut weather, Amara had decided, could suck it.

The two of them had reconciled shortly after Jake's talk with Ryan, and after she'd moved out of the apartment and into an extended-stay hotel about 15 miles out of Bridgeport, though she'd waited for him to initiate it. She'd quit her bartending job at The Bull and decided to focus her attention on her freelance writing, but she still kept in touch with Dani at least once a week.

"You haven't spoken to them at all? Nothing?" Jake had asked her, right after learning that she'd moved out.

"No. I haven't spoken to either of them since I left. Tyler checks in every few days with a 'You still alive?' text, to which I reply that I am, but aside from that? Nothing."

"When Ryan and I spoke, he had only amazing things to say, Amara. He cares about you."

"And I care about him too. So much, which is why I left."

"Just so you know, I'm fine with you staying friends with him, if that's something you feel you need to do. It's totally fine. It's still a little weird, but I'm fine with it."

"OK, Ross. I'm glad you're fine," she joked. *"What I need to do is move on with my life and let him move on with his."*

"You don't miss him?"

"I miss Ryan every damn day."

"Then why don't you talk to him?"

"Because," she'd told him. *"There's too much I need to say*

318

to him that I'm not ready to say yet."

And two months later, it all remained unsaid.

Aside from the occasional text exchange with Tyler, Amara hadn't spoken to either of them at all. Tyler wasn't happy about it, but he understood.

T: Mar, I told you, I'll do whatever I have to do if it means you're happy, and I meant it. Do what you gotta do, OK?

T: When you're ready, I'll be here. I told you, I'm not going anywhere.

"Here, sit down," Jake told her, taking a seat on a bench along the walking path, which overlooked the bay. "It's breathtaking out here, isn't it?"

"It really is," she said, running her hands up and down her arms. "It's so damn cold and windy, it takes your breath away."

"Interesting segue. So, the reason I brought you here is because..." he paused. "My construction company is relocating. To...Florida." He reached over and grabbed her hand.

"And I'm guessing that means you're relocating, too?"

"Yes," he said slowly. "And I was thinking that maybe...you would like to...relocate with me."

She laughed, shaking her head. "We've known each other for like, four months, Jake."

"And? If I didn't bail after the 'Never Have I Ever' debacle, I think we're good," he said with a wink. "Hey: I want you to come with me. There's nothing tying you here, Amara. This place served its purpose for you."

"I kinda like it here," she replied quietly.

"You'll like it in Florida, too. I promise. It's warm all year round, and where the company's moving is right on the Gulf Coast. Here," he said, pulling out his phone, typing for a bit, then handing it to her. "This is the house I'm buying."

She began scrolling through the pictures, mouth agape. It was an exquisite, elevated 1800-square-foot home directly on the water, complete with a dock and an enclosed swimming pool and hot tub combo. There was an elegant wooden gazebo that overlooked the Gulf with access to a private beach. He reached his finger over and started scrolling for her. "Hold on, this...where is it?" He stopped at a picture of an office. "I was thinking this could be your writing room."

"Wow. It's really something," she remarked, pretending she didn't see the $1.2 million listing price and $16,000 a year in property taxes.

"Come with me," he said, taking the phone from her, turning to face her, and grabbing both her hands. "I can make you happy."

"Happy," she repeated sarcastically. "What's that feel like?"

"It feels like you getting to live your life for *you*, Amara. Between your ex, then all the bullshit with Ryan, you've gotten so used to living for other people that you forgot that you deserve to live, too."

"I take care of people," she said sadly. "That's what I do."

"Then maybe it's time you let someone take care of *you*."

"I can take care of myself, Jake. Been doing it my whole life."

"I know you can. But just because you can doesn't mean you should have to. You don't have to decide right now. You can always come down later when you're ready."

"When are you leaving?"

He sighed. "Next week. The transfer is happening on Tuesday, and we're headed down right after."

"Wow. OK. That doesn't give me a whole..."

Her phone rang, and she checked the screen. "Yale New Haven Health? Who the hell?" She put up a finger as she took the call.

"Hello?...Yes, this is she...Uh huh...uh huh...Oh my God...Yeah, I'll be right there."

Horrified, she hung up and turned towards Jake.

"What's the matter?" he asked her, immediately taking notice of the tears streaming down her face.

"It's Ty."

THE INJURY (41)

They'd gotten to Bridgeport Hospital in a matter of minutes, thanks to Jake's Formula One-worthy driving performance.

"Text me and let me know what's going on. I'll be in the waiting room," he called, as he dropped her off at the emergency room entrance and went to park the car.

Running into the building, she immediately went to triage. "Hi, I'm here for Tyler Hayes." She tried to fight it, but she burst into tears. "I got a call that he...was brought here by ambulance from Total Mortgage Arena and...that he was unresponsive. I'm his emergency contact, Amara McDonough."

"Just a moment, ma'am," the woman said, typing and scrolling on her computer screen.

"Is he OK?"

"One moment." She continued typing on the computer for what felt like hours, then finally said, "He's stable now. You can go back and see him. Wait here, and I'll have someone bring you back as soon as I can."

"OK, thank you."

She apprehensively paced back and forth, unable to even consider sitting down, until finally, a nurse came out to get her. "For Tyler Hayes?"

She nodded.

"Follow me."

Heading down a long hallway past rows of patients, she finally made it to where Tyler was. When the nurse pulled the curtain back, he lay in a bed, hooked up to all sorts of monitors that were beeping and blinking a million different ways, with an IV in his arm.

"Mar," he whimpered upon seeing her, and she raced to his bedside, grabbing his hand as he began sobbing.

"Baby, what happened?"

Unable to get any words out, she waited for him to calm down a bit. "I don't know. The last thing I remember before waking up in the ambulance is that I was behind the net fightin' for the puck. I saw the guy comin' in from my peripheral, and I don't know what happened after that. They told me I was unconscious for a while. All I know is my shoulder is fuckin' killin' me. This could...Mar, if it's my shoulder again, this could be the end of my career."

"No, stop it. Don't even fucking talk like that!" she scolded him, caressing his hand as he began sobbing again. "They'll fix you right up this time just like they did last time. You're gonna be fine, OK?"

They sat together quietly for a bit, as she stared at his heart rate and blood pressure readings on the screen, both of which were bouncing wildly like a pinball. Suddenly, he sat up. "Mar, get the..." he heaved, "trash can."

Before she could grab it in time, he turned his head away from her and threw up onto the floor. She handed it to him so he could finish and ran out into the hallway.

"Hey! We need some fucking help in here!" she yelled.

A nurse approached her. "Ma'am, please keep your voice down and watch your language. What's the problem?"

"I'm sorry, it's...my friend. He was brought here after being hit in...his hockey game, and now he's vomiting. Please...help him!" she cried, remembering having heard somewhere that vomiting after a concussion was a bad sign.

"OK, we'll take care of it. Just calm down, OK? Why don't you wait out here while we get him cleaned up?" She pointed to a chair in the hallway, and Amara reluctantly took a seat, as she listened to him continuing to vomit.

Suddenly, it dawned on her.

Ryan.

Ryan must have been an absolute fucking mess right now.

Pulling out her phone to give Jake an update, she noticed there was already a message from him.

J: Ryan's here. I've got him, but he's flipping the fuck out.

* * *

The game had been an absolute barn burner, with Springfield and Bridgeport having been knotted five to five at the start of the third period. Both teams had been playing amazing hockey, but the tension was becoming thicker by the minute and emotions were beginning to get the better of both teams.

Hayes, in typical Hayes fashion, hadn't stopped running his big mouth from the moment the game had started, having taken two minutes for delay of game after yanking one of the Thunderbirds' sticks away from him and launching it into the crowd like a scud missile. The ref hadn't even known *what* to call him for, as he'd never seen anything like it, but decided that delay of game was probably most appropriate.

"Aww, come on! He deserved it, the fuckin' piece of shit," he'd argued with the ref as he skated backward towards the box. "You know why I did it, right?"

"Get in the box, Mouth," the ref ordered.

"He called me a fuckin' faggot. So, we're cool with that kind of homophobic language? You know I'm currently dating a dude, right? Fuckin' him right in the ass!" he yelled, as the ref skated away, and he entered the penalty box. "Thought hockey was for everyone, bitch!"

Skating back over to him, the ref said, "I'll address his language with him. But you can't toss your opponents' sticks into the crowd, and you can't call me a bitch. I'm giving you two more for unsportsmanlike conduct. Now shut your mouth unless you wanna make it a 10."

"Are you fucking kidding me?" Hayes screamed as Rizz skated over to the box.

"Hayes, shut the fuck up!" he barked, skating over to the ref to sort out the penalties. Moments later, he saw the other guy enter the box for a two-minute unsportsmanlike as well, so he backed off.

When he'd gotten out of the box with 12:25 left in the third, the stars had aligned and he'd ended up on a breakaway, taking it right into the offensive zone, where he was quickly met by their defense and ended up in a puck battle behind the net. His head was down, about two feet in front of the boards, and someone had screamed, "Hayes, look up, look up!"

It was too late.

There was a loud *crack,* followed by a *thud,* and Hayes lay motionless on the ice. Everyone immediately stopped playing, and the crowd went almost silent. Ryan, who'd watched in horror from the bench, was the first to his side, with Nick right behind him.

"Hayes! Hayes!" Ryan yelled, kneeling next to him. "He's not moving. He's not fucking moving!"

Rizz and Kasic skated over and pulled Ryan away. "Hey, let Nick get to him, OK? Let Nick do his job. He's gonna be alright. He just got his bell rung, brother."

Before long, the medics made their way onto the ice with a stretcher, had loaded Hayes onto it, and were wheeling him down the tunnel and toward the ambulance. They'd managed to get Ryan back to the bench, as Hastings came up behind him and grabbed onto both his shoulders. "He'll be OK, kid. Just keep your head on straight. He'll be OK."

The guy who'd charged Hayes, number 53, had somehow gotten away with only a double-minor for cross-checking, and the Islanders' bench lost its collective mind. Rizz had argued so hard with the ref, they were sure he was going to get a game misconduct, and Hastings took a bench penalty for calling the ref a "blind piece of flaming, decrepit monkey shit," or something along those lines.

Coach Reilly had benched Ryan for the remainder of the game for two reasons: first, because he knew his head wasn't on right, and second, because he didn't want him to catch a murder charge. When Hastings had called a timeout at the three-minute mark, Rizz and Ryan devised a little non-verbal agreement.

When it came time for the face-off, number 53 was out for a shift. Rizz nodded at Ryan, and as soon as the puck dropped, Rizz made a beeline for the bench, and Ryan launched himself over the boards.

"Baylor!" Reilly hollered. "Rislan, what the fuck?"

"Sorry. Skate issues, Coach." He shrugged.

Gripping his stick like a baseball bat, he raced up behind number 53 and cracked him right across the lower back, dropping him immediately. Throwing his stick and gloves to the ice, Ryan jumped on top of him and, with a flashback to Gilgo Beach, began pounding on his face. He'd gotten about three good punches in before two Thunderbirds yanked him off their teammate and proceeded to beat the ever-loving shit out of him, resulting in a bench-clearing brawl complete with Rock 'Em Sock 'Em goalies.

Ryan had been ejected, and after dragging himself to the locker room covered in blood, he tore off his gear, leaving it all on the floor of the locker room. He threw on his suit pants and dress shirt, snagged the Raptor keys from Hayes's stall, and hauled ass to the hospital, driving with the one of his eyes that wasn't swollen shut.

Ryan Baylor knew he was in deep shit, but at that moment, the only thing that mattered to him was Tyler fucking Hayes.

I DON'T HATE
YOU, TOO (42)

Amara could hear Ryan carrying on from the hallway, as she hurried back towards the ER waiting room. Rounding the corner, she saw Jake with his arms around him, trying to calm him down near the main entrance.

"Sir, you're gonna have to take it easy," one of the ER nurses told him.

"Why won't you let me see him?" he yelled, as Amara approached him. Jake let him go and Ryan threw himself into her arms. "They won't let me see him, Amara!"

"I'll take care of it. Don't worry," she told him softly, running her hands up and down his back and making a face at the foul stench that was coming off him. He hadn't had a chance to shower after the game, and it'd never been more obvious. Turns out, all the rumors about how repulsive hockey equipment smelled?

All true.

He pulled away from her and she examined him: his dress shirt had several blood stains on it, which she assumed were from his face, as his one eye was completely swollen shut and there was a bloody gash along his forehead that could probably use a stitch or two.

"Ma'am, does he need to be admitted?" the nurse asked her, looking him up and down. "He's not lookin' too good."

"No, he's fine. He's just here to visit his boyfriend, and apparently, he's being told he's not allowed to."

"One visitor per patient, ma'am. Emergency contacts only if they're available, unless the patient is a minor. That's our policy."

"OK, well since I'm not back there now, can he take my spot?"

"Please?" he begged. "I gotta...I gotta see him."

The nurse rolled her eyes. "Lemme see what I can do. Get him settled down, please. He can't be in here freakin' out like this."

"OK. Thank you very much." Amara turned towards a row of unoccupied chairs near the bathroom, away from the other people waiting, who'd been attentively watching all this go down.

They sat, Amara on one side of Ryan and Jake on the other.

"Thanks for staying with him," Amara told Jake.

"Of course."

Ryan collapsed forward, leaning on his arms against his knees and shaking. Jake reached his hand around his back, grabbed his shoulder, and squeezed, then patted it a few times. "It's gonna be OK, man. Just try to relax."

He lifted his head up and leaned back against the wall, before popping up out of his chair and beginning to pace back and forth in front of them. "He was unresponsive. I heard them saying something about a possible broken neck..."

"He's awake, Ryan. I was just talking to him back there. His neck isn't broken, and he's awake and alert."

Flopping back down into his chair, he leaned over onto Amara and began sobbing. "Really?"

"Yes, really. I haven't had a chance to talk to the doctor yet, but I don't think it's terrible. He was complaining about his shoulder, though, so I'm not sure if he reinjured it."

He sat back up in his chair, unable to keep still for more than 30 seconds at a time, but she was proud of him: he should've been in the throes of a full-blown panic attack at this point, and he wasn't, which defied all logic.

"Can we talk about what happened to you for a second, Ry?"

"Let's just say I'm in deep fucking shit."

"You get tossed?"

"Oh yeah. Coach Reilly benched me, but Rizz had my back. First chance I could, I went after him. Teed off on him with my stick and beat his ass, 'til his teammates got a hold of me and returned the favor." He motioned towards his battered face. "Both benches cleared, the goalies fought, the crowd was going insane. This is gonna be all over the news, social media. A complete shit show. It was a dirty fucking hit, Mar. Filthy. That dude charged him from the blue line, wasn't even in on the battle. Fucking stripes let him go with a double-minor for cross-checking. I wasn't having any of that shit."

"That's it? A double-minor? Charging should be at least a five, possibly with a game misconduct!" Amara exclaimed, causing both Ryan and Jake to whip their heads in her direction. She shrugged. "What? I've been doing some reading."

The nurse approached them, and both Amara and Ryan stood up. "So, we only allow one visitor, and you can't switch them out. But since you're his..." she winked at Amara, "mother?"

She nodded. "Yep. I'm Tyler's...mother."

"And since this is your other..." she winked at Ryan, "son?"

Ryan nodded. "Yeah. He's my...brother."

"Since you're both immediate family, I am going to make an exception and allow you both back." She turned to Jake. "You Dad?"

He shook his head. "Nope. I am definitely *not* Dad. Though she has been known to call me Daddy from time to time." The nurse pursed her lips and turned away, as Amara shot him a death glare. "Sorry. That...went over much better in my head."

"Follow me, family." They went with the nurse, with Amara turning back and running towards Jake.

"You don't have to stay if you don't want to," she said, giving him a quick hug and a kiss on the cheek.

"I'm not going anywhere."

She smiled at him. "Thanks...Daddy," she teased, running to catch up with Ryan and the nurse, who'd already begun making their way back to Tyler.

They got to Ty's room, and the nurse pulled back the curtain. "If he falls asleep, wake him up. They don't want him sleeping until he's been seen by the doctor."

"And is that going to happen soon?" Amara asked.

"As soon as it can, ma'am." She turned and left, and both Amara and Ryan entered the room, where the slight smell of vomit lingered, though it was somewhat of a welcome distraction from Ryan's post-game funk.

"Rook!" Ty whimpered, as Ryan hurried over to him, leaned down, and hugged all the life that remained out of him. Both boys immediately started crying, which, of course, triggered Amara's tears. Tyler's monitors began beeping wildly, and Amara pushed a chair over towards Ryan.

"Don't lean on him. You're pinching off his cords. Here, sit."

Ryan sat, grabbing Ty's hand with both of his. "Hey," he said. "You scared the fucking shit outta me, you know that?"

"Never mind me. The fuck happened to *you*?"

Ryan cocked his head. "What the fuck do you *think* happened to me?"

"So, when you say you're in deep shit, what do you mean?" Amara asked him, pulling a chair in from the hallway and sliding it over next to Ryan.

"I'm gonna have to go to hearing. I'll probably get suspended and fined. I might...what's it, March? They hit me with a 10 or 15-game, I'm done for the season."

"You sure you even got any hits in? Looks like you got your fuckin' ass handed to you like a little bitch."

"There's the Ty we all know and love," Amara teased.

"I chopped him with my stick, right in the kidneys. Dropped him."

"Yep, you're done for the season. Dude that hit me at least get tossed?"

"Nope. Double-minor. Cross-checking."

Ty shook his head. "Un-fuckin'-real. It's 'cause it's me. If it was anyone else, dude woulda been kicked outta the league and sent to a Russian gulag."

"So, FYI: if anyone asks? I'm your mother and Ry's your brother. That's the only way they'd let him back here."

"Wow. OK. Little West Virginia action goin' on, eh?"

"This is one fucked-up family right here," Ryan added.

Amara reached over, resting her hand on top of both of theirs. "It sure is." She noticed Ty was beginning to dip out, so she nudged Ryan. "Wake him up."

Ryan shook his arm gently.

"Fuck, Rook," Ty bitched. "I'm so tired."

"No sleeping until you see the doctor," Ryan added, leaning toward his face and kissing him lightly. "Need me to keep you awake?"

"Not until you shower, you fuckin' animal. I could smell you from the hallway."

Ryan laughed. "Well, you kinda taste like barf, so let's call it even. Also, um, I don't know if this is the best time to tell you this, but I smacked a median with your truck. Pretty sure I bent the rim."

"Of course you did. You finally learned to skate, now it's time to learn how to fuckin' drive!"

"You love me," he said softly, leaning in for another kiss just as the doctor came in. Amara cleared her throat loudly as Ryan pulled away.

"Hello, Hayes family. I'm Dr. Ramara..."

"Oh, shut the fuck up!" Ty yelled, laughing. "*Ramara*?"

Ryan shrugged. "I guess Ramara *is* happening after all."

"I'm sorry?" he asked, confused.

"Forget it, "Ty said. "So, am I fuckin' dyin' or what?"

"No, you're not dying. I understand you were hit during your hockey game. I've spoken to your athletic trainer, but do you remember anything?"

"Not a fuckin' thing. Was playin' hockey one minute and woke up in an ambulance the next."

"So, we're going to run a series of tests on you. In a moment, I'm going to ask your family to leave so I can perform a neurological examination and a series of cognitive tests, at which point we're going to send you for a CT scan, just to assess the brain, make sure there's no swelling or bleeding. You're not really exhibiting signs of a severe injury, but since you're an athlete and you vomited, we're going to err on the side of caution. More than likely, we're gonna keep you overnight for observation, and if there are no complications, you'll be released tomorrow."

"I've always heard vomiting is a bad sign after a concussion," Amara chimed in.

"Repeat vomiting is. It's possible this was caused by stress from an adrenaline dump. Since it was only once, I'm not too concerned about it."

"Why does he have an IV? You can't give him any pain medication yet, right?"

"For fluids. With concussions, especially when loss of consciousness is involved, there's always the risk of vomiting, so we usually don't allow patients to eat or drink. Any other pain, Tyler?"

"My shoulder. I had surgery for an AC separation about a year ago, and it's...I think I reinjured it."

"We'll get you an X-ray for that, as well. Mom, brother? I'm gonna ask you guys to step out so I can perform some tests now. You can wait in the hallway."

Ryan kissed his hand. "You got this," he said, getting up and walking towards the door. "Oh, by the way," he stopped in front of Dr. Ramara. "If you're looking for cognitive function?" Ryan shook his head. "He doesn't have that on a normal day."

"Fuck off, Rookie."

"I'll keep that in mind," he said with a smile. "Son, you should probably get some ice on that eye. Mom, stop by the nurse station, let them know you need an ice pack."

"Will do. Come on, son." She grabbed Ryan by the hand, and they left the room. Amara checked her phone, and there were a few messages from Jake.

J: There is a legitimate entourage of people here for Ty. Nick already notified his real mom, FYI. She's on her way.

The next message was a picture of the waiting room, where Nick, Hastings, Reilly, Osi, Kasic, Dalesy, and Rizz all sat waiting for Ty. She smiled, showing it to Ryan. "You guys really are like one big family."

"Yep. One big, fucked-up family," Ryan said, checking his

own messages and typing a quick update to Luke.

He looked over at her.

"So."

"So."

"You've been OK?" he asked.

She nodded. "You?"

He nodded, and they both moved to hug each other at the same time. She inhaled deeply out of habit, expecting to breathe in his signature cologne and deodorant combo, but quickly remembered the olfactory details of the current situation and pulled away.

"Thank you," he said quietly.

"For what?" she asked, confused.

"For moving out. I never got the chance to thank you. It had to happen. I fought it for a long time, but I know it...it needed to happen."

"I know. And you're welcome."

"So where are you living? Dani won't talk, and Ty swears you haven't told him."

"I haven't. But I can tell you where I *will* be living in about a week."

"And where's that?"

She hesitated, then finally said, "Florida."

"Florida?"

"Yep. Jake's company is relocating, and he asked me to go with him. I'm gonna...I'm gonna go."

Ryan sighed, sitting down on a nearby chair, as they'd both been standing. "Amara?" He closed his eyes, took a deep breath, exhaled loudly, then opened them. "I think that's a really good idea, and I'm happy for you."

"Yeah?" she asked, surprised. "You like him?"

"Very much."

"He likes you, too."

"I know," he said. "We talk."

"Oh, do you, now?"

"Yup. We're practically besties at this point."

"Right. Listen, Ryan, there's so much I have to say to you, I don't know..."

He shook his head and brought a finger to his lips.

"But I treated you like shit, Ryan..."

"You did the best you could with what you had in your

arsenal at the time, Amara. I don't hold anything against you. Nothing. No hard feelings, no ill will. You pulled so much out of me that I wasn't ready to deal with, refused to deal with, and you forced me to face some truths about myself. Sometimes, the universe has a fucked-up way of getting you to do what it needs you to do." He shrugged.

"So, you don't hate me?"

"No, I don't hate you, Amara McDonough. Quite the opposite."

"Well, I don't hate you, too, Ryan Baylor."

BREAKING RYAN BAYLOR (43)

"You nervous?" Hayes asked, as the ETA on the GPS now showed two minutes.

"Why would I be nervous?" Ryan asked.

"Um, let's see. Were you around for the last eight fuckin' months, or did I dream all this shit?"

"Why? Are you?"

"Nah. More excited than nervous. I miss her, man."

"Me too."

It was May, and hockey season had ended about a month ago with Bridgeport failing to make the post-season for the third year in a row.

Hayes had gotten lucky: there were no lingering complications from his concussion, and the hit hadn't reinjured his shoulder. The league had also reviewed the play and determined that number 53's hit was, in fact, dirty. He was given a $2,000 fine and a three-game suspension for it. After only having to sit out for a week, Hayes played the rest of the season flawlessly and was immediately called up to New York for the Islanders' post-season, which had ended very quickly after they'd gotten swept in round one by the Devils.

It'd become very clear to everyone that Hayes had played in his last game as a Bridgeport Islander and would be on the opening night roster for New York when October rolled around.

"No one deserves it more than you, kid. No one," Hastings had told him, pulling him in for a hug after the final game at Total Mortgage Arena.

Ryan had also gotten somewhat lucky. At his hearing, he'd only been assessed a $3,000 fine and a five-game suspension, allowing him to finish his season with Bridgeport.

His future there, however, hung in the balance.

"Baylor, we love you. We really do, but there's no question you're a liability," Hastings had said to him during his post-season review meeting. *"You fly off the handle too quickly. You gotta learn to get your emotions under control."*

"Coach, I'm not some loose cannon. Everything I did was to protect the people I love the most. If that makes me a liability, then so be it. I'll never apologize for that."

"Fair enough. Listen, you've got heart. That much is for sure. You played your ass off, you worked on whatever we asked you to work on without hesitation, and I respect that about you, Baylor. I don't know what Sellars has planned for you, but whatever it is, and as much of a pain the fucking dick you've been? It's been an honor coaching you, kid. I mean that."

"Holy shit," Hayes remarked, as they made a right onto the street and pulled into the driveway. "Mar got herself a fuckin' sugar daddy, eh?"

"Good for her. She deserves to be happy," Ryan said, parking the car they'd rented, as they both got out and he grabbed a briefcase from the trunk.

"The fuck's in there anyway?" Hayes asked, pointing to it. "You servin' her with court papers or some shit?

Ryan laughed. "Don't worry about it."

"Oh, you got secrets now? That's fine, Rook. I see how it is. Five months in and we're gonna start hidin' shit from each other?"

"Stop being so damn dramatic, will you? Jesus, you're

like a teenage girl."

"Yeah, you weren't sayin' that last night when I was swallowin' on your cock, were you?"

They approached the house that Amara and Jake shared, having been invited to attend a sort of months-late housewarming party. They'd been lucky to find a parking spot, as there were cars and people everywhere, with tons of kids running around and a huge blow-up waterslide on the front lawn.

As they came to the door, Ryan turned to Hayes. "You see all these children? You need to behave. You can't be droppin' F-bombs every other word, OK? Behave." They opened the screen door and walked into the beautifully decorated, spotless home, looking around and taking it all in.

"I bet she's so fuckin' happy here," Hayes said. "This is amazing."

"Yo, boys!" a familiar voice called, coming around the corner. "Thought that was you. Mar told me you guys were gonna be here."

"Dunny, what's good?" Hayes went in for a hug, then extended his hand to shake Mark's, with Ryan doing the same.

"This is beautiful, huh? Did you see the pool and the private beach? It's like something out of a fairy tale." Nick turned to Mark. "We need to step our game up, babe. Come on, let me take you guys out back. I think she's out by the pool."

There was an area in the foyer where people had been leaving their bags and purses, so Ryan set the briefcase down before following Nick and Hayes through the kitchen, out the sliding glass doors, and to the pool area.

He stopped dead in his tracks when he saw her.

She donned a sexy, yet modest black, one-piece bathing suit with a sheer black cover-up wrapped around her waist and huge red sunglasses. She leaned down, consoling a little girl who was crying because she'd scraped her knee. Jake had shown up and handed her a bandage and some towels, and she quickly cleaned the wound and applied the bandage.

"See? Good as new! You got this." She kissed her on the top of the head. "Now get back out there and play with your friends, sweetie."

"Thanks, Aunt Mar!" she called, before running off. Amara gathered up the towels and trash, turned towards the patio, and that's when she spotted him.

Their eyes met, and Hayes immediately looked over at Ryan. "Aaaand, there it is," he teased, as he watched Ryan's eyes fill, then overflow onto his cheeks within seconds.

He didn't move, but she hurried over to him, and the two hugged for what seemed like hours, both of them in tears.

"Hi," she finally said, wiping her eyes and taking a step back from him.

"Hi."

"I'm so glad you came."

"Me too."

"So, like, what the fuck am I, some asshole off the street?" Hayes bitched, as Amara grabbed him and pulled him in for a hug.

"Hi, Tyler." She leaned into his ear. "Watch your mouth, please. There are kids everywhere."

"Sorry, babe," he apologized. "I'll do my best."

She reached over to Ryan, inviting him to join them, and the three of them stood silently hugging for a bit.

"This kid," Hayes said, pointing at Ryan as they finally broke away from each other. "Every time he sees you, he bawls. Stop bein' such a bitch, man."

"Sorry, I can't help it," he said, wiping his eyes. "This...Mar, wow. It's unbelievable."

"Tell me about it. I still pinch myself daily to make sure I'm not dreaming."

"Baylor and Hayes!" Jake yelled, appearing behind them and placing one hand on each of their shoulders. "Glad you could make it down here, gentlemen."

"I see you're takin' care of our girl quite well," Hayes said.

"You know it," he said, looking at Amara. "You give 'em the tour yet?"

"No, but let's go. Honestly," she turned to Ryan, "I need to get away for a bit. You know me and people."

"Catch up with you guys later," Jake called, heading over to the pool as they turned to go inside the house.

She'd led them around, showing them the downstairs, then the upstairs, including their master suite complete with his and hers walk-in closets. "It's not a huge house, but the space is maximized to perfection. And this," she said, opening the last in the hallway on the right, "is my respite."

There was a huge desk in the middle of the room with bookshelves holding color-coordinated spines along the back wall. A small couch was positioned under the bay window that overlooked the beach, and the walls were decorated with some of her favorite published pieces of writing that Jake had framed for her. "It's nice having a place all to myself where I can just sit and read or write," she said.

"You mean where you don't have two needy, dickhead hockey boys up your ass 24/7?" Hayes joked. "Don't lie. You miss that shit."

She shrugged. "Sometimes, I suppose."

Just then, a muffled, high-pitched bark echoed throughout the hallway.

"Oh my God. *And* you have a fuckin' dog? Bitch is out here livin' the literal American dream!"

She laughed. "Be right back," she said, leaving for a few seconds before returning with the teeniest, fluffiest golden retriever puppy. She shut the door behind her and plopped him onto the floor, where he took off right towards Ryan. The pup began sniffing him and immediately mounted his leg and went to town. "Baylor! No!"

"What'd I do?" Ryan said, throwing his hands up, confused.

"No, it's...his name. We named him...Baylor."

"Oh, for fuck's sake! All I'm sayin'? You better bust out another one of those fuzzy 'lil fuckers named Hayes, woman, or I'm outta here."

Ryan blushed. "I'm flattered. But, um, why?"

"Well, Jake and I couldn't come up with a name for him. We fought over just about every single one of them. Then it dawned on us: he's adorable, he's sweet but with a bit of an attitude, he's blonde, he cries a lot, and he literally never stops humping things. So," she shrugged. "Baylor."

"That's...actually perfect." Ryan got down on his hands and knees and rolled onto his back, giggling as the dog crawled all over him and shooing him away when he began humping various parts of his body. "Oh, I love him!"

"He's due to go outside. Can you take him out for me?" she asked Ryan. "His leash and collar are right next to the patio doors."

"Yup. Come on, buddy." He scooped the puppy up and

kissed it. "God, I fucking love dogs so much!" he said, as he left the room.

Amara had a seat next to Hayes on the couch, and he put his arm around her, kissing the top of her head. "You're OK?" he asked.

"I'm *so* OK, Ty. I miss you guys so much, but I do look forward to our little Facetime chats every couple of weeks. They help ease the pain a bit."

"I like 'em, too. And hey: just so you know? You fuckin' deserve all of this."

"I know."

He picked up her left hand and examined it. "And, uh...nah?"

"Nope, not yet," she laughed. "Still got just under two years of alimony payments to collect first. Then, maybe someday."

"Well, I better be in the wedding since I can't even get a puppy named after me."

She smiled. "You'd be my man of honor. You know, because I don't have one single female friend, sad as that is."

"I mean, you got Rook. Close enough."

"True," she laughed. "But you really are my best friend, Ty."

"I know that," he said, as Ryan came back in without the puppy, but holding the briefcase and three beers.

"I was brutally attacked by a mob of children, and they took the puppy. Who are all these kids, anyway? It's like a fucking daycare down there."

"Jake's business partners' kids, mostly, and some are the neighbors. Jake knew everyone's life story within two weeks. I'm still trying to learn names. I only come out when he forces me to. I'd much rather be in here writing."

Ryan handed Hayes a beer. "I need some fuckin' food first, man. I'm gonna head down, and," he said, taking note of the briefcase, "leave you two to catch up."

Hayes left the room, and Ryan sat down next to Amara, handing her the beer. "Hey. Here's to new beginnings," he said, clinking his bottle with hers and taking a sip. She set hers down on the end table without taking a sip. "No? Won't drink to that?"

"It's perfect, really. And it's not that I *won't* drink to that.

I, uh, *can't* drink to that. Or at all, for that matter."

He shot her a puzzled look. "Give it up for lent or something? Is it even lent? I don't fucking know."

She put her palm flat against her stomach. "Yeah. Or something."

She could see the wheels turning pretty hard, followed by his eyes bulging out of his skull. "No!"

She nodded.

"No!"

"Yes."

He jumped up, running his fingers through his hair. "Oh my God. How? I mean, I know *how*. Oh my God. I mean, how long until, like..."

"It's super-early. I'm only about eight weeks. I...Ryan, you're the first person I've told. I haven't even told Jake yet."

"Mar? You have to tell him!" he yelled excitedly.

"Shhh. Calm down. I will."

"Shit," he said, turning away from her. When he turned back around, he had tears streaming down his face again. "Apparently I'm just never gonna stop crying today!" He sat back down next to her, wrapping her in his arms. "You're gonna be a *mom*, Mar!"

"I know," she said, resting her head on his shoulder. "How fucking terrifying is *that*?" she laughed, wiping her eyes.

"Not terrifying at all. You're gonna...you're gonna be such an amazing mom."

"I hope so," she said. "But look at me: no one knows but you. No one. So you can't even tell Ty, OK?"

He nodded. "Of course."

"So, listen," he said after they'd sat quietly for a few minutes. "I have a...proposition for you. Feel free to say no, but I'm really hoping you'll say yes because there's no one else in the world I'd trust to do it."

"No pressure," she joked, as he got up, grabbed a manila envelope from the briefcase, and brought it to her. "What's this?"

"Open it."

She pulled the metal tab apart, lifted the flap, and pulled out a stack of papers. She read the first page:

Breaking Ryan Baylor

The memoir of a gay, sex-addicted, anxiety-riddled professional hockey player

"Will you ghostwrite my memoir with me?" he asked softly. "I'll pay you whatever you want, name your price. You're just, you're such a talented writer, and you know all about my strengths and weaknesses. You could add a ton of perspective that I couldn't. I've thought a lot about everything that I've been through, and Amara, I really think telling my story could help a lot of people like me."

He sat down next to her as she continued to flip through the pages. "Right now, it's just a lot of my random thoughts, but I know you could take them and turn them into a beautiful story. So? What do you think?"

She'd taken notice of some of the preliminary chapter titles: *Your Dad is Dead. Her. Him. Her and Him. The Sad Wife in the Red Dress. Self-Deprecation.*

Knowing this would be one hell of a rollercoaster ride, she sighed and placed the manuscript on her lap. "I'll do it, Ryan. But only on one condition."

"Name it."

"You're not paying me one cent. I'm doing it for free."

"I can't ask you to do that…"

"You're not asking. I'm demanding. I won't take money from you, Ryan. I took enough from you. Let me…let this be me making it right by you, OK?"

"If that's what you want."

"It is."

"Then it's a go?"

She nodded. "It's a go."

He reached over, flipped through the pages, and stopped. "I wanna start with this quote," he said excitedly, pointing to it. "What do you think?"

She read it:

"I don't think we talk enough about the in-betweens. The part when you know you want to change something but don't yet know how, don't yet feel strong enough, don't yet know what your first step is. So, to the people in the in-betweens: don't be disheartened, don't give up. You've done the hard part. Now you just need to take it one small step at a time." -ALLYISLIA

(Instagram)

    "Ryan. I think it's perfect."

❋ ❋ ❋

ACKNOWLEDGEMENT

Can I please tell you how amazing it feels to publish a book?

It's something I've aspired to do my whole life. I hope it does well and others enjoy it, but regardless of what happens, at least I can now finally say **"I DID IT!"**

It wouldn't have been possible without the help of some amazing people.

To My husband: thank you for your support and for the hours you held down the fort while I wrote, read, and edited. And thank you for attempting to read this, even though it's "definitely not for boys."

To My besties (CR and GR): thank you for being my very first readers, for giving me feedback, and for being my biggest cheerleaders through this process. I love you both. And thank you for indulging my silly ass with all the Tyler Seguin pictures and GIFs.

To My beta readers: thank you so much for taking the time to read my story and give me crucial feedback. I appreciate all of you more than you'll ever know. Your support and encouragement kept me going and made this possible.

To My Parents: thank you for always loving me, supporting me, and encouraging me to write a book...even if it ended up being about gay hockey boys.

To All the Hockey Boys: thank you for being beautiful and fabulous. You inspire us (Ryan and Tyler were loosely inspired by my two favorite AHL boys, who are every bit as gorgeous as my characters) and you keep old bitches like me young.

To My Readers: thank you for giving me and my characters a chance to tell you our story. It means the world to me, and please feel free to contact me anytime.

Instagram: @author_chmaddington

Email: chmaddington@gmail.com

If you enjoyed this story, please consider giving it a positive review on Amazon, Goodreads, Instagram, Storygraph, TikTok, or Facebook. Your support is much appreciated!

THANK YOU FOR READING!

COMING SOON...

Did you love reading Tyler Hayes as much as I loved writing him? He very quickly weaseled his cocky little way into my heart and became my favorite character, which is why I feel compelled to tell his story next.

What makes Tyler tick? What made him so insanely cocky and obsessed with older women? What happens when he makes it to the show? What becomes of him and Ryan? What about Mar, Jake, and the baby?

If you found yourself asking any of these questions, then stay tuned for my next book, ***Taming Tyler Hayes.***

Details coming soon!

Instagram: @author_chmaddington

Email: chmaddington@gmail.com

Made in the USA
Las Vegas, NV
29 January 2025

17196370R00208